# SUIT YOUR SELFIE

# SUIT YOUR SELFIE

Stephan T. Pastis

**Andrews McMeel**
PUBLISHING®

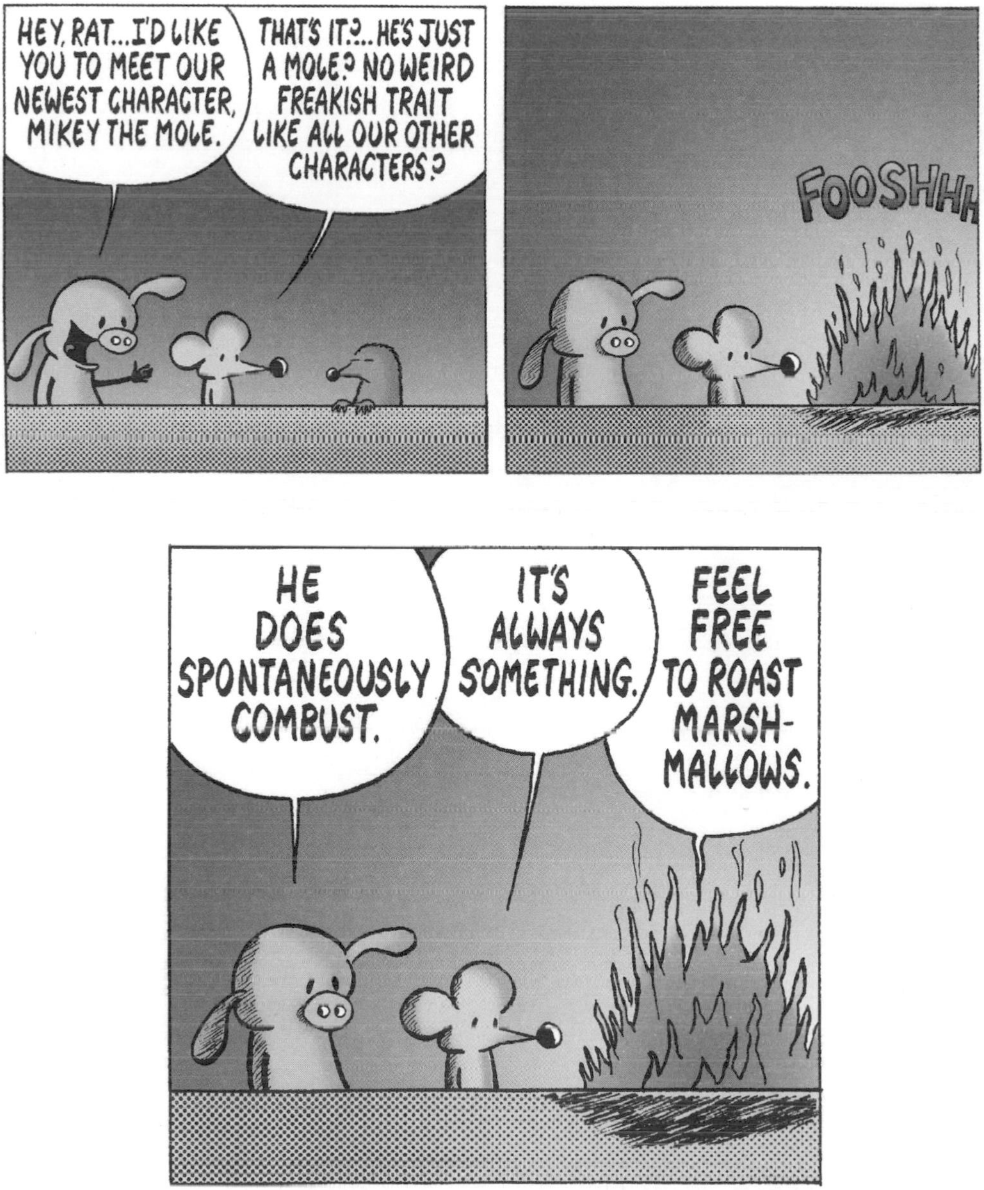
HEY, RAT...I'D LIKE YOU TO MEET OUR NEWEST CHARACTER, MIKEY THE MOLE.
THAT'S IT?...HE'S JUST A MOLE? NO WEIRD FREAKISH TRAIT LIKE ALL OUR OTHER CHARACTERS?
FOOSHHH
HE DOES SPONTANEOUSLY COMBUST.
IT'S ALWAYS SOMETHING.
FEEL FREE TO ROAST MARSH-MALLOWS.

OOOOOOHH...
Ahhhhh.
WHAT ARE YOU WATCHING, PIG?
A 3D FILM... IT'S INCREDIBLE.
WHY DOES EVERYTHING HAVE TO BE IN 3D NOW? IT'S BORING IF YOU ASK ME.
THAT'S WHAT I THOUGHT UNTIL I WATCHED THIS ONE RAT TOLD ME TO WATCH... IT'S GREAT.

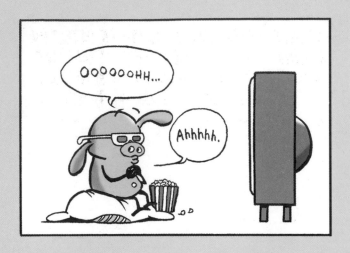

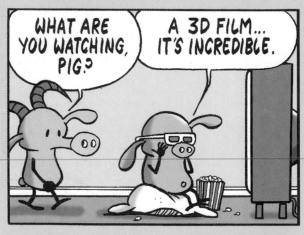

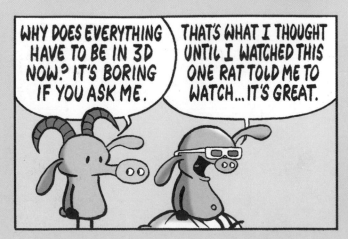

WHAT'S SO GREAT ABOUT IT?
WELL, WHEN YOU SEE AN OBJECT ON THE SCREEN, IT REALLY FEELS LIKE IT'S FLYING RIGHT TOWARD YOUR FACE...LIKE, LOOK AT THAT CAN...
CLANG
WOW! THAT WAS JUST LIKE THE SHOE!
PIG....THAT'S JUST—
SHHHHH

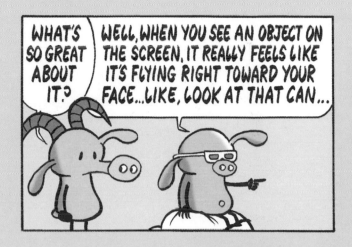

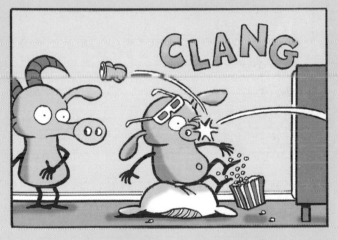

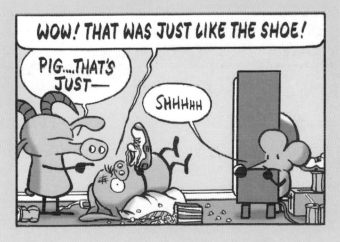

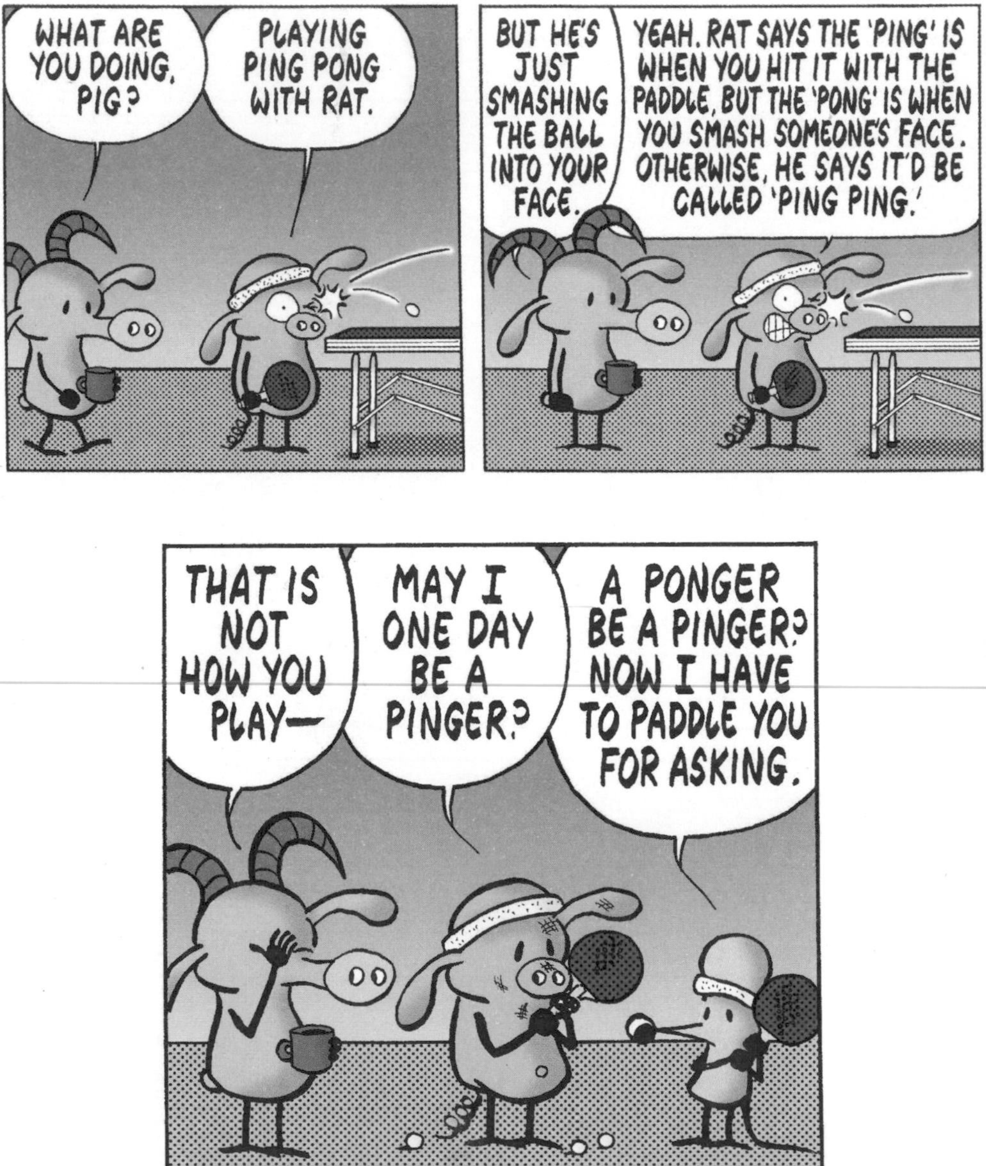
WHAT ARE YOU DOING, PIG?
PLAYING PING PONG WITH RAT.
BUT HE'S JUST SMASHING THE BALL INTO YOUR FACE.
YEAH. RAT SAYS THE 'PING' IS WHEN YOU HIT IT WITH THE PADDLE, BUT THE 'PONG' IS WHEN YOU SMASH SOMEONE'S FACE. OTHERWISE, HE SAYS IT'D BE CALLED 'PING PING.'
THAT IS NOT HOW YOU PLAY—
MAY I ONE DAY BE A PINGER?
A PONGER BE A PINGER? NOW I HAVE TO PADDLE YOU FOR ASKING.

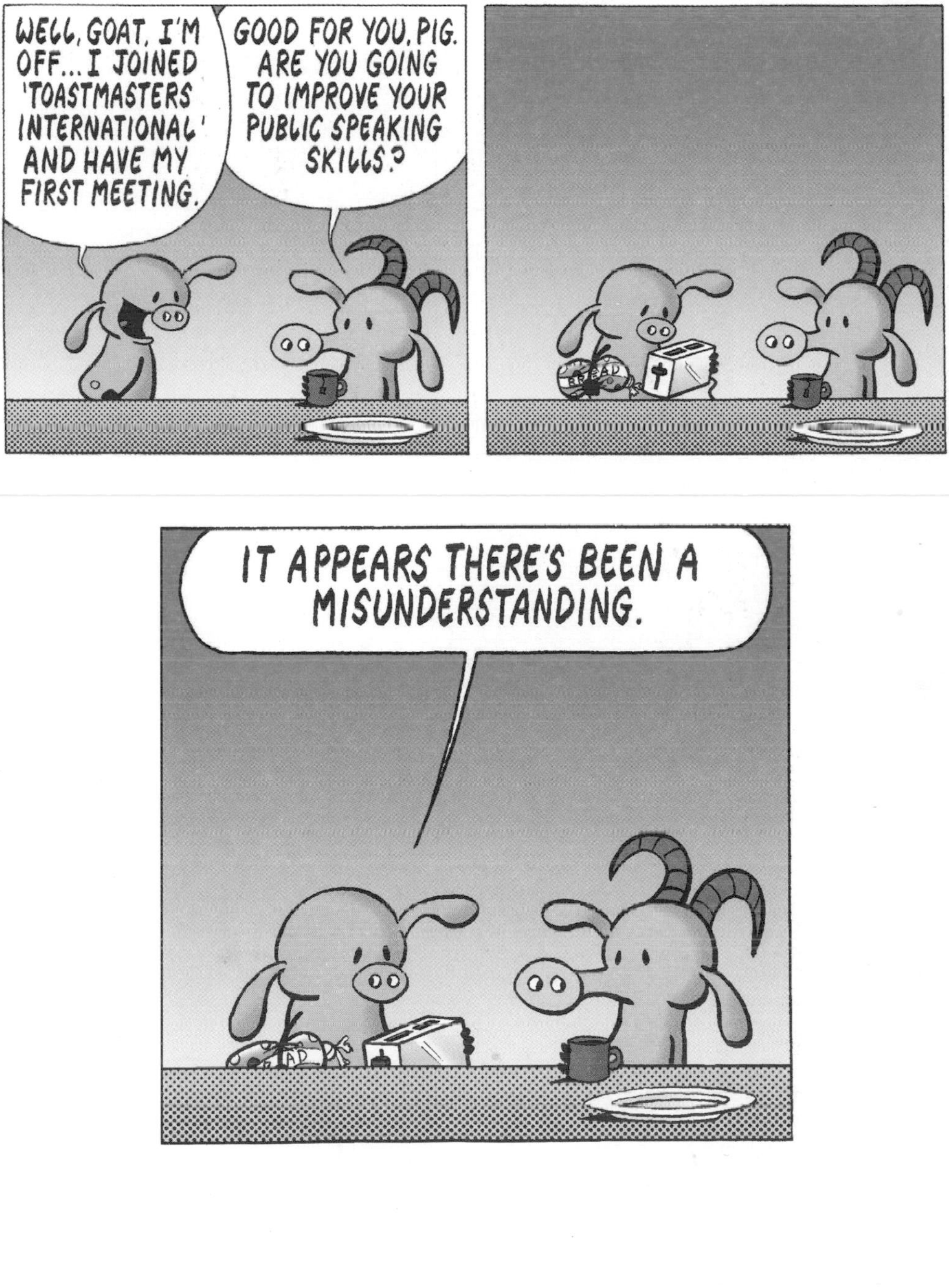
WELL, GOAT, I'M OFF... I JOINED 'TOASTMASTERS INTERNATIONAL' AND HAVE MY FIRST MEETING.
GOOD FOR YOU, PIG. ARE YOU GOING TO IMPROVE YOUR PUBLIC SPEAKING SKILLS?
IT APPEARS THERE'S BEEN A MISUNDERSTANDING.

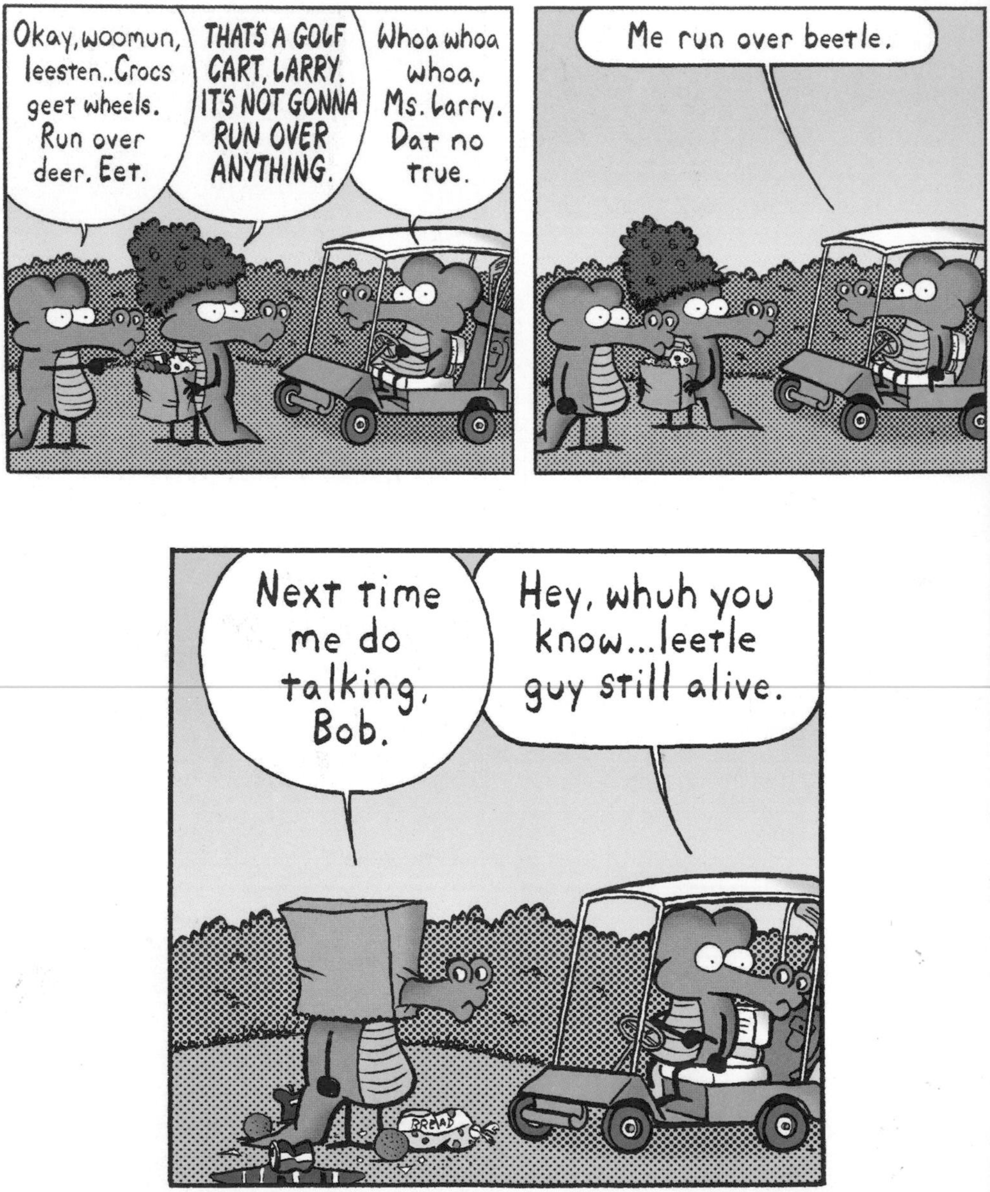
Okay, woomun, leesten..Crocs geet wheels. Run over deer. Eet.
THAT'S A GOLF CART, LARRY. IT'S NOT GONNA RUN OVER ANYTHING.
Whoa whoa whoa, Ms. Larry. Dat no true.
Me run over beetle.
Next time me do talking, Bob.
Hey, whuh you know...leetle guy still alive.
BREAD

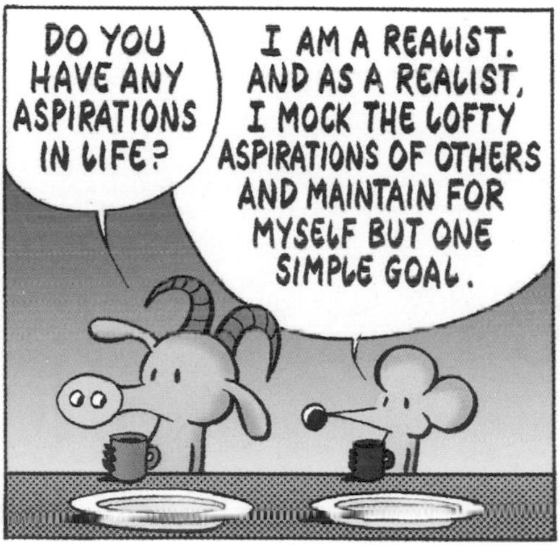
DO YOU HAVE ANY ASPIRATIONS IN LIFE?
I AM A REALIST. AND AS A REALIST, I MOCK THE LOFTY ASPIRATIONS OF OTHERS AND MAINTAIN FOR MYSELF BUT ONE SIMPLE GOAL.

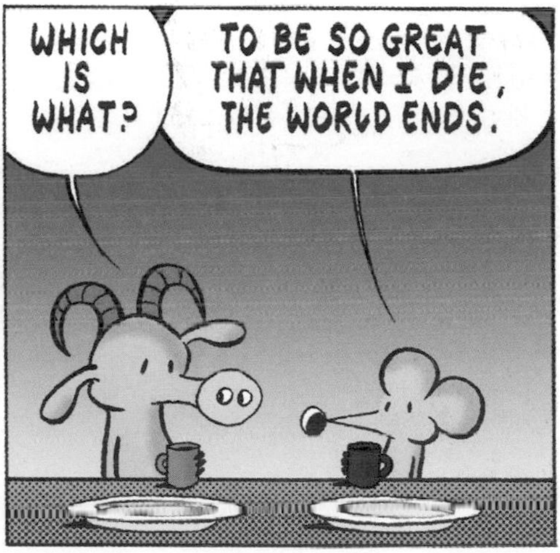
WHICH IS WHAT?
TO BE SO GREAT THAT WHEN I DIE, THE WORLD ENDS.

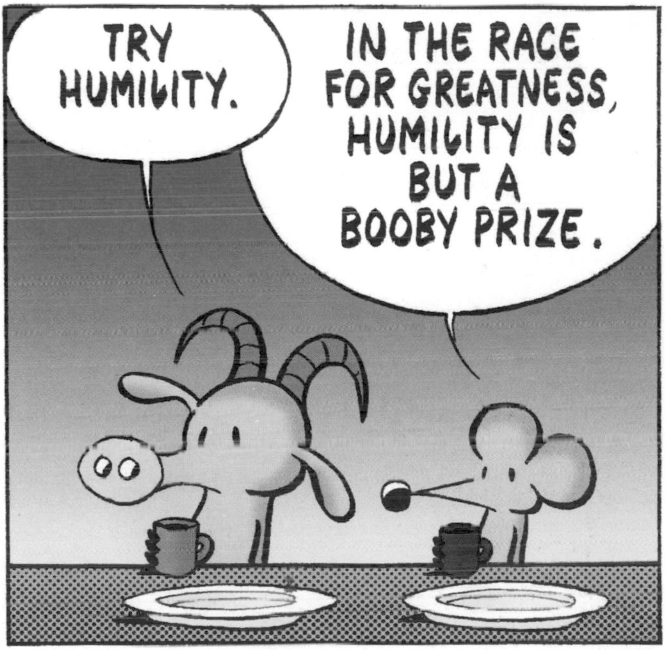
TRY HUMILITY.
IN THE RACE FOR GREATNESS, HUMILITY IS BUT A BOOBY PRIZE.

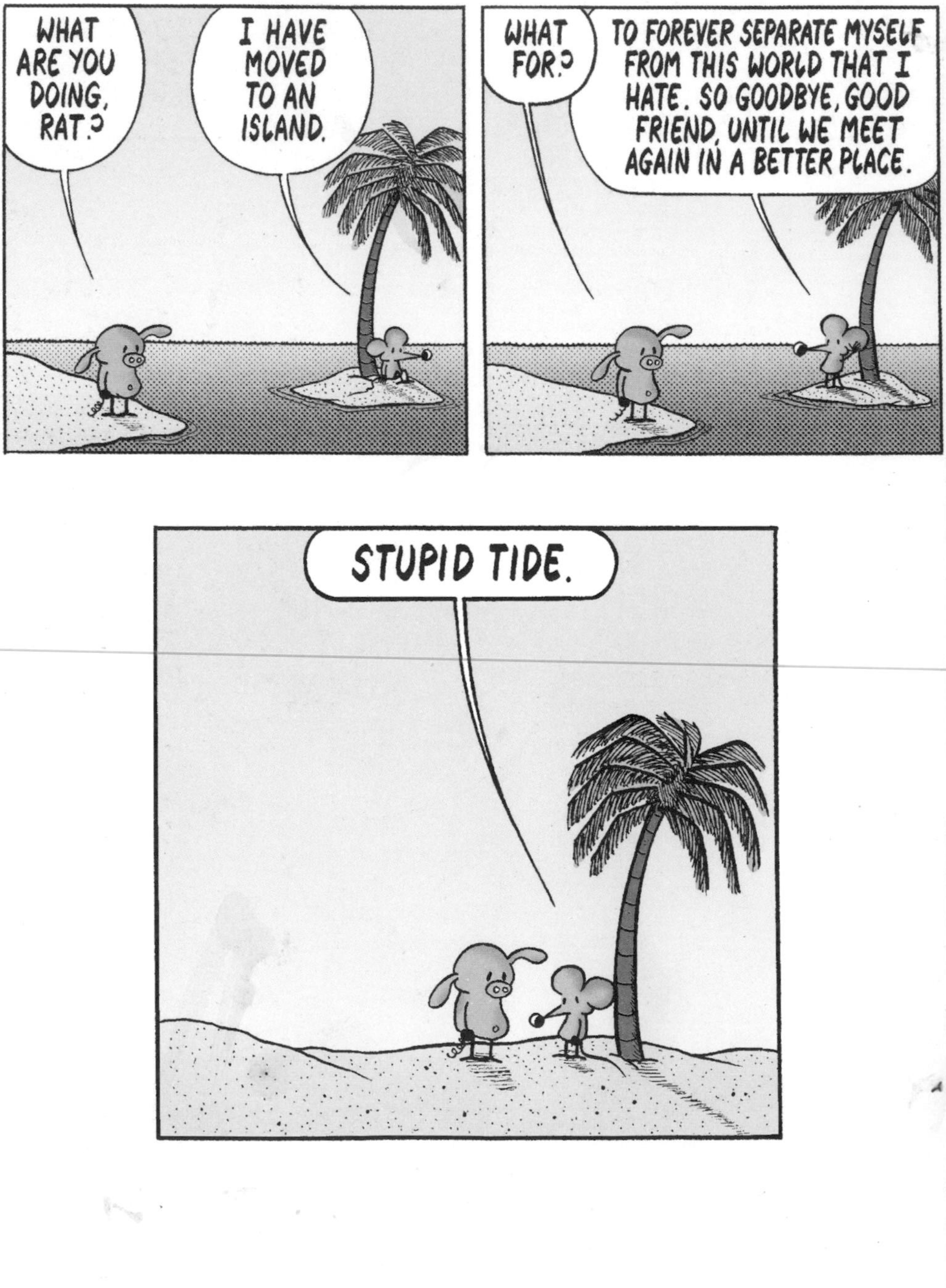
WHAT ARE YOU DOING, RAT?
I HAVE MOVED TO AN ISLAND.
WHAT FOR?
TO FOREVER SEPARATE MYSELF FROM THIS WORLD THAT I HATE. SO GOODBYE, GOOD FRIEND, UNTIL WE MEET AGAIN IN A BETTER PLACE.
STUPID TIDE.

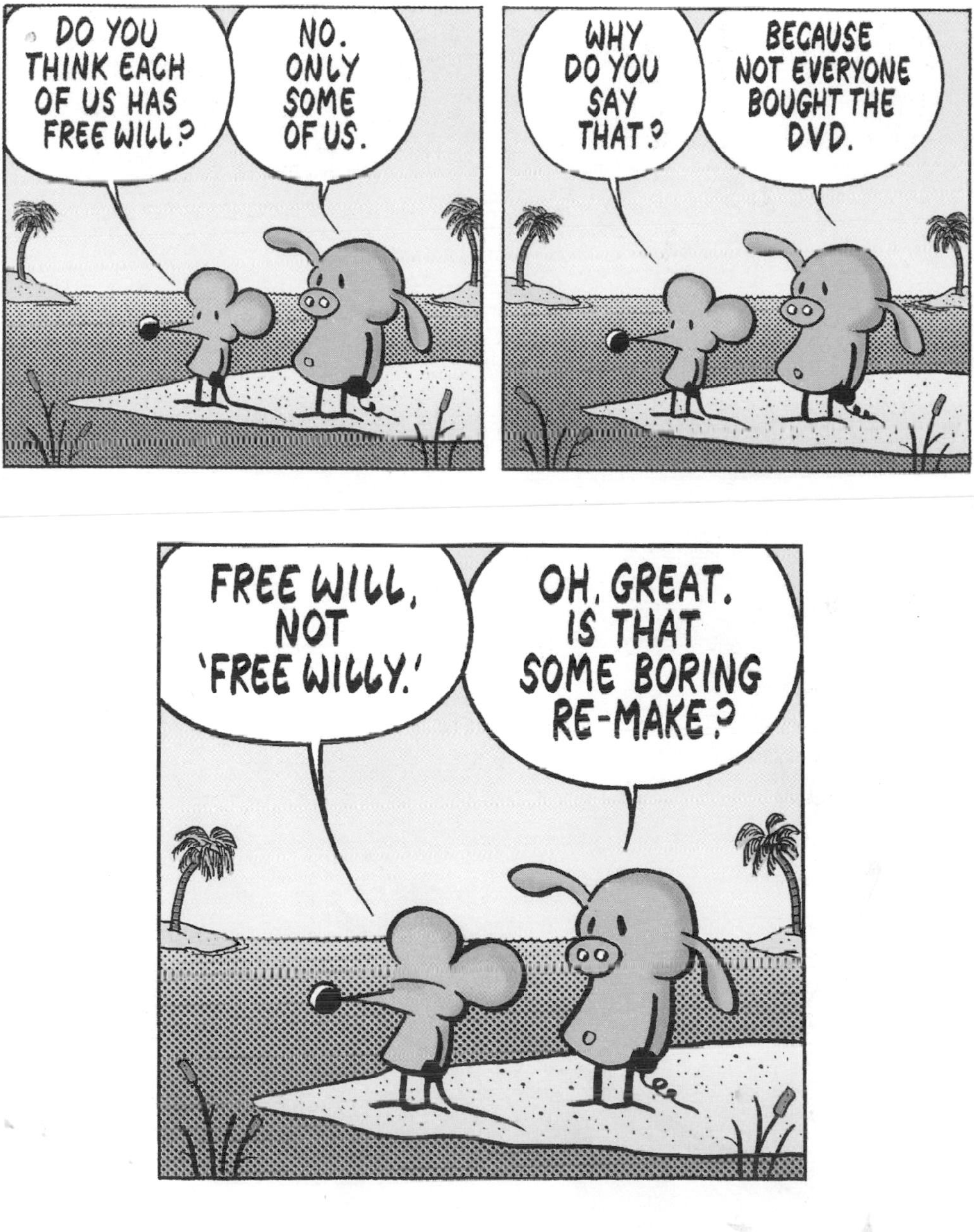
DO YOU THINK EACH OF US HAS FREE WILL?
NO. ONLY SOME OF US.
WHY DO YOU SAY THAT?
BECAUSE NOT EVERYONE BOUGHT THE DVD.
FREE WILL, NOT 'FREE WILLY.'
OH, GREAT. IS THAT SOME BORING RE-MAKE?

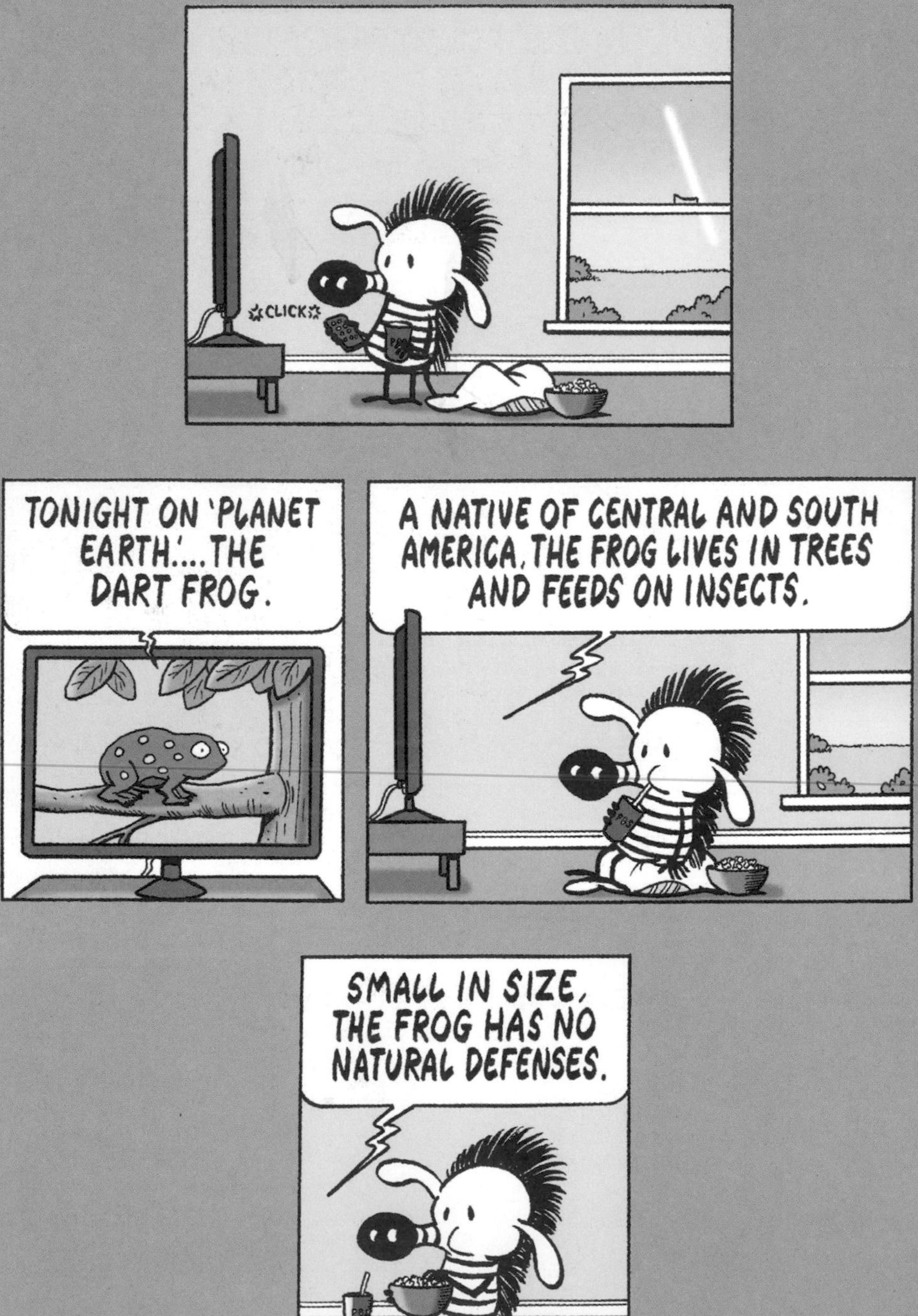

☼CLICK☼
TONIGHT ON 'PLANET EARTH.'... THE DART FROG.
A NATIVE OF CENTRAL AND SOUTH AMERICA, THE FROG LIVES IN TREES AND FEEDS ON INSECTS.
SMALL IN SIZE, THE FROG HAS NO NATURAL DEFENSES.

THUS, IT MUST RELY SOLELY ON ITS BRIGHTLY COLORED SKIN, A SIGNAL TO PREDATORS THAT IT IS POISONOUS AND THAT TO EAT IT IS TO SUFFER A SLOW, PAINFUL DEATH...

Dat guy fashion-challenged.

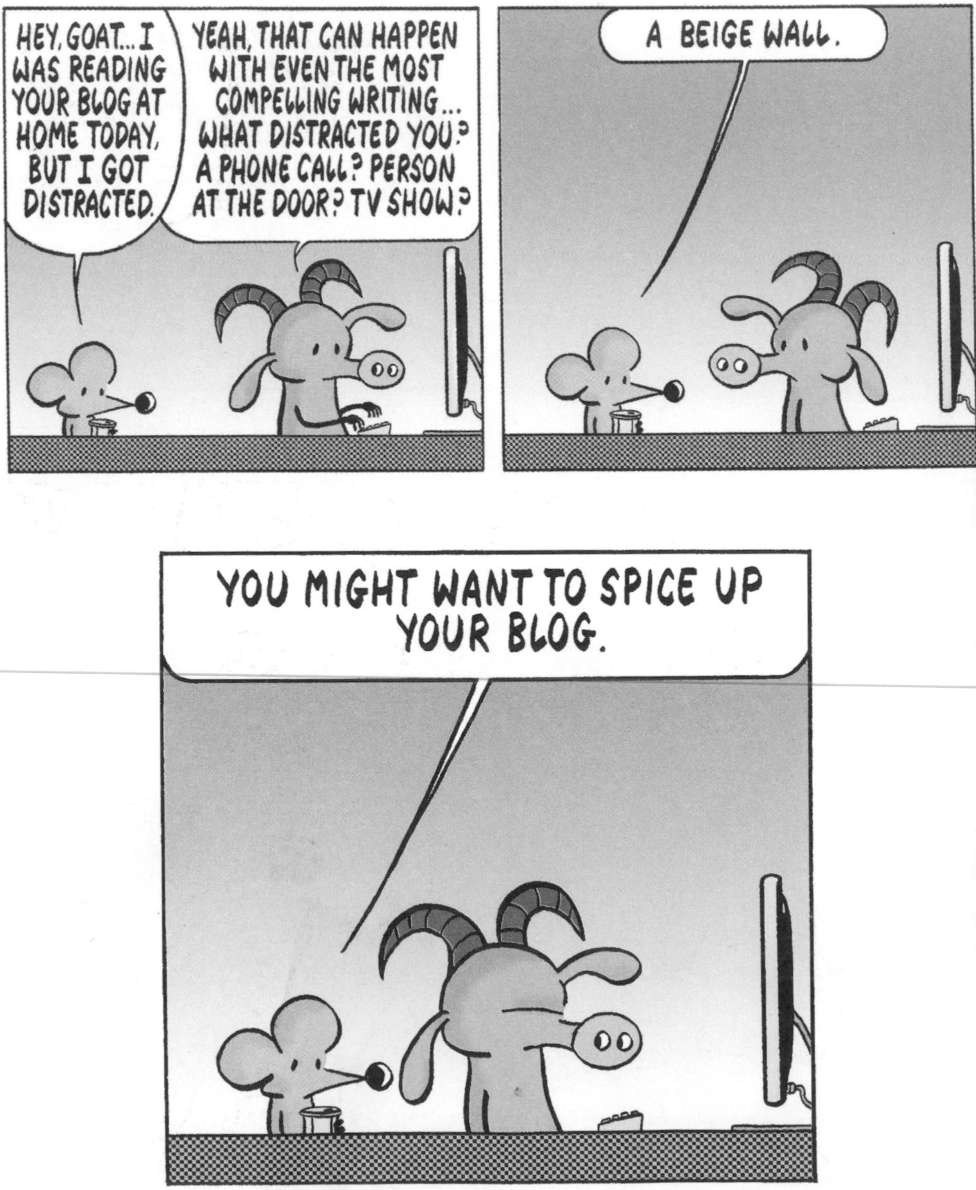
HEY, GOAT... I WAS READING YOUR BLOG AT HOME TODAY, BUT I GOT DISTRACTED.
YEAH, THAT CAN HAPPEN WITH EVEN THE MOST COMPELLING WRITING... WHAT DISTRACTED YOU? A PHONE CALL? PERSON AT THE DOOR? TV SHOW?
A BEIGE WALL.
YOU MIGHT WANT TO SPICE UP YOUR BLOG.

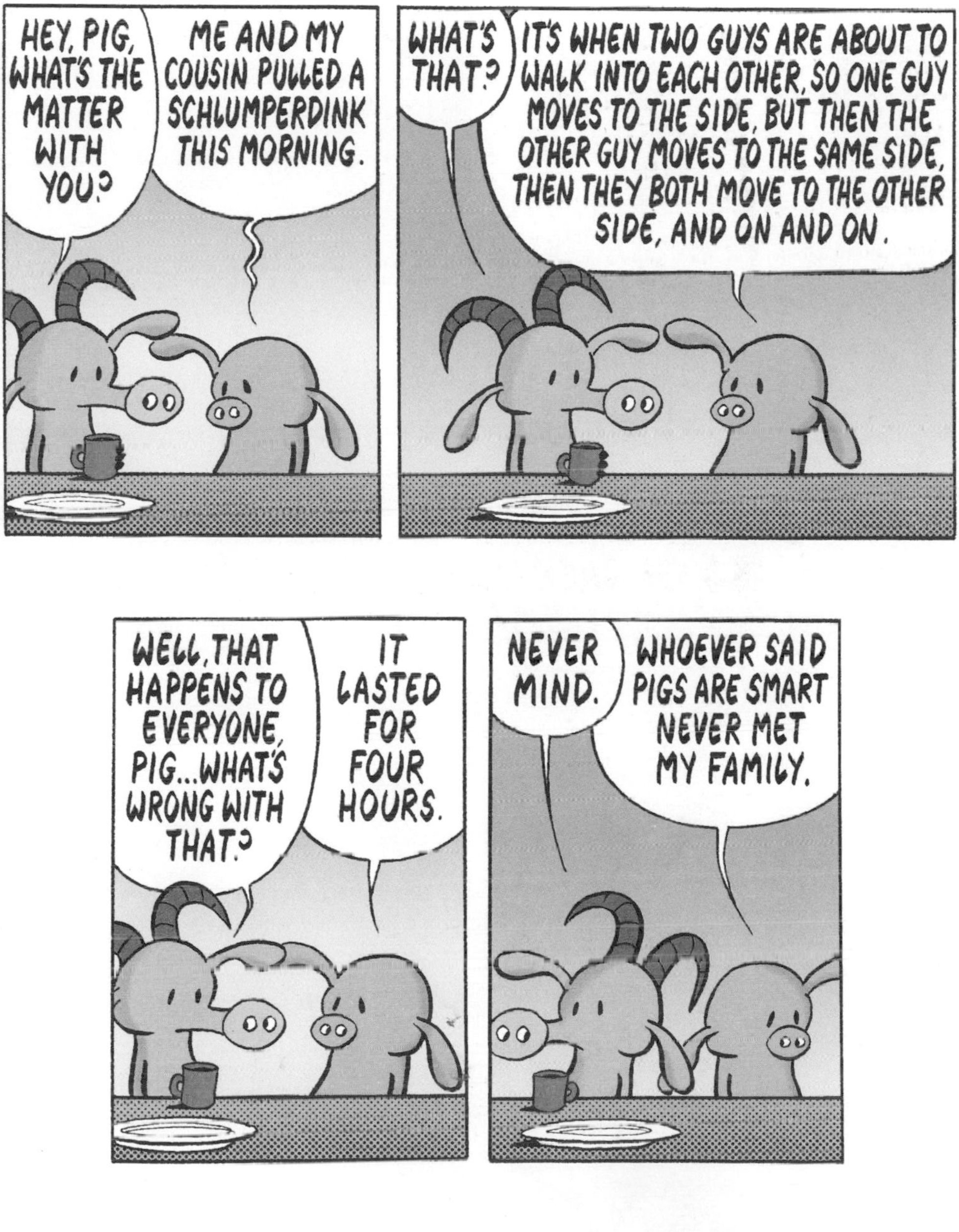
HEY, PIG, WHAT'S THE MATTER WITH YOU?
ME AND MY COUSIN PULLED A SCHLUMPERDINK THIS MORNING.
WHAT'S THAT?
IT'S WHEN TWO GUYS ARE ABOUT TO WALK INTO EACH OTHER, SO ONE GUY MOVES TO THE SIDE, BUT THEN THE OTHER GUY MOVES TO THE SAME SIDE, THEN THEY BOTH MOVE TO THE OTHER SIDE, AND ON AND ON.
WELL, THAT HAPPENS TO EVERYONE, PIG...WHAT'S WRONG WITH THAT?
IT LASTED FOR FOUR HOURS.
NEVER MIND.
WHOEVER SAID PIGS ARE SMART NEVER MET MY FAMILY.

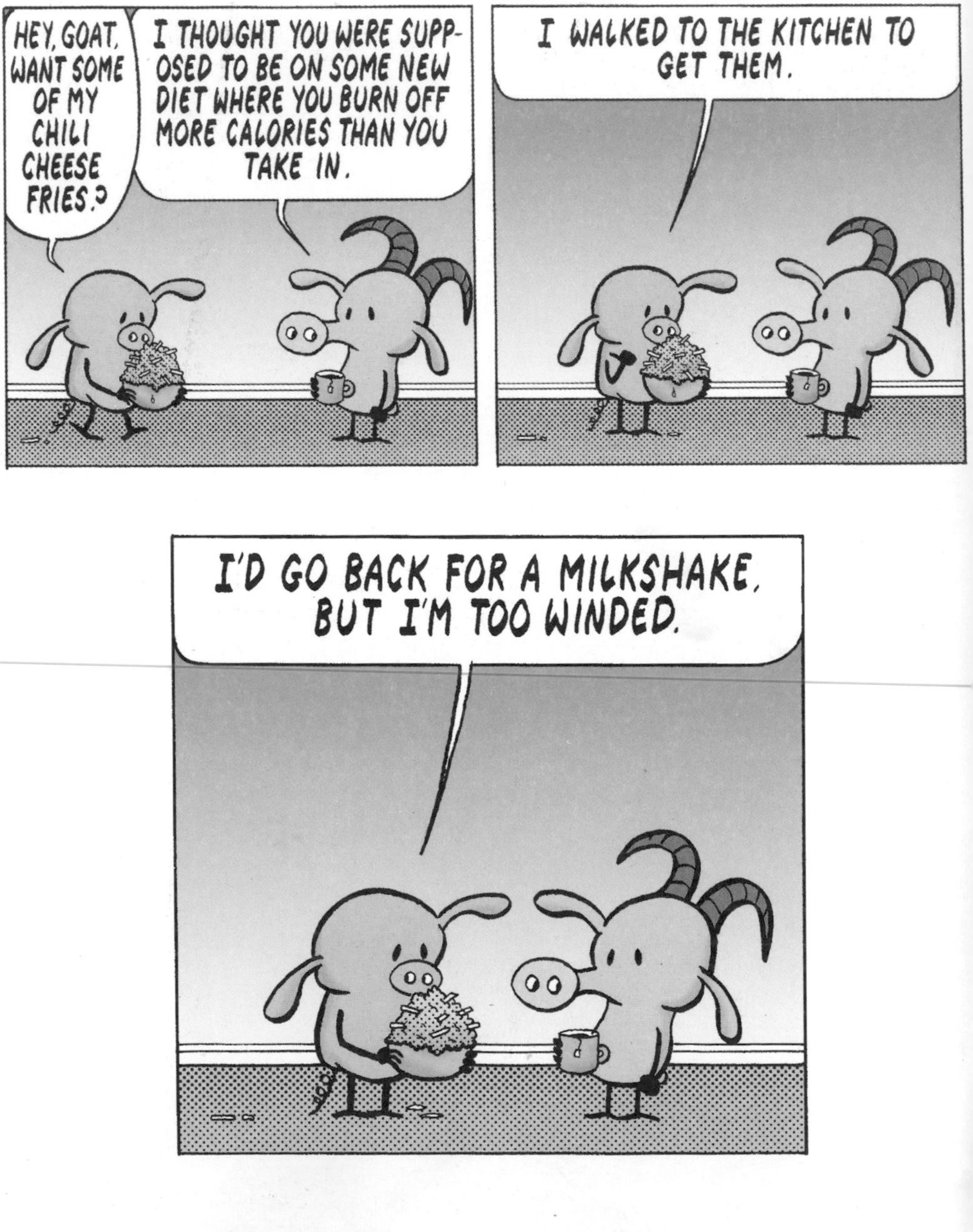
HEY, GOAT, WANT SOME OF MY CHILI CHEESE FRIES?
I THOUGHT YOU WERE SUPP-OSED TO BE ON SOME NEW DIET WHERE YOU BURN OFF MORE CALORIES THAN YOU TAKE IN.
I WALKED TO THE KITCHEN TO GET THEM.
I'D GO BACK FOR A MILKSHAKE, BUT I'M TOO WINDED.

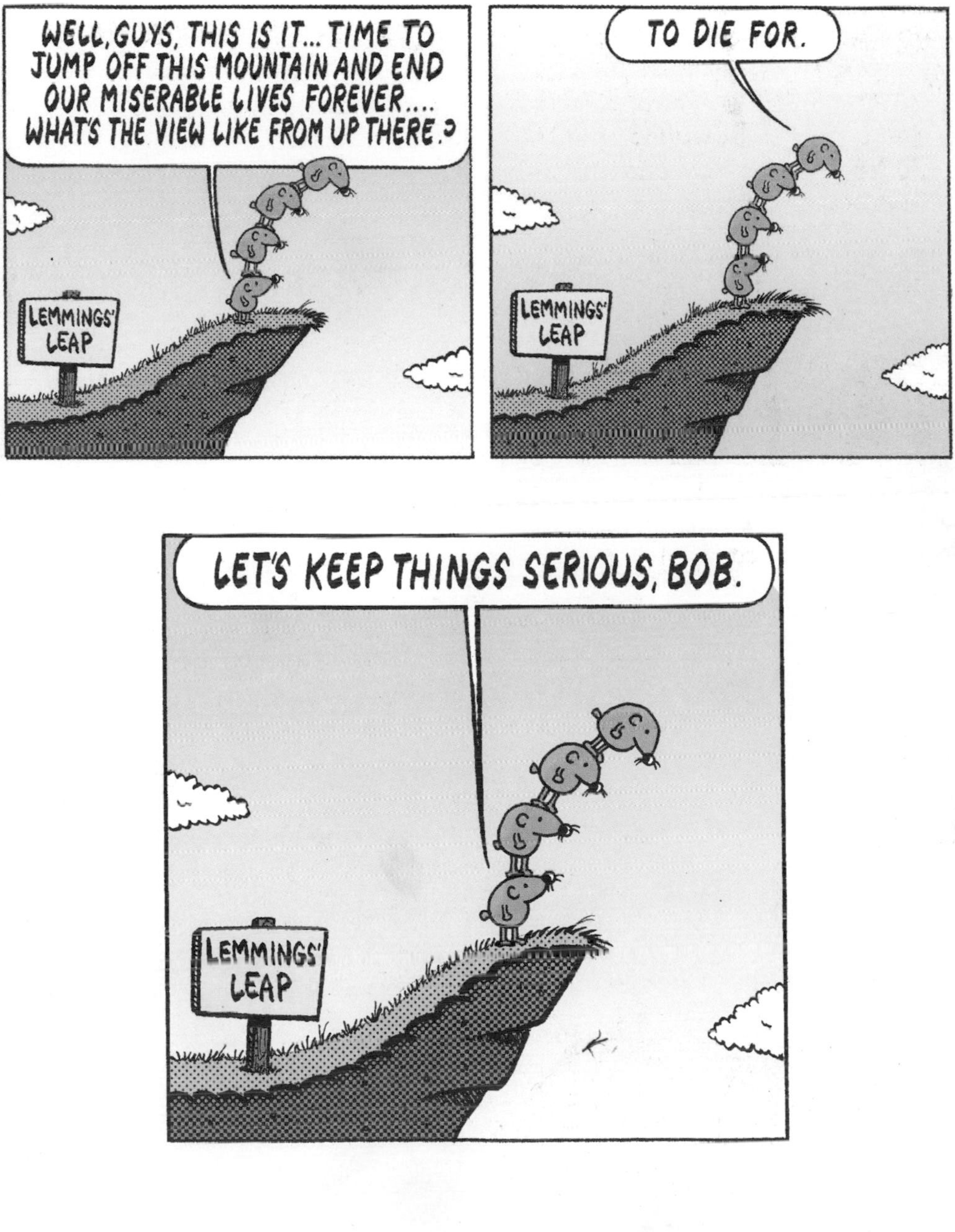
WELL, GUYS, THIS IS IT... TIME TO JUMP OFF THIS MOUNTAIN AND END OUR MISERABLE LIVES FOREVER.... WHAT'S THE VIEW LIKE FROM UP THERE?
LEMMINGS' LEAP
TO DIE FOR.
LEMMINGS' LEAP
LET'S KEEP THINGS SERIOUS, BOB.
LEMMINGS' LEAP

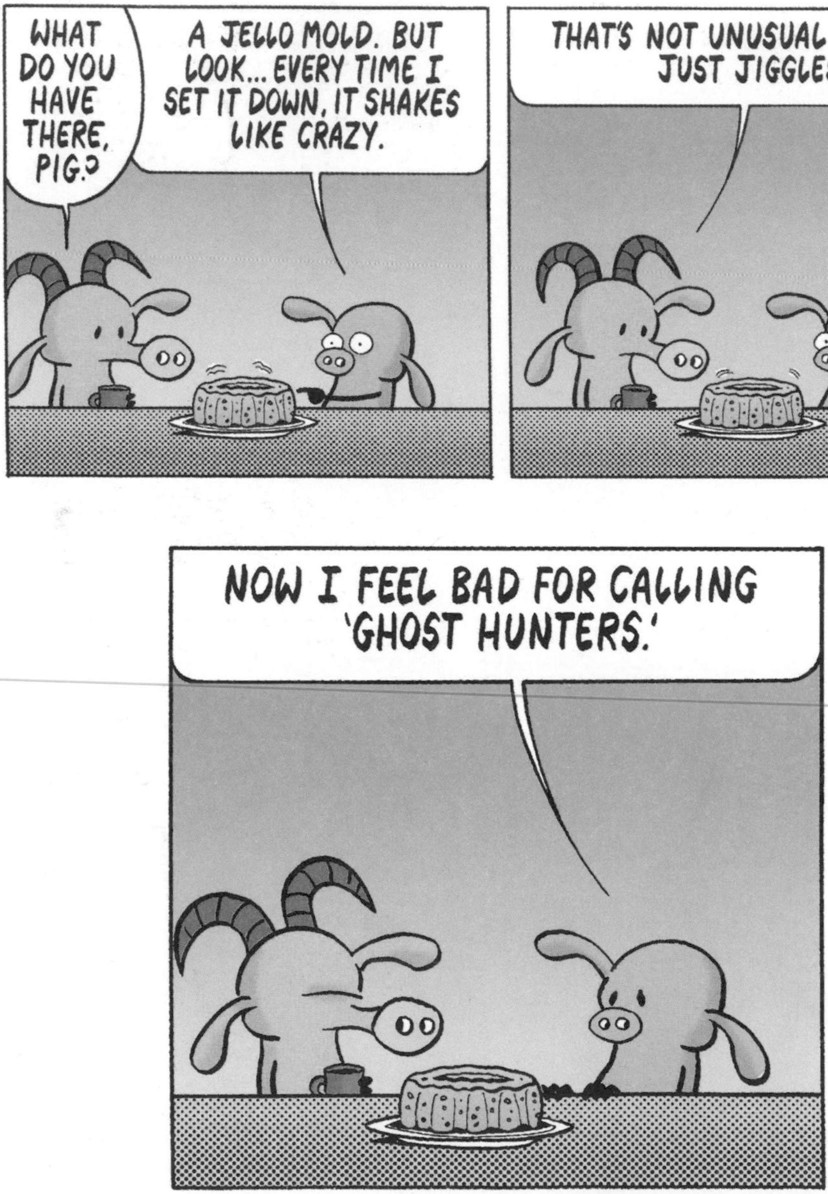
WHAT DO YOU HAVE THERE, PIG?
A JELLO MOLD. BUT LOOK... EVERY TIME I SET IT DOWN, IT SHAKES LIKE CRAZY.
THAT'S NOT UNUSUAL. JELLO JUST JIGGLES.
NOW I FEEL BAD FOR CALLING 'GHOST HUNTERS.'

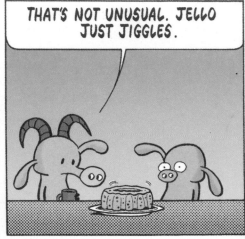

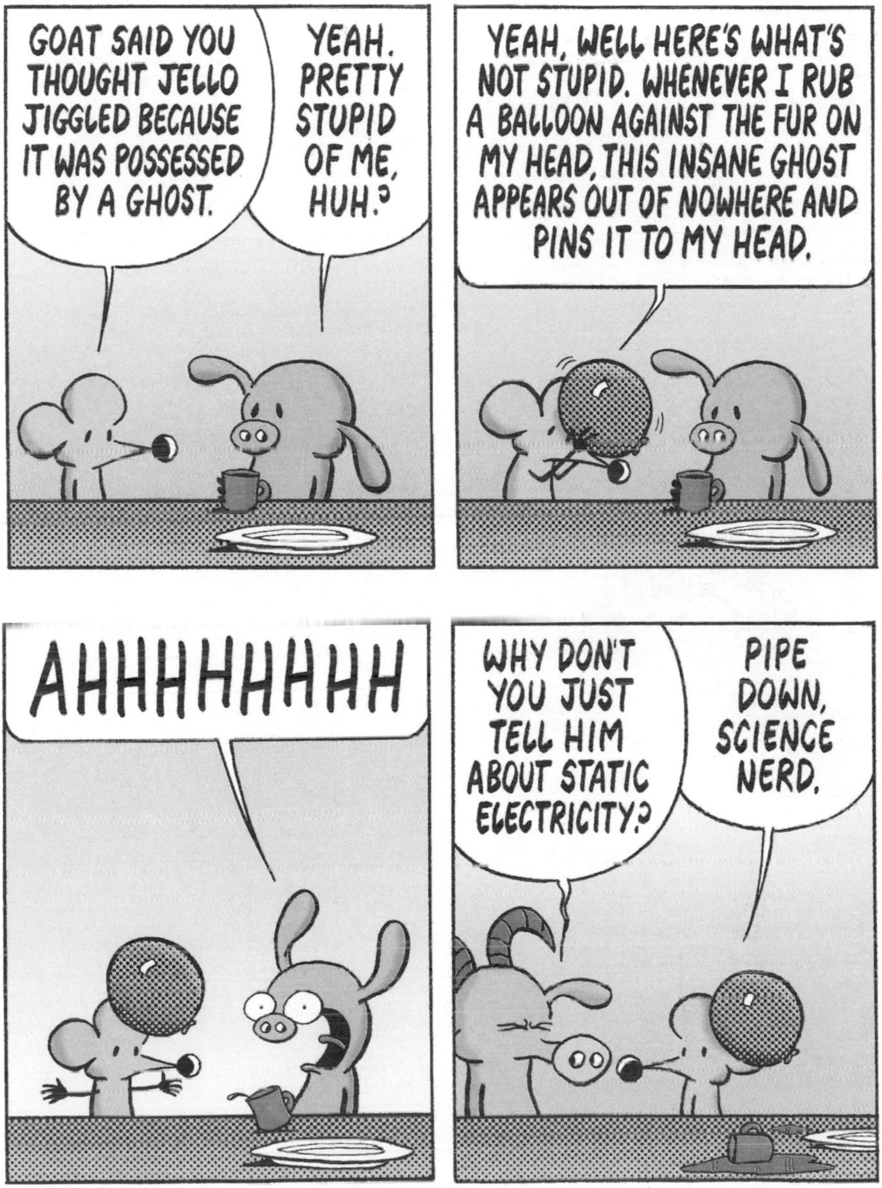
GOAT SAID YOU THOUGHT JELLO JIGGLED BECAUSE IT WAS POSSESSED BY A GHOST.
YEAH. PRETTY STUPID OF ME, HUH?
YEAH, WELL HERE'S WHAT'S NOT STUPID. WHENEVER I RUB A BALLOON AGAINST THE FUR ON MY HEAD, THIS INSANE GHOST APPEARS OUT OF NOWHERE AND PINS IT TO MY HEAD.
AHHHHHHHH
WHY DON'T YOU JUST TELL HIM ABOUT STATIC ELECTRICITY?
PIPE DOWN, SCIENCE NERD.

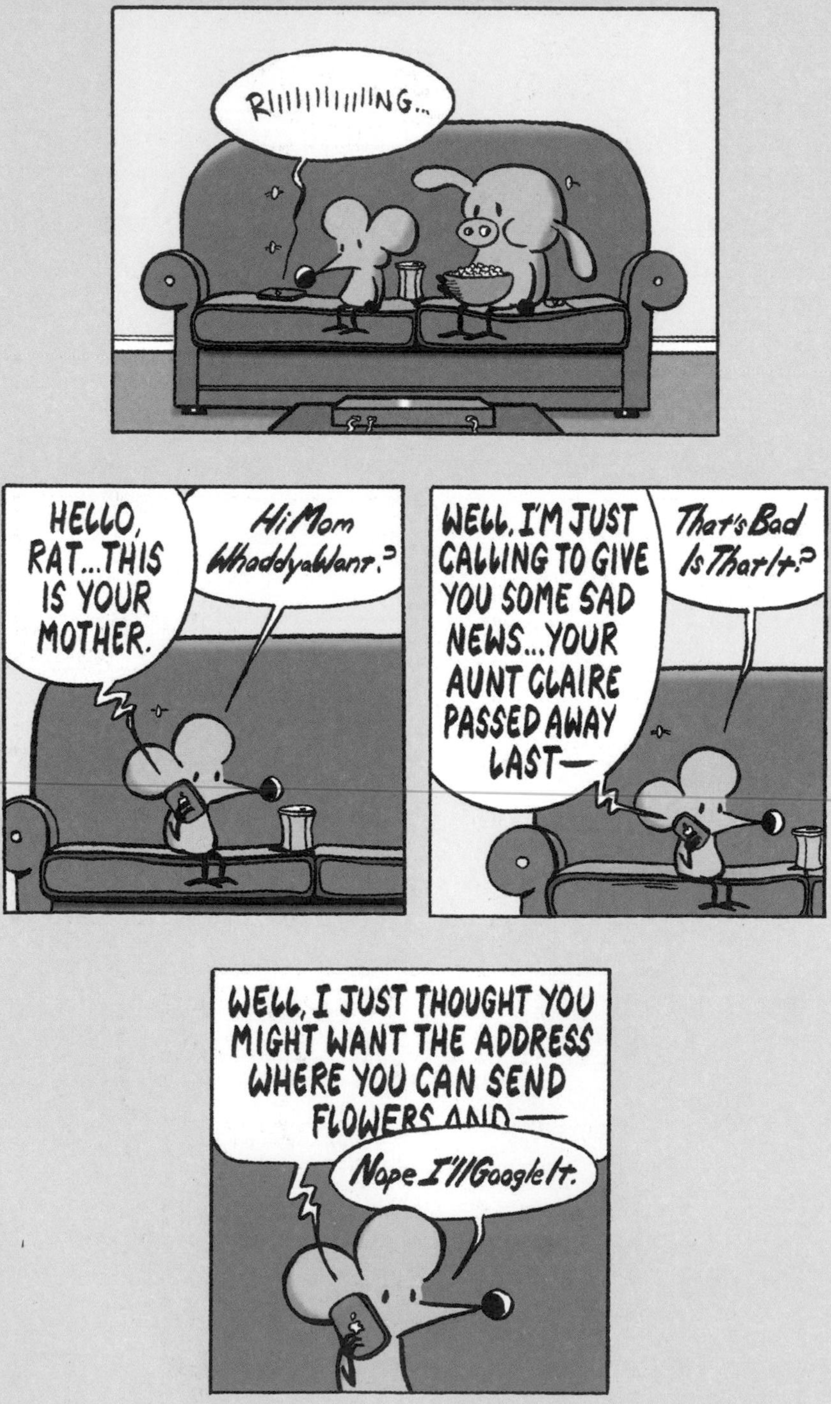
RIIIIIIIIIIING...
HELLO, RAT...THIS IS YOUR MOTHER.
Hi Mom WhaddyaWant.?
WELL, I'M JUST CALLING TO GIVE YOU SOME SAD NEWS...YOUR AUNT CLAIRE PASSED AWAY LAST—
That's Bad Is That It?
WELL, I JUST THOUGHT YOU MIGHT WANT THE ADDRESS WHERE YOU CAN SEND FLOWERS AND—
Nope I'll Google It.

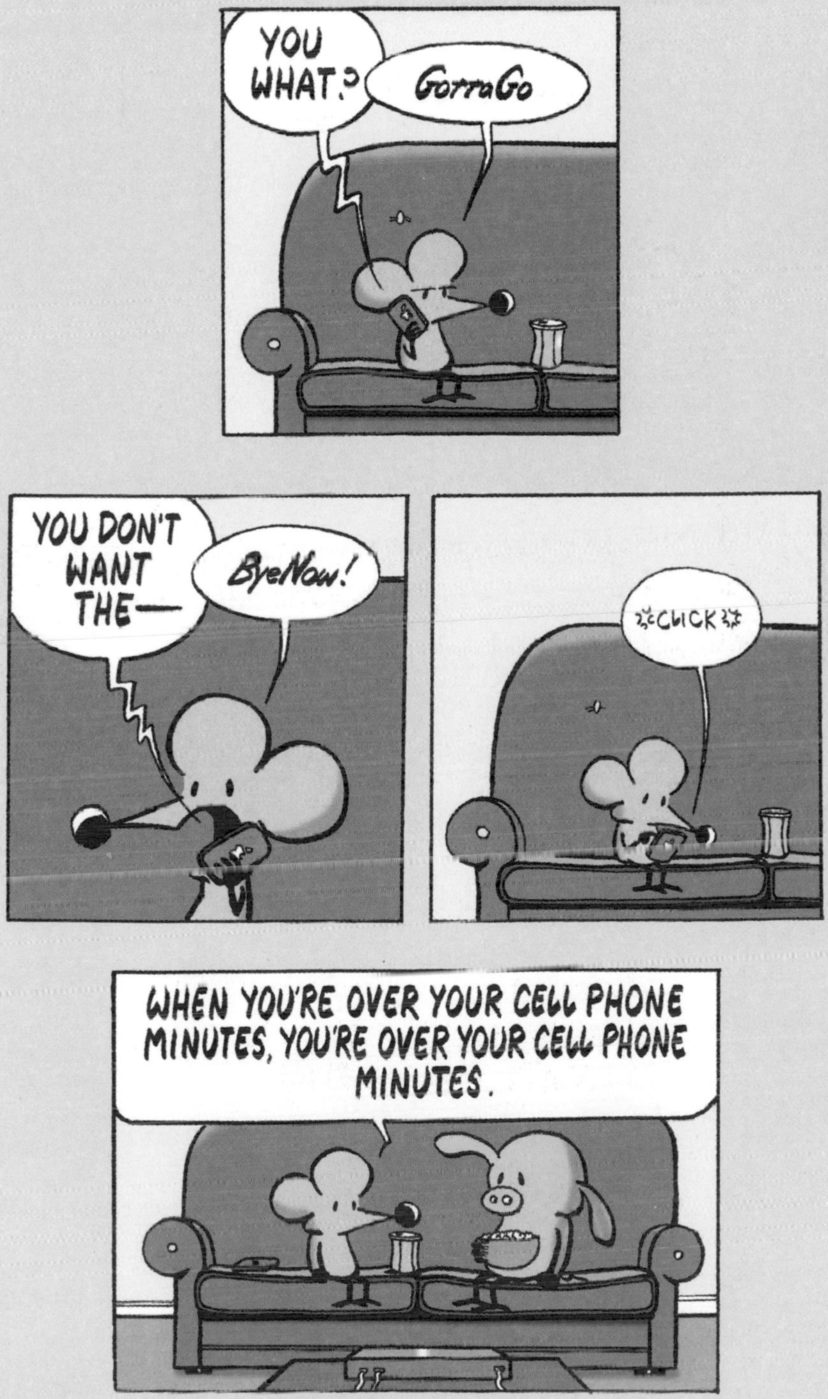
YOU WHAT?
GottaGo
YOU DON'T WANT THE—
ByeNow!
CLICK
WHEN YOU'RE OVER YOUR CELL PHONE MINUTES, YOU'RE OVER YOUR CELL PHONE MINUTES.

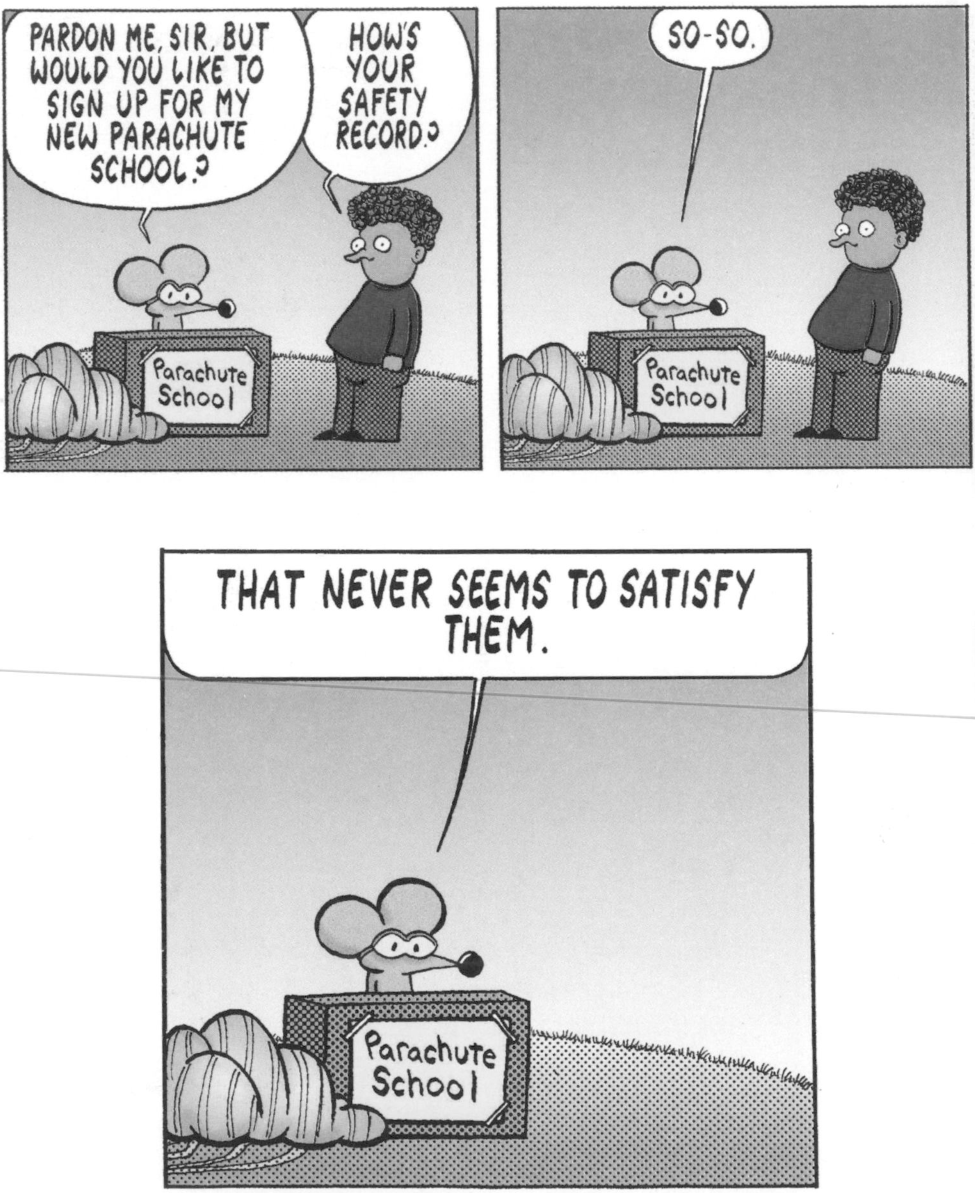
PARDON ME, SIR, BUT WOULD YOU LIKE TO SIGN UP FOR MY NEW PARACHUTE SCHOOL?
HOW'S YOUR SAFETY RECORD?
Parachute School
SO-SO.
Parachute School
THAT NEVER SEEMS TO SATISFY THEM.
Parachute School

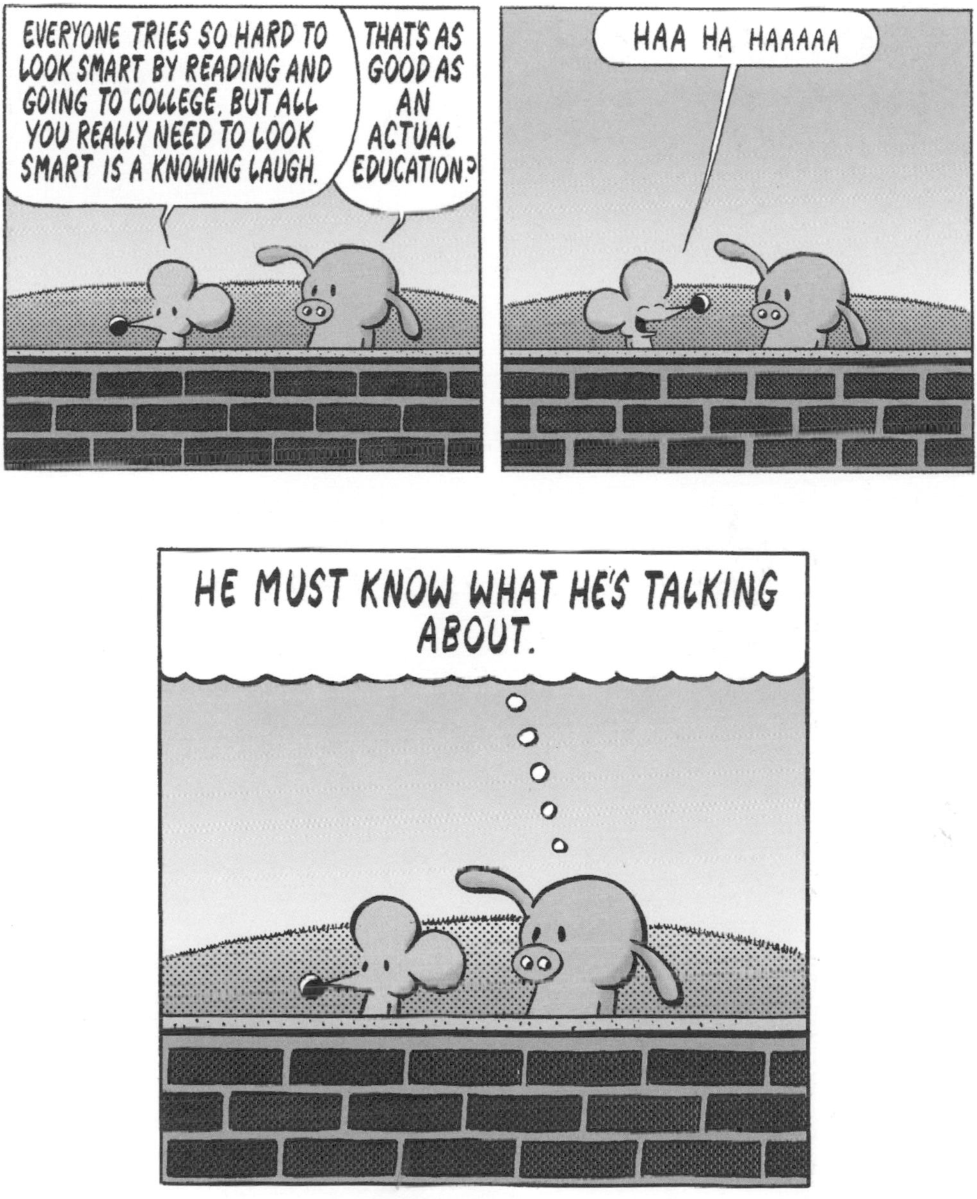
EVERYONE TRIES SO HARD TO LOOK SMART BY READING AND GOING TO COLLEGE. BUT ALL YOU REALLY NEED TO LOOK SMART IS A KNOWING LAUGH.
THAT'S AS GOOD AS AN ACTUAL EDUCATION?
HAA HA HAAAAA
HE MUST KNOW WHAT HE'S TALKING ABOUT.

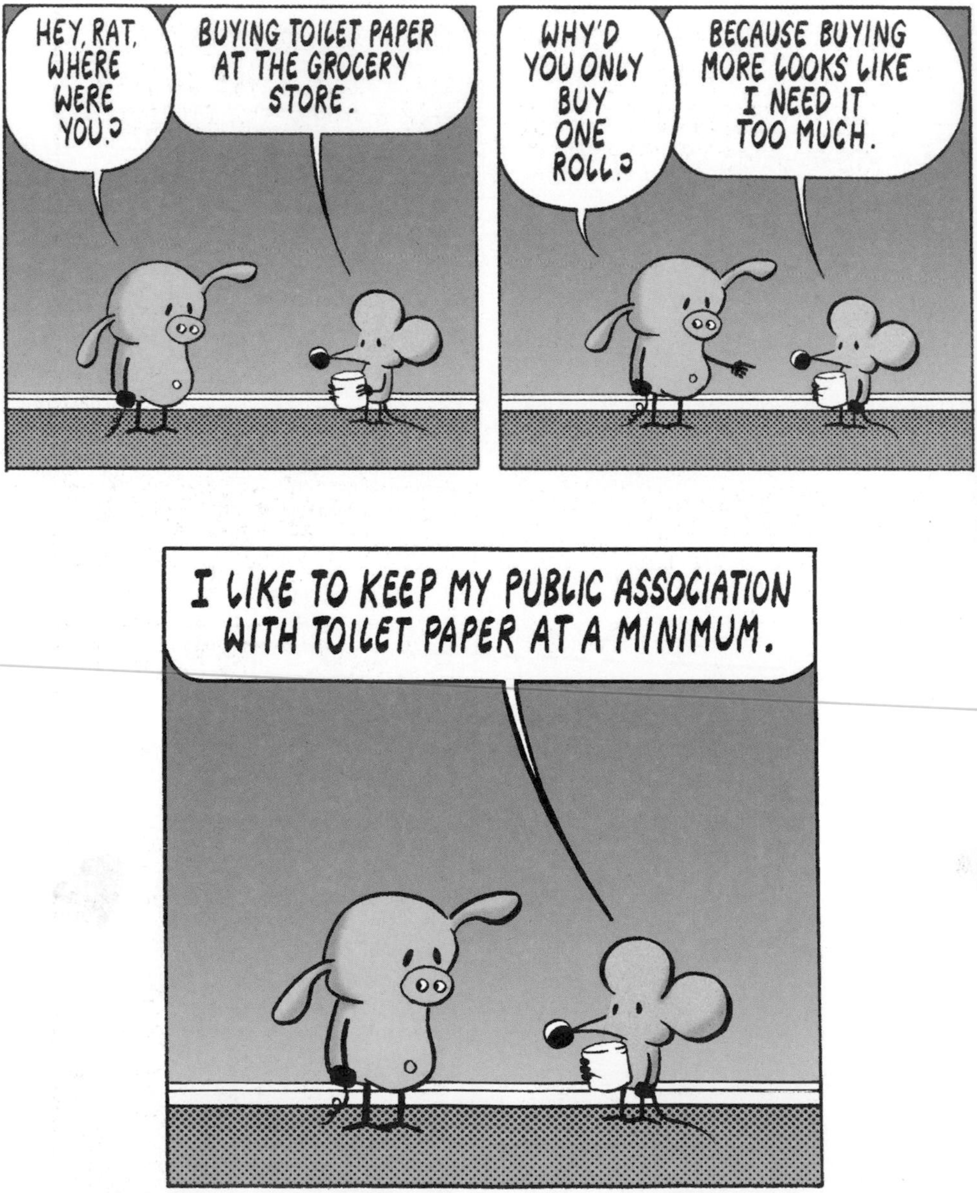
HEY, RAT, WHERE WERE YOU?
BUYING TOILET PAPER AT THE GROCERY STORE.
WHY'D YOU ONLY BUY ONE ROLL?
BECAUSE BUYING MORE LOOKS LIKE I NEED IT TOO MUCH.
I LIKE TO KEEP MY PUBLIC ASSOCIATION WITH TOILET PAPER AT A MINIMUM.

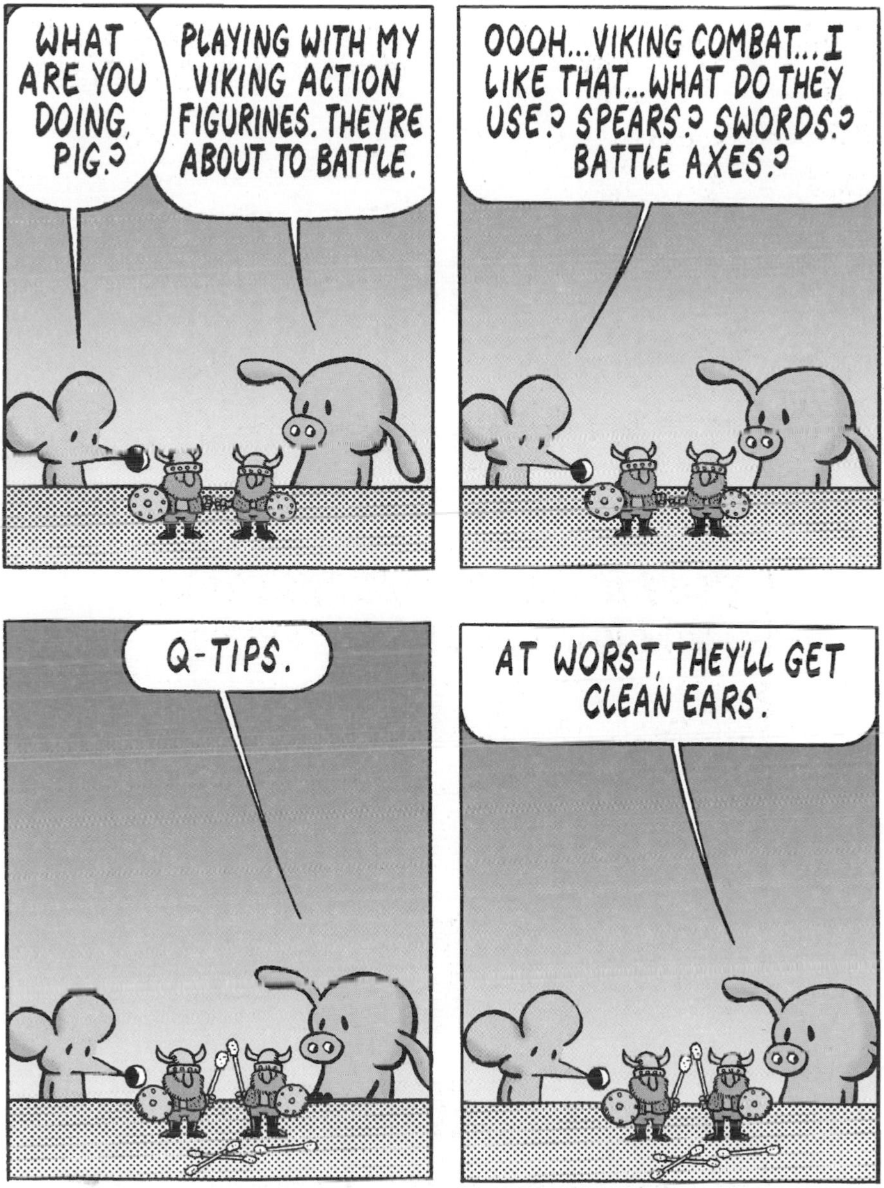
WHAT ARE YOU DOING, PIG?
PLAYING WITH MY VIKING ACTION FIGURINES. THEY'RE ABOUT TO BATTLE.
OOOH... VIKING COMBAT... I LIKE THAT... WHAT DO THEY USE? SPEARS? SWORDS? BATTLE AXES?
Q-TIPS.
AT WORST, THEY'LL GET CLEAN EARS.

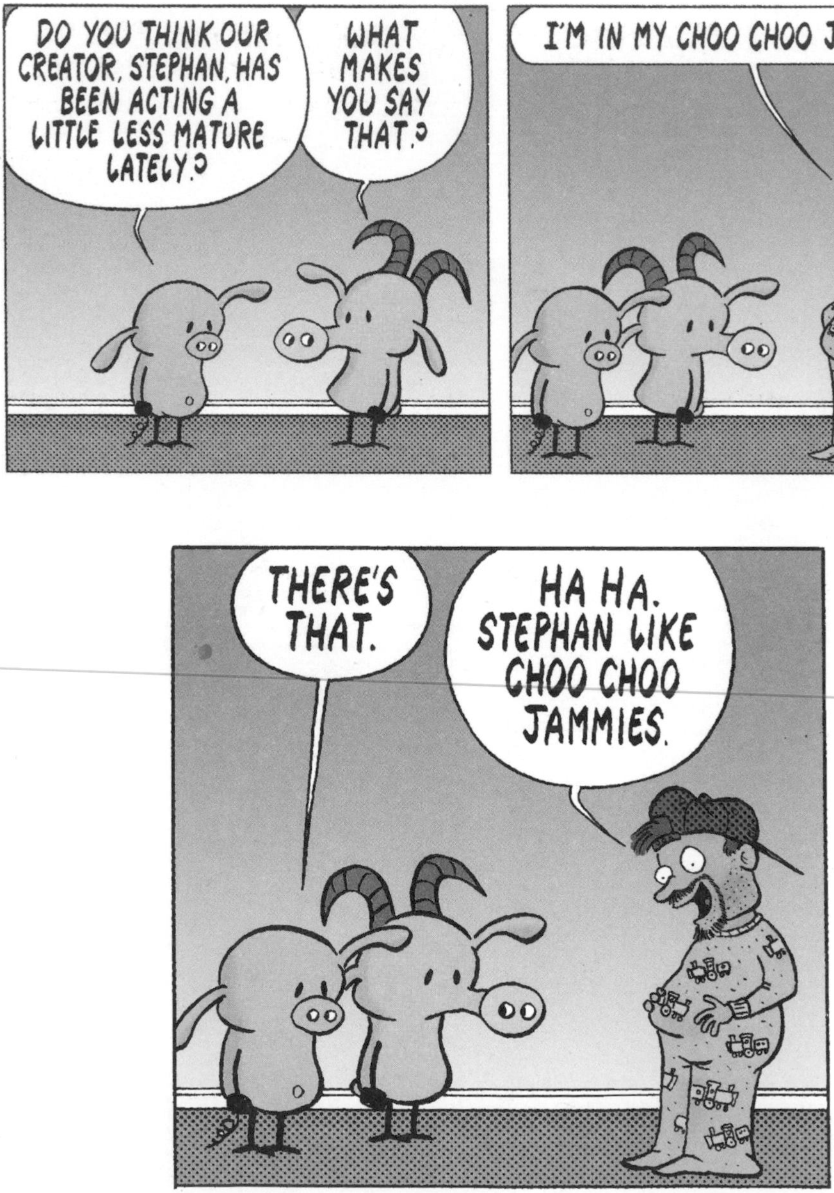
DO YOU THINK OUR CREATOR, STEPHAN, HAS BEEN ACTING A LITTLE LESS MATURE LATELY?
WHAT MAKES YOU SAY THAT?
I'M IN MY CHOO CHOO JAMMIES.
THERE'S THAT.
HA HA. STEPHAN LIKE CHOO CHOO JAMMIES.

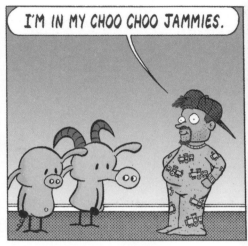

OUR CREATOR, STEPHAN, IS HAVING SOME SORT OF MIDLIFE CRISIS.
YOU MEAN LIKE WHERE HE BUYS A SPORTS CAR AND TRIES TO RELIVE HIS 20s?
I THINK HE'S AIMING FOR A LITTLE YOUNGER THAN THAT.

PEEK-A-BOO! I SEE YOU!
PLEASE GO AWAY.

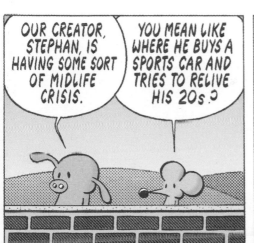

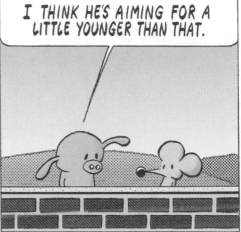

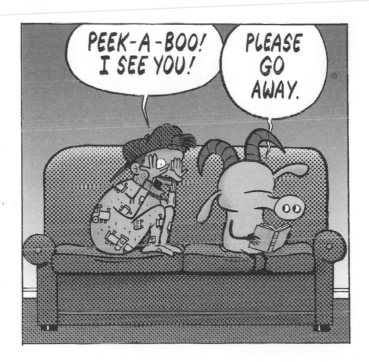

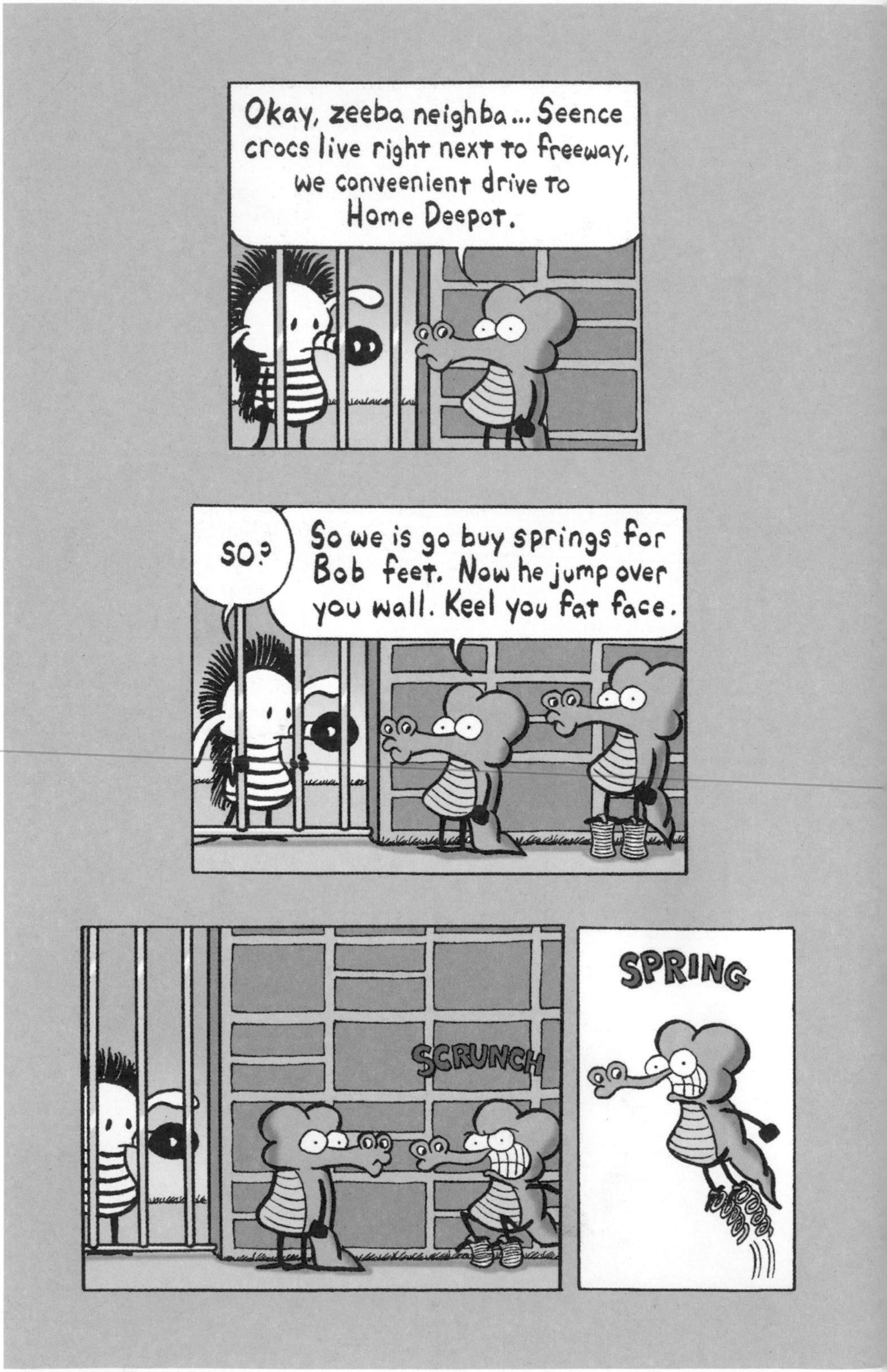
Okay, zeeba neighba... Seence crocs live right next to freeway, we conveenient drive to Home Deepot.
SO?
So we is go buy springs for Bob feet. Now he jump over you wall. Keel you fat face.
SCRUNCH
SPRING

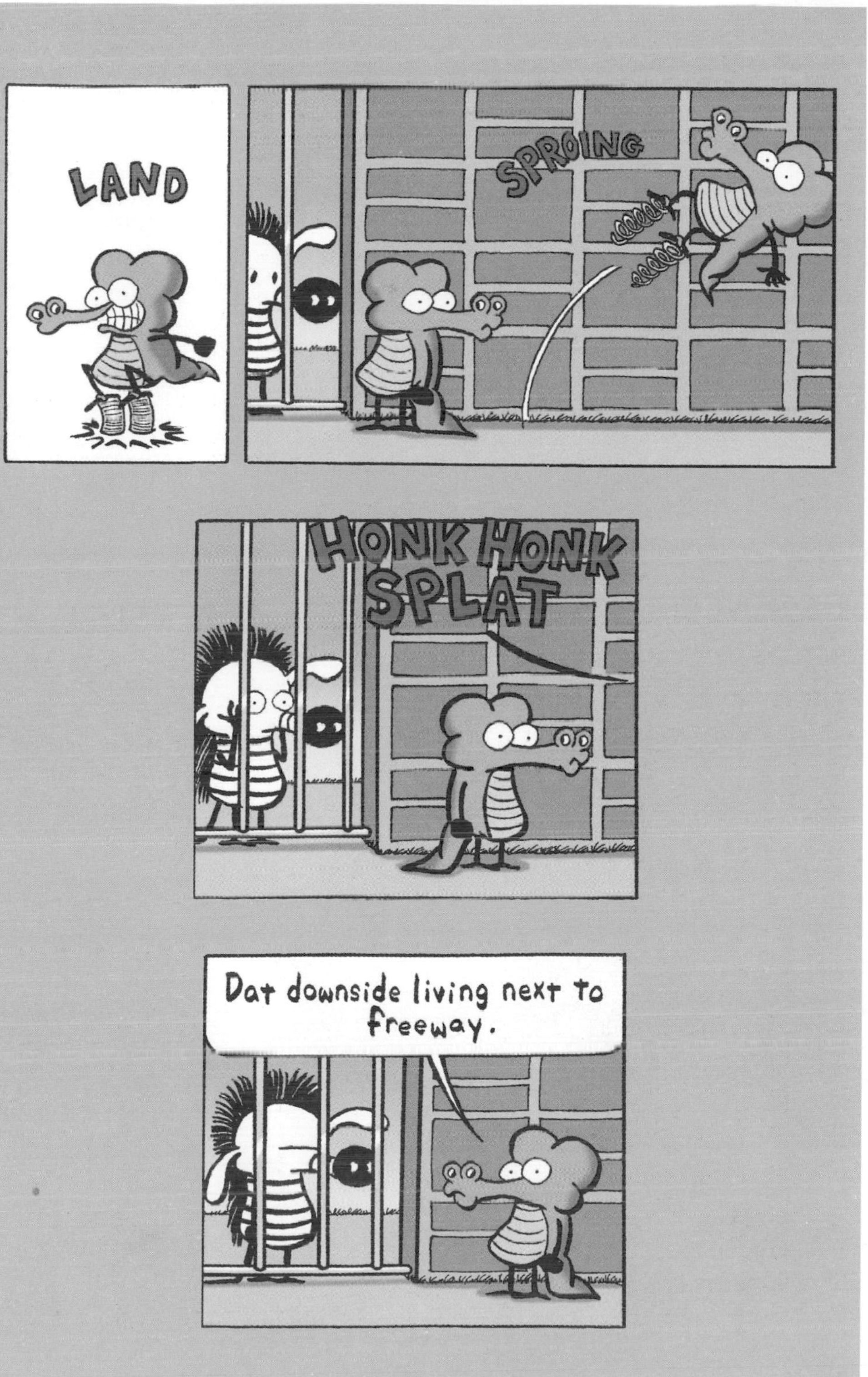
LAND
SPROING
HONK HONK
SPLAT
Dat downside living next to freeway.

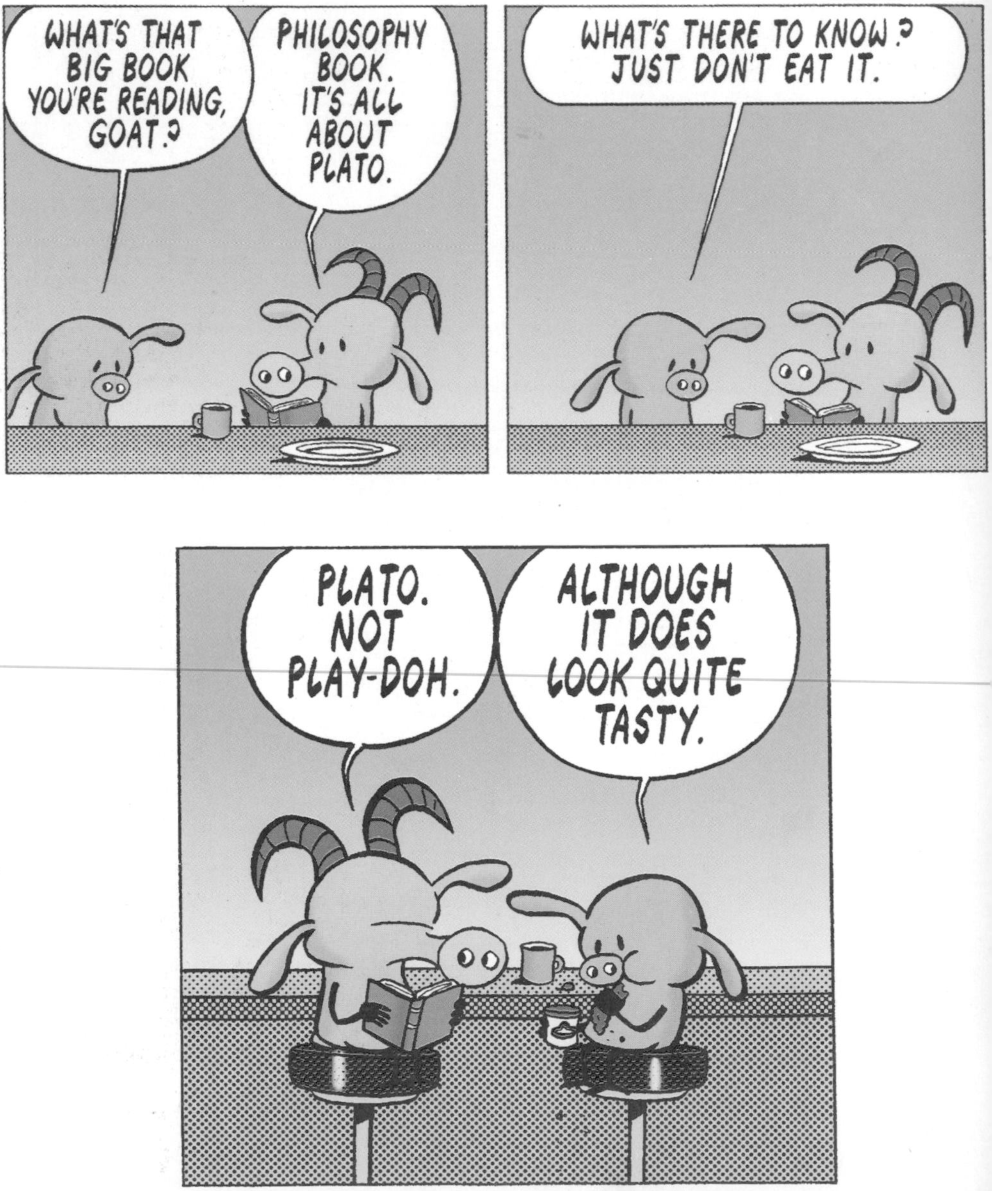
WHAT'S THAT BIG BOOK YOU'RE READING, GOAT?
PHILOSOPHY BOOK. IT'S ALL ABOUT PLATO.
WHAT'S THERE TO KNOW? JUST DON'T EAT IT.
PLATO. NOT PLAY-DOH.
ALTHOUGH IT DOES LOOK QUITE TASTY.

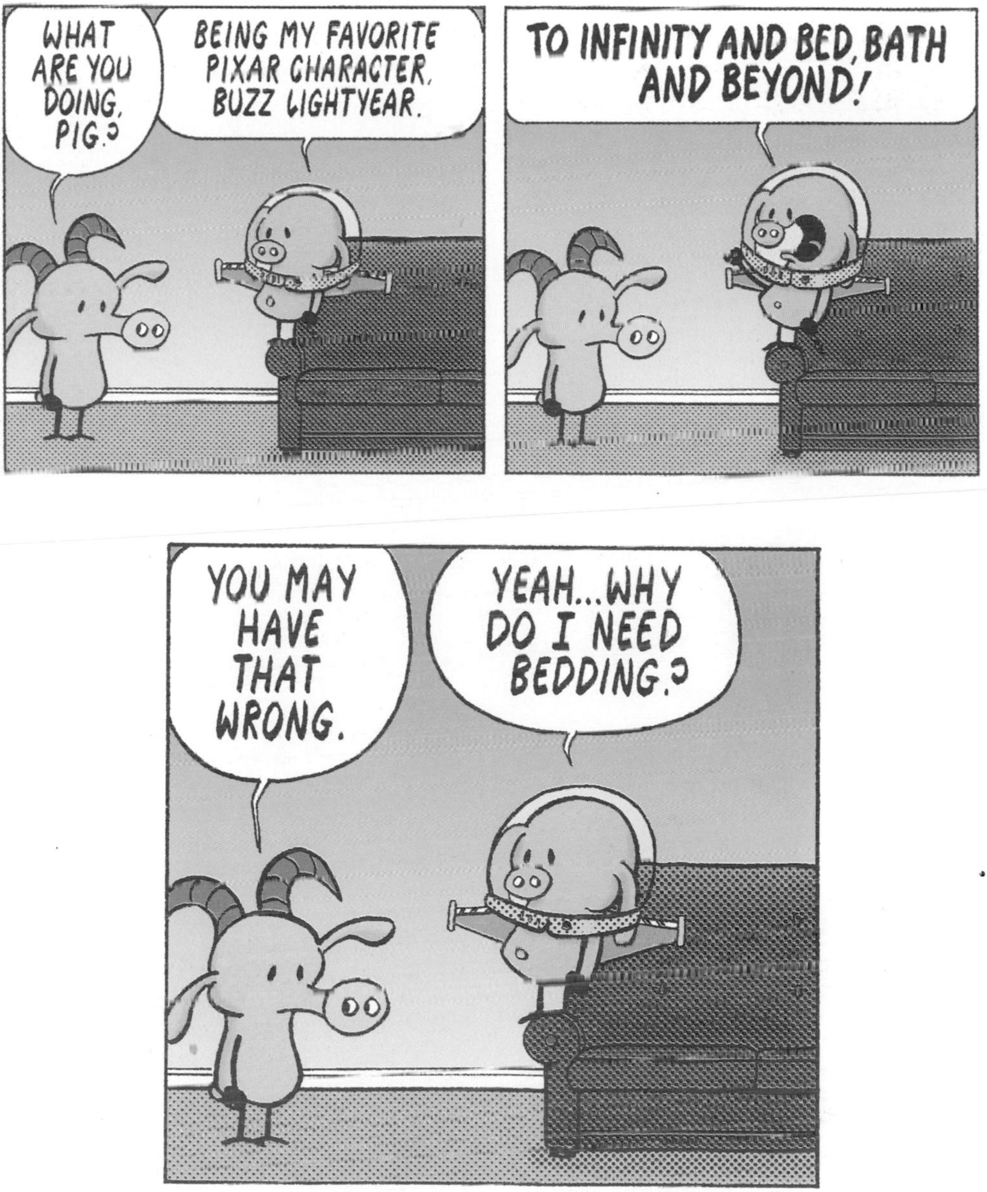
WHAT ARE YOU DOING, PIG?
BEING MY FAVORITE PIXAR CHARACTER, BUZZ LIGHTYEAR.
TO INFINITY AND BED, BATH AND BEYOND!
YOU MAY HAVE THAT WRONG.
YEAH...WHY DO I NEED BEDDING?

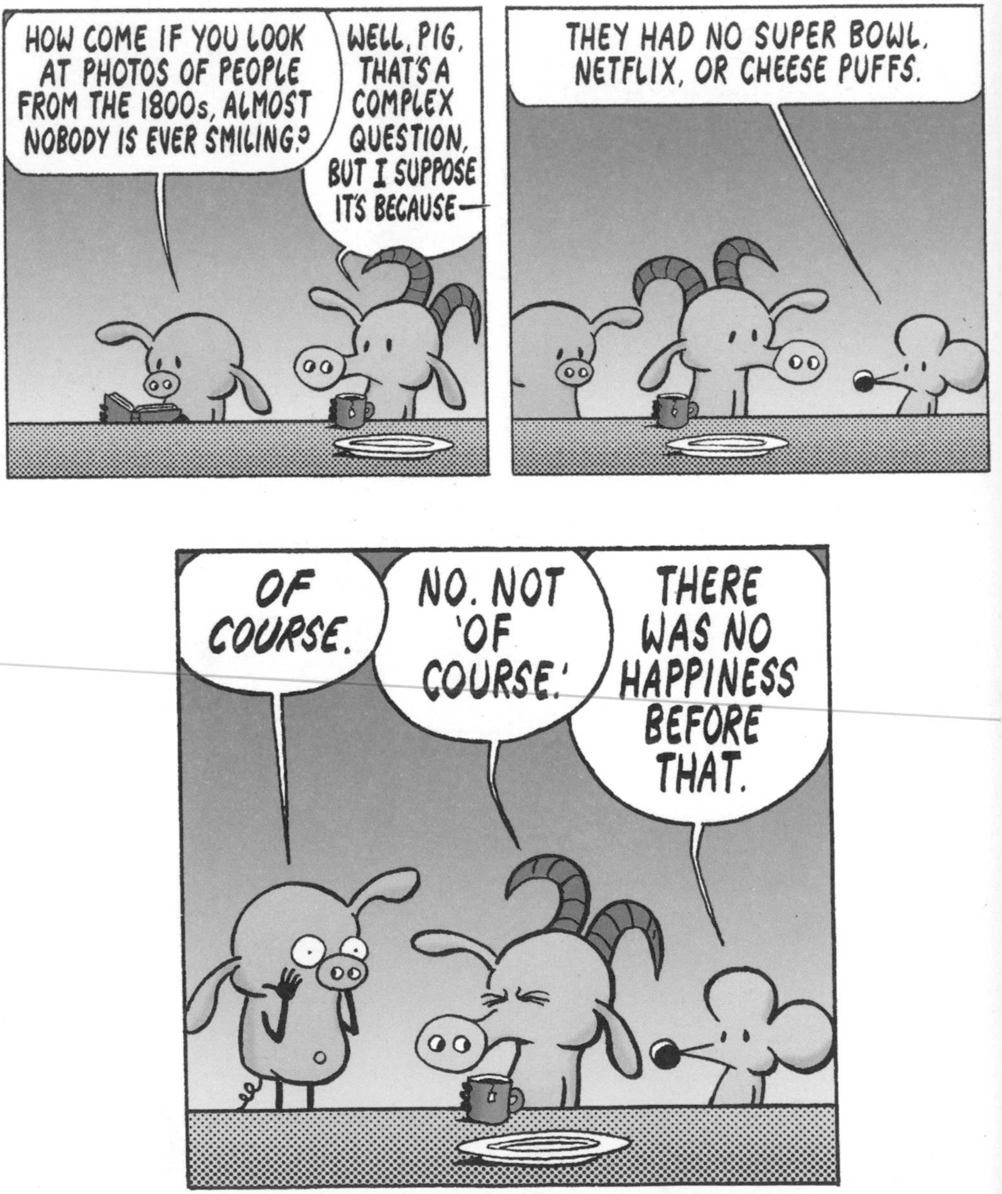
HOW COME IF YOU LOOK AT PHOTOS OF PEOPLE FROM THE 1800s, ALMOST NOBODY IS EVER SMILING?
WELL, PIG, THAT'S A COMPLEX QUESTION, BUT I SUPPOSE IT'S BECAUSE—
THEY HAD NO SUPER BOWL, NETFLIX, OR CHEESE PUFFS.
OF COURSE.
NO. NOT 'OF COURSE.'
THERE WAS NO HAPPINESS BEFORE THAT.

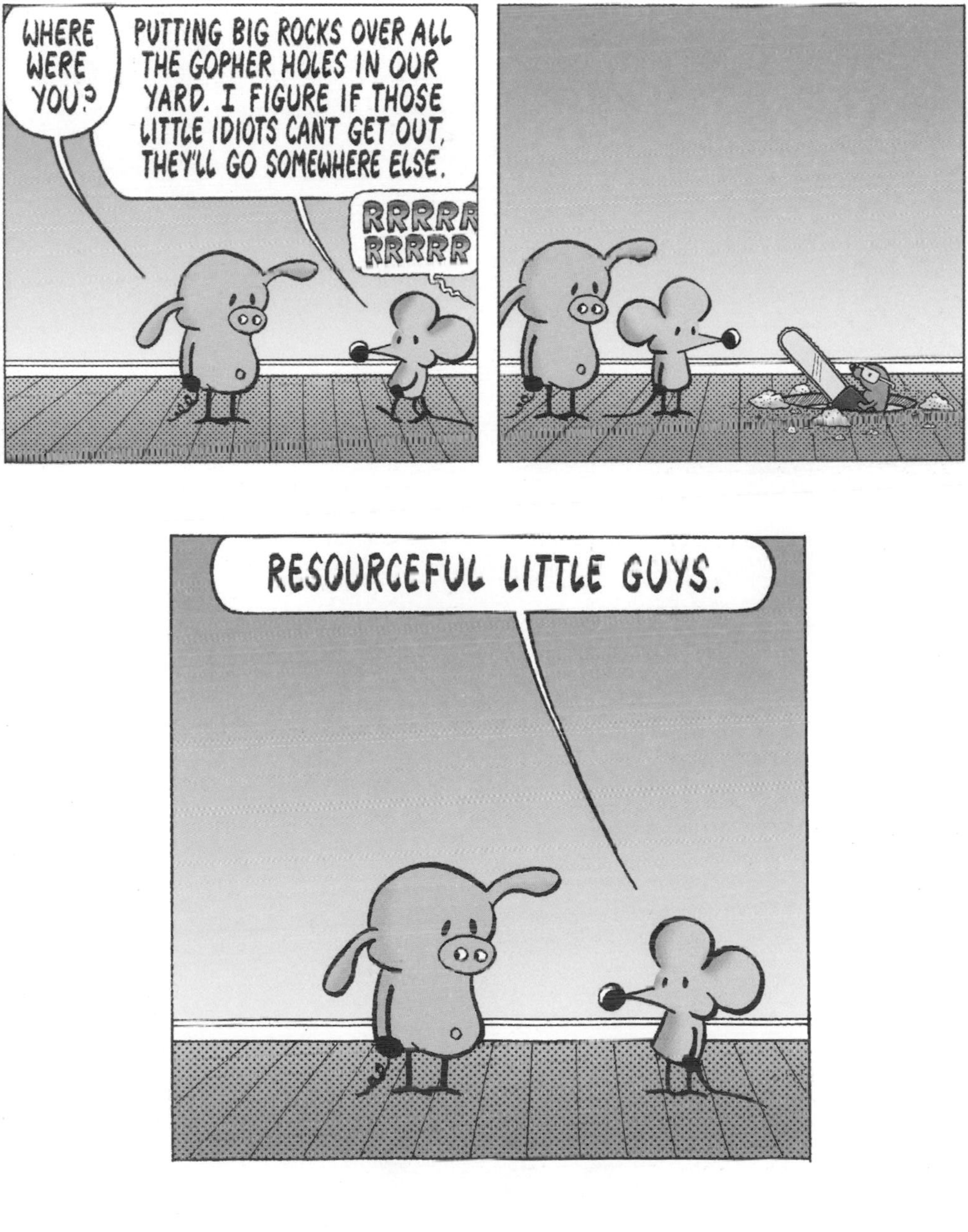
WHERE WERE YOU?
PUTTING BIG ROCKS OVER ALL THE GOPHER HOLES IN OUR YARD. I FIGURE IF THOSE LITTLE IDIOTS CAN'T GET OUT, THEY'LL GO SOMEWHERE ELSE.
RRRRR RRRRR
RESOURCEFUL LITTLE GUYS.

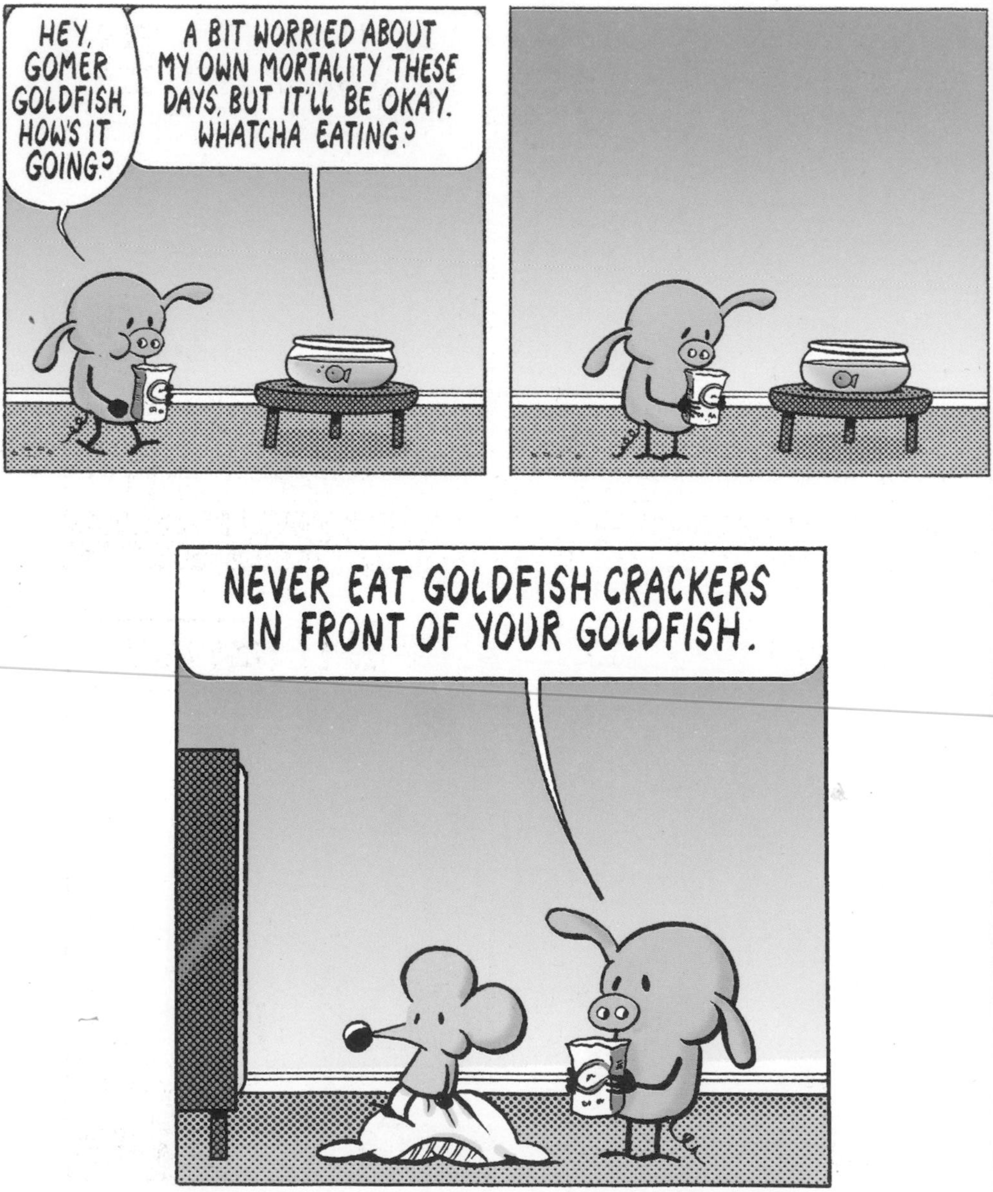
HEY, GOMER GOLDFISH, HOW'S IT GOING?
A BIT WORRIED ABOUT MY OWN MORTALITY THESE DAYS, BUT IT'LL BE OKAY. WHATCHA EATING?
NEVER EAT GOLDFISH CRACKERS IN FRONT OF YOUR GOLDFISH.

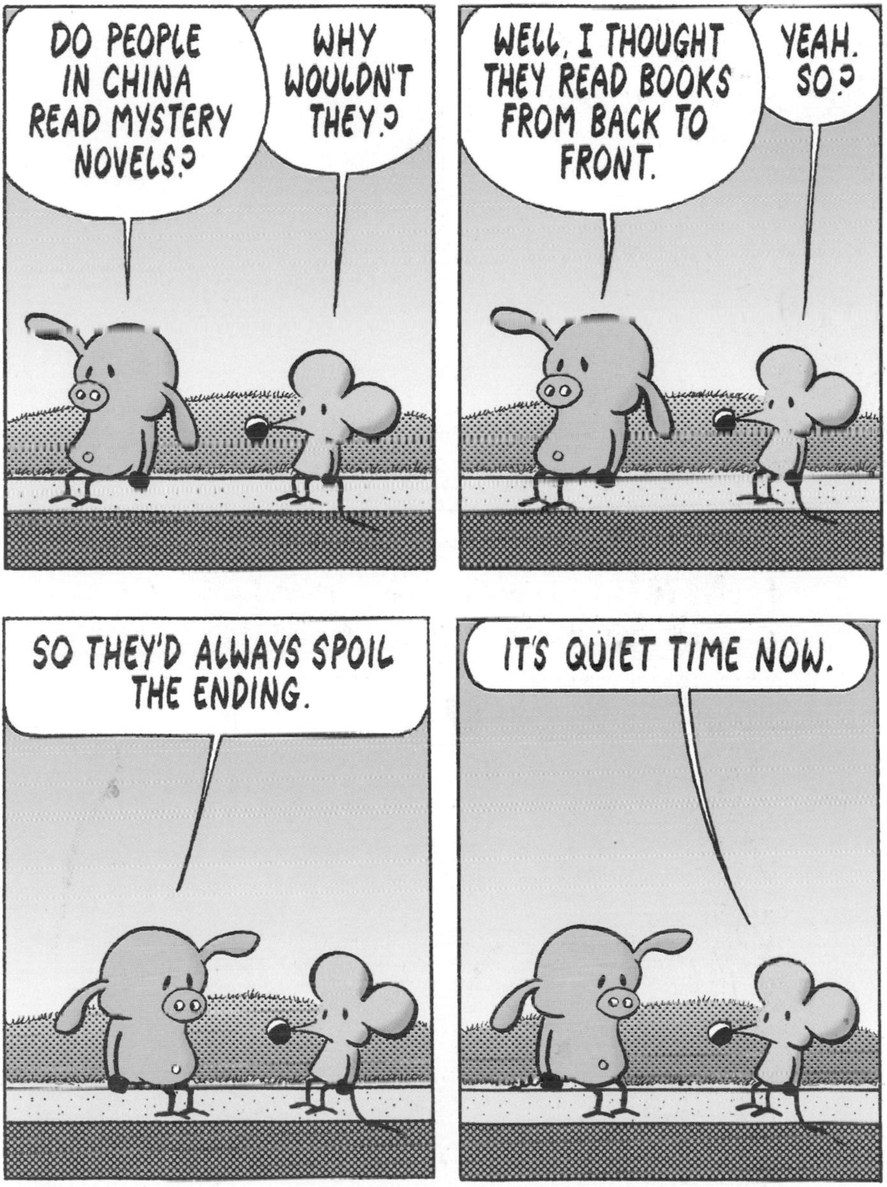

DO PEOPLE IN CHINA READ MYSTERY NOVELS?
WHY WOULDN'T THEY?
WELL, I THOUGHT THEY READ BOOKS FROM BACK TO FRONT.
YEAH. SO?
SO THEY'D ALWAYS SPOIL THE ENDING.
IT'S QUIET TIME NOW.

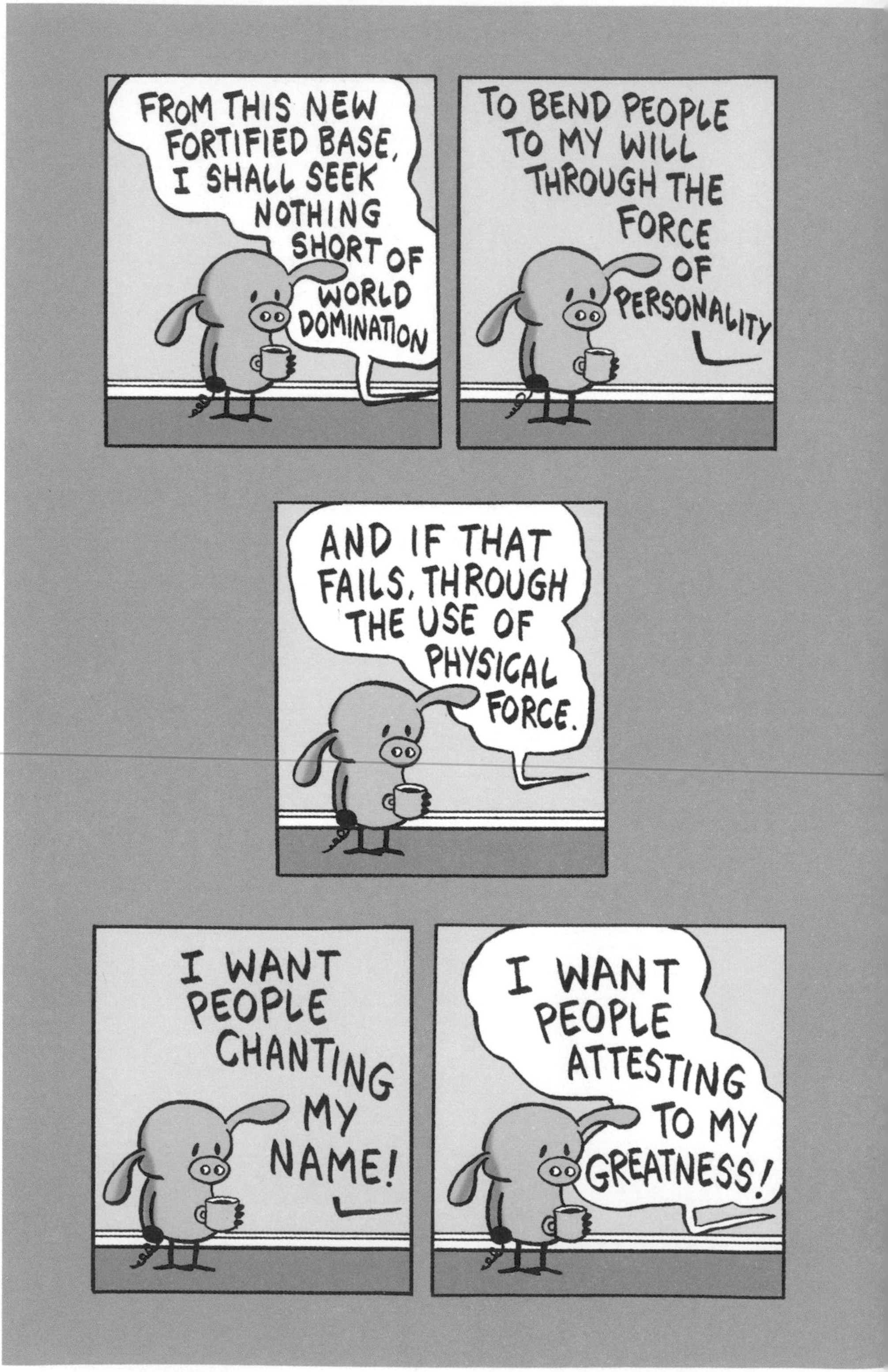
FROM THIS NEW FORTIFIED BASE, I SHALL SEEK NOTHING SHORT OF WORLD DOMINATION
TO BEND PEOPLE TO MY WILL THROUGH THE FORCE OF PERSONALITY
AND IF THAT FAILS, THROUGH THE USE OF PHYSICAL FORCE.
I WANT PEOPLE CHANTING MY NAME!
I WANT PEOPLE ATTESTING TO MY GREATNESS!

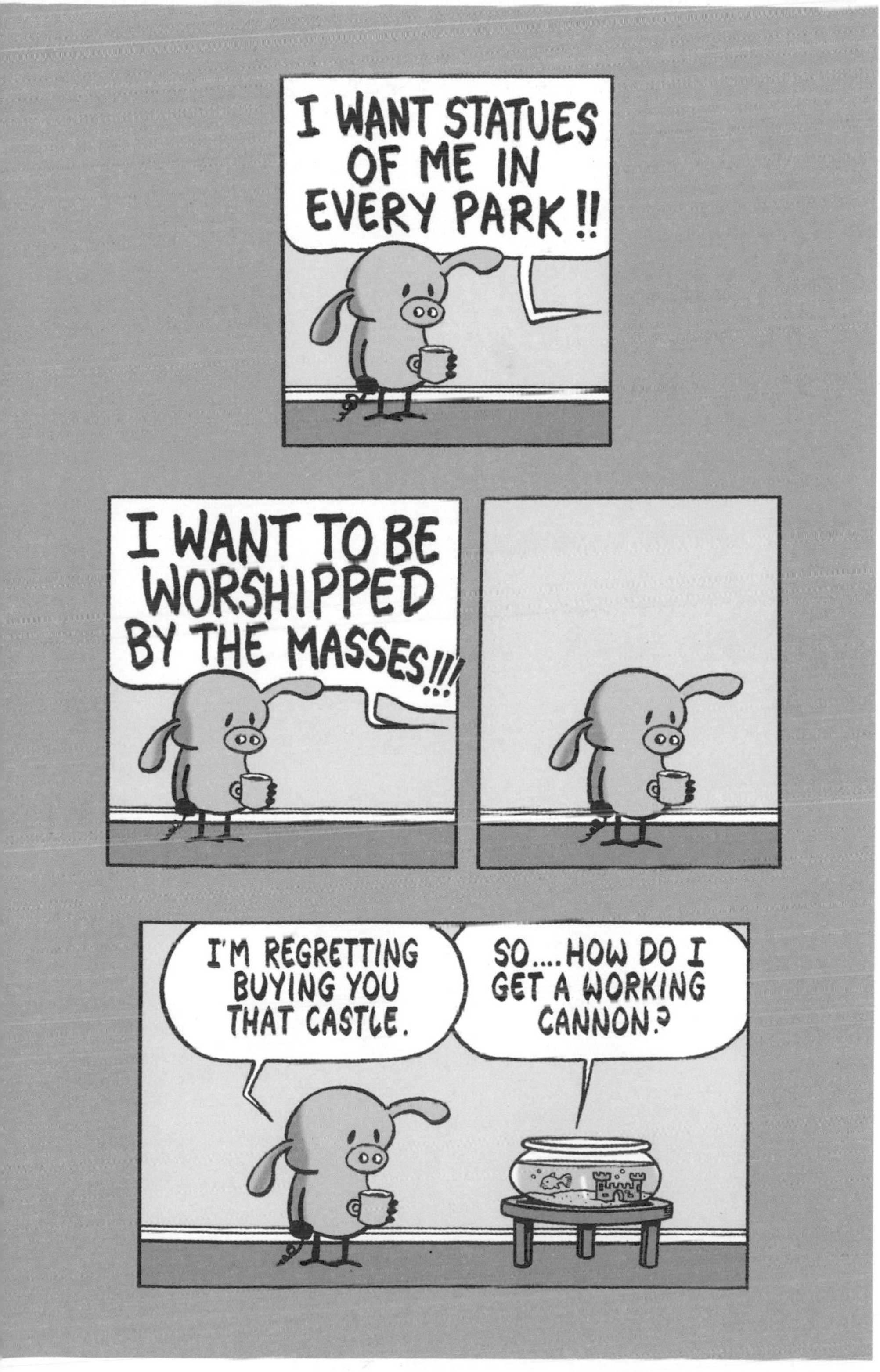
I WANT STATUES OF ME IN EVERY PARK !!
I WANT TO BE WORSHIPPED BY THE MASSES!!!
I'M REGRETTING BUYING YOU THAT CASTLE.
SO.... HOW DO I GET A WORKING CANNON?

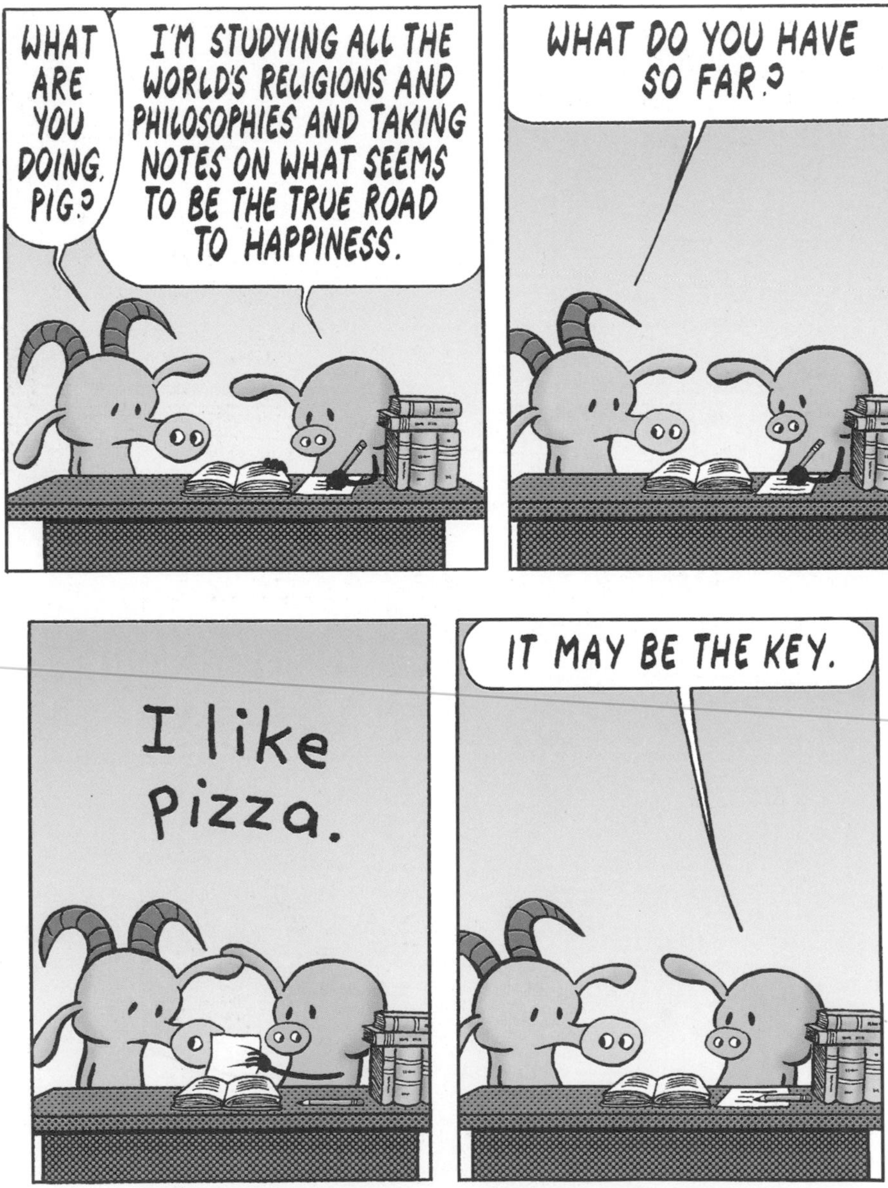
WHAT ARE YOU DOING, PIG?
I'M STUDYING ALL THE WORLD'S RELIGIONS AND PHILOSOPHIES AND TAKING NOTES ON WHAT SEEMS TO BE THE TRUE ROAD TO HAPPINESS.
WHAT DO YOU HAVE SO FAR?
I like pizza.
IT MAY BE THE KEY.

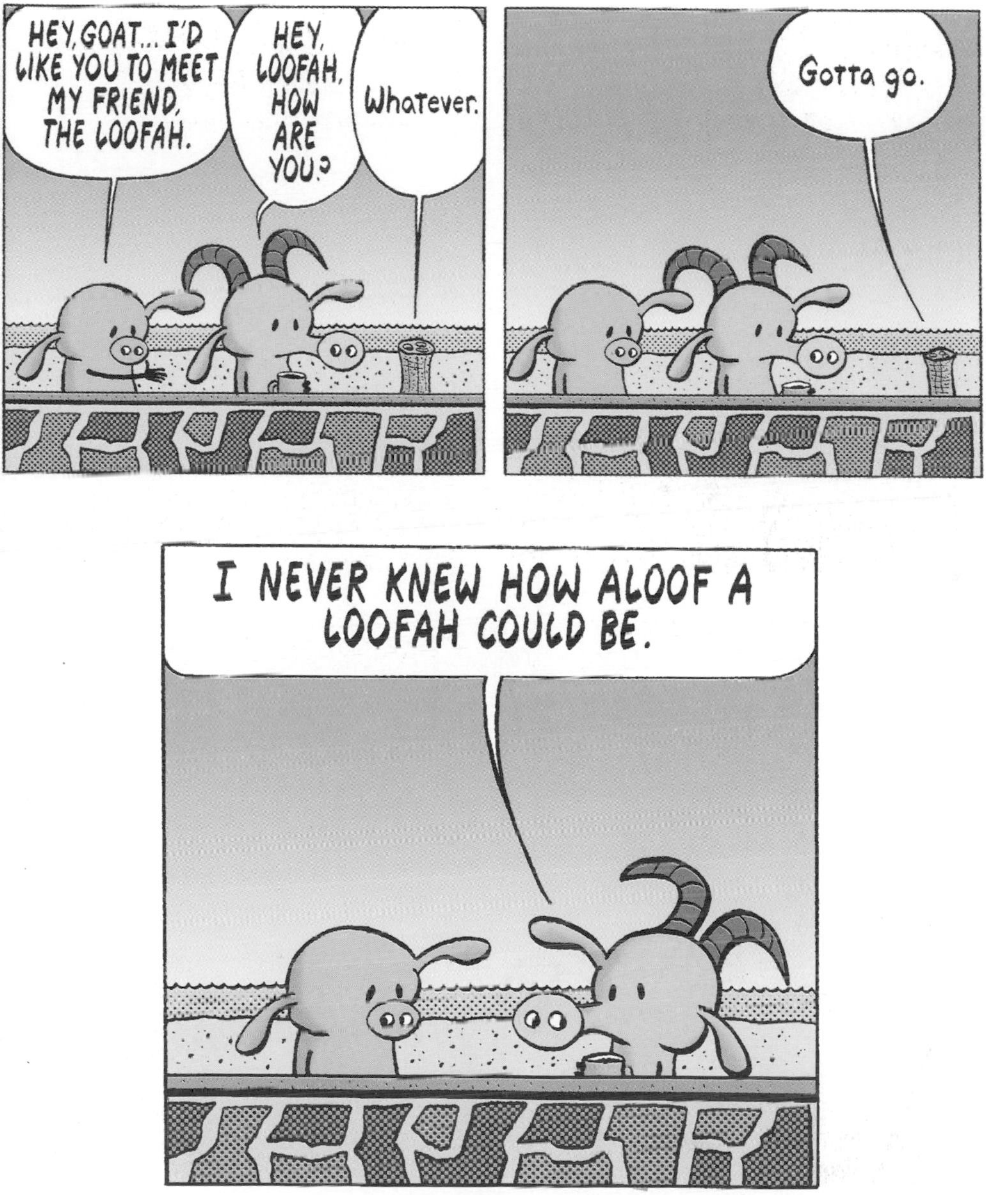
HEY, GOAT... I'D LIKE YOU TO MEET MY FRIEND, THE LOOFAH.
HEY, LOOFAH, HOW ARE YOU?
Whatever.
Gotta go.
I NEVER KNEW HOW ALOOF A LOOFAH COULD BE.

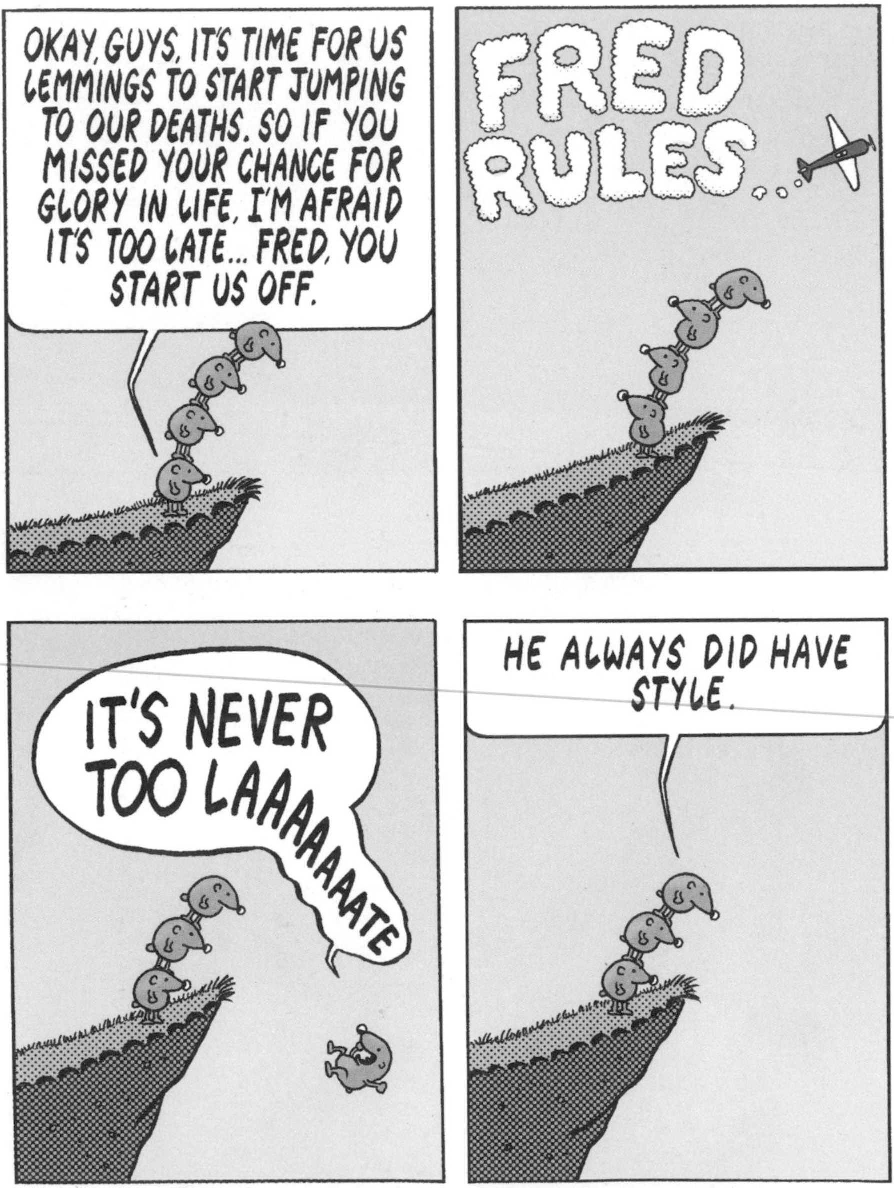
OKAY, GUYS, IT'S TIME FOR US LEMMINGS TO START JUMPING TO OUR DEATHS. SO IF YOU MISSED YOUR CHANCE FOR GLORY IN LIFE, I'M AFRAID IT'S TOO LATE... FRED, YOU START US OFF.
FRED RULES...
IT'S NEVER TOO LAAAAAAATE
HE ALWAYS DID HAVE STYLE.

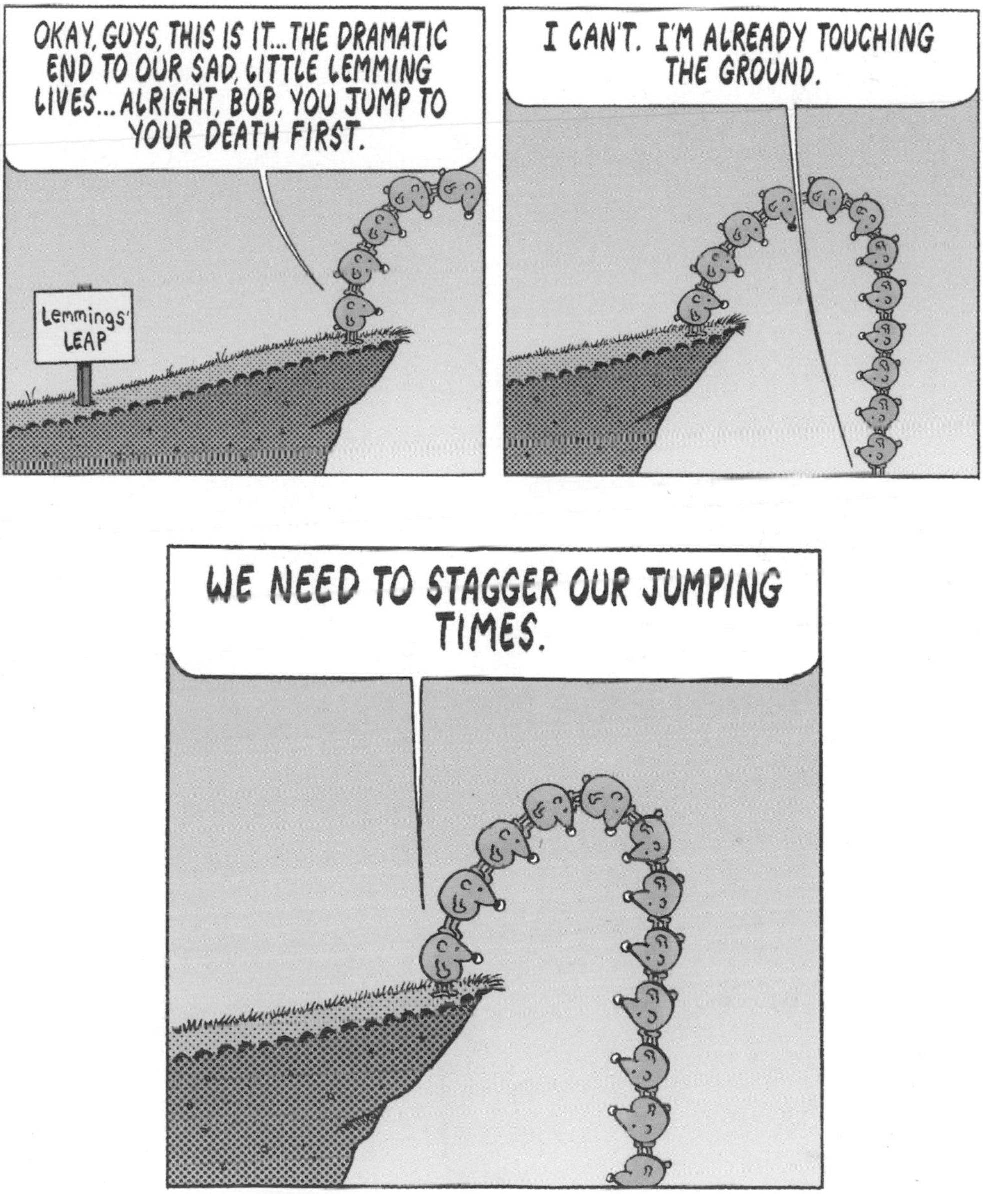
OKAY, GUYS, THIS IS IT...THE DRAMATIC END TO OUR SAD, LITTLE LEMMING LIVES... ALRIGHT, BOB, YOU JUMP TO YOUR DEATH FIRST.
Lemmings' LEAP
I CAN'T. I'M ALREADY TOUCHING THE GROUND.
WE NEED TO STAGGER OUR JUMPING TIMES.

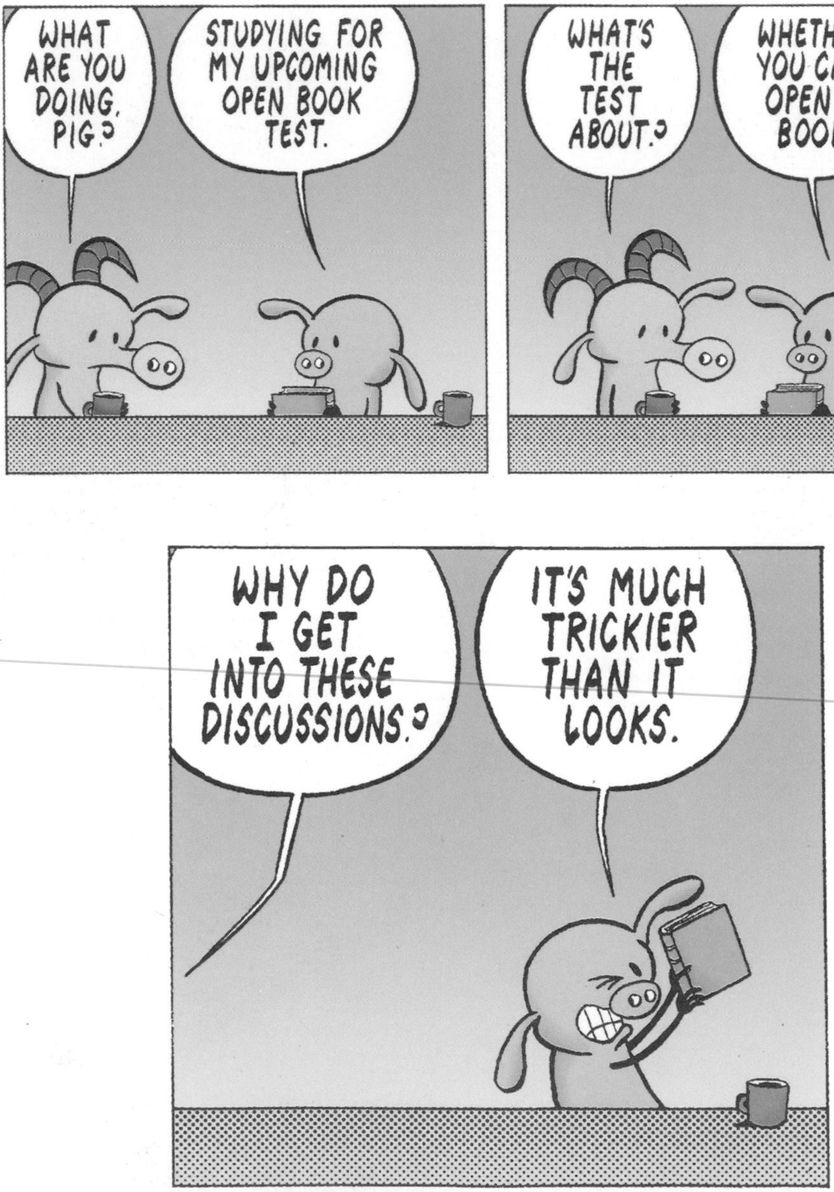
WHAT ARE YOU DOING, PIG?
STUDYING FOR MY UPCOMING OPEN BOOK TEST.
WHAT'S THE TEST ABOUT?
WHETHER YOU CAN OPEN A BOOK.
WHY DO I GET INTO THESE DISCUSSIONS?
IT'S MUCH TRICKIER THAN IT LOOKS.

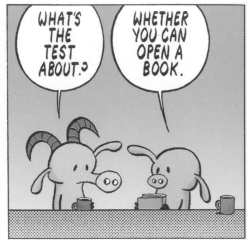

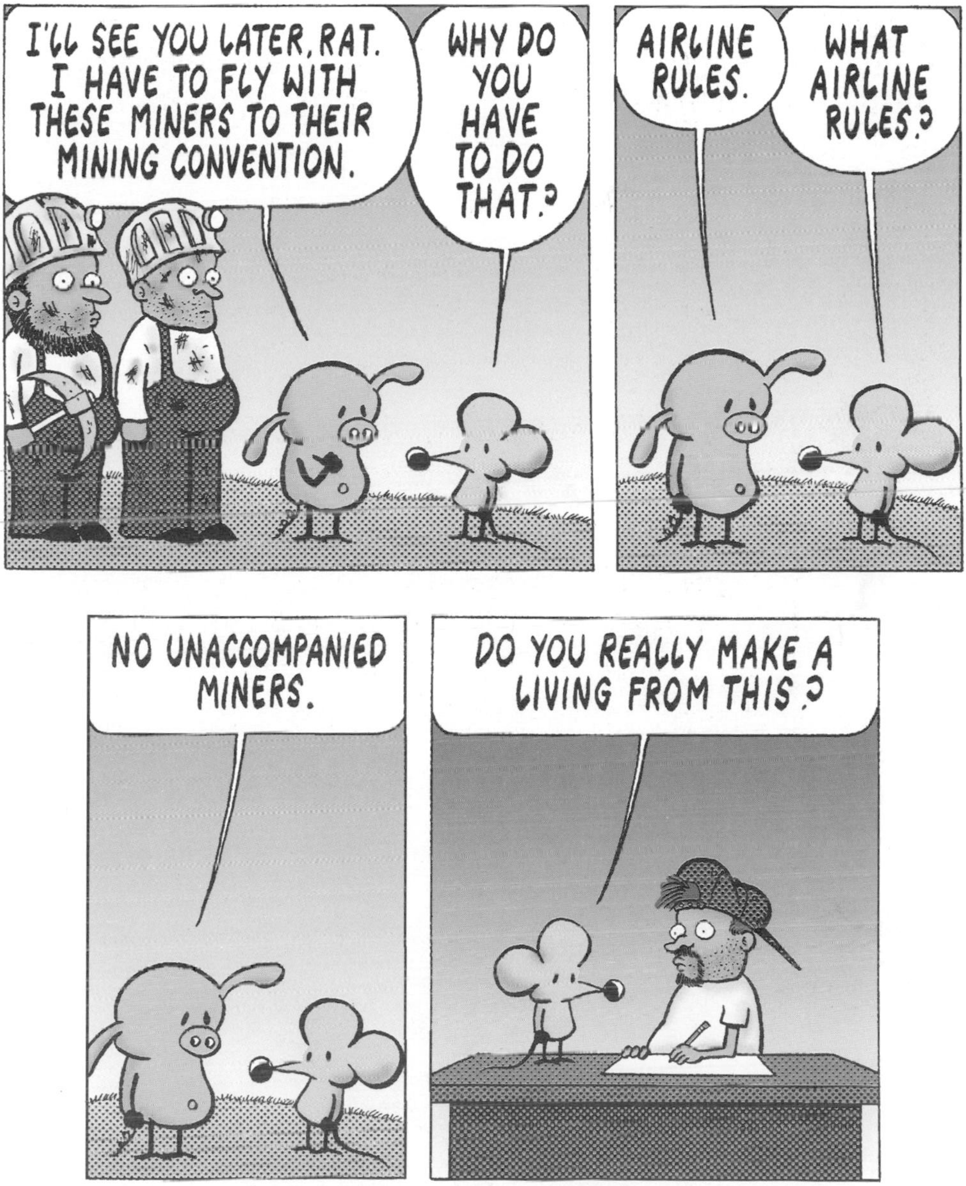
I'LL SEE YOU LATER, RAT. I HAVE TO FLY WITH THESE MINERS TO THEIR MINING CONVENTION.
WHY DO YOU HAVE TO DO THAT?
AIRLINE RULES.
WHAT AIRLINE RULES?
NO UNACCOMPANIED MINERS.
DO YOU REALLY MAKE A LIVING FROM THIS?

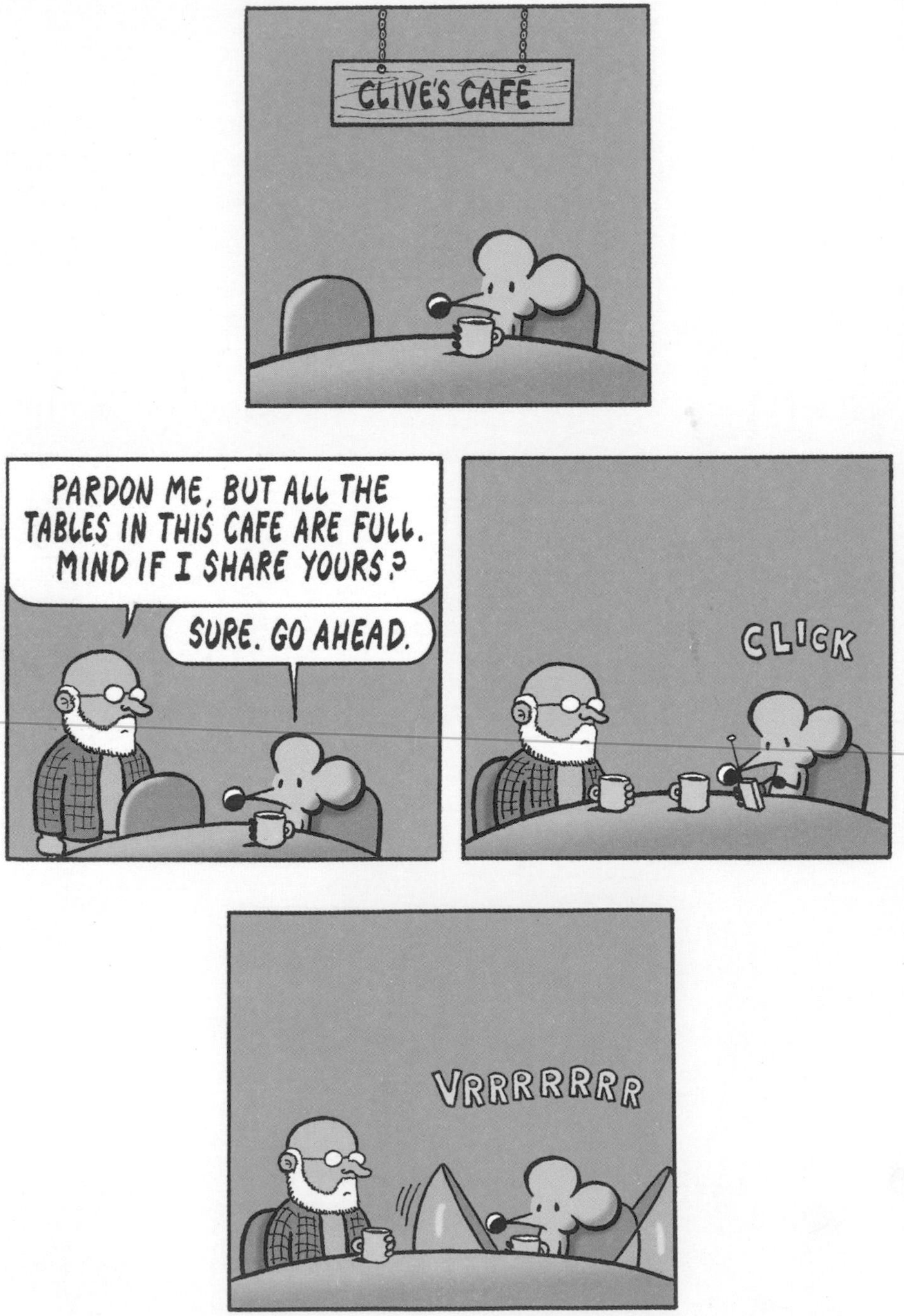
CLIVE'S CAFE
PARDON ME, BUT ALL THE TABLES IN THIS CAFE ARE FULL. MIND IF I SHARE YOURS?
SURE. GO AHEAD.
CLICK
VRRRRRRR

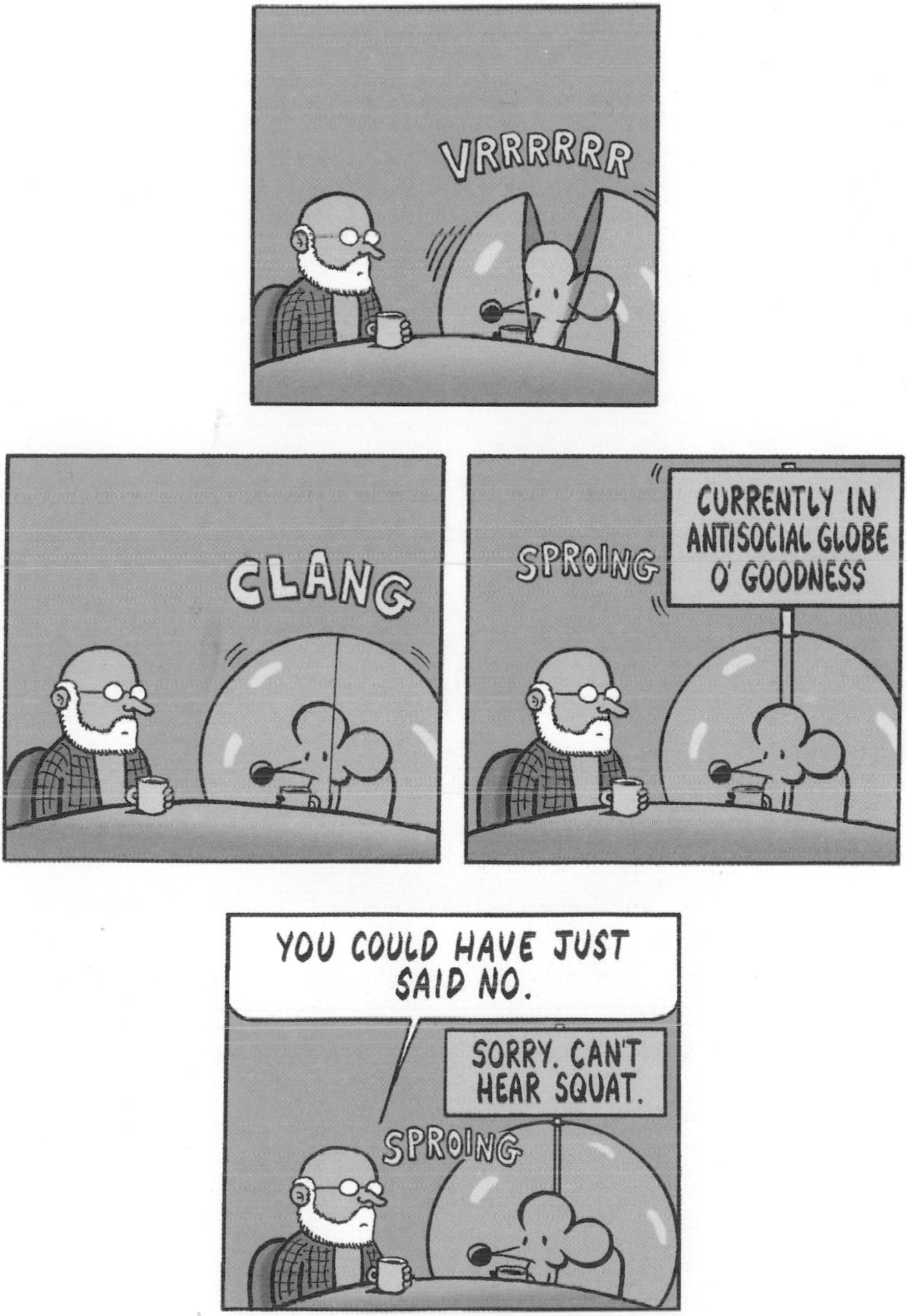
VRRRRRR
CLANG
SPROING
CURRENTLY IN ANTISOCIAL GLOBE O' GOODNESS
YOU COULD HAVE JUST SAID NO.
SORRY. CAN'T HEAR SQUAT.
SPROING

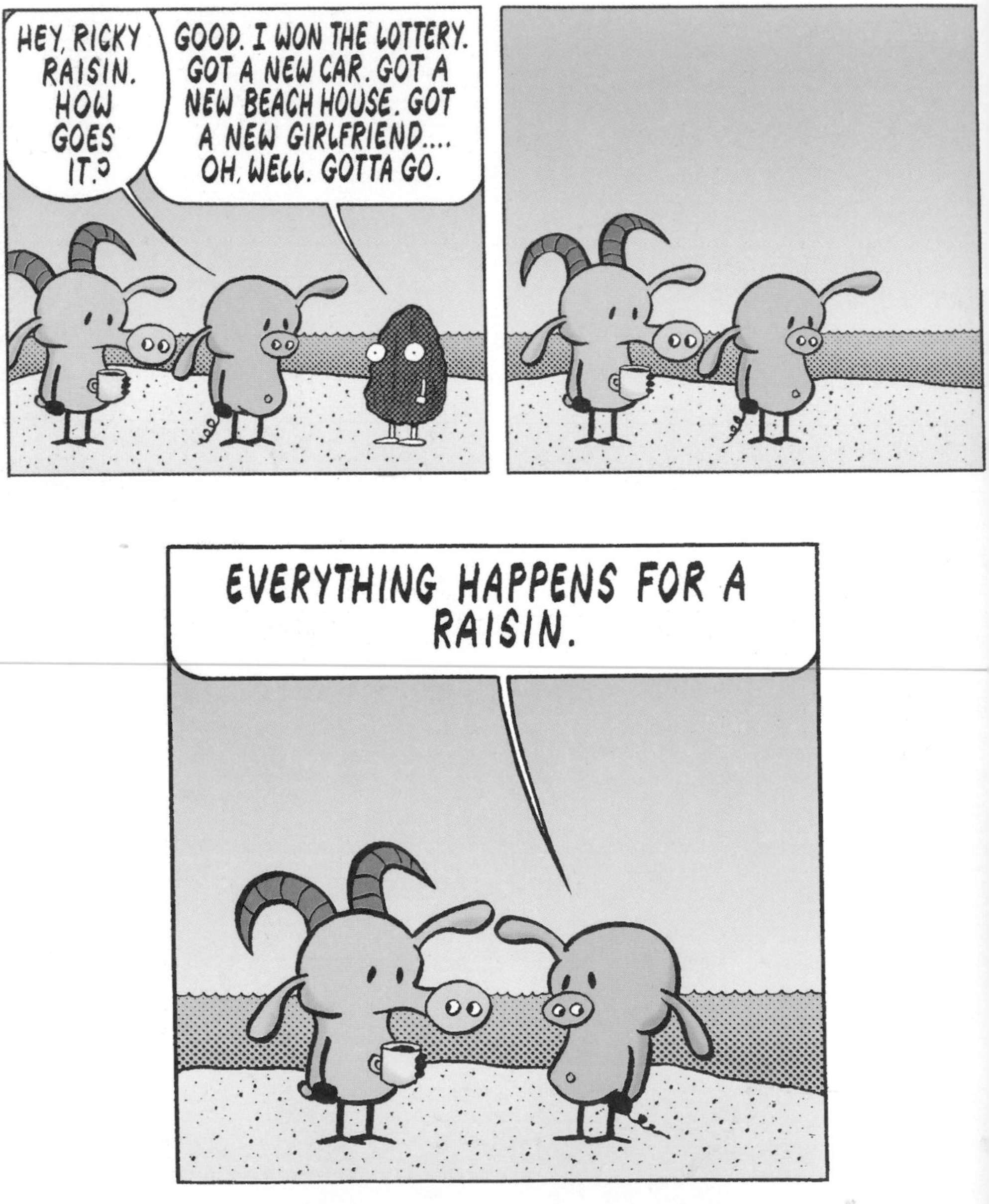
HEY, RICKY RAISIN. HOW GOES IT?
GOOD. I WON THE LOTTERY. GOT A NEW CAR. GOT A NEW BEACH HOUSE. GOT A NEW GIRLFRIEND.... OH, WELL. GOTTA GO.
EVERYTHING HAPPENS FOR A RAISIN.

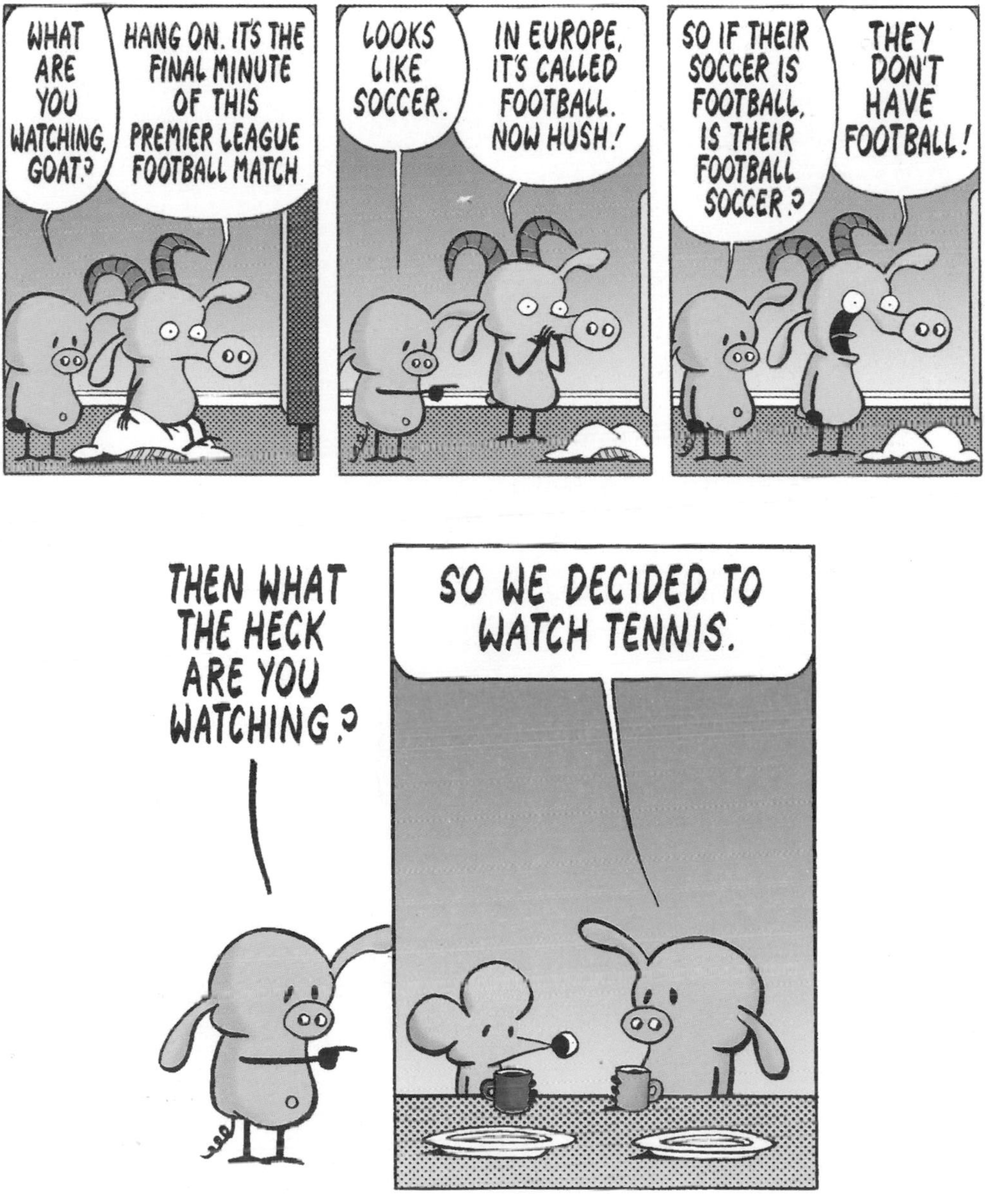
WHAT ARE YOU WATCHING, GOAT?
HANG ON. IT'S THE FINAL MINUTE OF THIS PREMIER LEAGUE FOOTBALL MATCH.
LOOKS LIKE SOCCER.
IN EUROPE, IT'S CALLED FOOTBALL. NOW HUSH!
SO IF THEIR SOCCER IS FOOTBALL, IS THEIR FOOTBALL SOCCER?
THEY DON'T HAVE FOOTBALL!
THEN WHAT THE HECK ARE YOU WATCHING?
SO WE DECIDED TO WATCH TENNIS.

HEY CHIEF... WE ALWAYS SWIM IN SCHOOLS, HOPING THAT THE OTHER GUY GETS EATEN, BUT HOW 'BOUT SOMETHING MORE ORGANIZED, LIKE DYING ALPHABETICALLY?

MAKES SENSE TO ME. ANYONE OPPOSED?

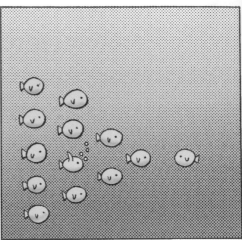

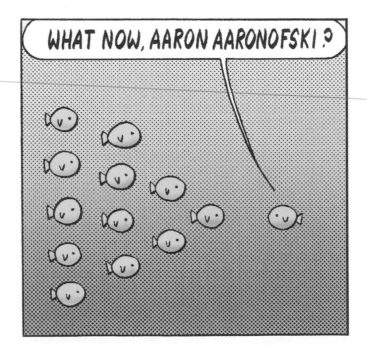

WHAT NOW, AARON AARONOFSKI?

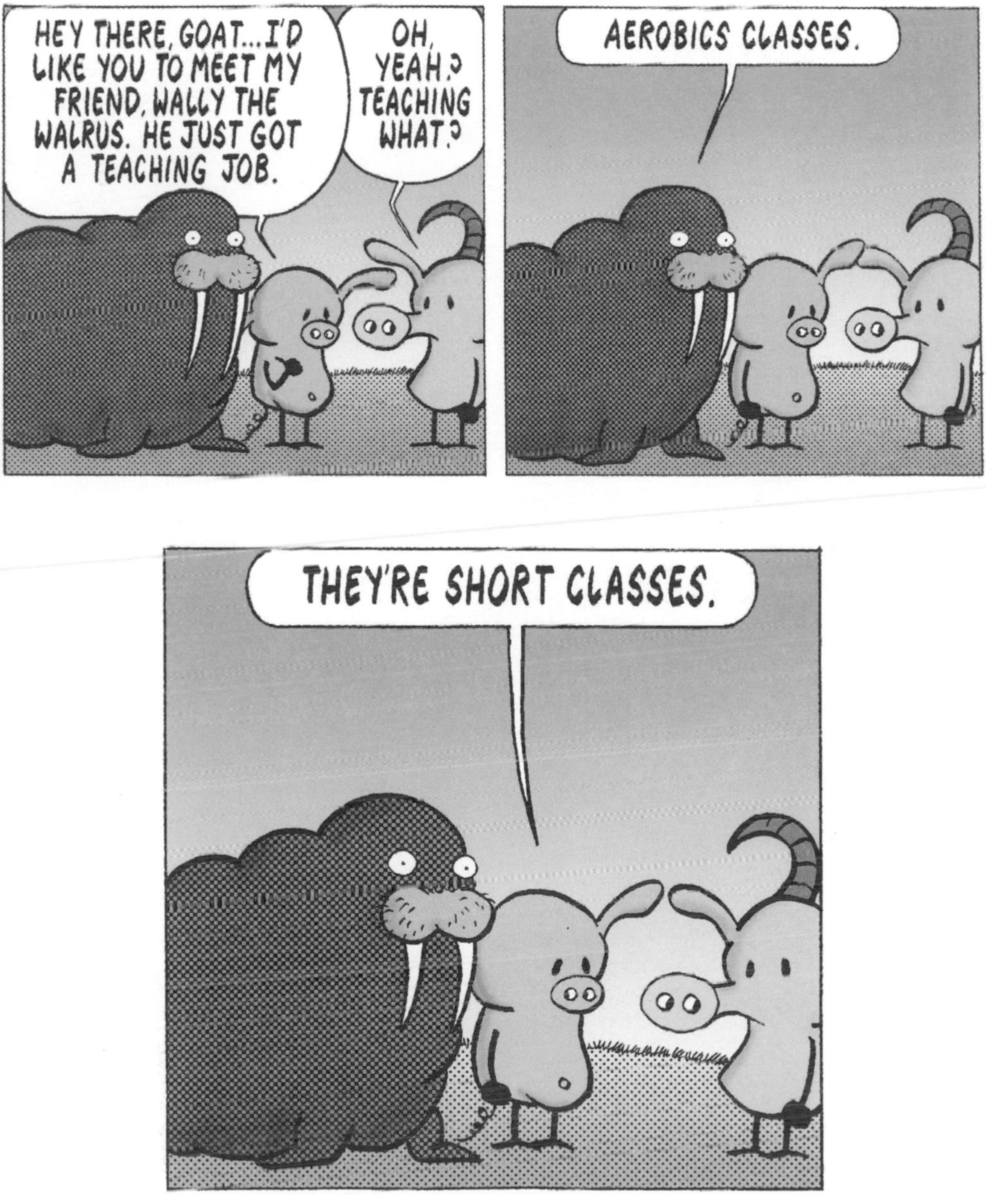
HEY THERE, GOAT...I'D LIKE YOU TO MEET MY FRIEND, WALLY THE WALRUS. HE JUST GOT A TEACHING JOB.
OH, YEAH? TEACHING WHAT?
AEROBICS CLASSES.
THEY'RE SHORT CLASSES.

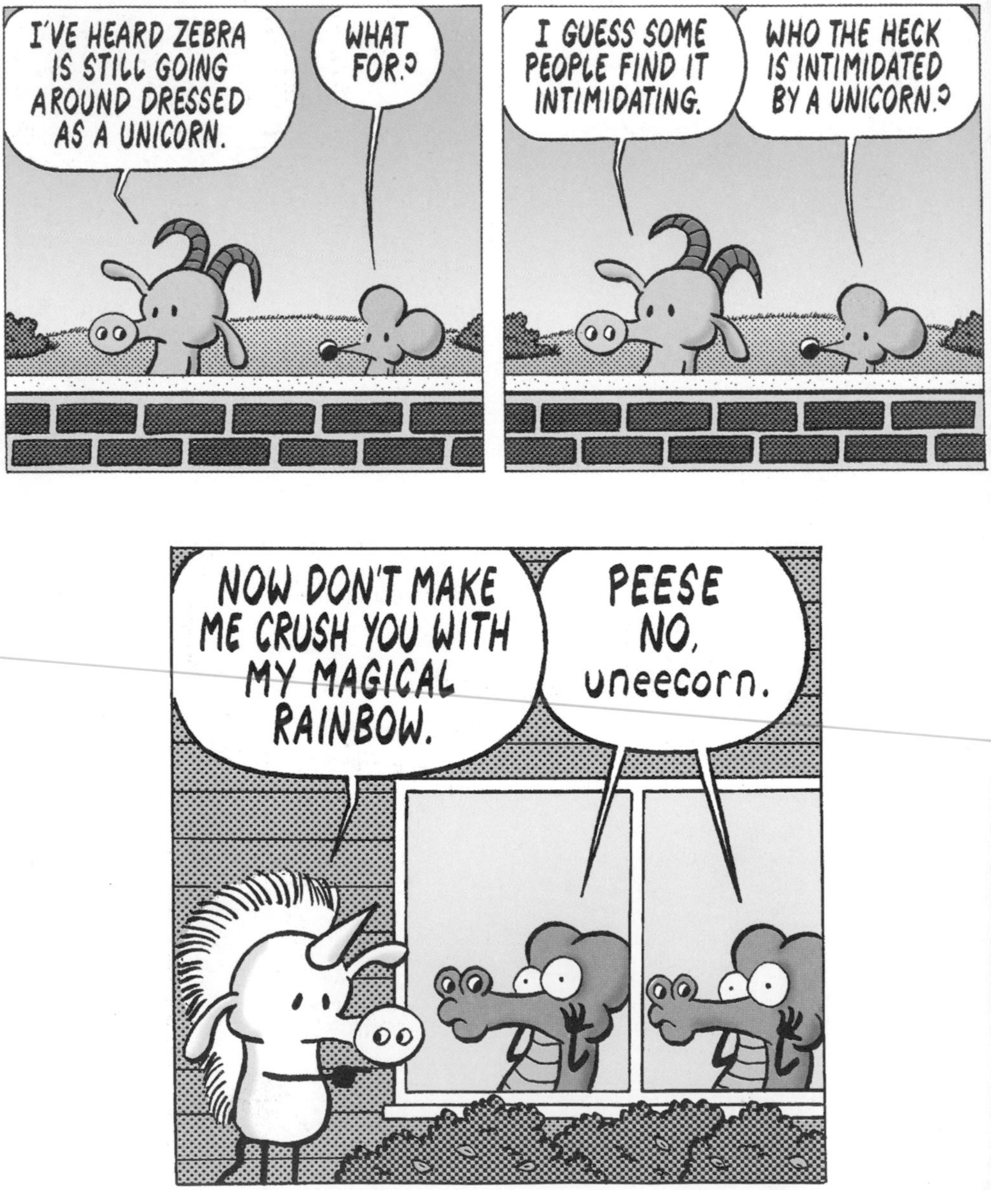
I'VE HEARD ZEBRA IS STILL GOING AROUND DRESSED AS A UNICORN.
WHAT FOR?
I GUESS SOME PEOPLE FIND IT INTIMIDATING.
WHO THE HECK IS INTIMIDATED BY A UNICORN?
NOW DON'T MAKE ME CRUSH YOU WITH MY MAGICAL RAINBOW.
PEESE NO, uneecorn.

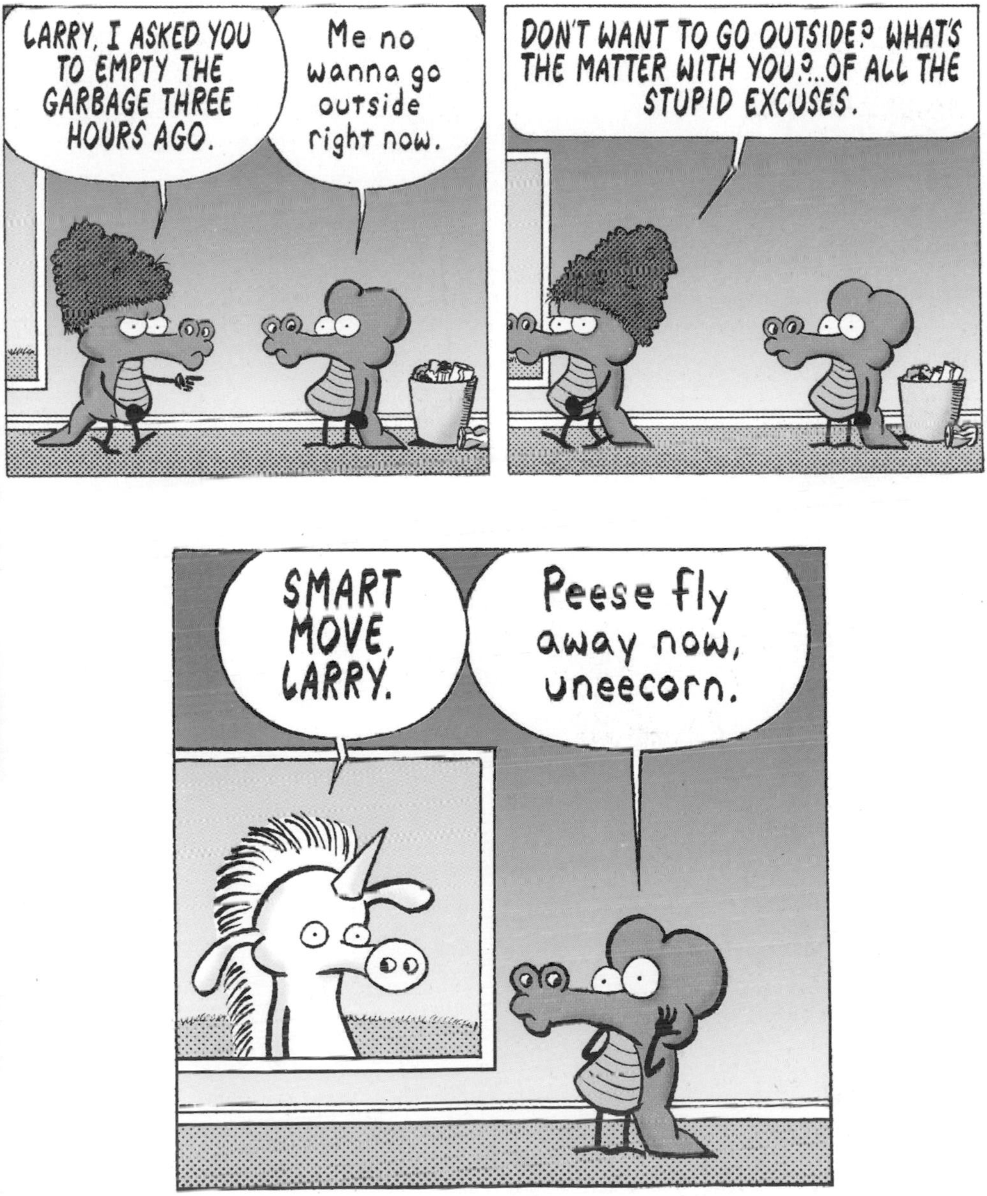
LARRY, I ASKED YOU TO EMPTY THE GARBAGE THREE HOURS AGO.
Me no wanna go outside right now.
DON'T WANT TO GO OUTSIDE? WHAT'S THE MATTER WITH YOU?...OF ALL THE STUPID EXCUSES.
SMART MOVE, LARRY.
Peese fly away now, uneecorn.

OKAY, LITTLE WILLY, I'M HAPPY TO TAKE YOU TO THE FAIR, BUT THERE'S A LOT OF PEOPLE HERE, AND WE NEED A PLAN IN CASE WE GET SEPARATED.
NOW WHEN I WAS LITTLE AND MY MOM TOOK ME TO THE FAIR, SHE ALWAYS CARRIED A BRIGHT YELLOW BALLOON SO I COULD SEE HER ABOVE THE CROWD.
AND SHE WORE A BRIGHT RED SHIRT LIKE THIS, SO I COULD SEE HER EASIER.
BUT IF WE DO STILL GET SEPARATED, WE NEED A PLAN.

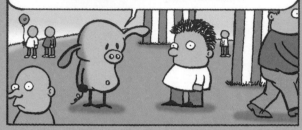

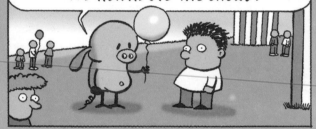

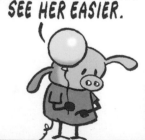

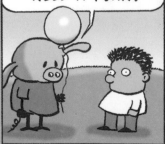

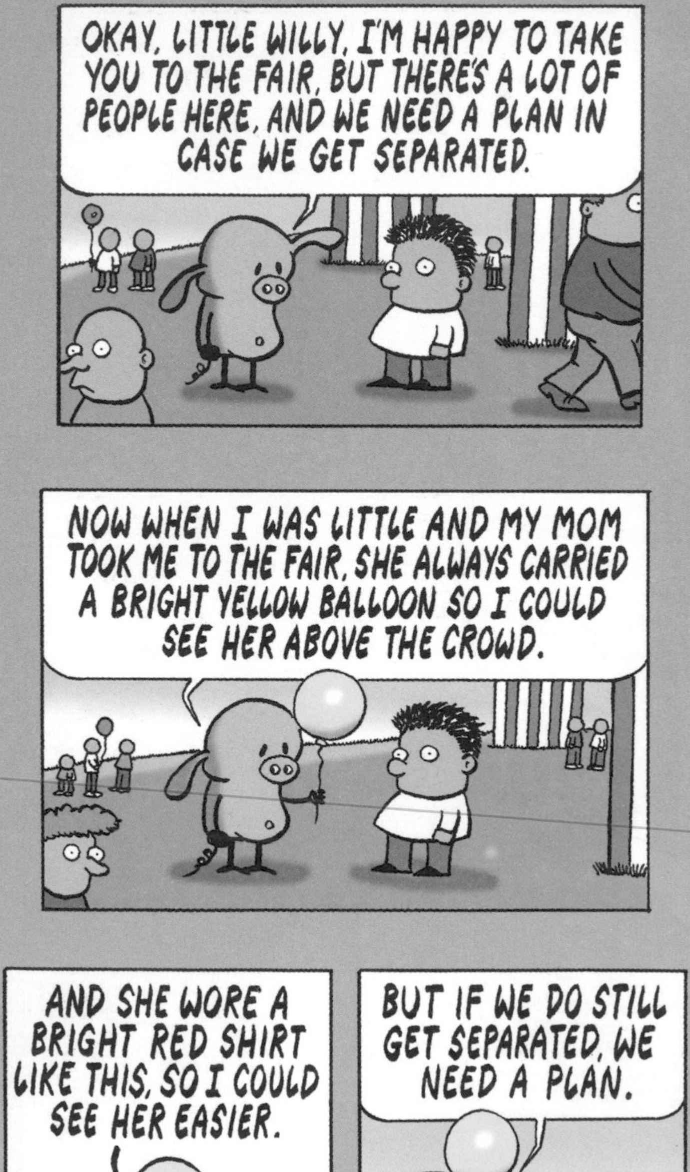

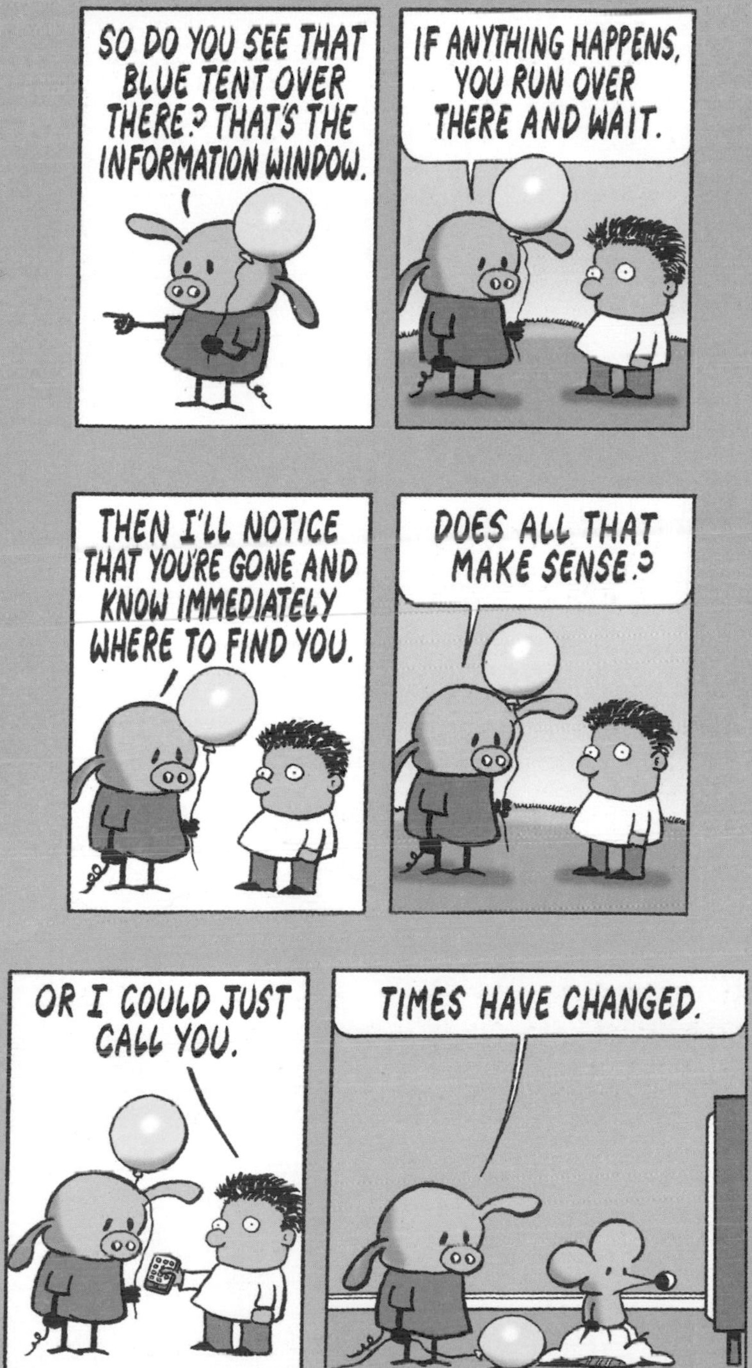
SO DO YOU SEE THAT BLUE TENT OVER THERE? THAT'S THE INFORMATION WINDOW.
IF ANYTHING HAPPENS, YOU RUN OVER THERE AND WAIT.
THEN I'LL NOTICE THAT YOU'RE GONE AND KNOW IMMEDIATELY WHERE TO FIND YOU.
DOES ALL THAT MAKE SENSE?
OR I COULD JUST CALL YOU.
TIMES HAVE CHANGED.

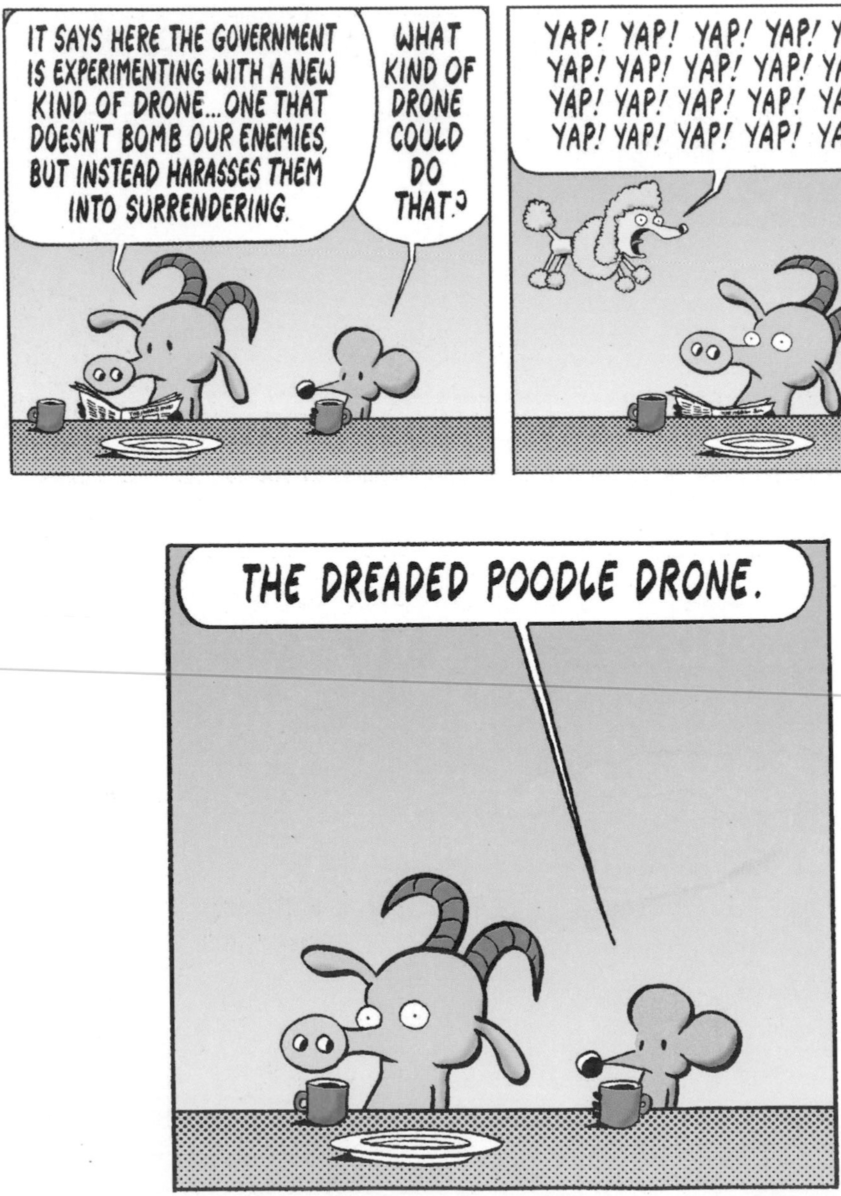
IT SAYS HERE THE GOVERNMENT IS EXPERIMENTING WITH A NEW KIND OF DRONE... ONE THAT DOESN'T BOMB OUR ENEMIES, BUT INSTEAD HARASSES THEM INTO SURRENDERING.
WHAT KIND OF DRONE COULD DO THAT?
YAP! YAP! YAP! YAP! YAP! YAP! YAP! YAP! YAP! YAP! YAP! YAP! YAP! YAP! YAP! YAP! YAP! YAP! YAP! YAP! YAP! YAP! YAP! YAP!
THE DREADED POODLE DRONE.

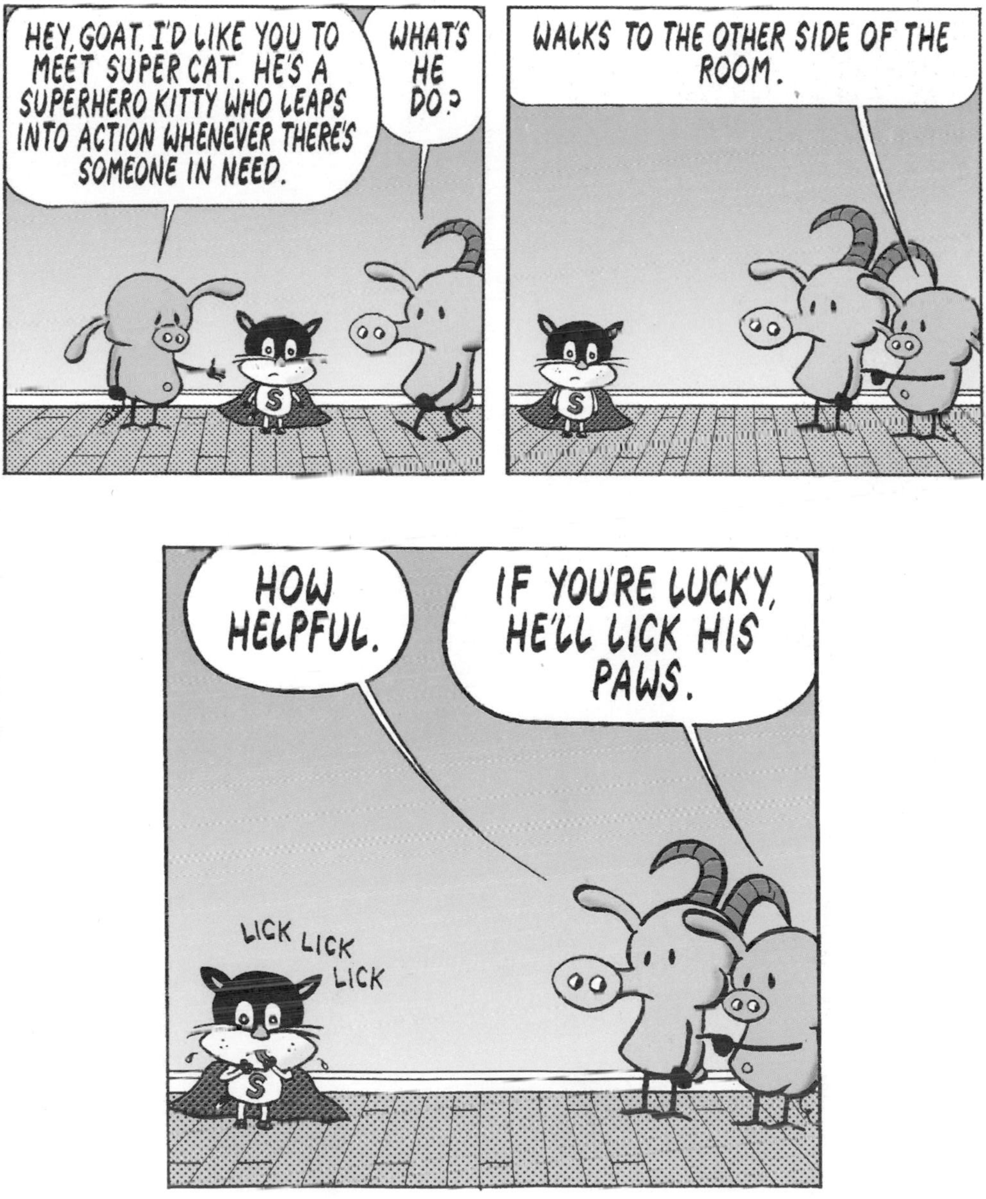
HEY, GOAT, I'D LIKE YOU TO MEET SUPER CAT. HE'S A SUPERHERO KITTY WHO LEAPS INTO ACTION WHENEVER THERE'S SOMEONE IN NEED.
WHAT'S HE DO?
WALKS TO THE OTHER SIDE OF THE ROOM.
HOW HELPFUL.
IF YOU'RE LUCKY, HE'LL LICK HIS PAWS.
LICK LICK LICK

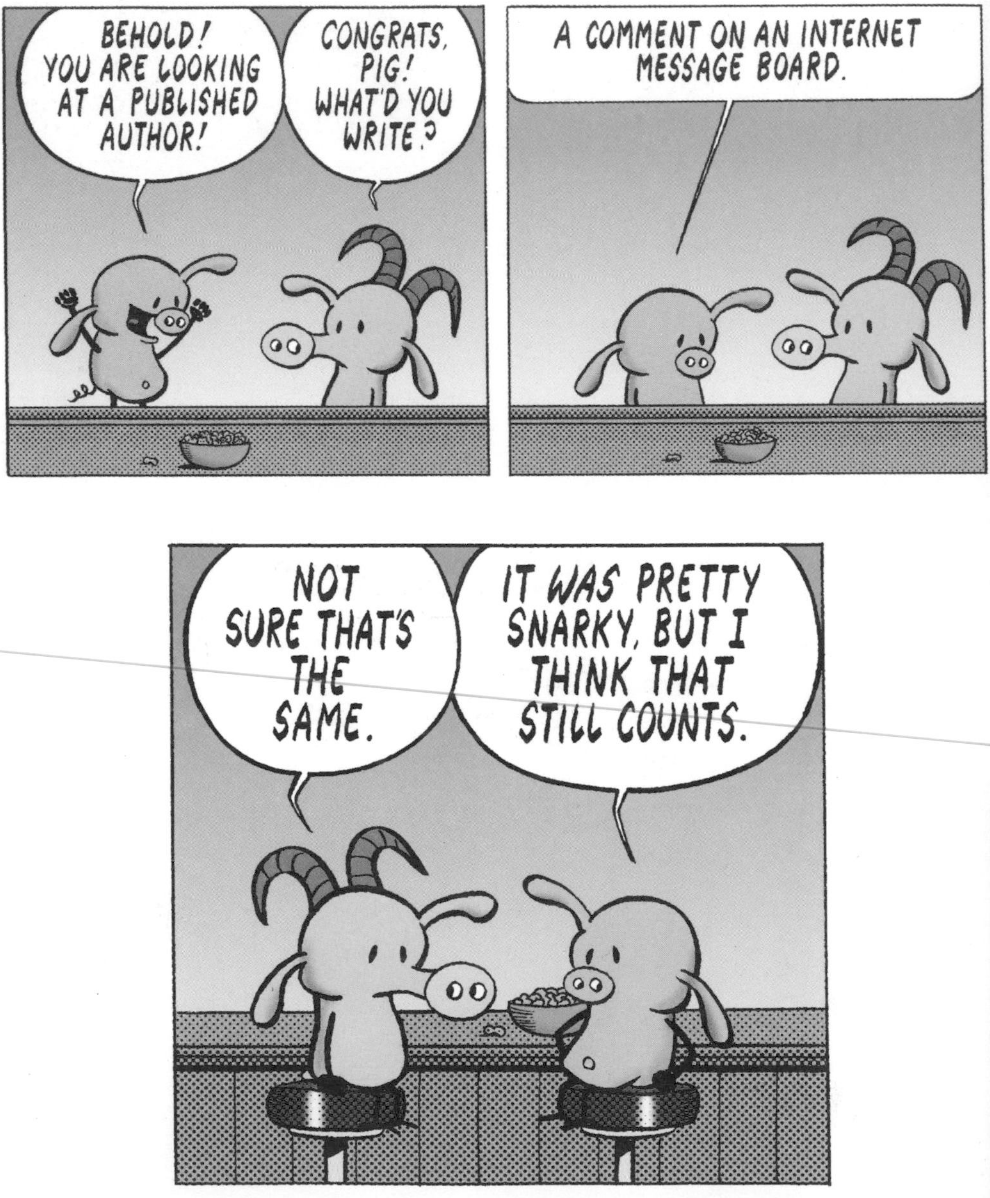
BEHOLD! YOU ARE LOOKING AT A PUBLISHED AUTHOR!
CONGRATS, PIG! WHAT'D YOU WRITE?
A COMMENT ON AN INTERNET MESSAGE BOARD.
NOT SURE THAT'S THE SAME.
IT WAS PRETTY SNARKY, BUT I THINK THAT STILL COUNTS.

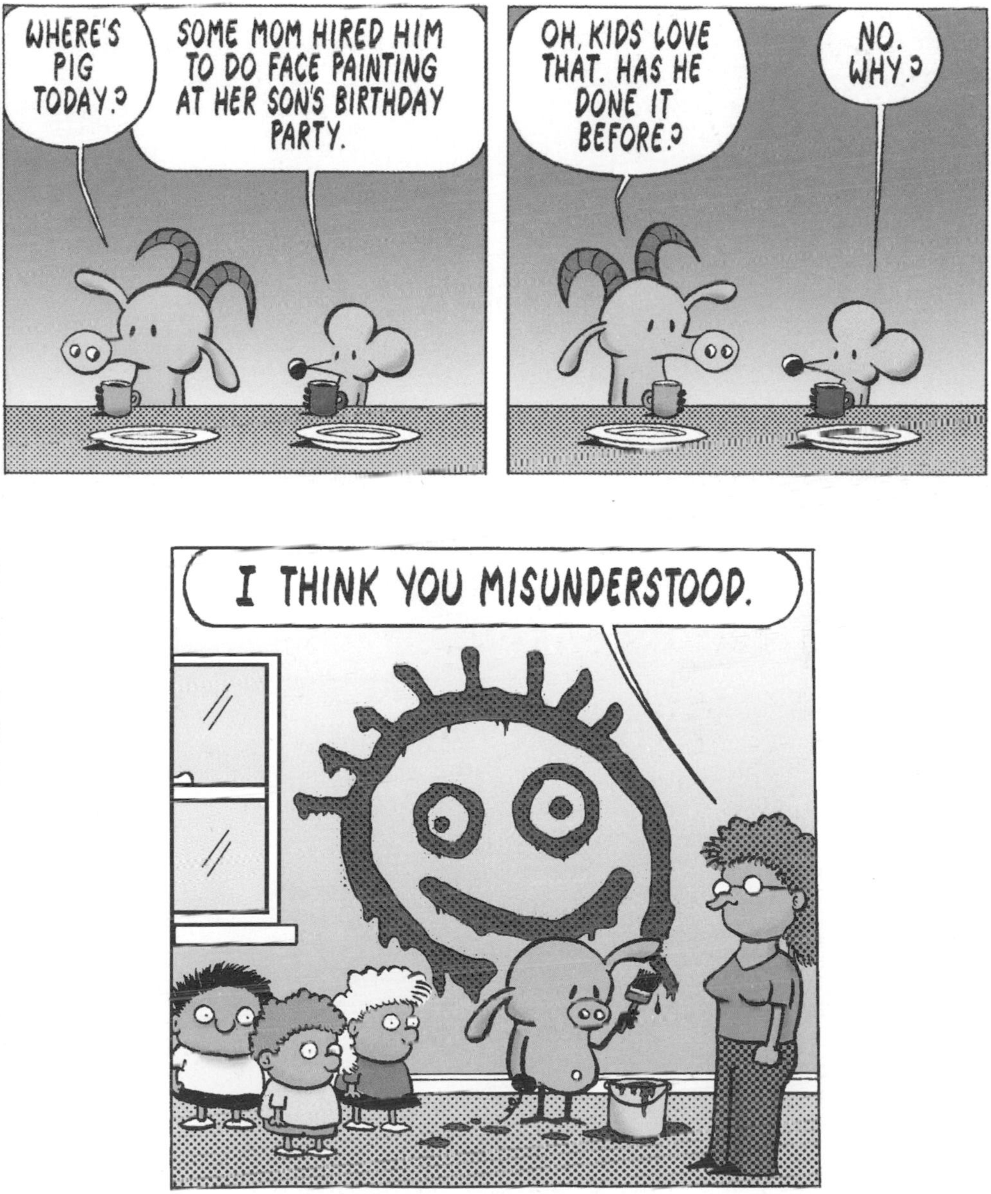
WHERE'S PIG TODAY?
SOME MOM HIRED HIM TO DO FACE PAINTING AT HER SON'S BIRTHDAY PARTY.
OH, KIDS LOVE THAT. HAS HE DONE IT BEFORE?
NO. WHY?
I THINK YOU MISUNDERSTOOD.

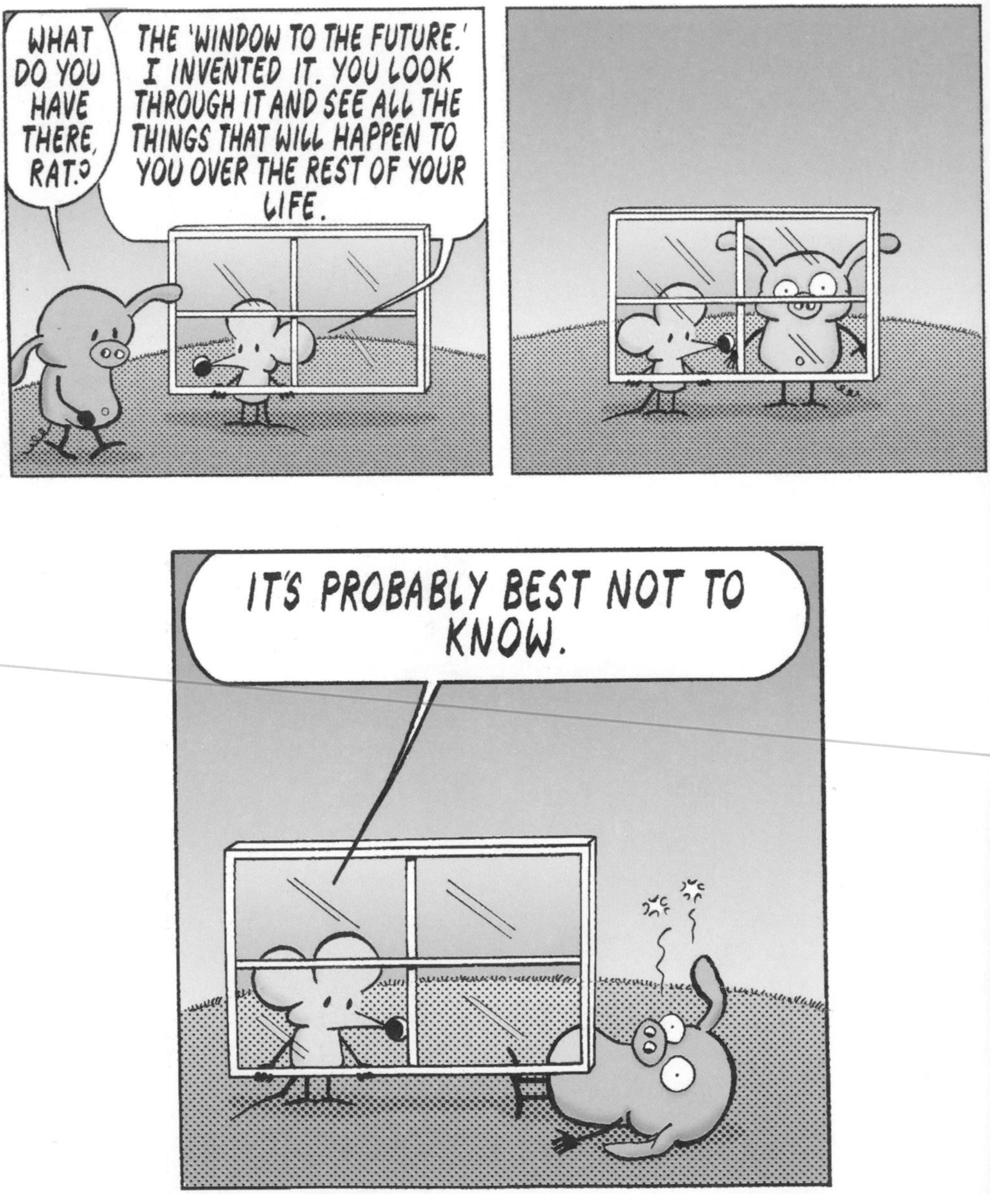
WHAT DO YOU HAVE THERE, RAT?
THE 'WINDOW TO THE FUTURE.' I INVENTED IT. YOU LOOK THROUGH IT AND SEE ALL THE THINGS THAT WILL HAPPEN TO YOU OVER THE REST OF YOUR LIFE.
IT'S PROBABLY BEST NOT TO KNOW.

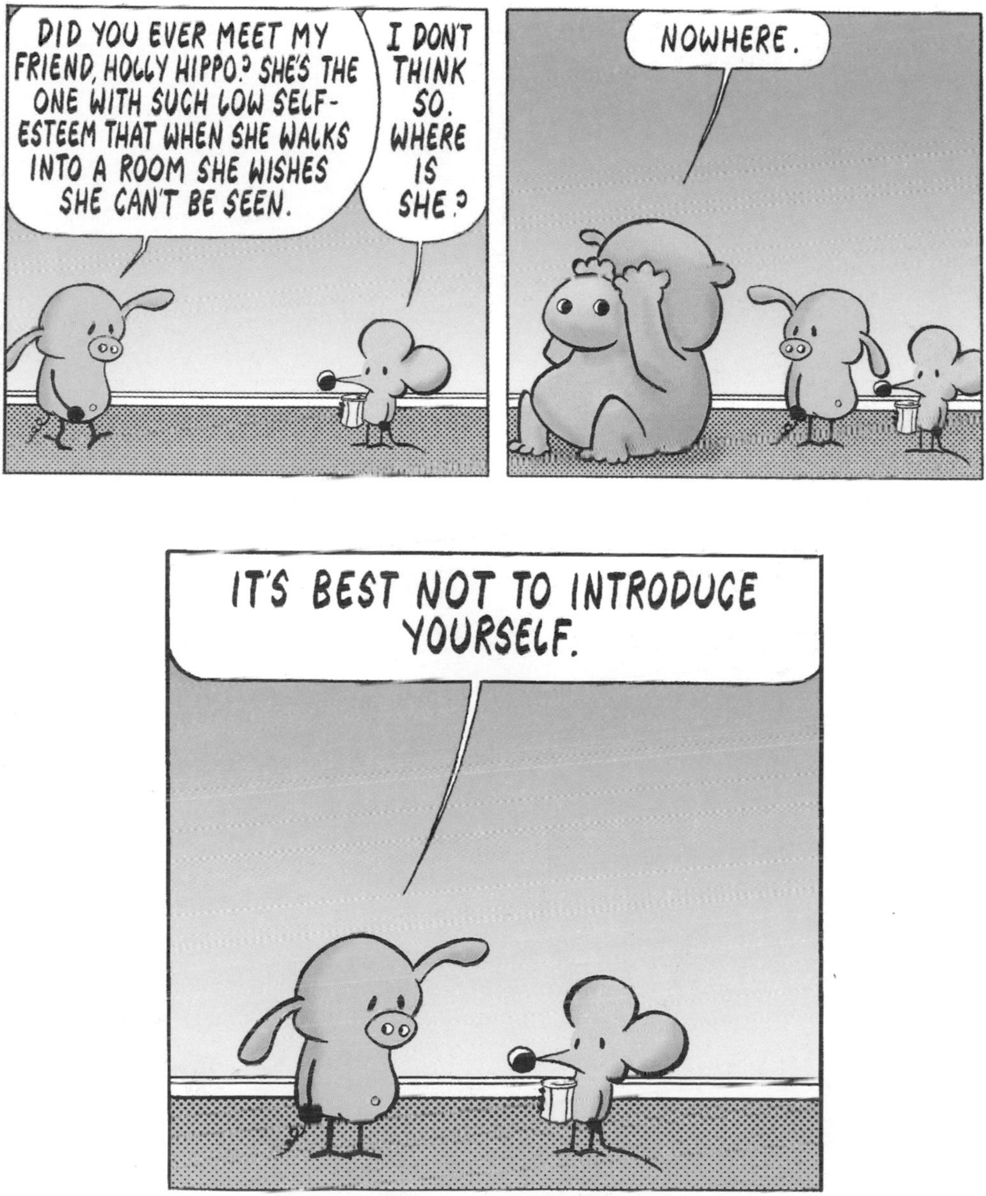
DID YOU EVER MEET MY FRIEND, HOLLY HIPPO? SHE'S THE ONE WITH SUCH LOW SELF-ESTEEM THAT WHEN SHE WALKS INTO A ROOM SHE WISHES SHE CAN'T BE SEEN.
I DON'T THINK SO. WHERE IS SHE?
NOWHERE.
IT'S BEST NOT TO INTRODUCE YOURSELF.

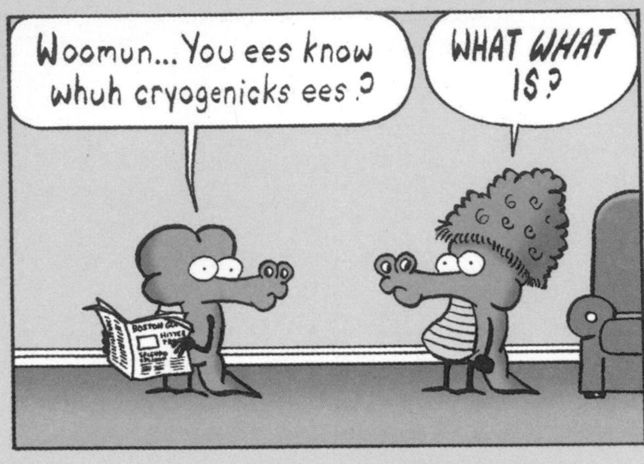
Woomun... You ees know whuh cryogenicks ees.?
WHAT WHAT IS?

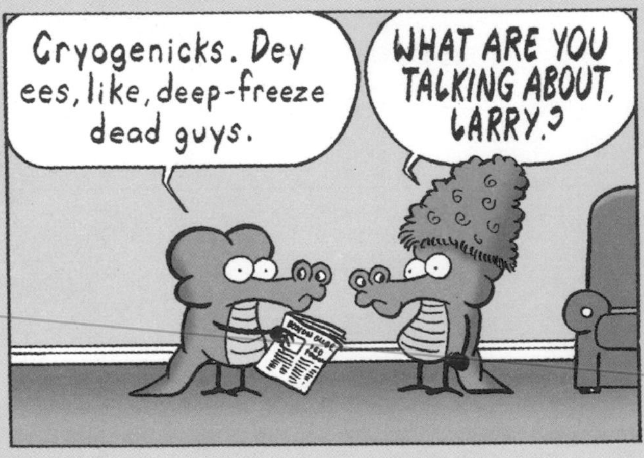
Cryogenicks. Dey ees, like, deep-freeze dead guys.
WHAT ARE YOU TALKING ABOUT, LARRY?

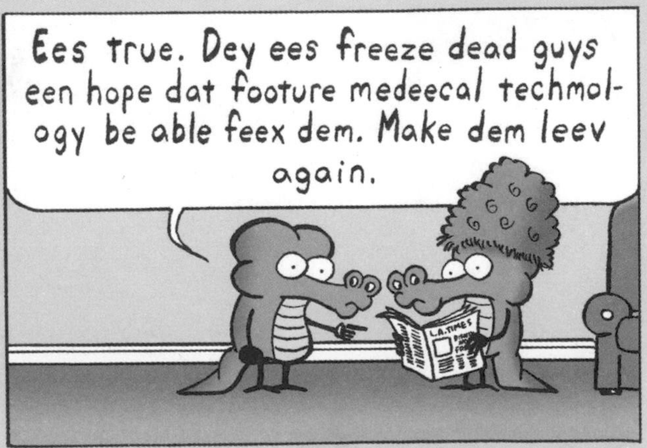
Ees true. Dey ees freeze dead guys een hope dat footure medeecal techmol-ogy be able feex dem. Make dem leev again.

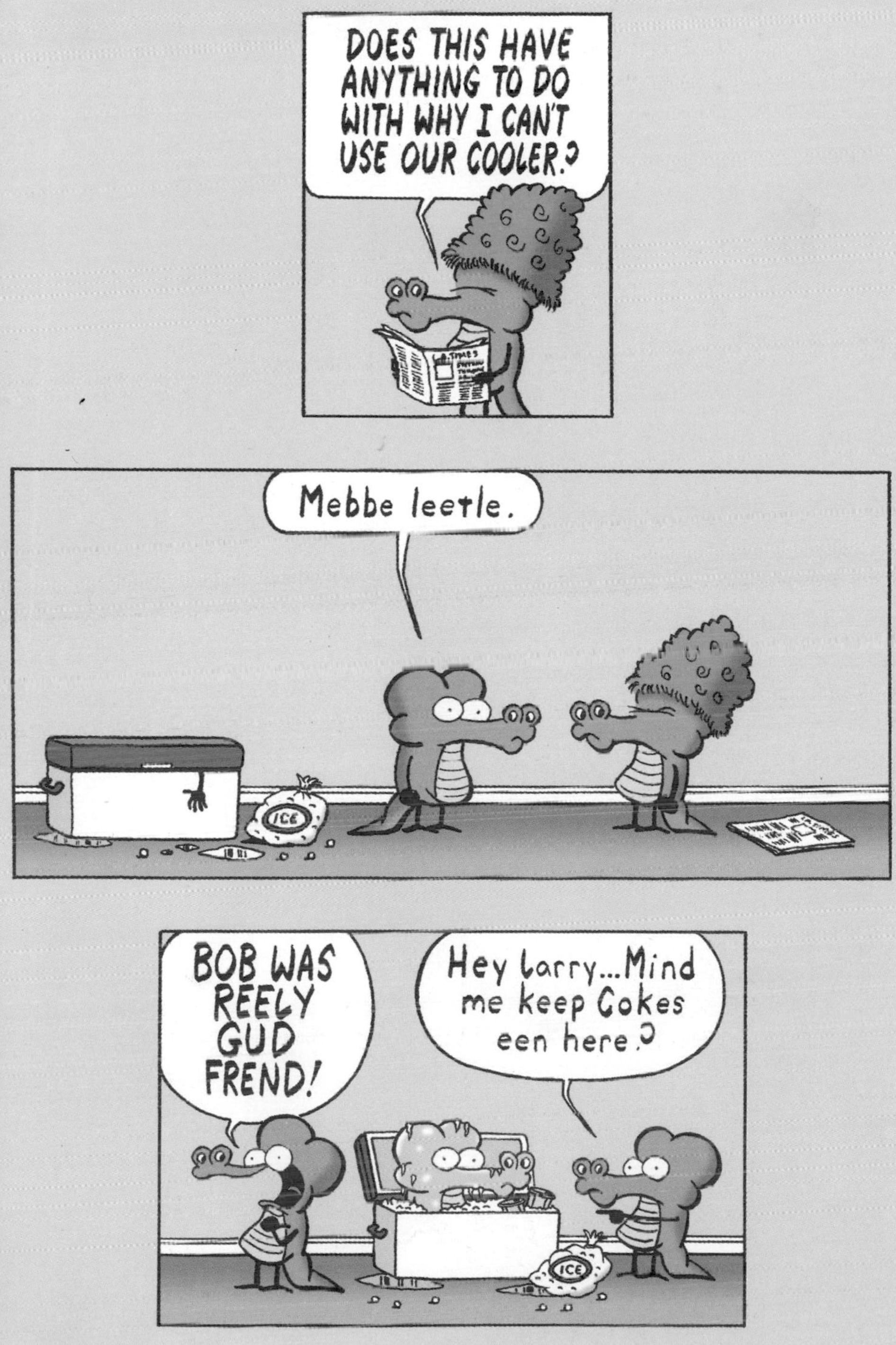
DOES THIS HAVE ANYTHING TO DO WITH WHY I CAN'T USE OUR COOLER?
Mebbe leetle.
BOB WAS REELY GUD FREND!
Hey Larry...Mind me keep Cokes een here?
ICE
ICE

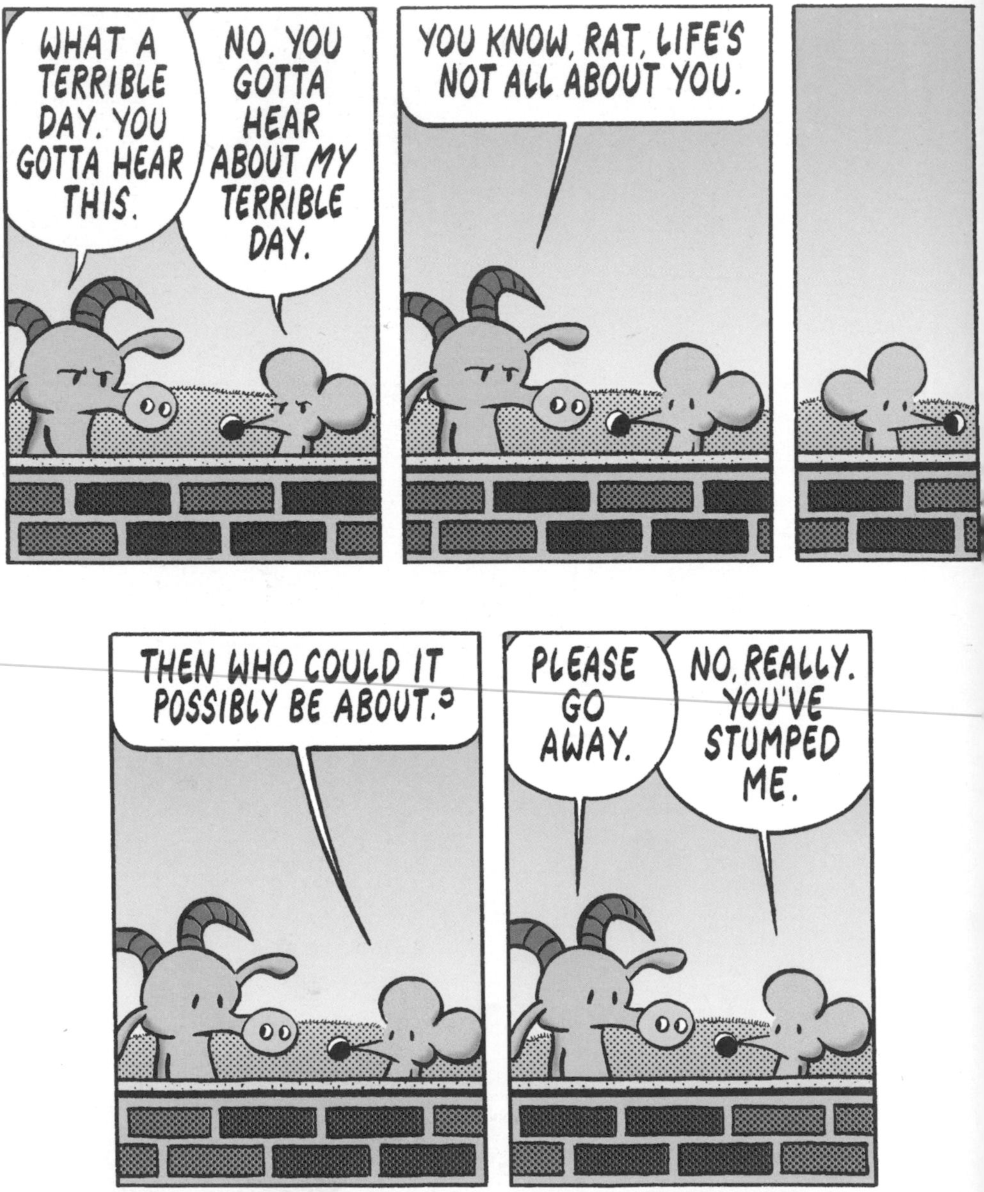
WHAT A TERRIBLE DAY. YOU GOTTA HEAR THIS.
NO. YOU GOTTA HEAR ABOUT MY TERRIBLE DAY.
YOU KNOW, RAT, LIFE'S NOT ALL ABOUT YOU.
THEN WHO COULD IT POSSIBLY BE ABOUT?
PLEASE GO AWAY.
NO, REALLY. YOU'VE STUMPED ME.

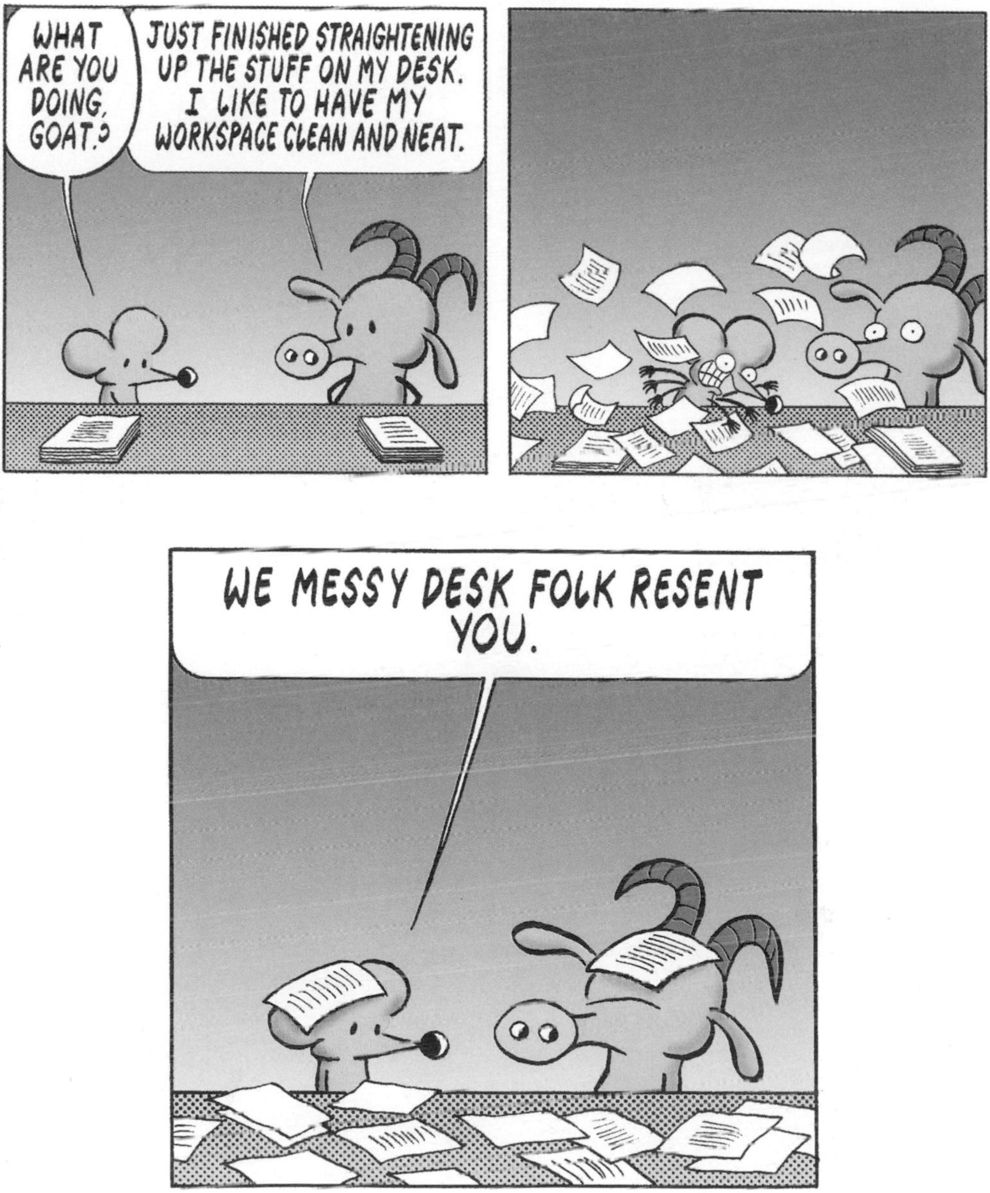
WHAT ARE YOU DOING, GOAT.?
JUST FINISHED STRAIGHTENING UP THE STUFF ON MY DESK. I LIKE TO HAVE MY WORKSPACE CLEAN AND NEAT.
WE MESSY DESK FOLK RESENT YOU.

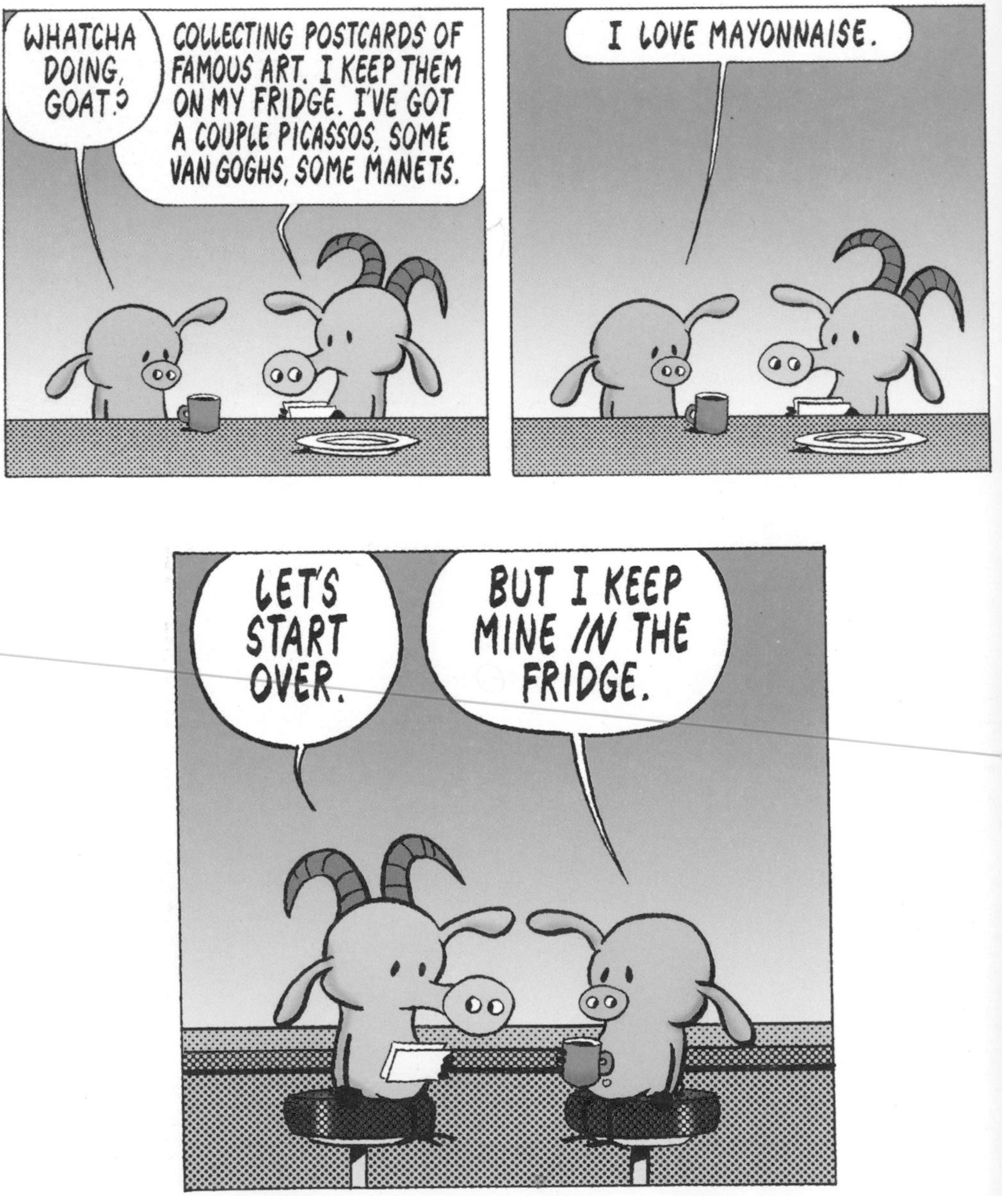
WHATCHA DOING, GOAT?
COLLECTING POSTCARDS OF FAMOUS ART. I KEEP THEM ON MY FRIDGE. I'VE GOT A COUPLE PICASSOS, SOME VAN GOGHS, SOME MANETS.
I LOVE MAYONNAISE.
LET'S START OVER.
BUT I KEEP MINE *IN* THE FRIDGE.

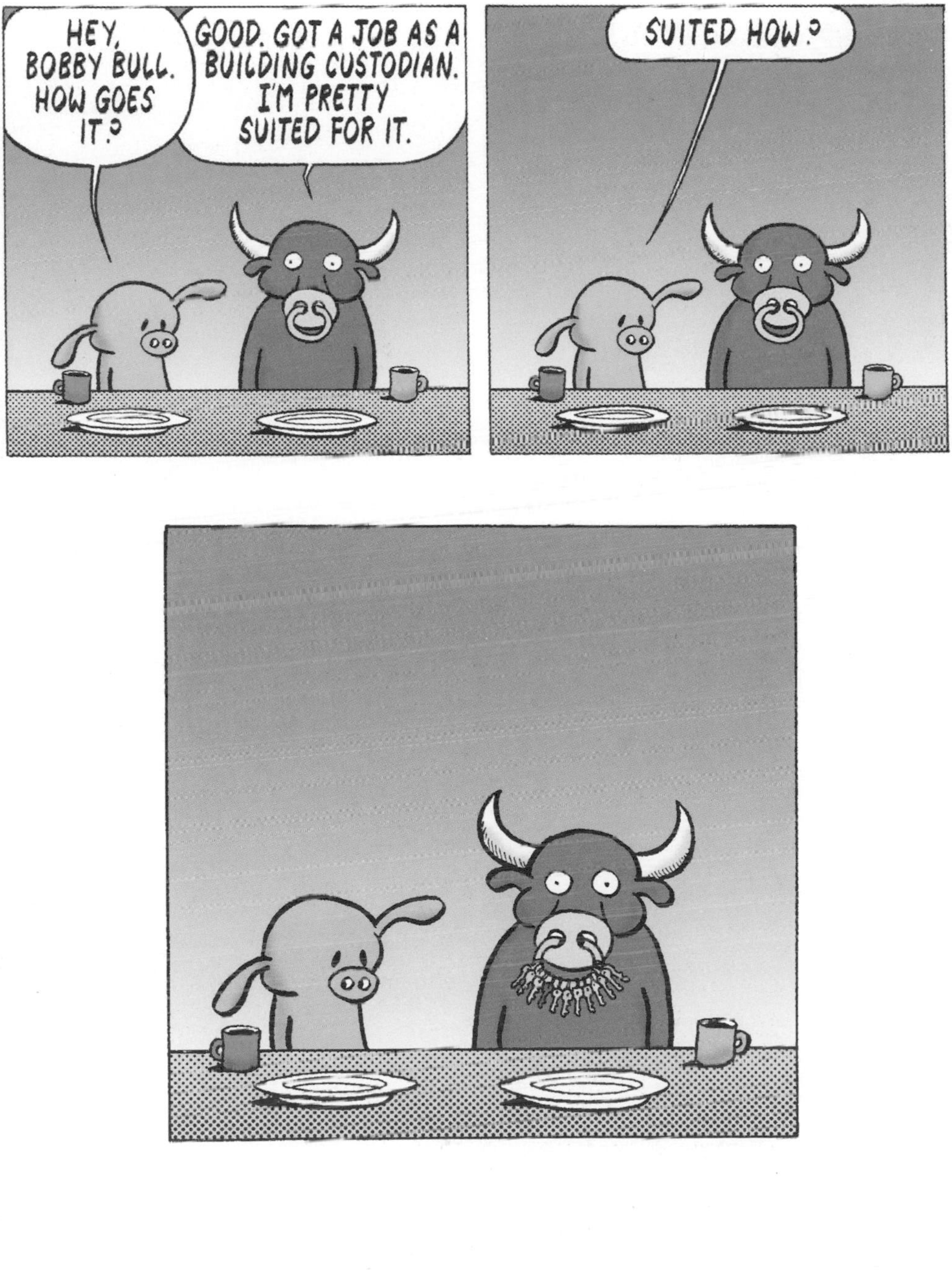
HEY, BOBBY BULL. HOW GOES IT?
GOOD. GOT A JOB AS A BUILDING CUSTODIAN. I'M PRETTY SUITED FOR IT.
SUITED HOW?

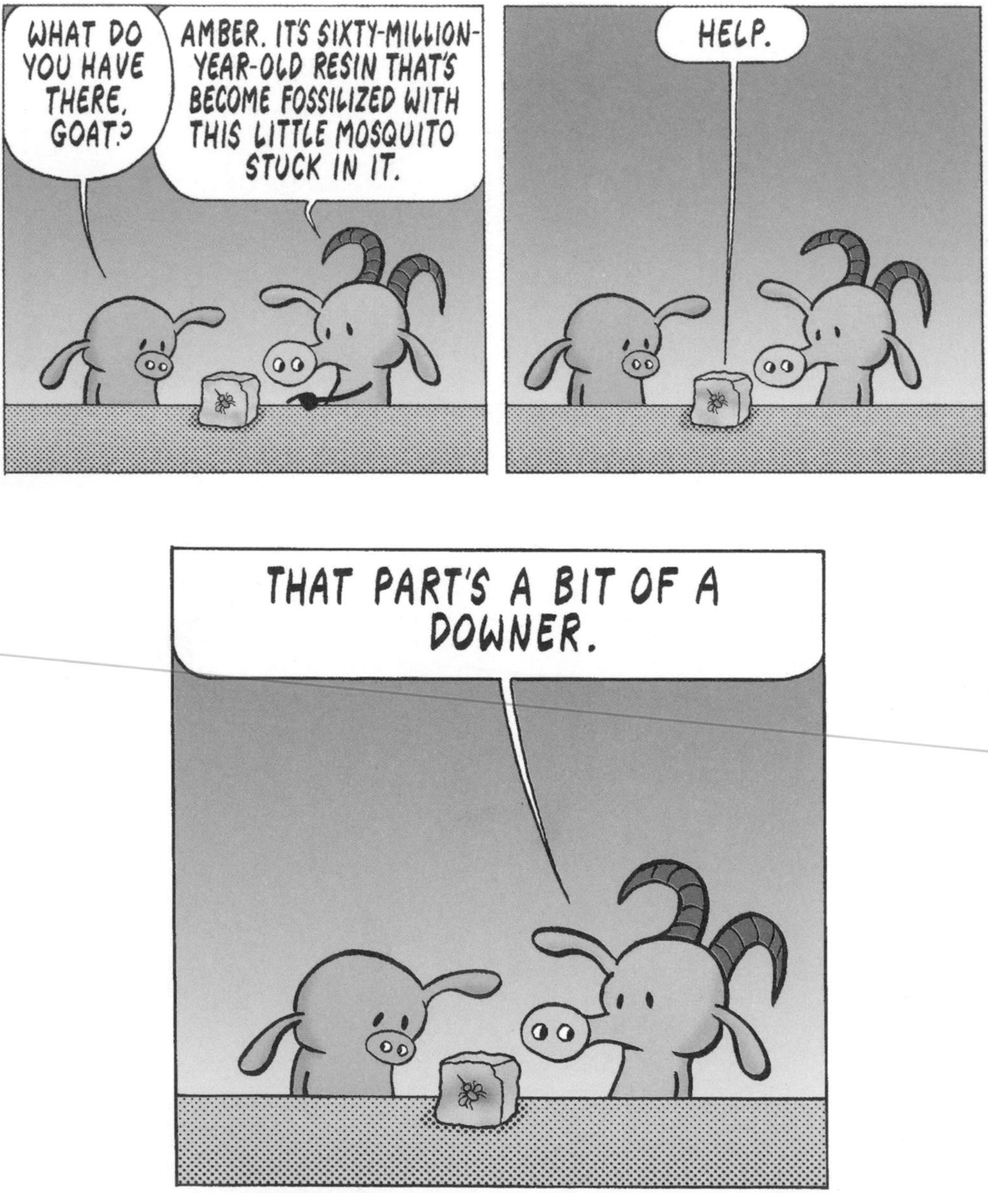
WHAT DO YOU HAVE THERE, GOAT?
AMBER. IT'S SIXTY-MILLION-YEAR-OLD RESIN THAT'S BECOME FOSSILIZED WITH THIS LITTLE MOSQUITO STUCK IN IT.
HELP.
THAT PART'S A BIT OF A DOWNER.

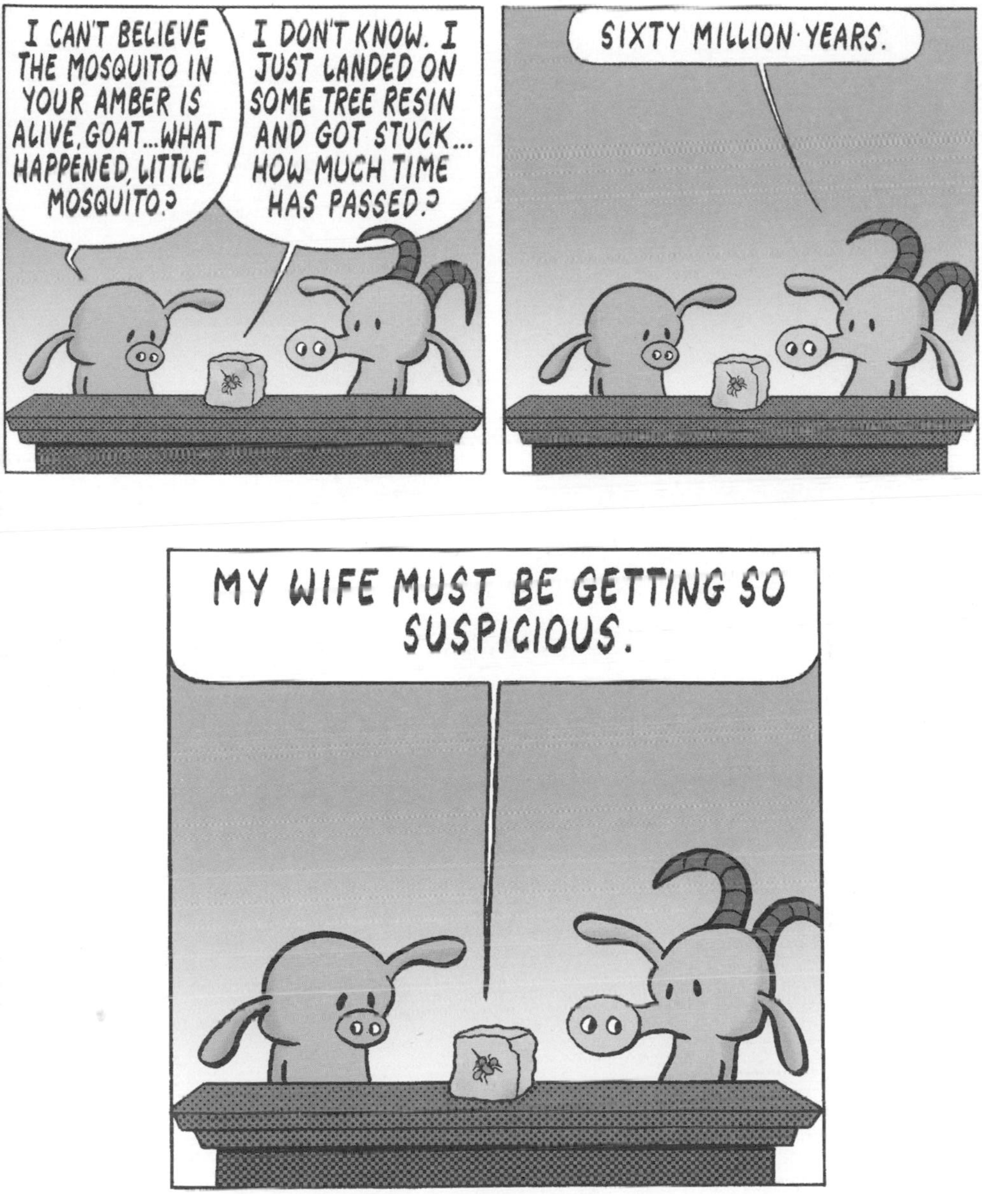
I CAN'T BELIEVE THE MOSQUITO IN YOUR AMBER IS ALIVE, GOAT...WHAT HAPPENED, LITTLE MOSQUITO?
I DON'T KNOW. I JUST LANDED ON SOME TREE RESIN AND GOT STUCK... HOW MUCH TIME HAS PASSED?
SIXTY MILLION YEARS.
MY WIFE MUST BE GETTING SO SUSPICIOUS.

I CAN'T BELIEVE THAT LITTLE MOSQUITO HAS BEEN ENCASED IN THAT AMBER FOR SIXTY MILLION YEARS.
IT'S STRANGE, HUH?
YEAH. AND HE'S BEEN TOTALLY PRESERVED.
THAT'S TRUE. PROBABLY DOESN'T LOOK MUCH DIFFERENT THAN HE WAS THEN.

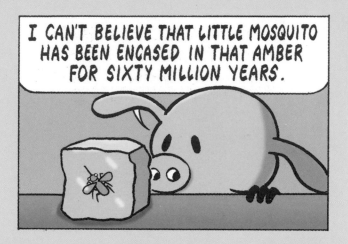

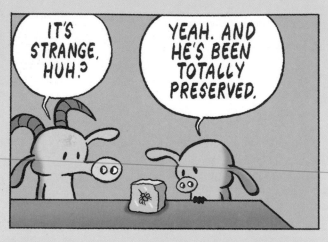

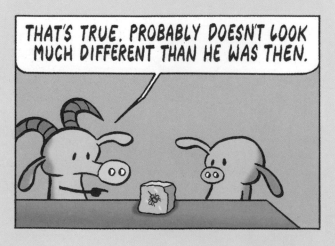

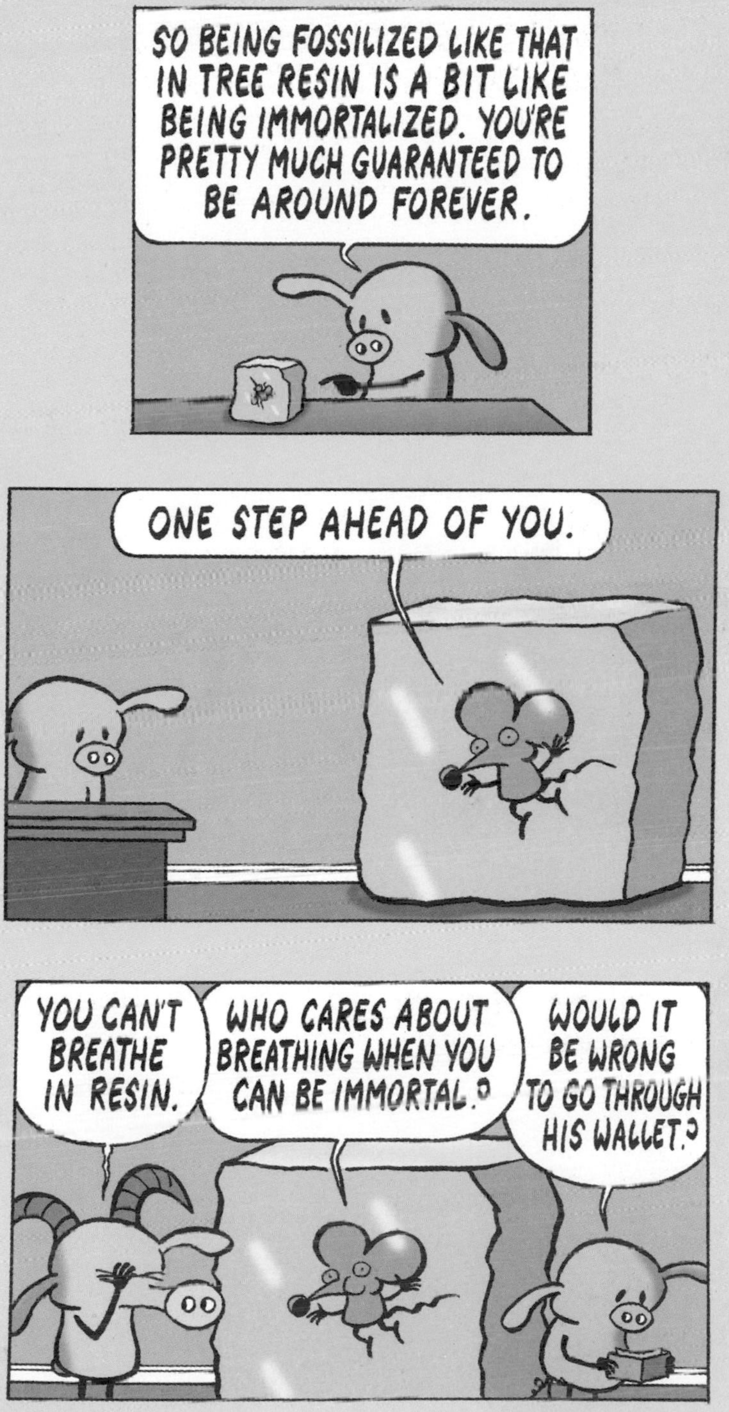
SO BEING FOSSILIZED LIKE THAT IN TREE RESIN IS A BIT LIKE BEING IMMORTALIZED. YOU'RE PRETTY MUCH GUARANTEED TO BE AROUND FOREVER.
ONE STEP AHEAD OF YOU.
YOU CAN'T BREATHE IN RESIN.
WHO CARES ABOUT BREATHING WHEN YOU CAN BE IMMORTAL?
WOULD IT BE WRONG TO GO THROUGH HIS WALLET?

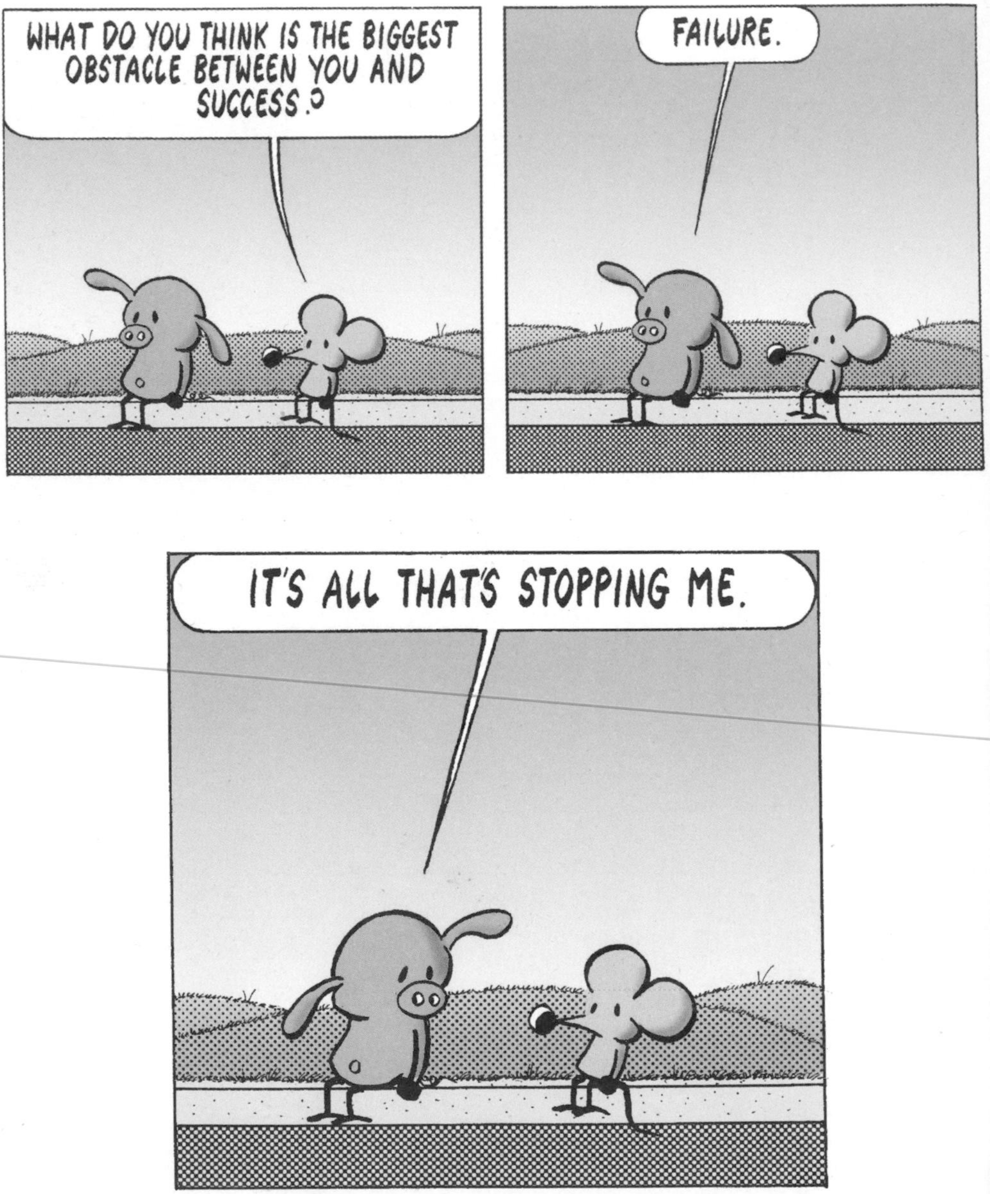
WHAT DO YOU THINK IS THE BIGGEST OBSTACLE BETWEEN YOU AND SUCCESS?
FAILURE.
IT'S ALL THAT'S STOPPING ME.

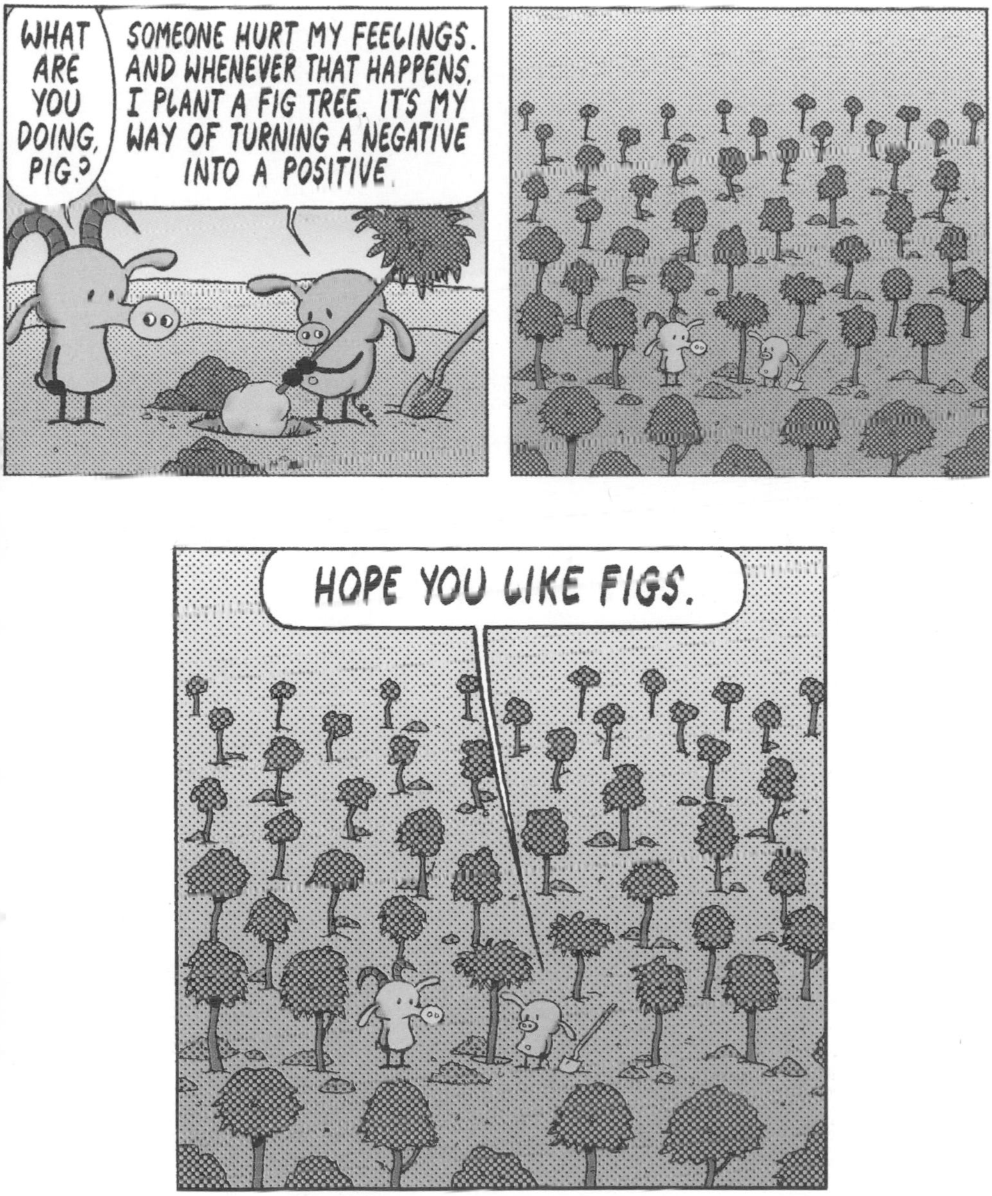
WHAT ARE YOU DOING, PIG?
SOMEONE HURT MY FEELINGS. AND WHENEVER THAT HAPPENS, I PLANT A FIG TREE. IT'S MY WAY OF TURNING A NEGATIVE INTO A POSITIVE.
HOPE YOU LIKE FIGS.

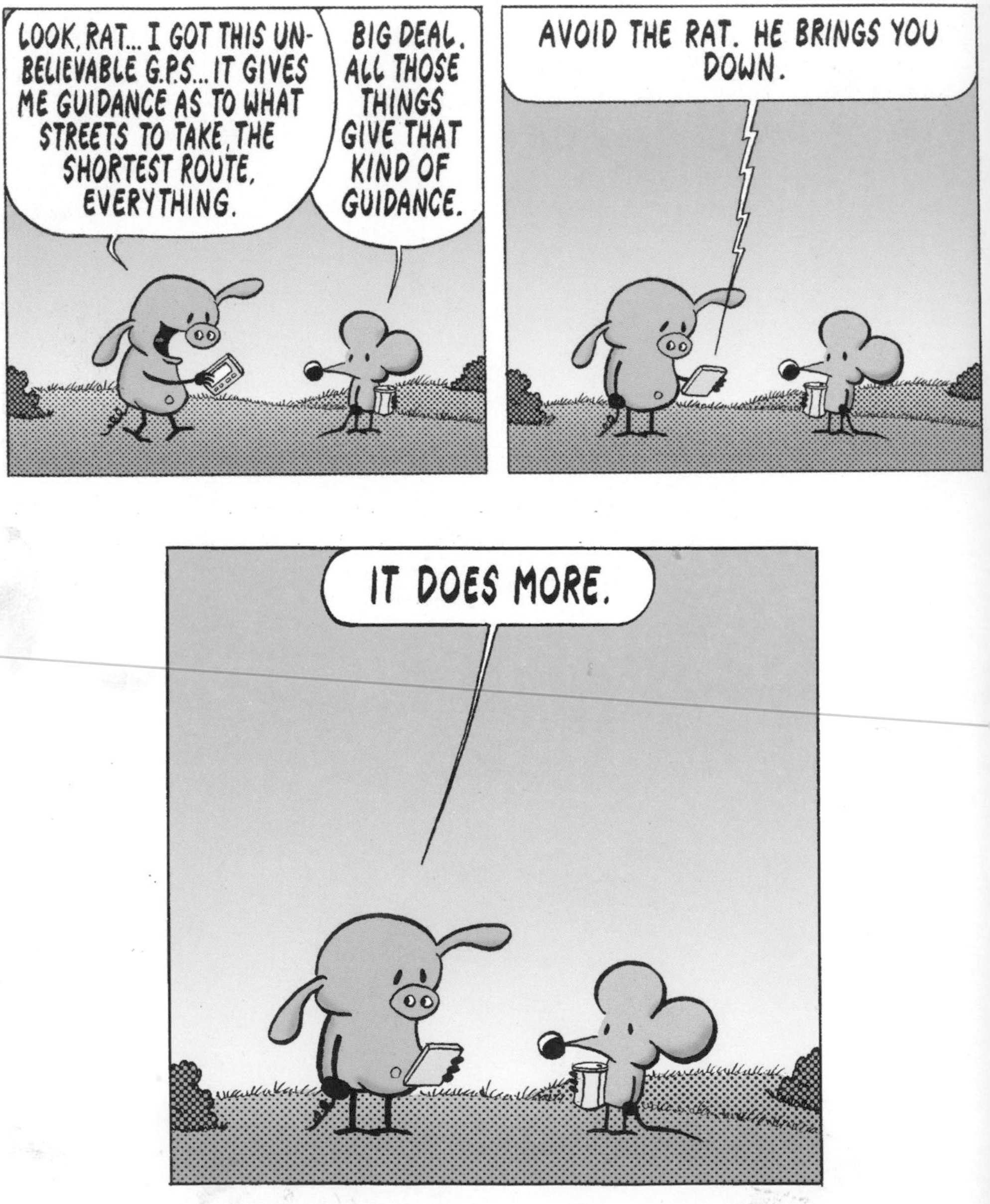
LOOK, RAT... I GOT THIS UN-BELIEVABLE G.P.S... IT GIVES ME GUIDANCE AS TO WHAT STREETS TO TAKE, THE SHORTEST ROUTE, EVERYTHING.
BIG DEAL. ALL THOSE THINGS GIVE THAT KIND OF GUIDANCE.
AVOID THE RAT. HE BRINGS YOU DOWN.
IT DOES MORE.

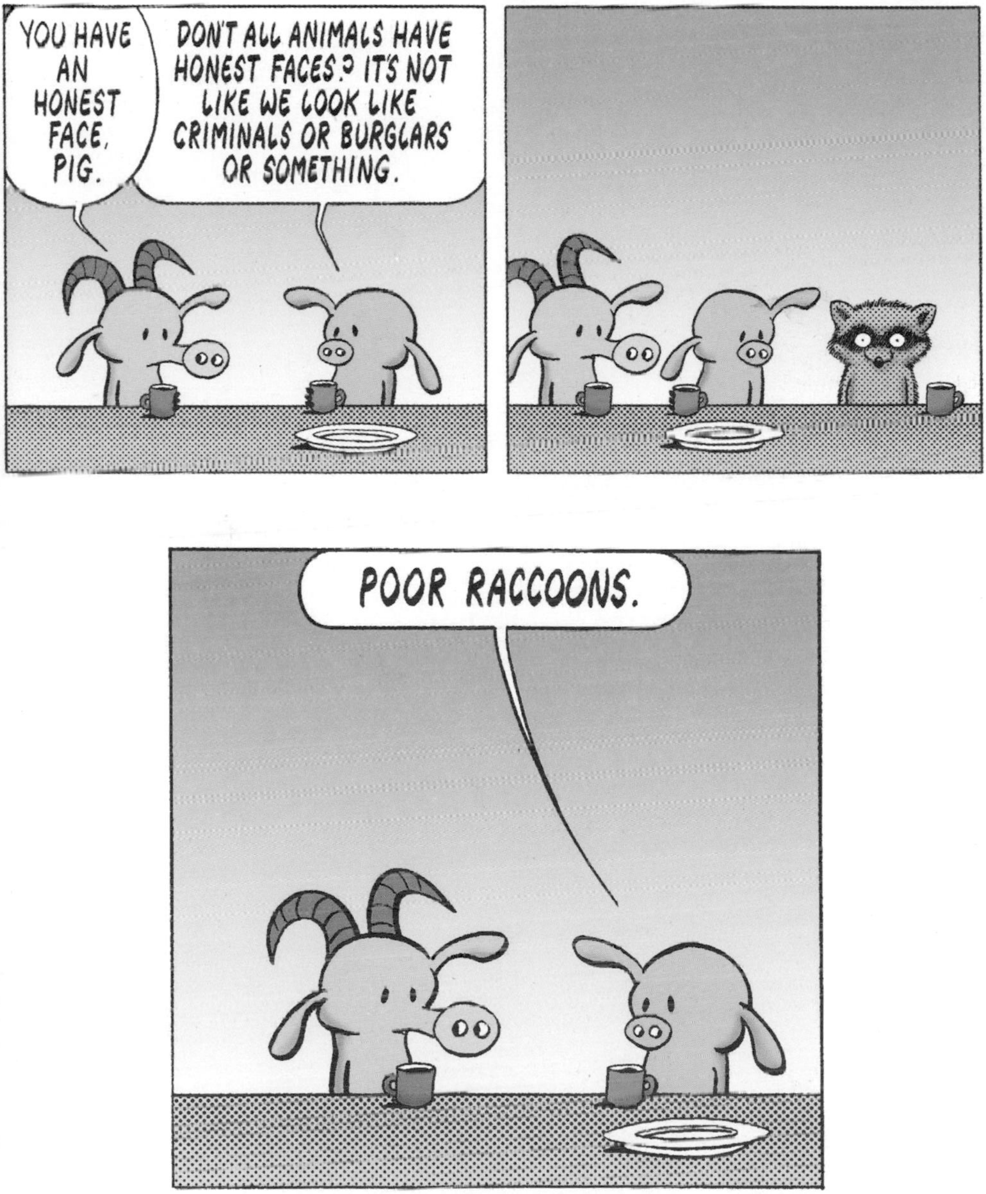
YOU HAVE AN HONEST FACE, PIG.
DON'T ALL ANIMALS HAVE HONEST FACES? IT'S NOT LIKE WE LOOK LIKE CRIMINALS OR BURGLARS OR SOMETHING.
POOR RACCOONS.

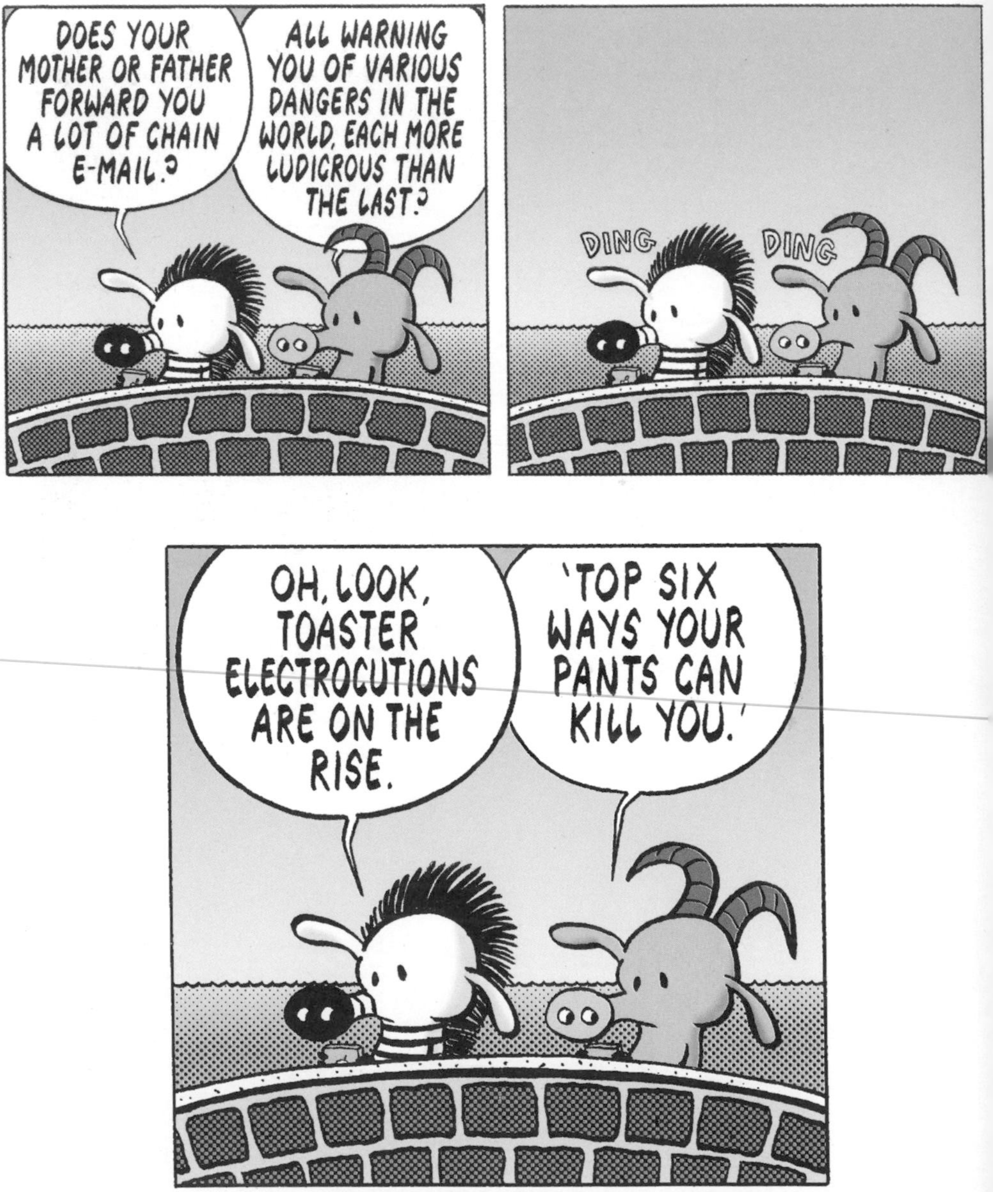
DOES YOUR MOTHER OR FATHER FORWARD YOU A LOT OF CHAIN E-MAIL?
ALL WARNING YOU OF VARIOUS DANGERS IN THE WORLD, EACH MORE LUDICROUS THAN THE LAST?
DING
DING
OH, LOOK, TOASTER ELECTROCUTIONS ARE ON THE RISE.
'TOP SIX WAYS YOUR PANTS CAN KILL YOU.'

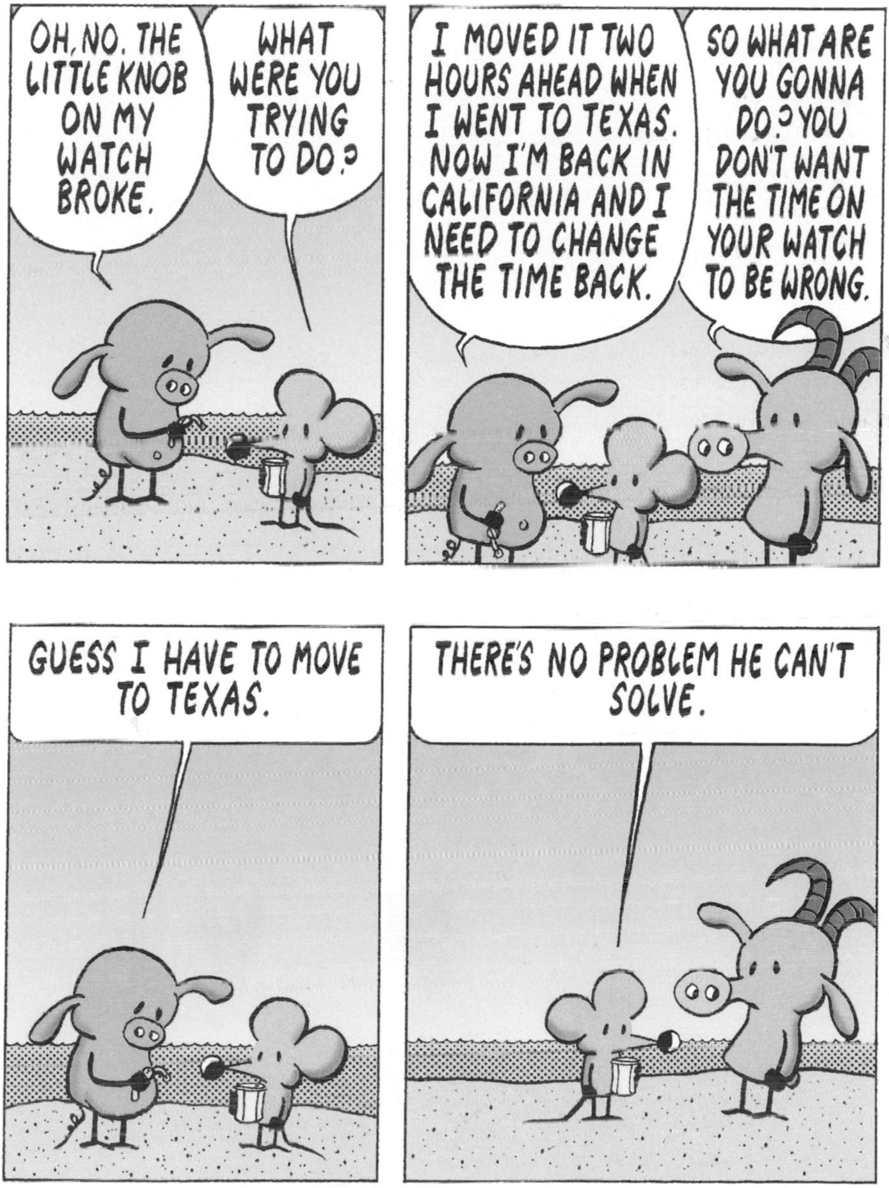
OH, NO. THE LITTLE KNOB ON MY WATCH BROKE.
WHAT WERE YOU TRYING TO DO?
I MOVED IT TWO HOURS AHEAD WHEN I WENT TO TEXAS. NOW I'M BACK IN CALIFORNIA AND I NEED TO CHANGE THE TIME BACK.
SO WHAT ARE YOU GONNA DO? YOU DON'T WANT THE TIME ON YOUR WATCH TO BE WRONG.
GUESS I HAVE TO MOVE TO TEXAS.
THERE'S NO PROBLEM HE CAN'T SOLVE.

# IF ABRAHAM LINCOLN HAD TWEETED....

## — An Alternative History —

Take that, you little troll, Stephen Douglas.

## THE GETTYSBURG ADDRESS

 **Abraham Lincoln**
@Honest_Abe

🐦 Follow

**87 yrs ago, our fathers did stuff. Now big war. Govt by people good.**

## ON THE SOUTH'S FIRING UPON FORT SUMTER

**Abraham Lincoln**
@Honest_Abe

🐦 Follow

**OH NO YOU DI'INT**

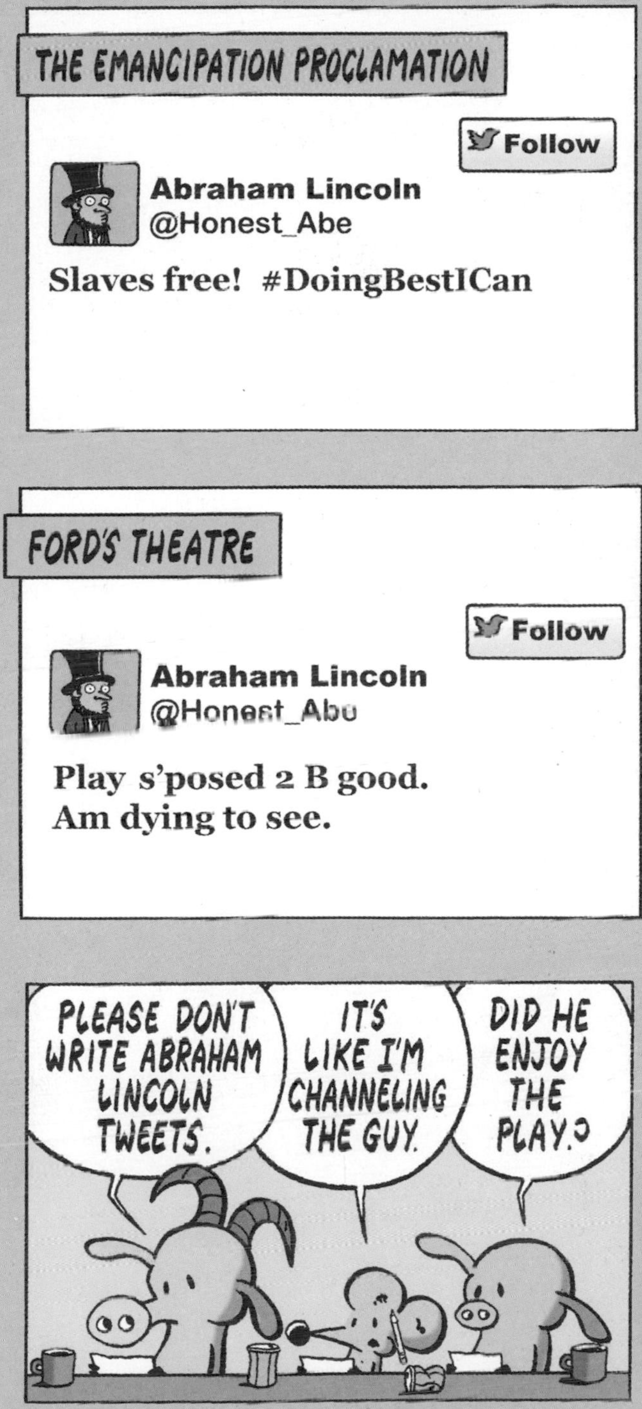
THE EMANCIPATION PROCLAMATION
Follow
Abraham Lincoln
@Honest_Abe
Slaves free! #DoingBestICan
FORD'S THEATRE
Follow
Abraham Lincoln
@Honest_Abe
Play s'posed 2 B good.
Am dying to see.
PLEASE DON'T WRITE ABRAHAM LINCOLN TWEETS.
IT'S LIKE I'M CHANNELING THE GUY.
DID HE ENJOY THE PLAY?

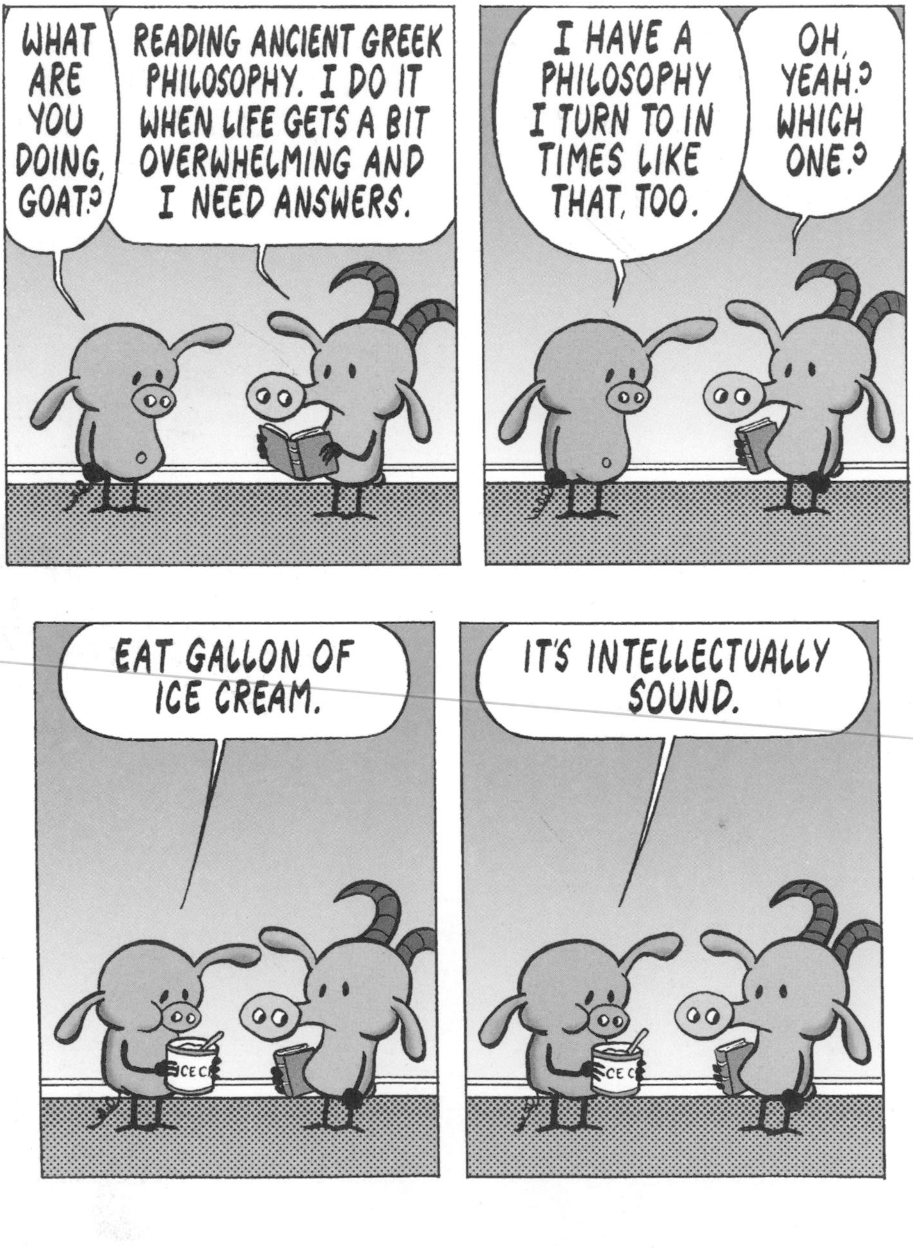
WHAT ARE YOU DOING, GOAT?
READING ANCIENT GREEK PHILOSOPHY. I DO IT WHEN LIFE GETS A BIT OVERWHELMING AND I NEED ANSWERS.
I HAVE A PHILOSOPHY I TURN TO IN TIMES LIKE THAT, TOO.
OH, YEAH? WHICH ONE?
EAT GALLON OF ICE CREAM.
IT'S INTELLECTUALLY SOUND.

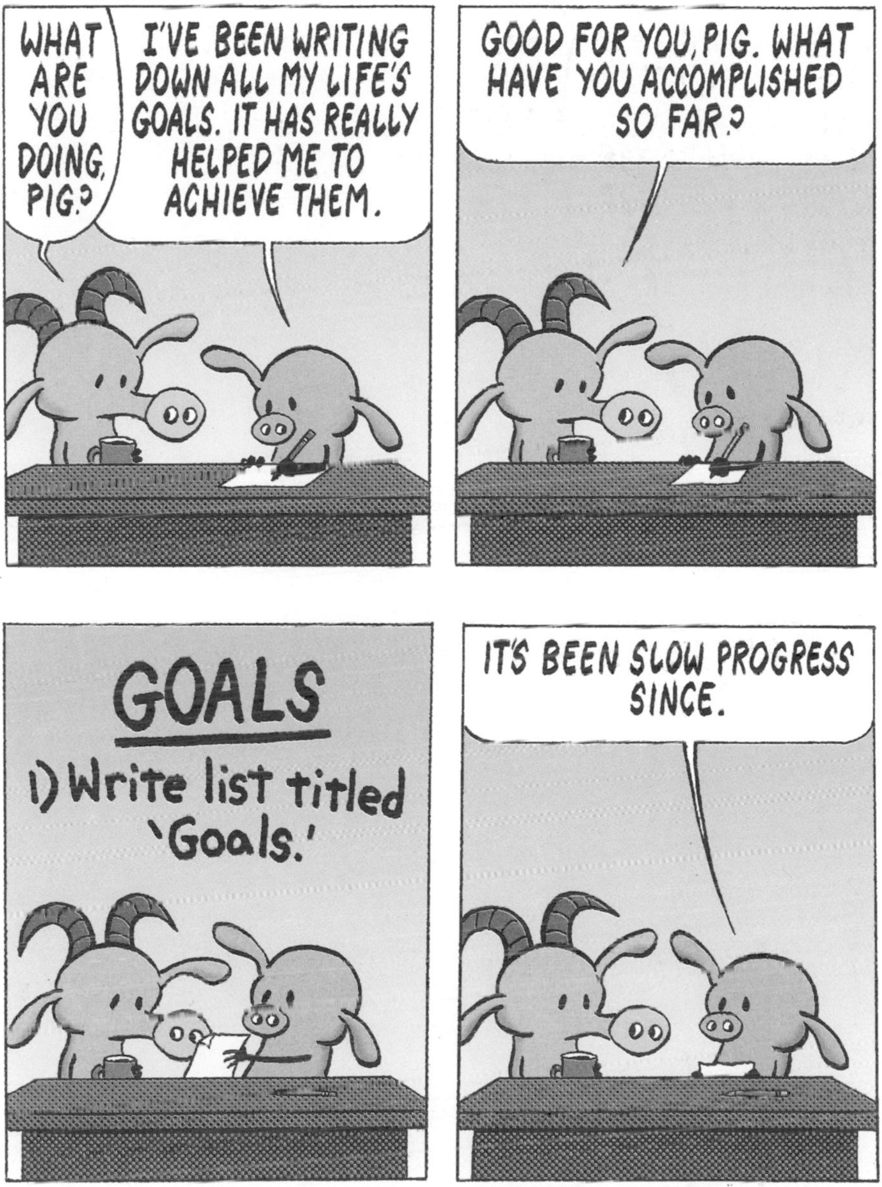
WHAT ARE YOU DOING, PIG?
I'VE BEEN WRITING DOWN ALL MY LIFE'S GOALS. IT HAS REALLY HELPED ME TO ACHIEVE THEM.
GOOD FOR YOU, PIG. WHAT HAVE YOU ACCOMPLISHED SO FAR?
GOALS
1) Write list titled 'Goals.'
IT'S BEEN SLOW PROGRESS SINCE.

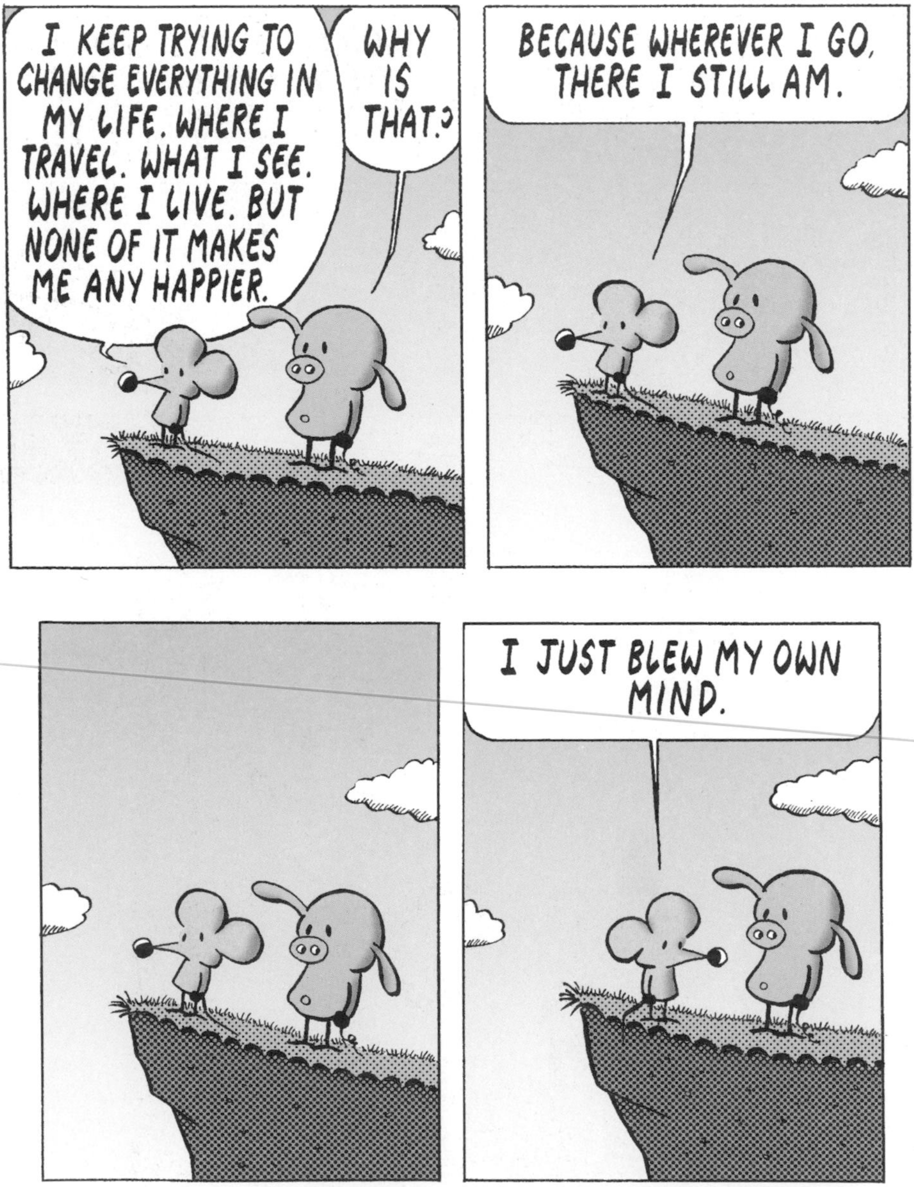
I KEEP TRYING TO CHANGE EVERYTHING IN MY LIFE. WHERE I TRAVEL. WHAT I SEE. WHERE I LIVE. BUT NONE OF IT MAKES ME ANY HAPPIER.
WHY IS THAT?
BECAUSE WHEREVER I GO, THERE I STILL AM.
I JUST BLEW MY OWN MIND.

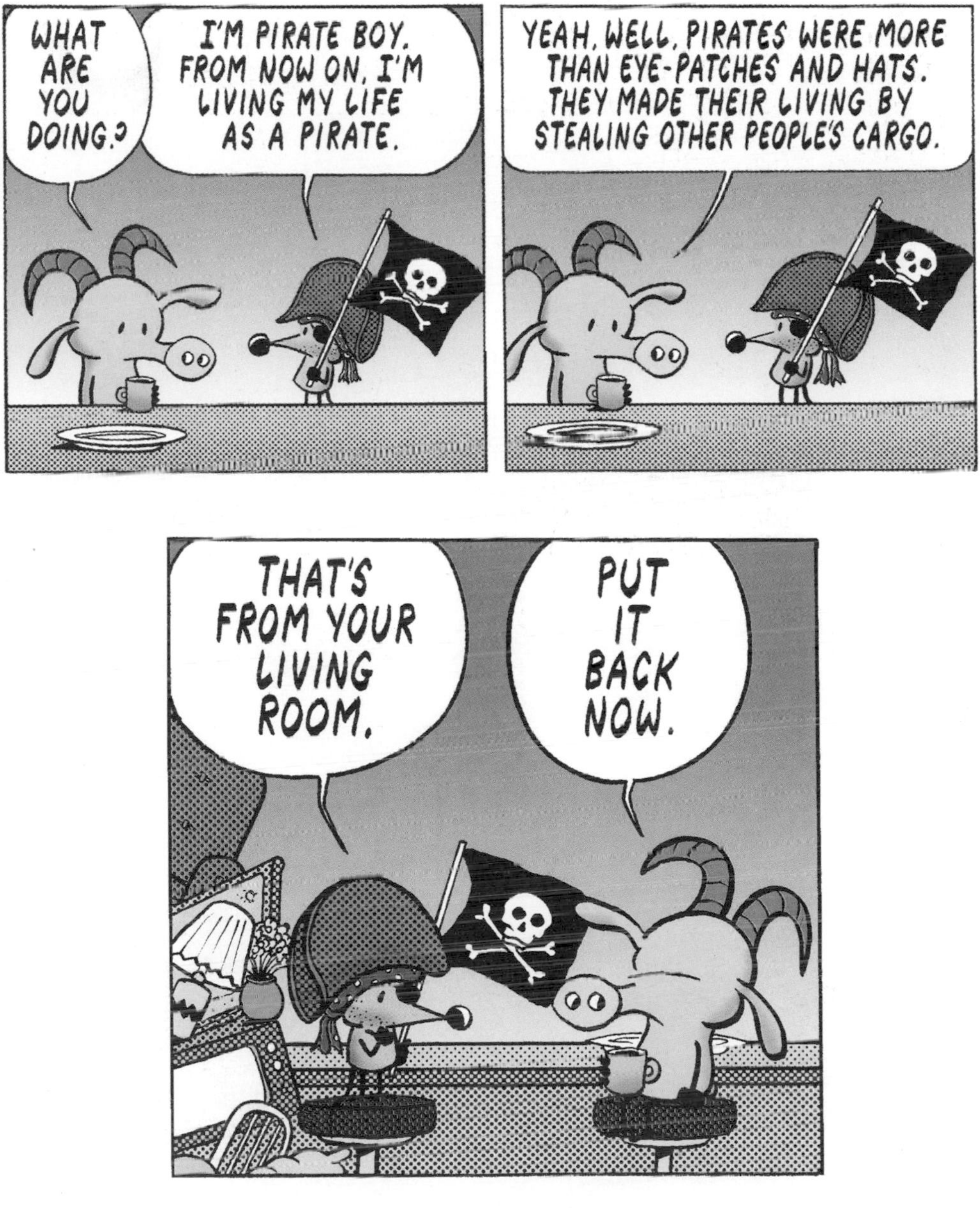
WHAT ARE YOU DOING.?
I'M PIRATE BOY. FROM NOW ON, I'M LIVING MY LIFE AS A PIRATE.
YEAH, WELL, PIRATES WERE MORE THAN EYE-PATCHES AND HATS. THEY MADE THEIR LIVING BY STEALING OTHER PEOPLE'S CARGO.
THAT'S FROM YOUR LIVING ROOM.
PUT IT BACK NOW.

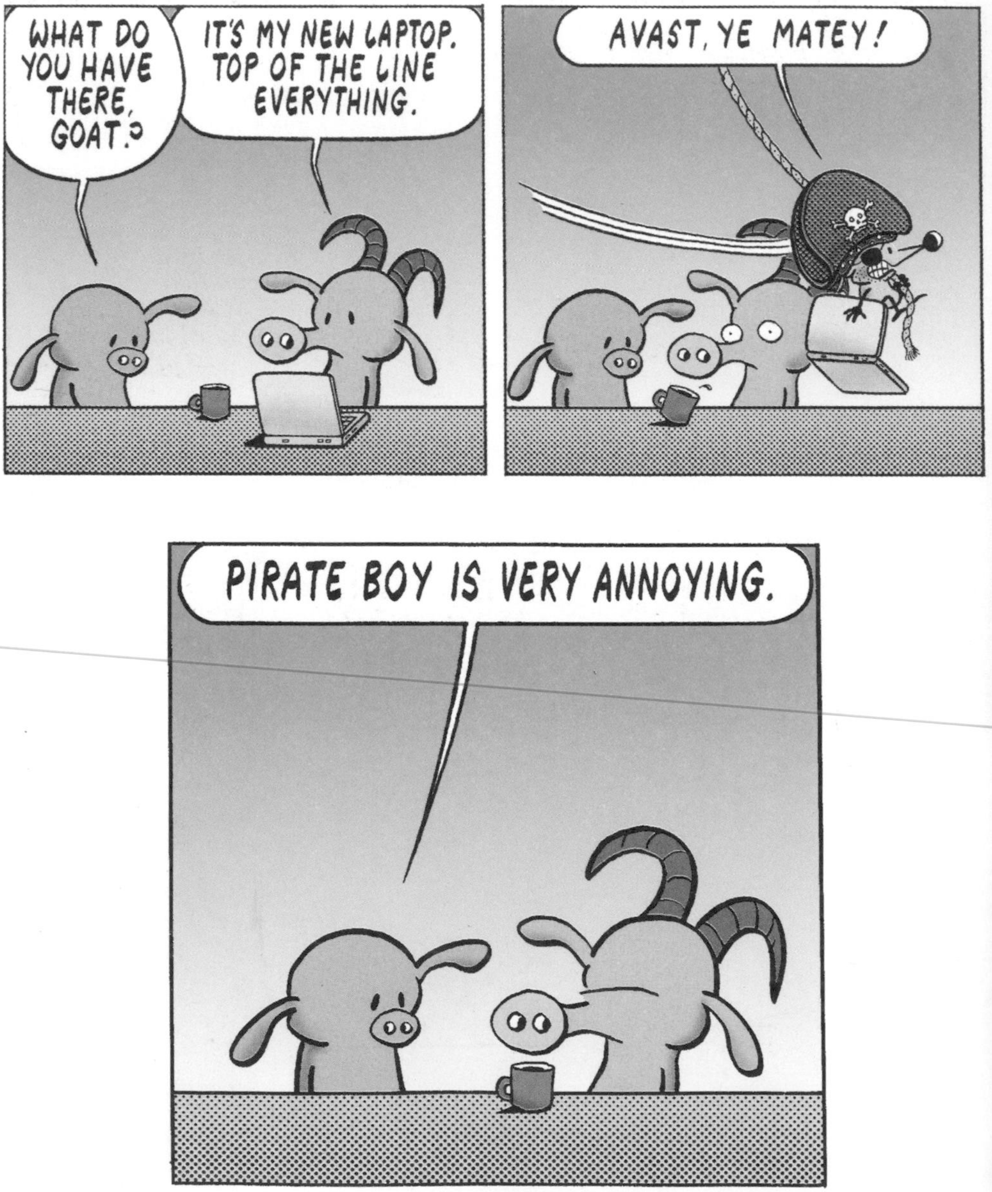
WHAT DO YOU HAVE THERE, GOAT?
IT'S MY NEW LAPTOP. TOP OF THE LINE EVERYTHING.
AVAST, YE MATEY!
PIRATE BOY IS VERY ANNOYING.

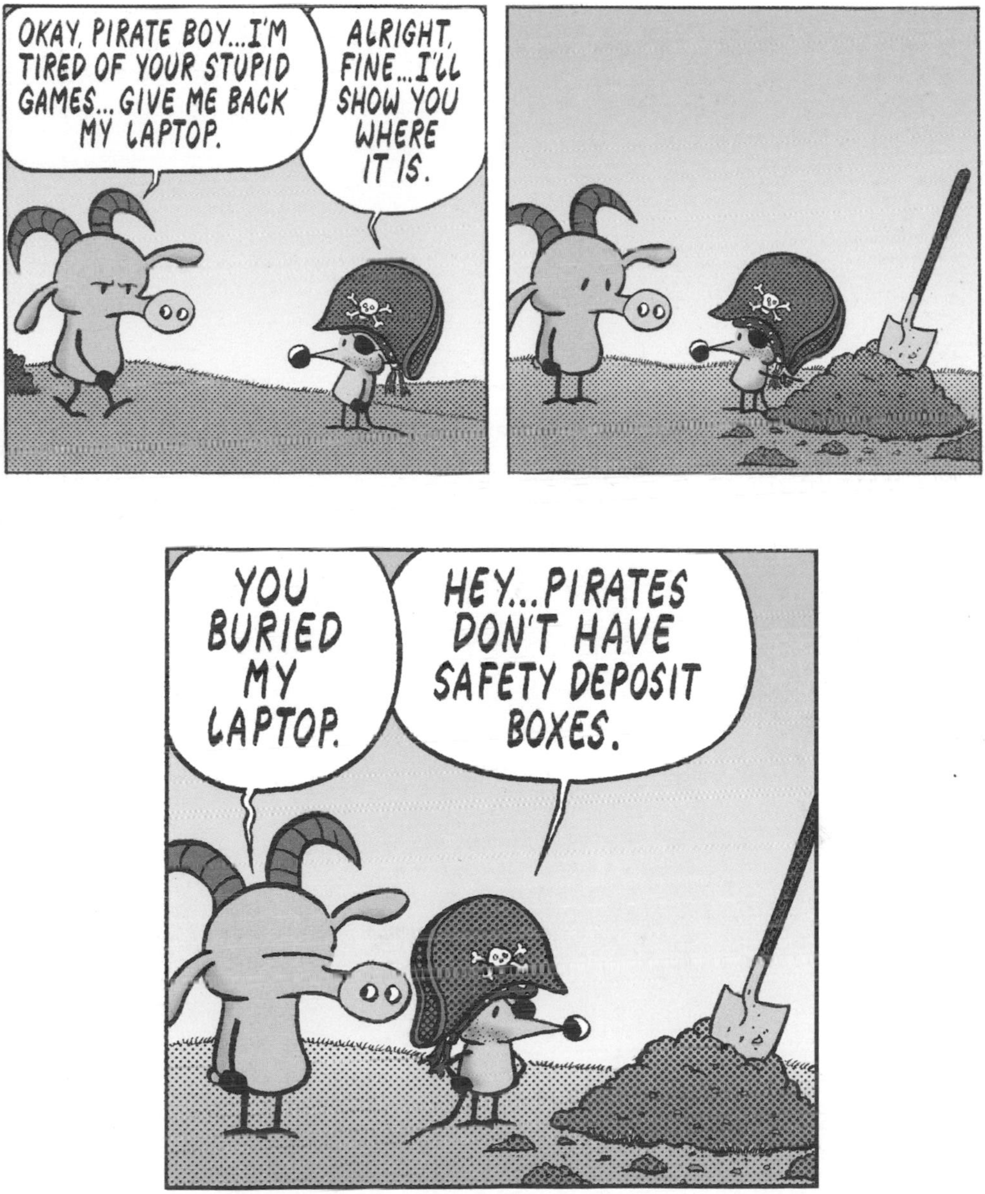
OKAY, PIRATE BOY...I'M TIRED OF YOUR STUPID GAMES...GIVE ME BACK MY LAPTOP.
ALRIGHT, FINE...I'LL SHOW YOU WHERE IT IS.
YOU BURIED MY LAPTOP.
HEY...PIRATES DON'T HAVE SAFETY DEPOSIT BOXES.

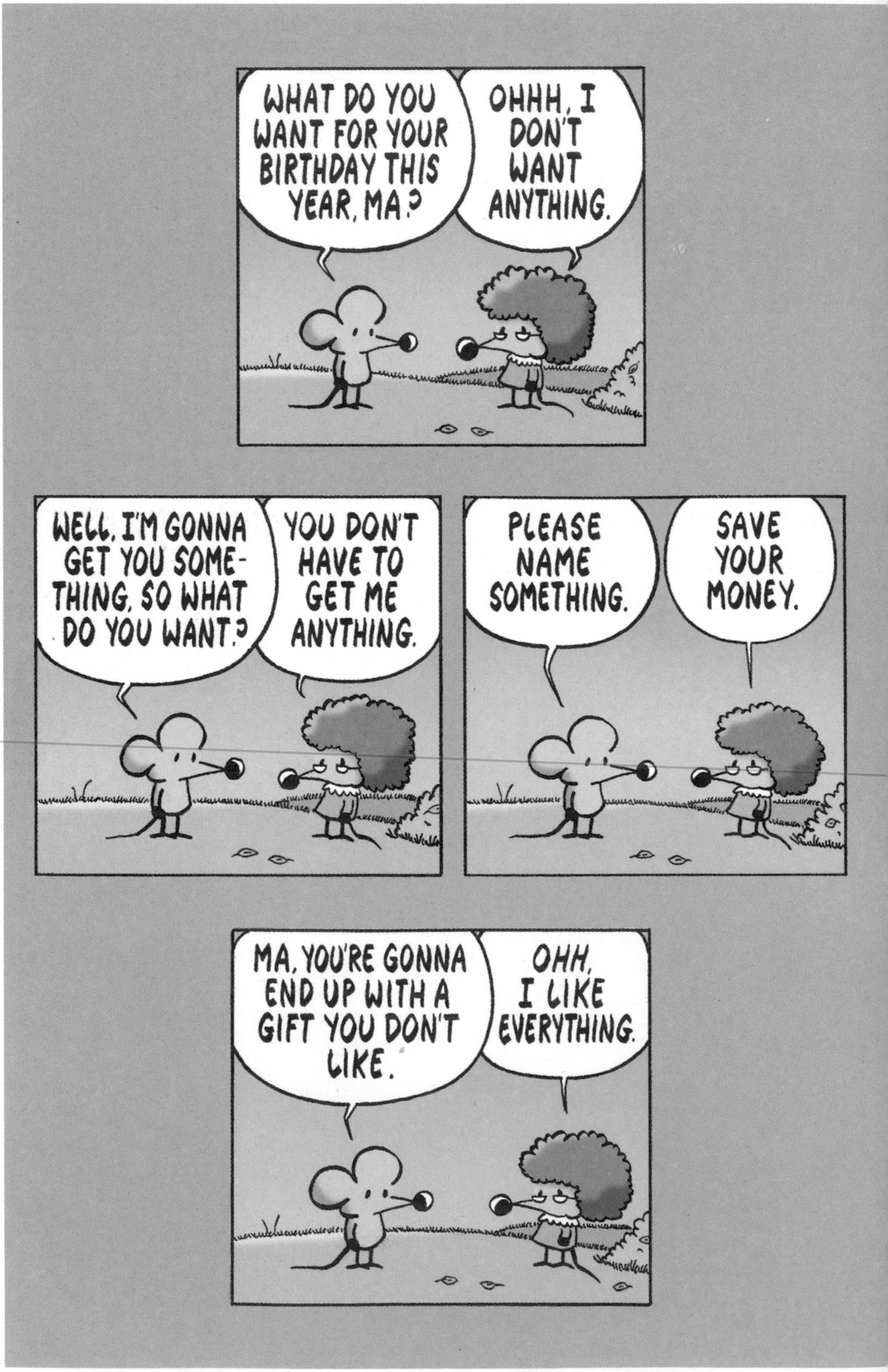
WHAT DO YOU WANT FOR YOUR BIRTHDAY THIS YEAR, MA?
OHHH, I DON'T WANT ANYTHING.
WELL, I'M GONNA GET YOU SOME-THING, SO WHAT DO YOU WANT?
YOU DON'T HAVE TO GET ME ANYTHING.
PLEASE NAME SOMETHING.
SAVE YOUR MONEY.
MA, YOU'RE GONNA END UP WITH A GIFT YOU DON'T LIKE.
OHH, I LIKE EVERYTHING.

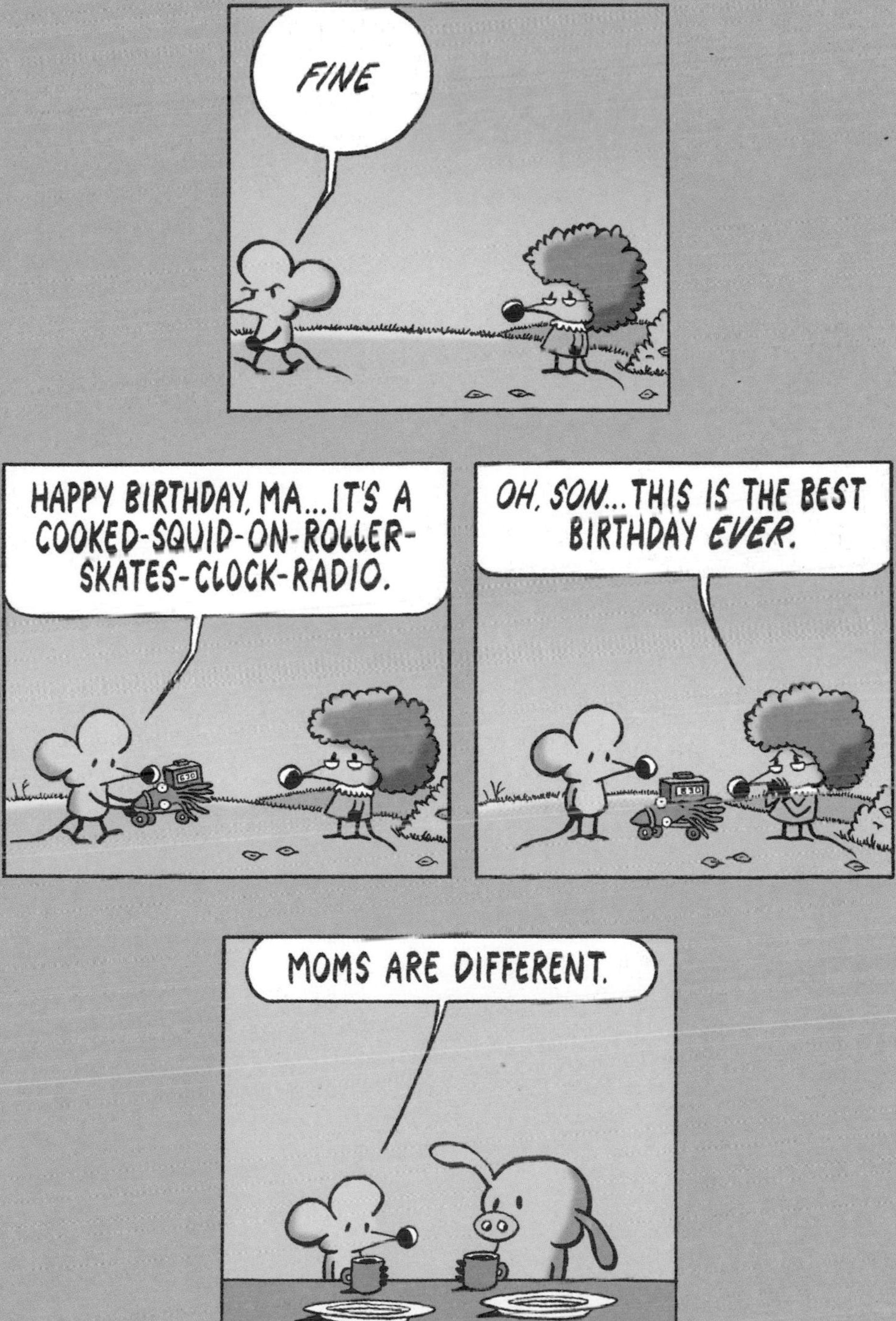
FINE
HAPPY BIRTHDAY, MA...IT'S A COOKED-SQUID-ON-ROLLER-SKATES-CLOCK-RADIO.
OH, SON...THIS IS THE BEST BIRTHDAY EVER.
MOMS ARE DIFFERENT.

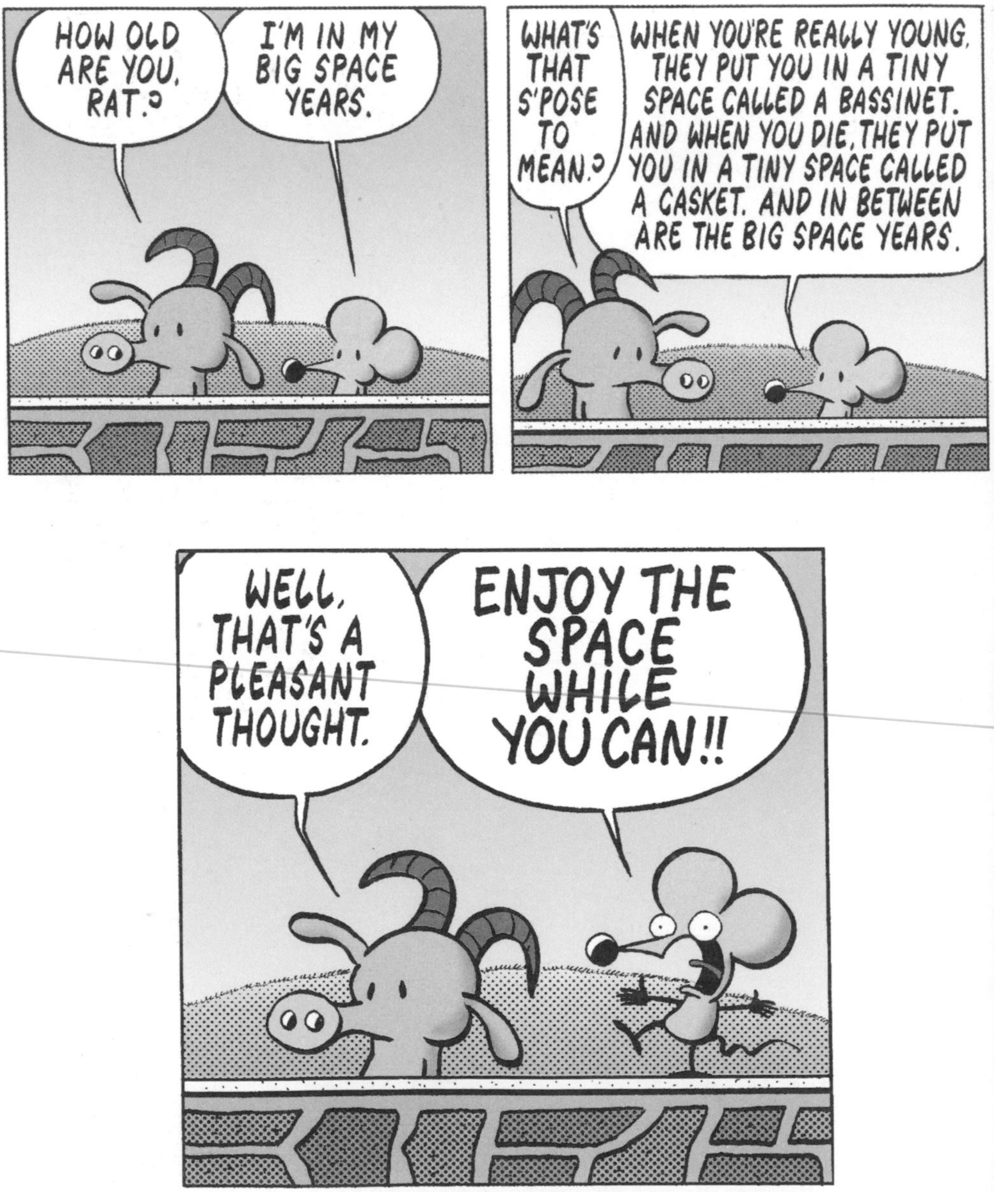
HOW OLD ARE YOU, RAT?
I'M IN MY BIG SPACE YEARS.
WHAT'S THAT S'POSE TO MEAN?
WHEN YOU'RE REALLY YOUNG, THEY PUT YOU IN A TINY SPACE CALLED A BASSINET. AND WHEN YOU DIE, THEY PUT YOU IN A TINY SPACE CALLED A CASKET. AND IN BETWEEN ARE THE BIG SPACE YEARS.
WELL, THAT'S A PLEASANT THOUGHT.
ENJOY THE SPACE WHILE YOU CAN!!

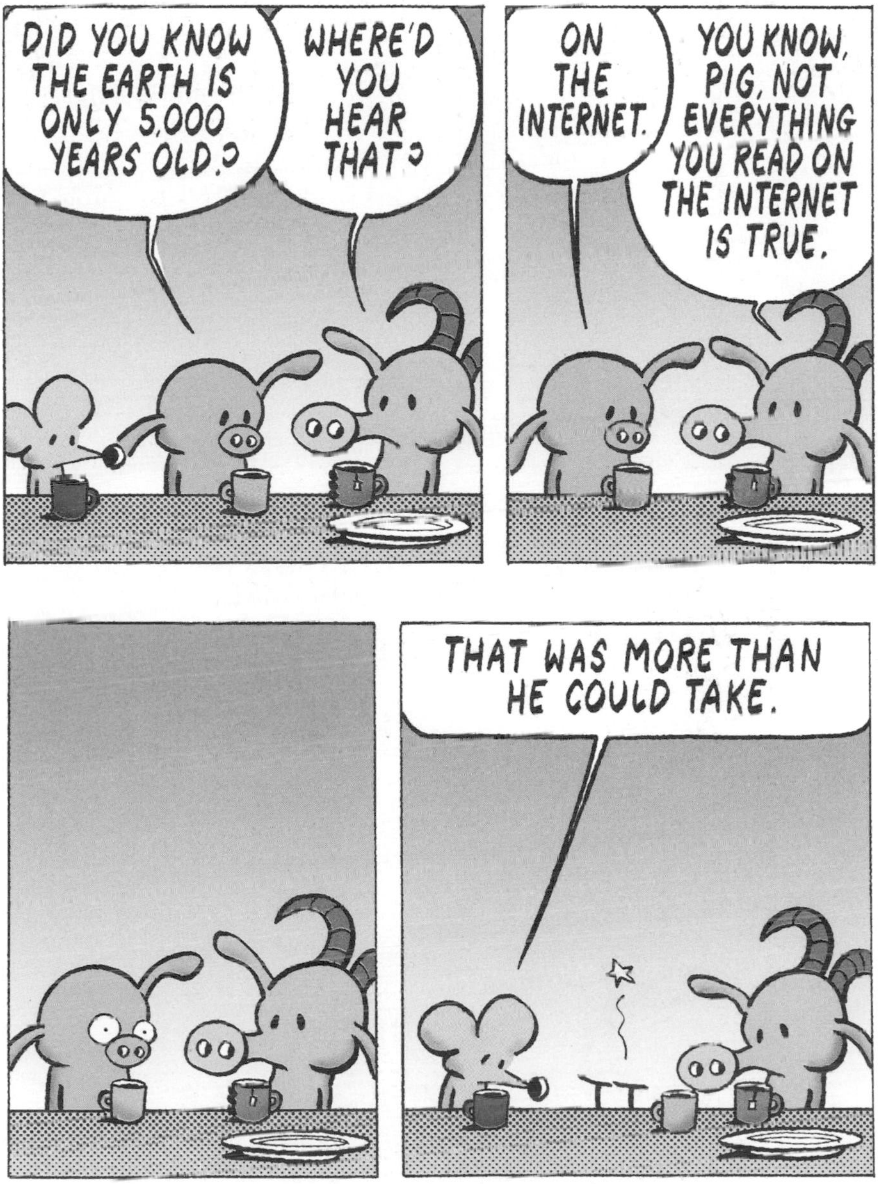
DID YOU KNOW THE EARTH IS ONLY 5,000 YEARS OLD?
WHERE'D YOU HEAR THAT?
ON THE INTERNET.
YOU KNOW, PIG, NOT EVERYTHING YOU READ ON THE INTERNET IS TRUE.
THAT WAS MORE THAN HE COULD TAKE.

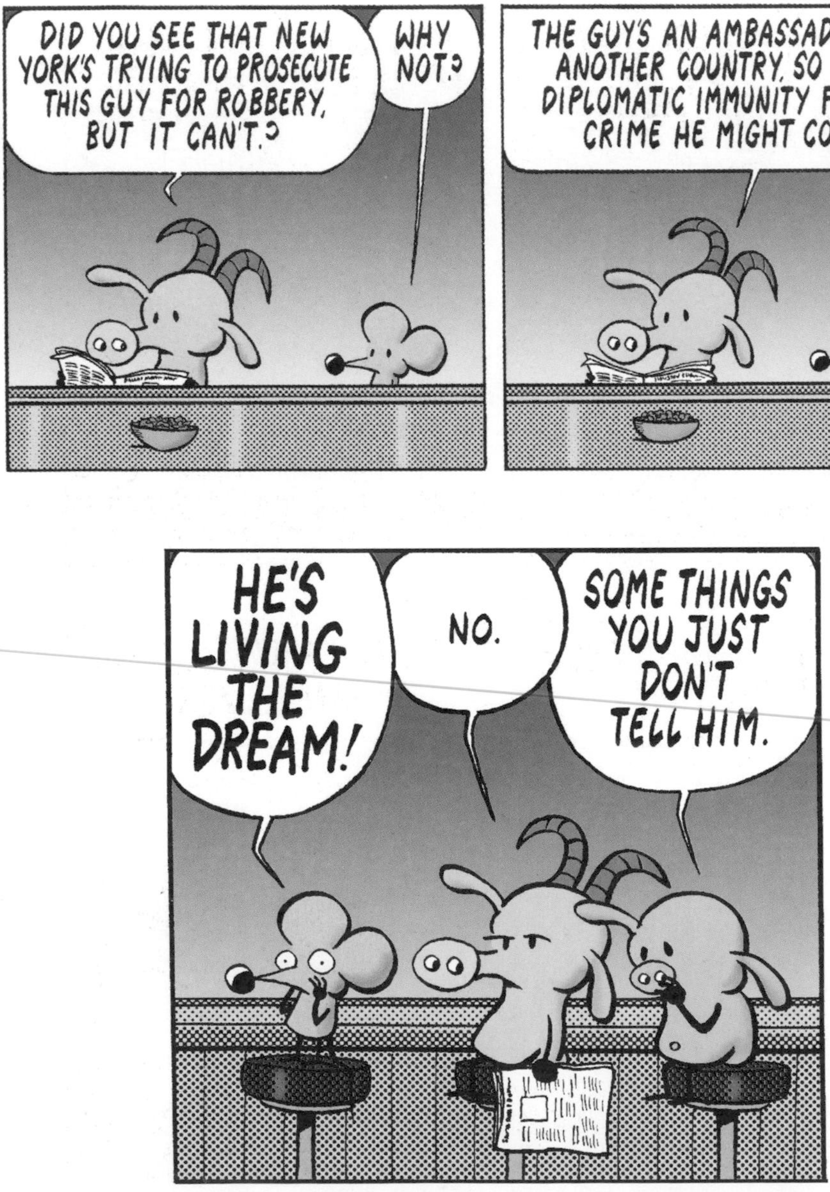
DID YOU SEE THAT NEW YORK'S TRYING TO PROSECUTE THIS GUY FOR ROBBERY, BUT IT CAN'T?
WHY NOT?
THE GUY'S AN AMBASSADOR FROM ANOTHER COUNTRY, SO HE HAS DIPLOMATIC IMMUNITY FOR ANY CRIME HE MIGHT COMMIT.
HE'S LIVING THE DREAM!
NO.
SOME THINGS YOU JUST DON'T TELL HIM.

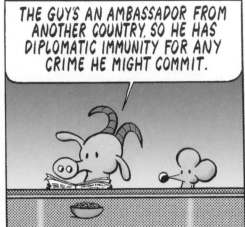

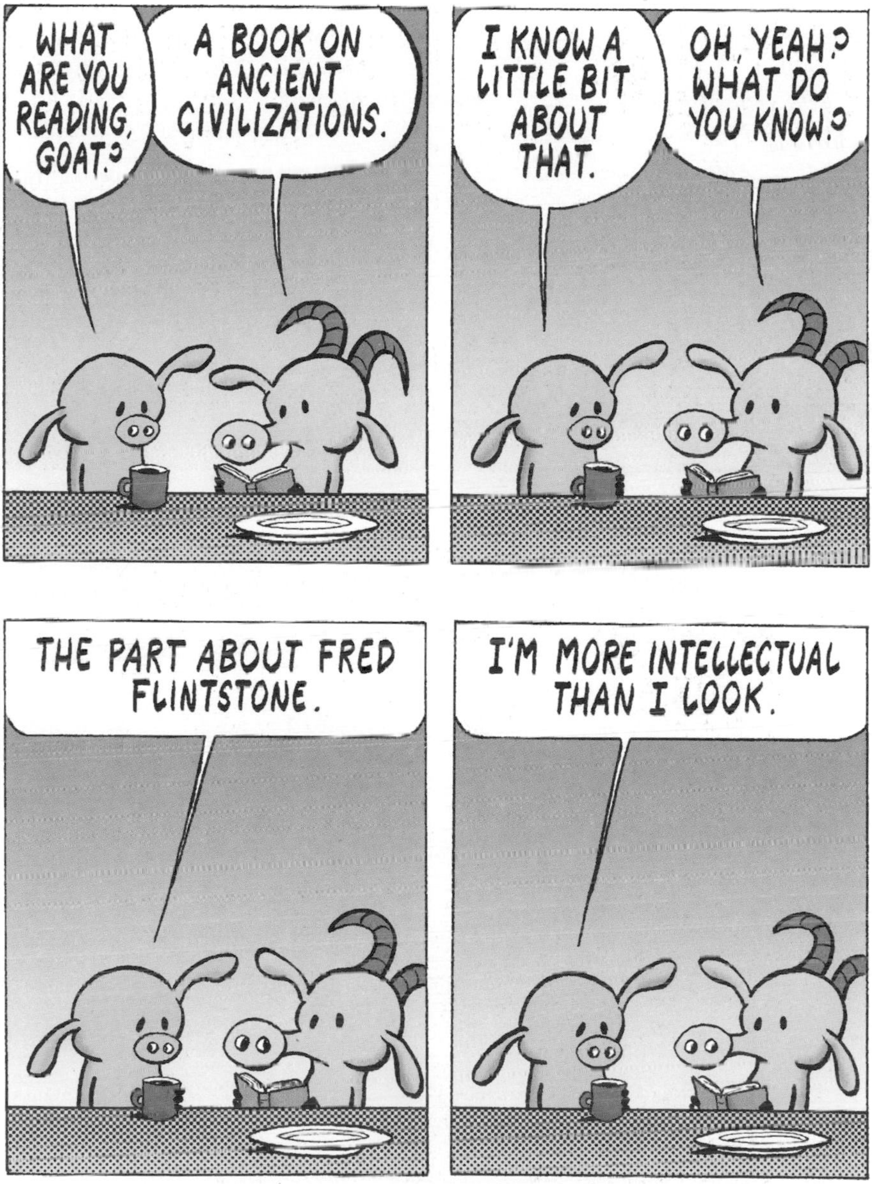
WHAT ARE YOU READING, GOAT?
A BOOK ON ANCIENT CIVILIZATIONS.
I KNOW A LITTLE BIT ABOUT THAT.
OH, YEAH? WHAT DO YOU KNOW?
THE PART ABOUT FRED FLINTSTONE.
I'M MORE INTELLECTUAL THAN I LOOK.

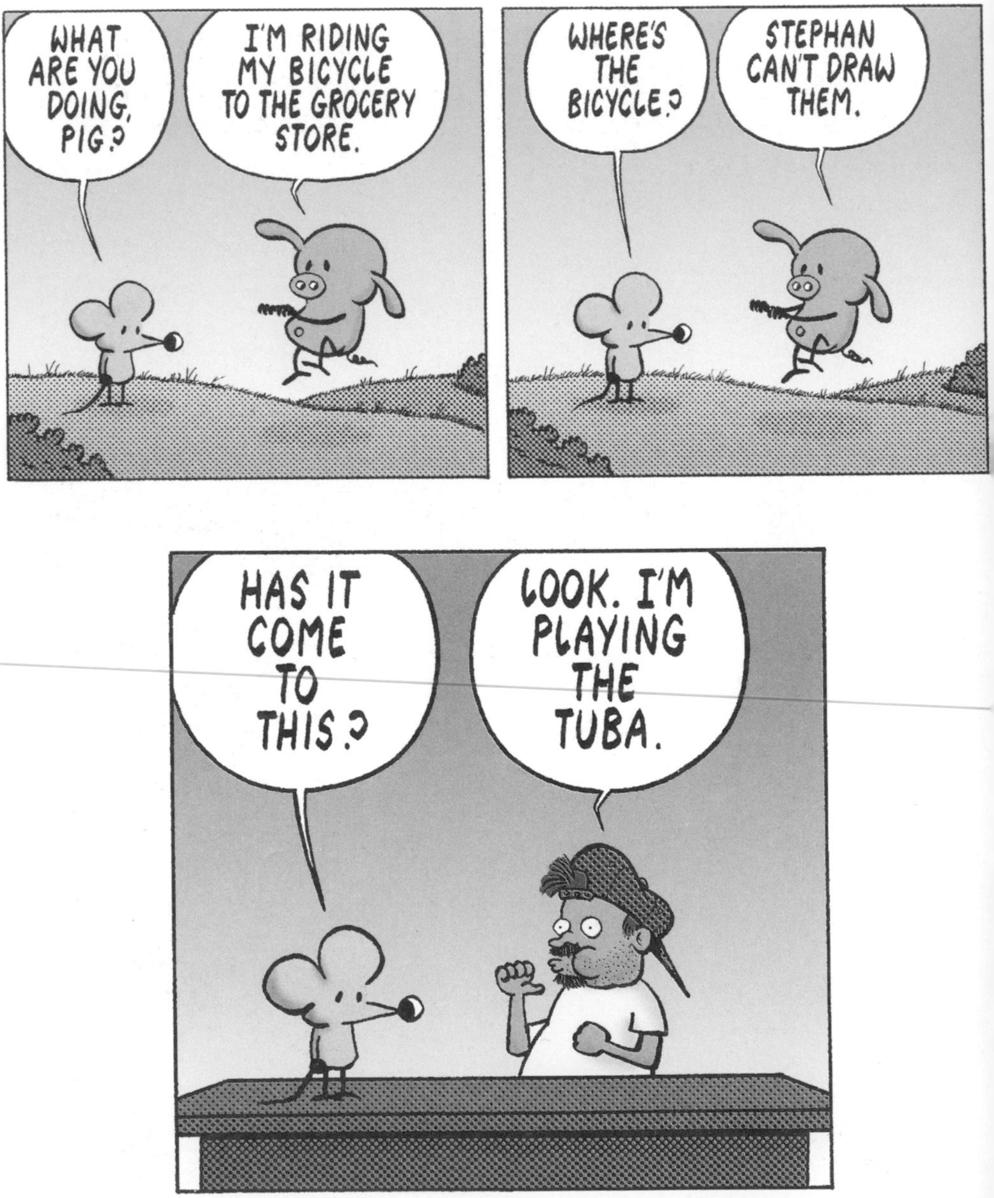
WHAT ARE YOU DOING, PIG?
I'M RIDING MY BICYCLE TO THE GROCERY STORE.
WHERE'S THE BICYCLE?
STEPHAN CAN'T DRAW THEM.
HAS IT COME TO THIS?
LOOK. I'M PLAYING THE TUBA.

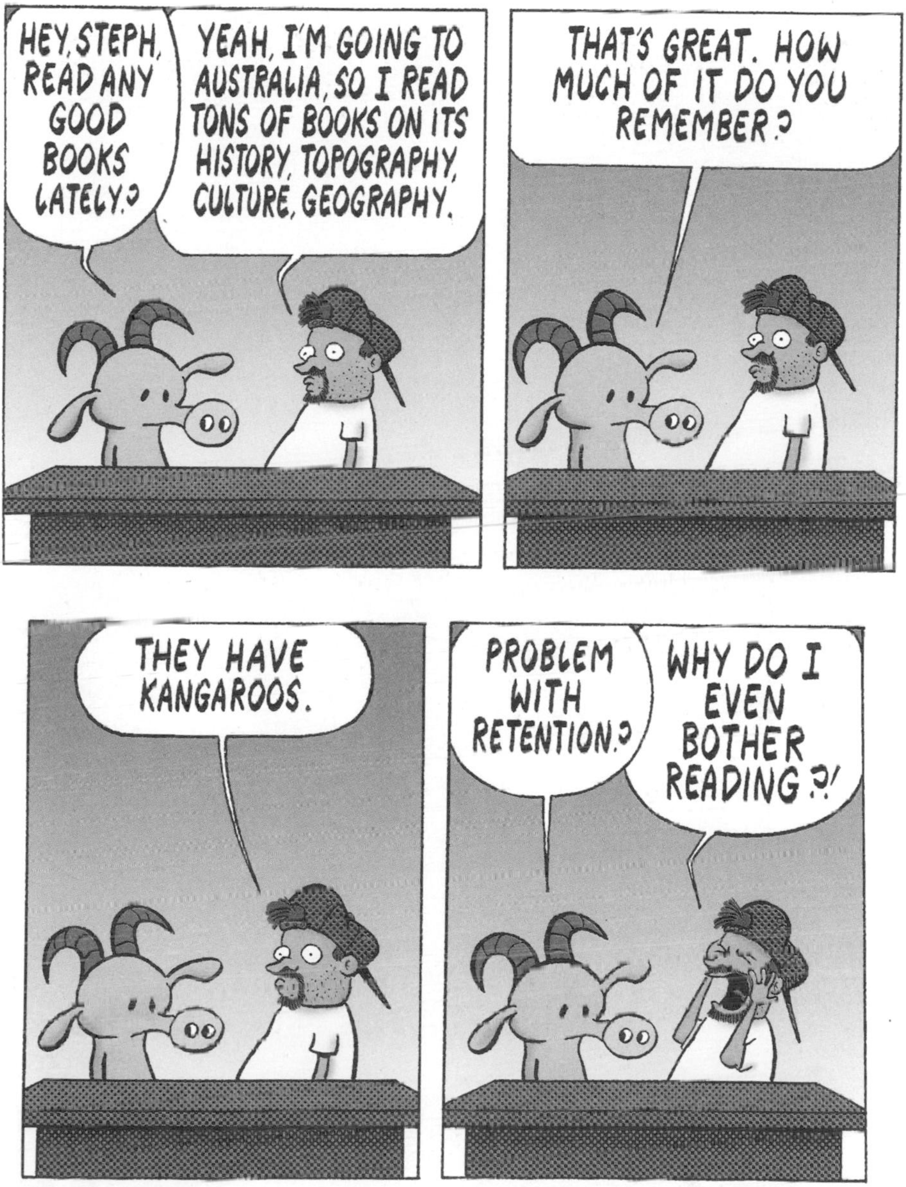
HEY, STEPH, READ ANY GOOD BOOKS LATELY?
YEAH, I'M GOING TO AUSTRALIA, SO I READ TONS OF BOOKS ON ITS HISTORY, TOPOGRAPHY, CULTURE, GEOGRAPHY.
THAT'S GREAT. HOW MUCH OF IT DO YOU REMEMBER?
THEY HAVE KANGAROOS.
PROBLEM WITH RETENTION?
WHY DO I EVEN BOTHER READING?!

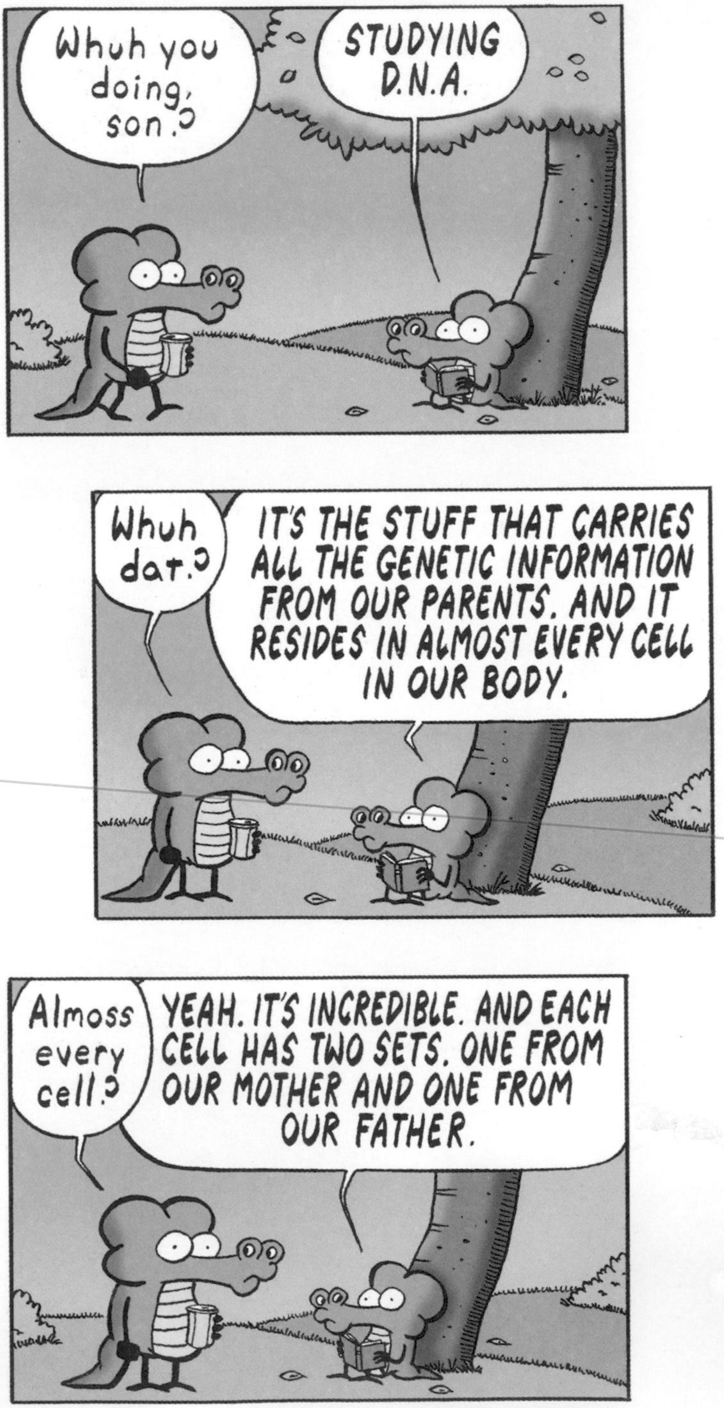
Whuh you doing, son?
STUDYING D.N.A.
Whuh dat?
IT'S THE STUFF THAT CARRIES ALL THE GENETIC INFORMATION FROM OUR PARENTS. AND IT RESIDES IN ALMOST EVERY CELL IN OUR BODY.
Almoss every cell?
YEAH. IT'S INCREDIBLE. AND EACH CELL HAS TWO SETS. ONE FROM OUR MOTHER AND ONE FROM OUR FATHER.

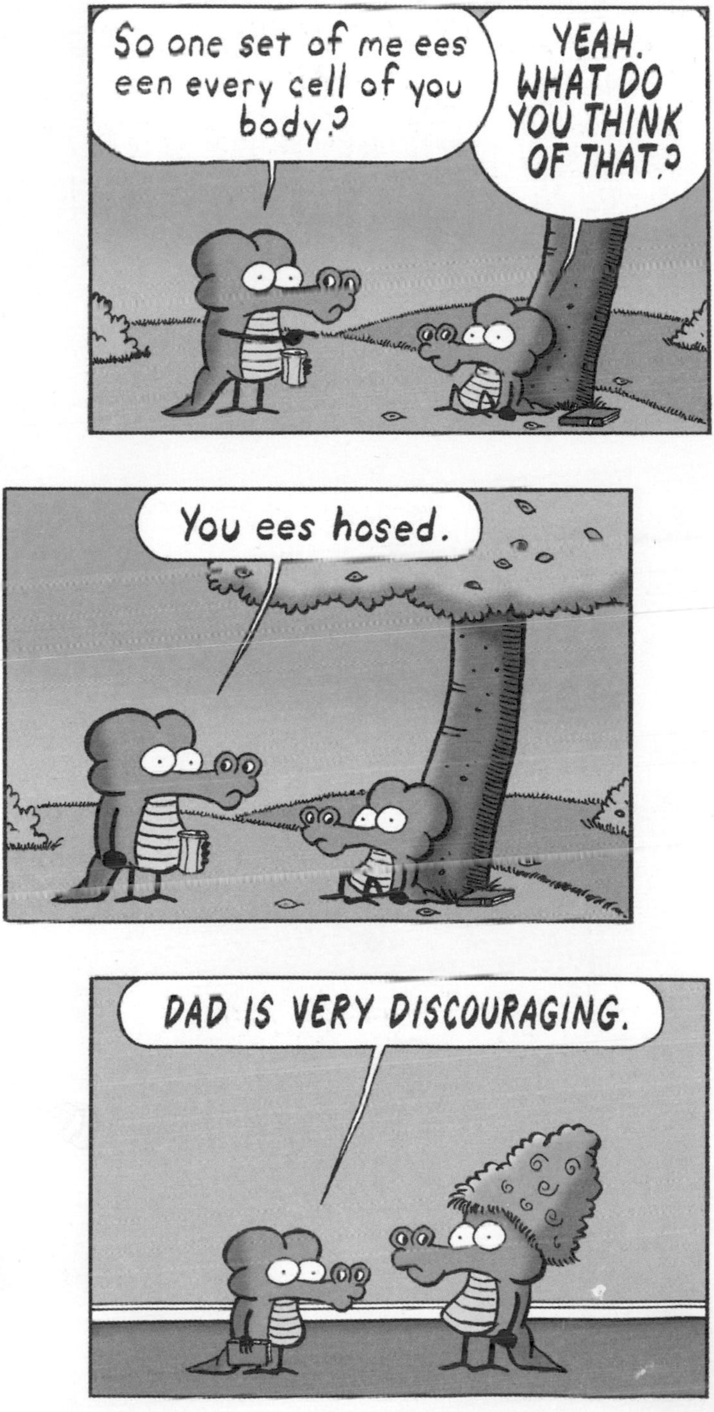
So one set of me ees een every cell of you body?
YEAH. WHAT DO YOU THINK OF THAT?
You ees hosed.
DAD IS VERY DISCOURAGING.

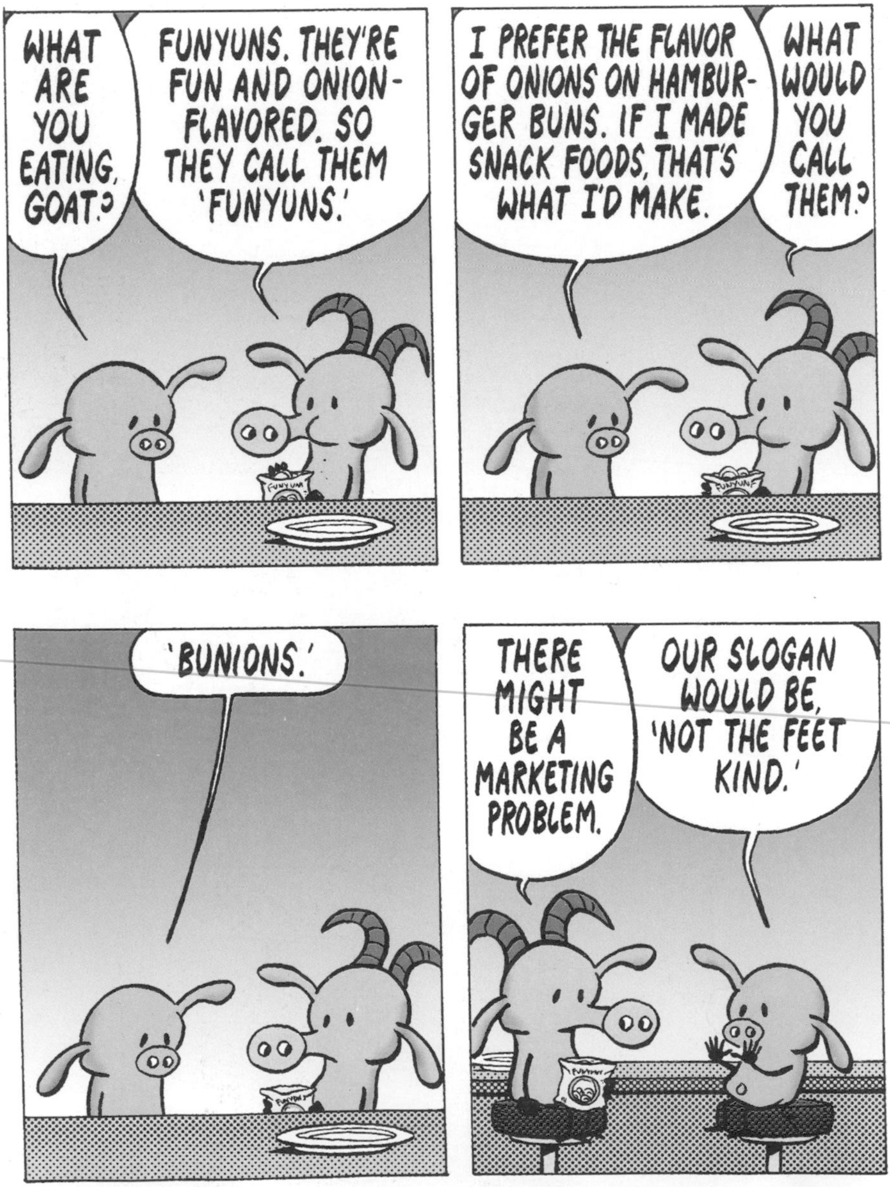
WHAT ARE YOU EATING, GOAT?
FUNYUNS. THEY'RE FUN AND ONION-FLAVORED. SO THEY CALL THEM 'FUNYUNS.'
I PREFER THE FLAVOR OF ONIONS ON HAMBURGER BUNS. IF I MADE SNACK FOODS, THAT'S WHAT I'D MAKE.
WHAT WOULD YOU CALL THEM?
'BUNIONS.'
THERE MIGHT BE A MARKETING PROBLEM.
OUR SLOGAN WOULD BE, 'NOT THE FEET KIND.'

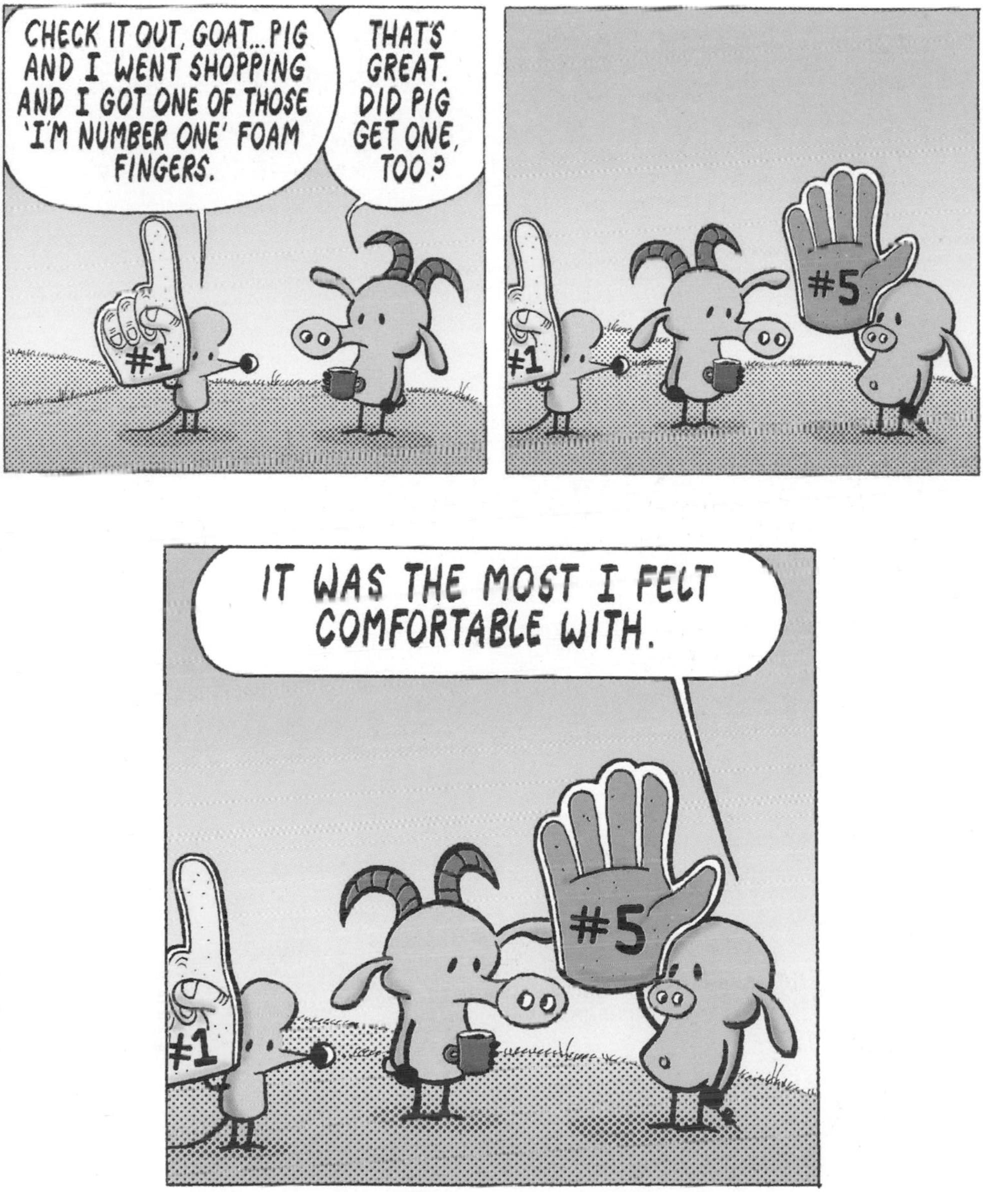
CHECK IT OUT, GOAT...PIG AND I WENT SHOPPING AND I GOT ONE OF THOSE 'I'M NUMBER ONE' FOAM FINGERS.
THAT'S GREAT. DID PIG GET ONE, TOO?
#1
#5
IT WAS THE MOST I FELT COMFORTABLE WITH.

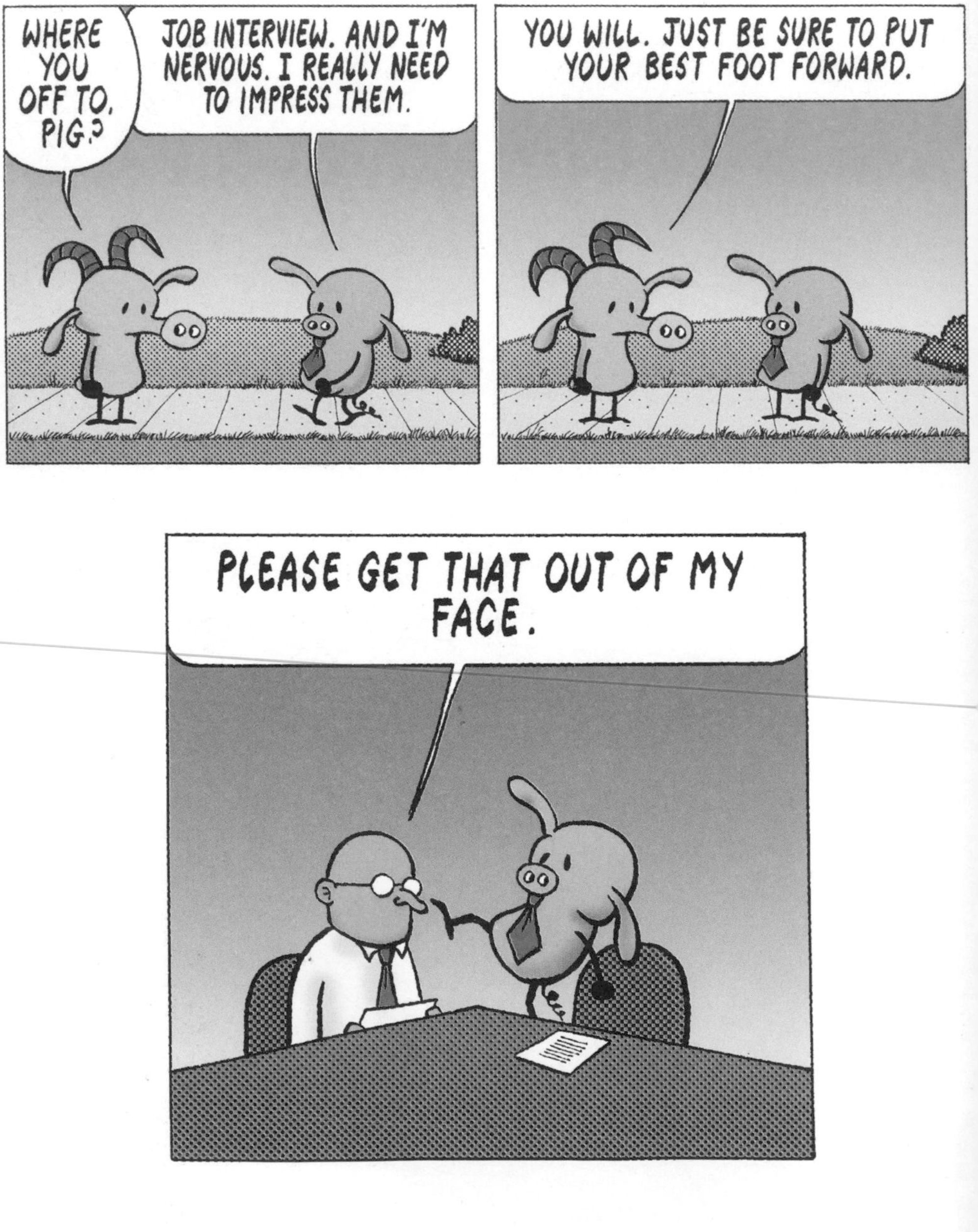
WHERE YOU OFF TO, PIG?
JOB INTERVIEW. AND I'M NERVOUS. I REALLY NEED TO IMPRESS THEM.
YOU WILL. JUST BE SURE TO PUT YOUR BEST FOOT FORWARD.
PLEASE GET THAT OUT OF MY FACE.

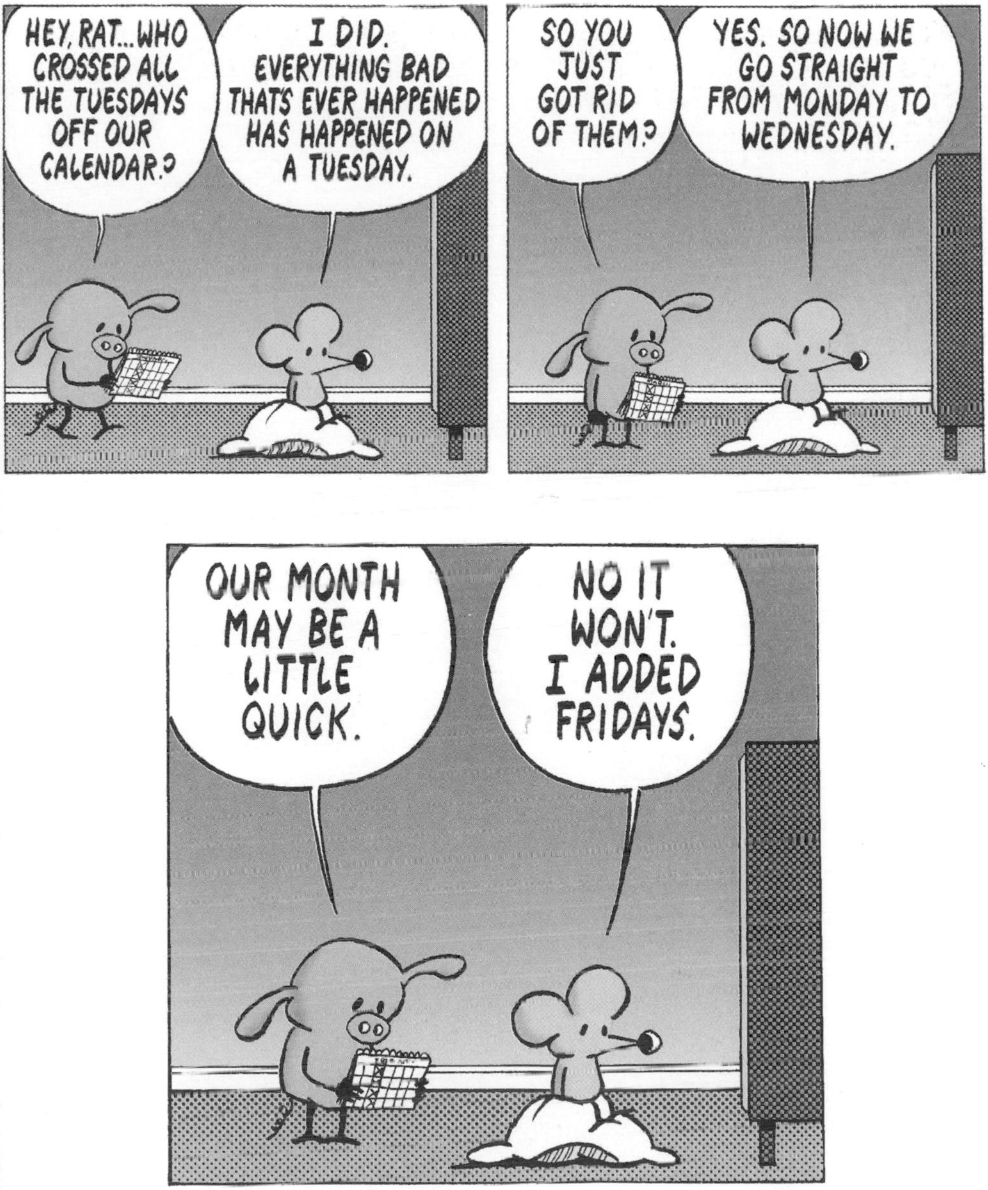
HEY, RAT...WHO CROSSED ALL THE TUESDAYS OFF OUR CALENDAR?
I DID. EVERYTHING BAD THAT'S EVER HAPPENED HAS HAPPENED ON A TUESDAY.
SO YOU JUST GOT RID OF THEM?
YES. SO NOW WE GO STRAIGHT FROM MONDAY TO WEDNESDAY.
OUR MONTH MAY BE A LITTLE QUICK.
NO IT WON'T. I ADDED FRIDAYS.

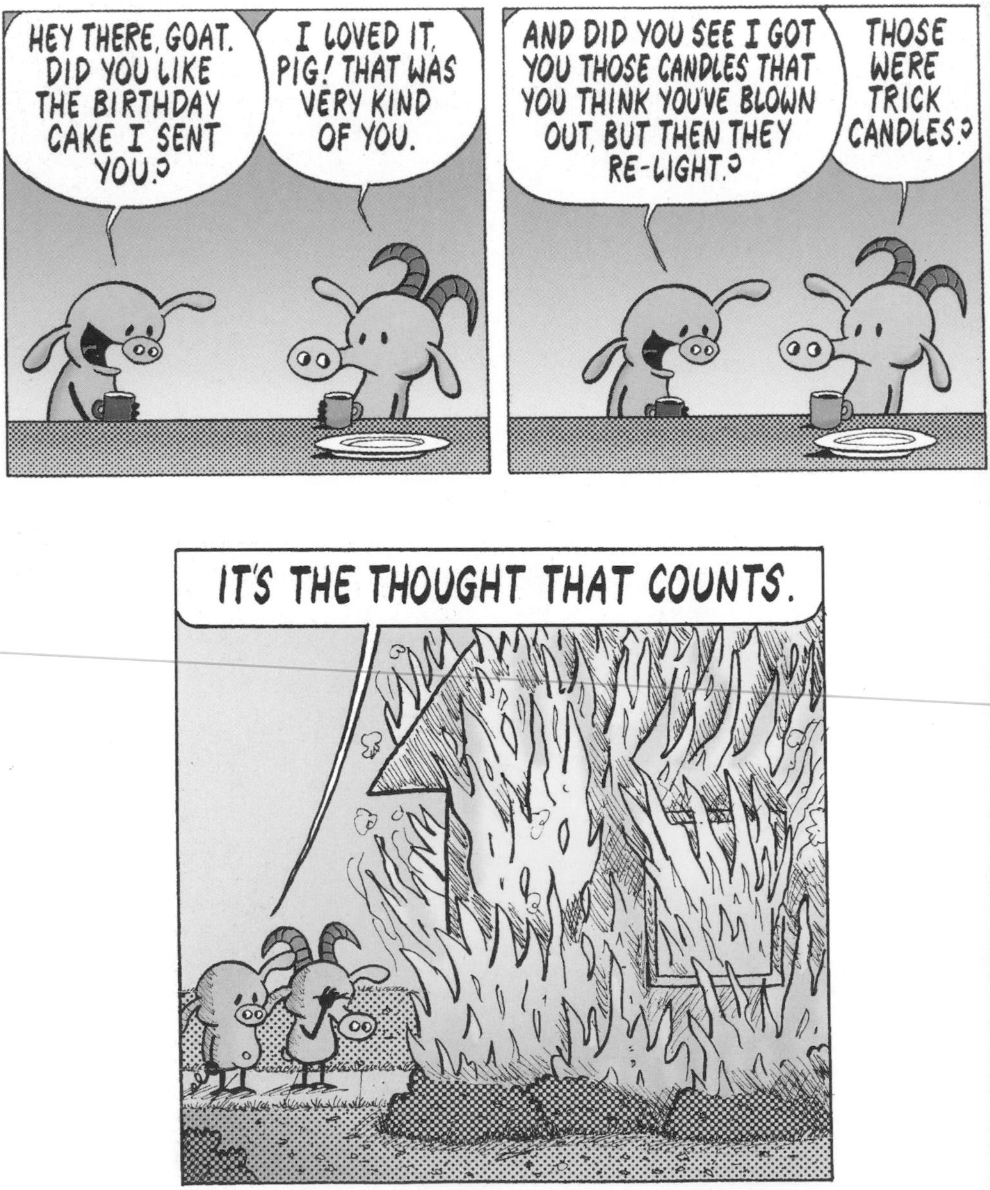
HEY THERE, GOAT. DID YOU LIKE THE BIRTHDAY CAKE I SENT YOU?
I LOVED IT, PIG! THAT WAS VERY KIND OF YOU.
AND DID YOU SEE I GOT YOU THOSE CANDLES THAT YOU THINK YOU'VE BLOWN OUT, BUT THEN THEY RE-LIGHT?
THOSE WERE TRICK CANDLES?
IT'S THE THOUGHT THAT COUNTS.

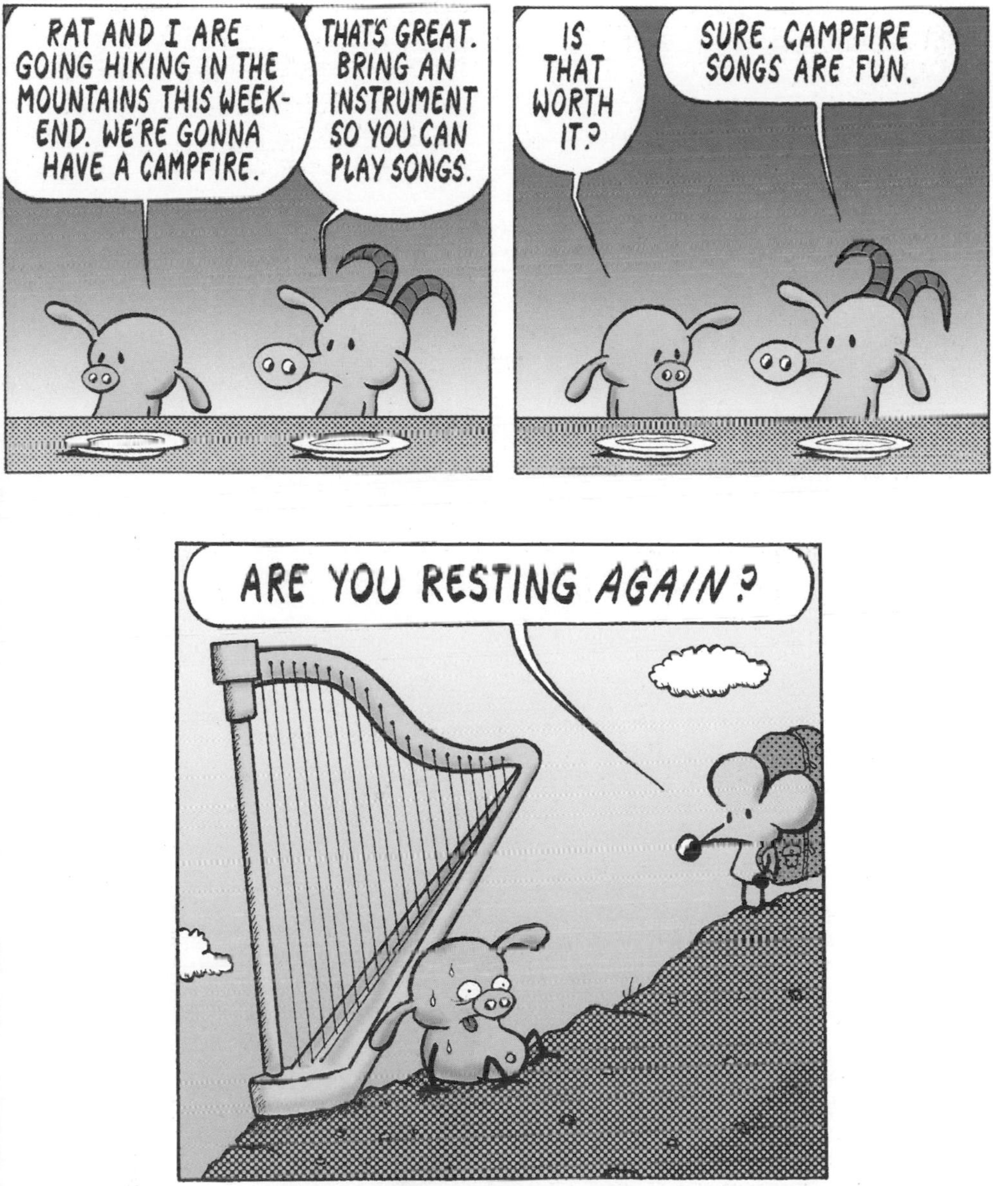

RAT AND I ARE GOING HIKING IN THE MOUNTAINS THIS WEEK-END. WE'RE GONNA HAVE A CAMPFIRE.
THAT'S GREAT. BRING AN INSTRUMENT SO YOU CAN PLAY SONGS.
IS THAT WORTH IT?
SURE. CAMPFIRE SONGS ARE FUN.
ARE YOU RESTING *AGAIN*?

WHAT ARE YOU DOING, RAT?
I'M SITTING IN THE 'BOX O' PEOPLE WHO ENJOY SUCCESS.'
People Who ENJOY SUCCESS
WHAT'S THAT?
WHAT'S IT LOOK LIKE? IT'S A BOX FOR PEOPLE WHO ENJOY SUCCESS.
People Who ENJOY SUCCESS
GEE, I'D LIKE TO GET IN, BUT IT LOOKS PRETTY PACKED.
OF COURSE IT'S PACKED. *EVERYONE* LOVES SUCCESS.
People Who ENJOY SUCCESS

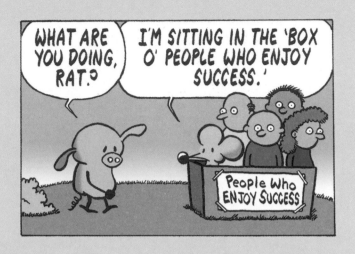

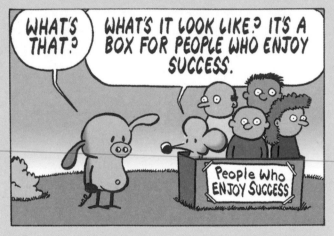

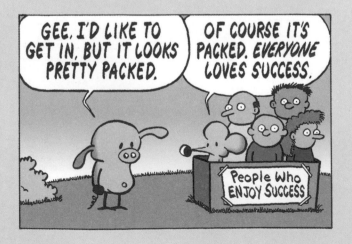

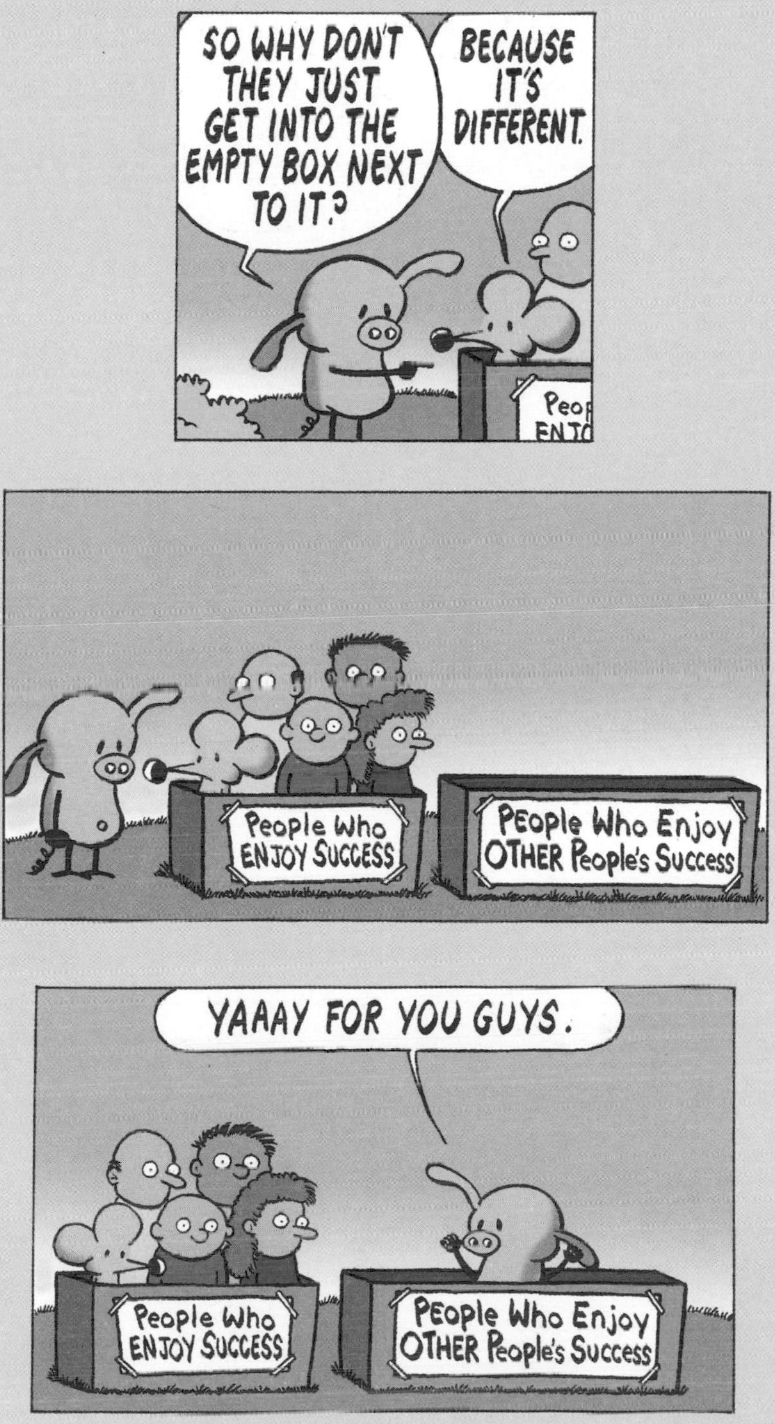
SO WHY DON'T THEY JUST GET INTO THE EMPTY BOX NEXT TO IT?
BECAUSE IT'S DIFFERENT.
People Who ENJOY SUCCESS
PEOPLE Who Enjoy OTHER People's Success
YAAAY FOR YOU GUYS.
People Who ENJOY SUCCESS
PEOPLE Who Enjoy OTHER People's Success

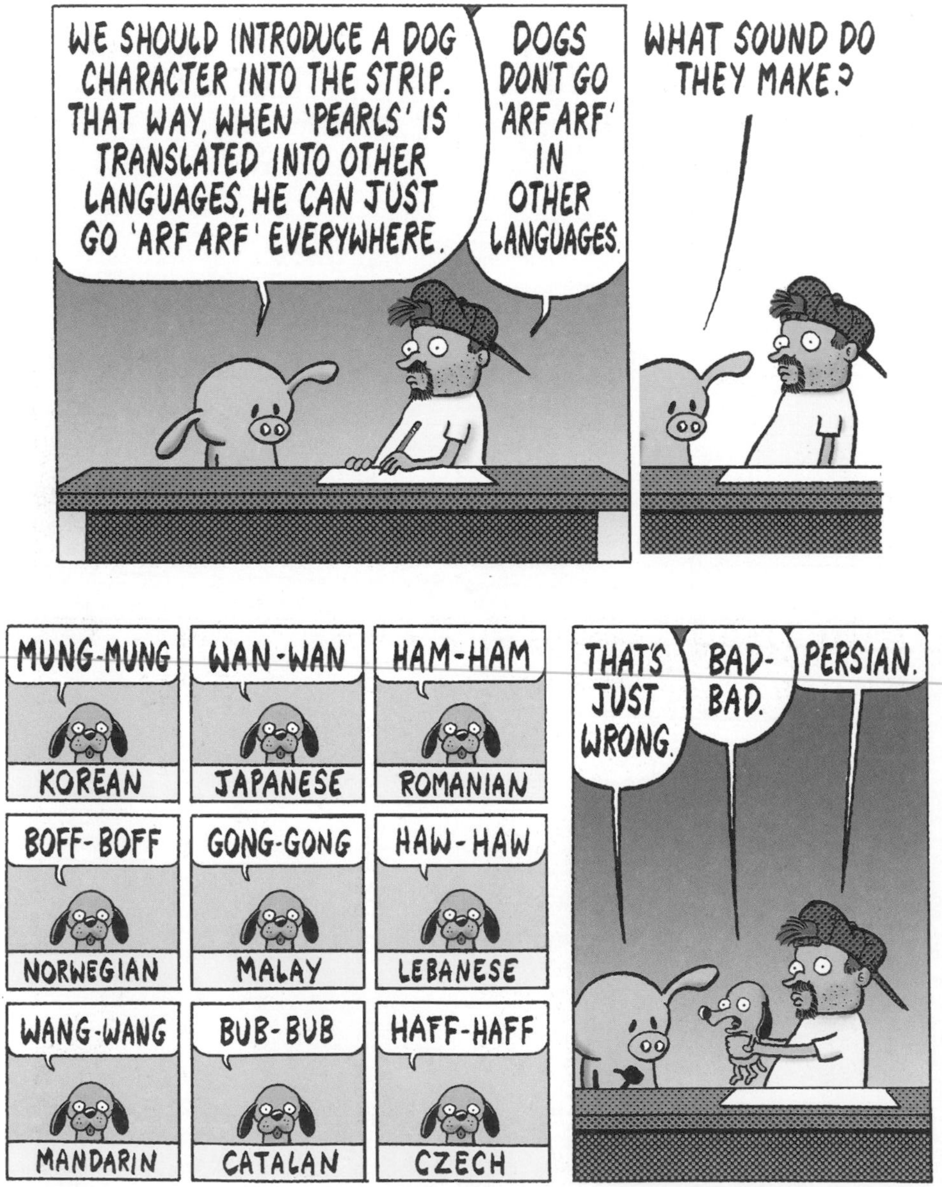
WE SHOULD INTRODUCE A DOG CHARACTER INTO THE STRIP. THAT WAY, WHEN 'PEARLS' IS TRANSLATED INTO OTHER LANGUAGES, HE CAN JUST GO 'ARF ARF' EVERYWHERE.
DOGS DON'T GO 'ARF ARF' IN OTHER LANGUAGES.
WHAT SOUND DO THEY MAKE?
MUNG-MUNG
KOREAN
WAN-WAN
JAPANESE
HAM-HAM
ROMANIAN
BOFF-BOFF
NORWEGIAN
GONG-GONG
MALAY
HAW-HAW
LEBANESE
WANG-WANG
MANDARIN
BUB-BUB
CATALAN
HAFF-HAFF
CZECH
THAT'S JUST WRONG.
BAD-BAD.
PERSIAN.

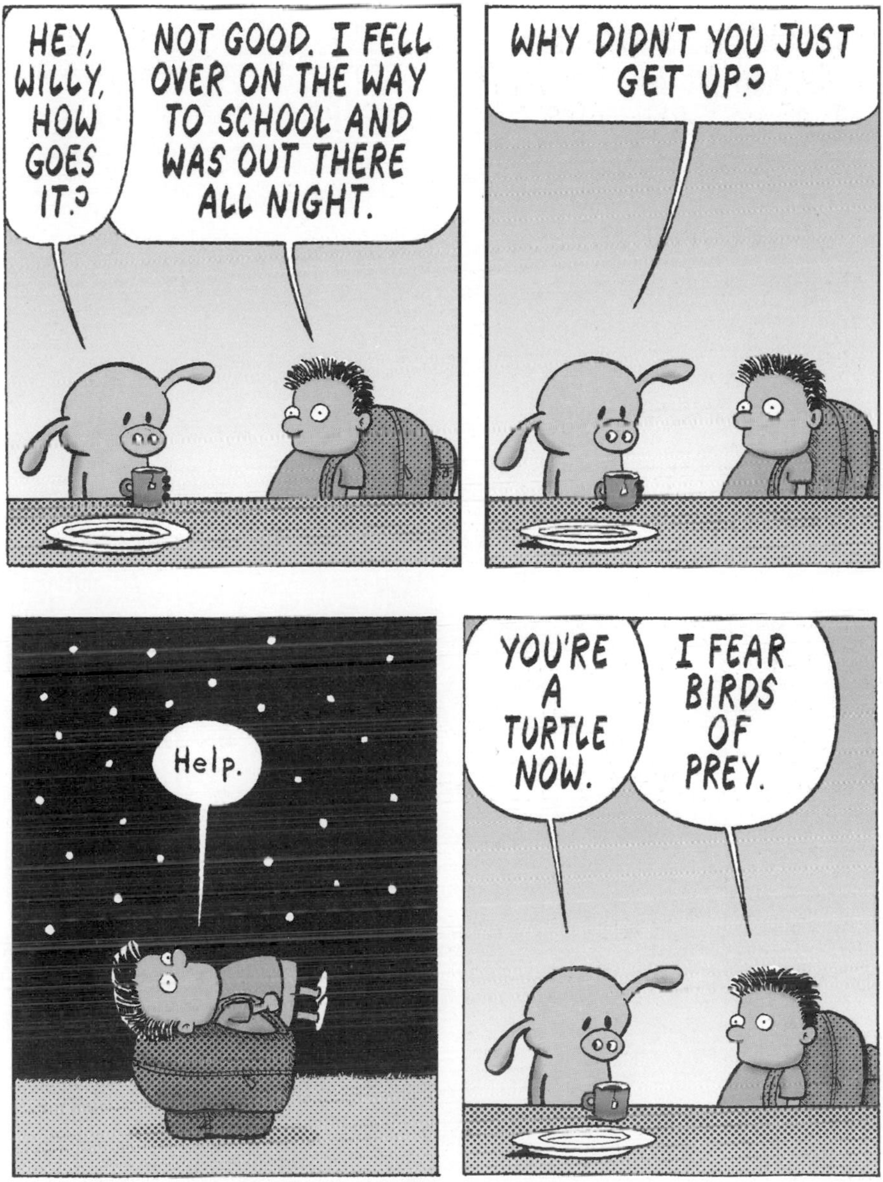
HEY, WILLY, HOW GOES IT?
NOT GOOD. I FELL OVER ON THE WAY TO SCHOOL AND WAS OUT THERE ALL NIGHT.
WHY DIDN'T YOU JUST GET UP?
Help.
YOU'RE A TURTLE NOW.
I FEAR BIRDS OF PREY.

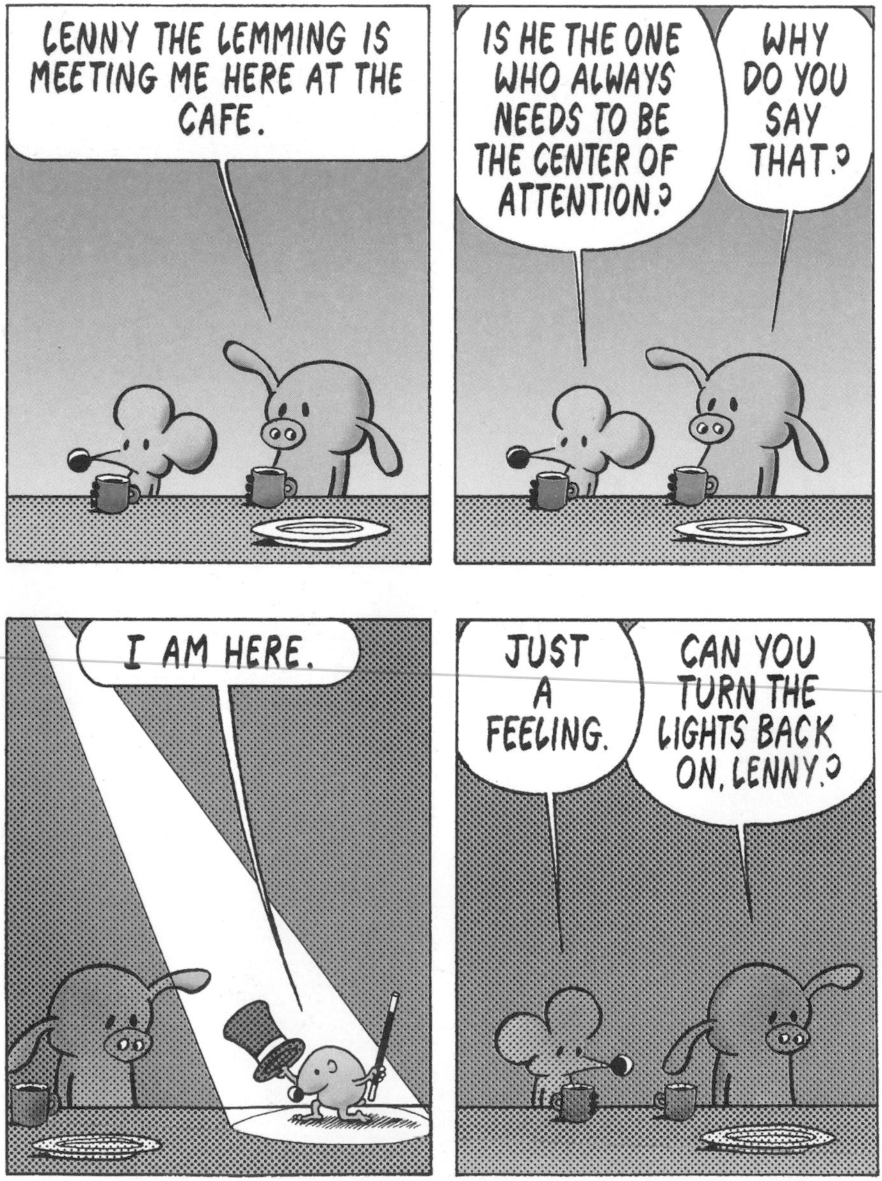
LENNY THE LEMMING IS MEETING ME HERE AT THE CAFE.
IS HE THE ONE WHO ALWAYS NEEDS TO BE THE CENTER OF ATTENTION?
WHY DO YOU SAY THAT?
I AM HERE.
JUST A FEELING.
CAN YOU TURN THE LIGHTS BACK ON, LENNY?

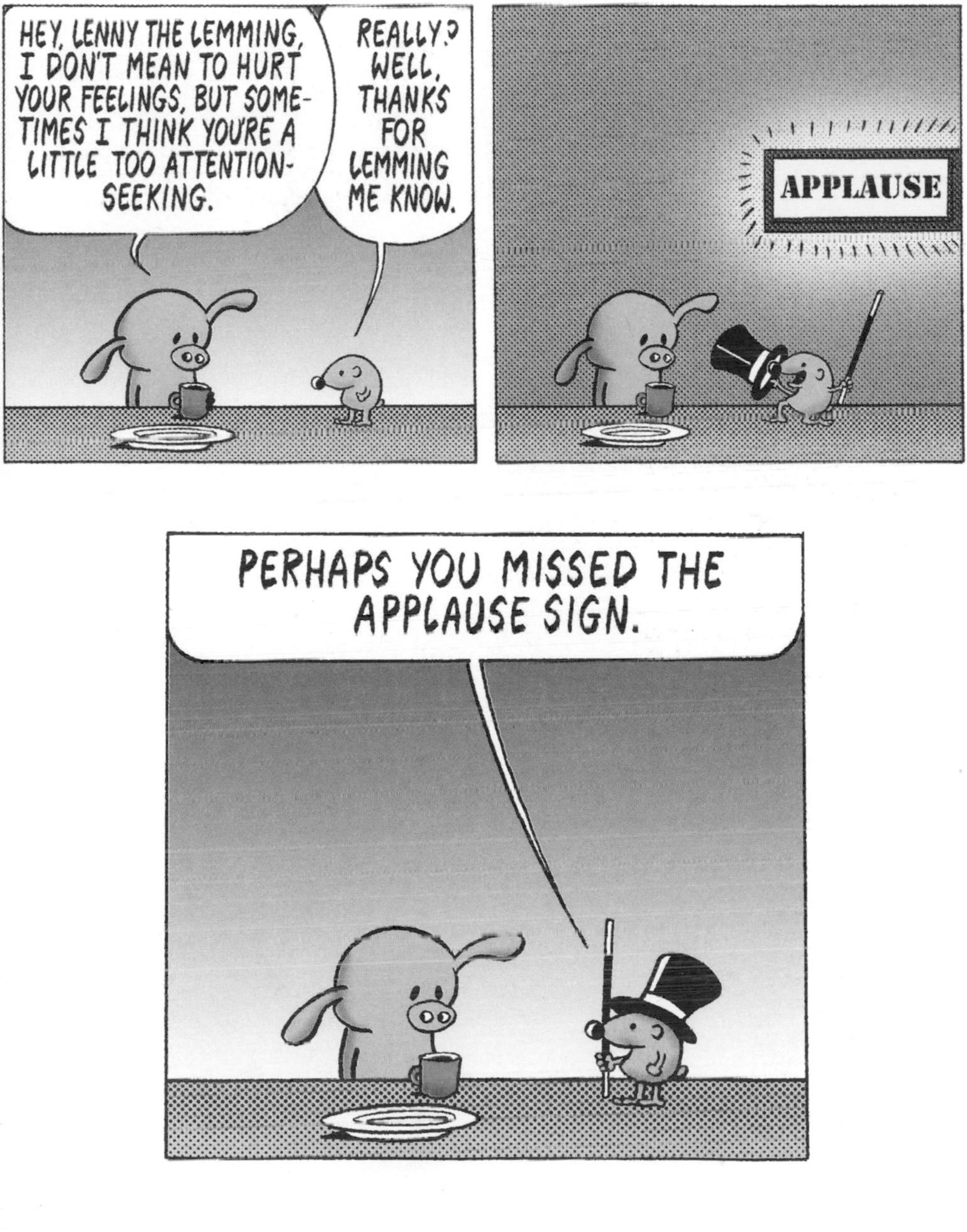
HEY, LENNY THE LEMMING, I DON'T MEAN TO HURT YOUR FEELINGS, BUT SOMETIMES I THINK YOU'RE A LITTLE TOO ATTENTION-SEEKING.
REALLY? WELL, THANKS FOR LEMMING ME KNOW.
APPLAUSE
PERHAPS YOU MISSED THE APPLAUSE SIGN.

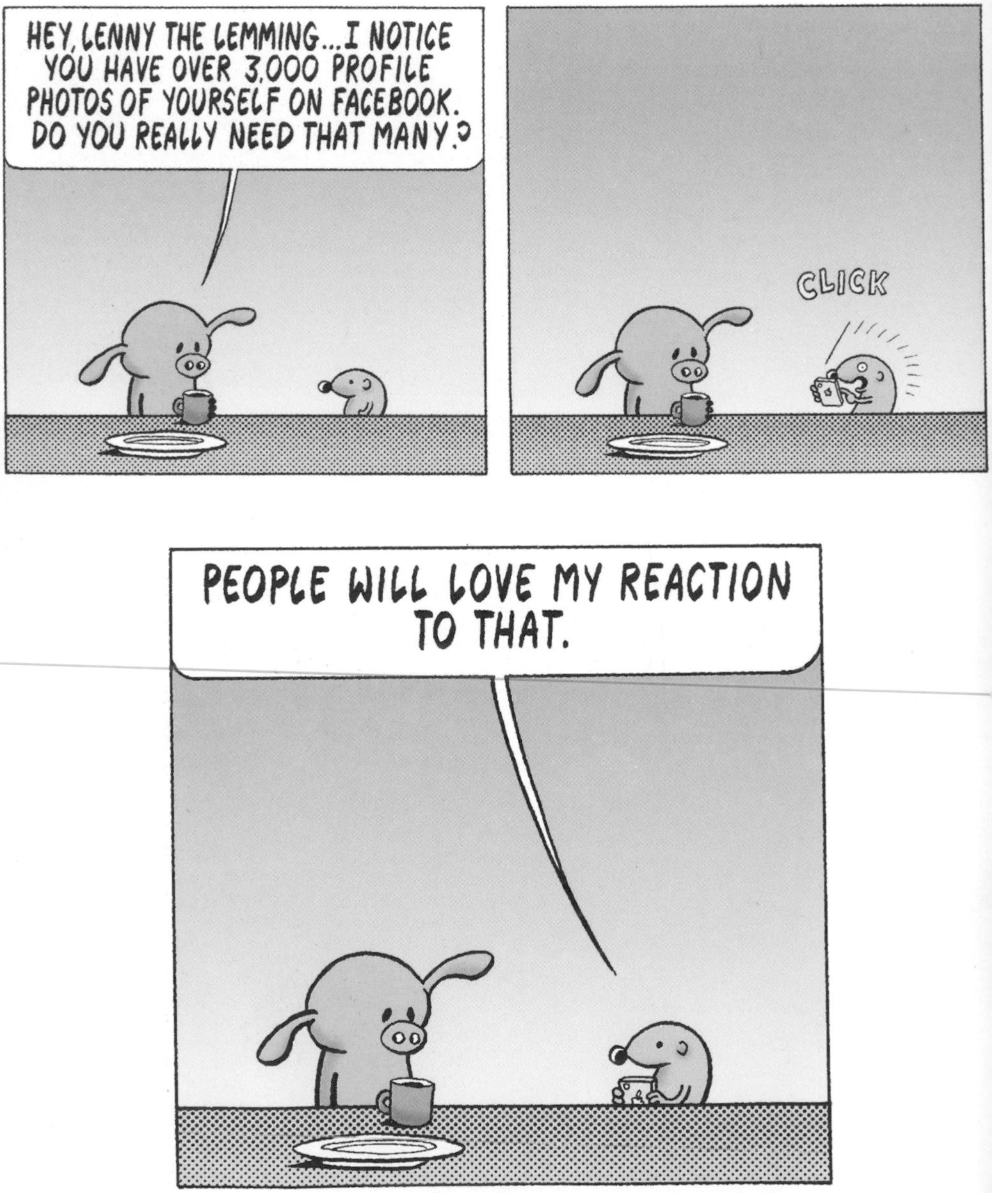
HEY, LENNY THE LEMMING... I NOTICE YOU HAVE OVER 3,000 PROFILE PHOTOS OF YOURSELF ON FACEBOOK. DO YOU REALLY NEED THAT MANY?
CLICK
PEOPLE WILL LOVE MY REACTION TO THAT.

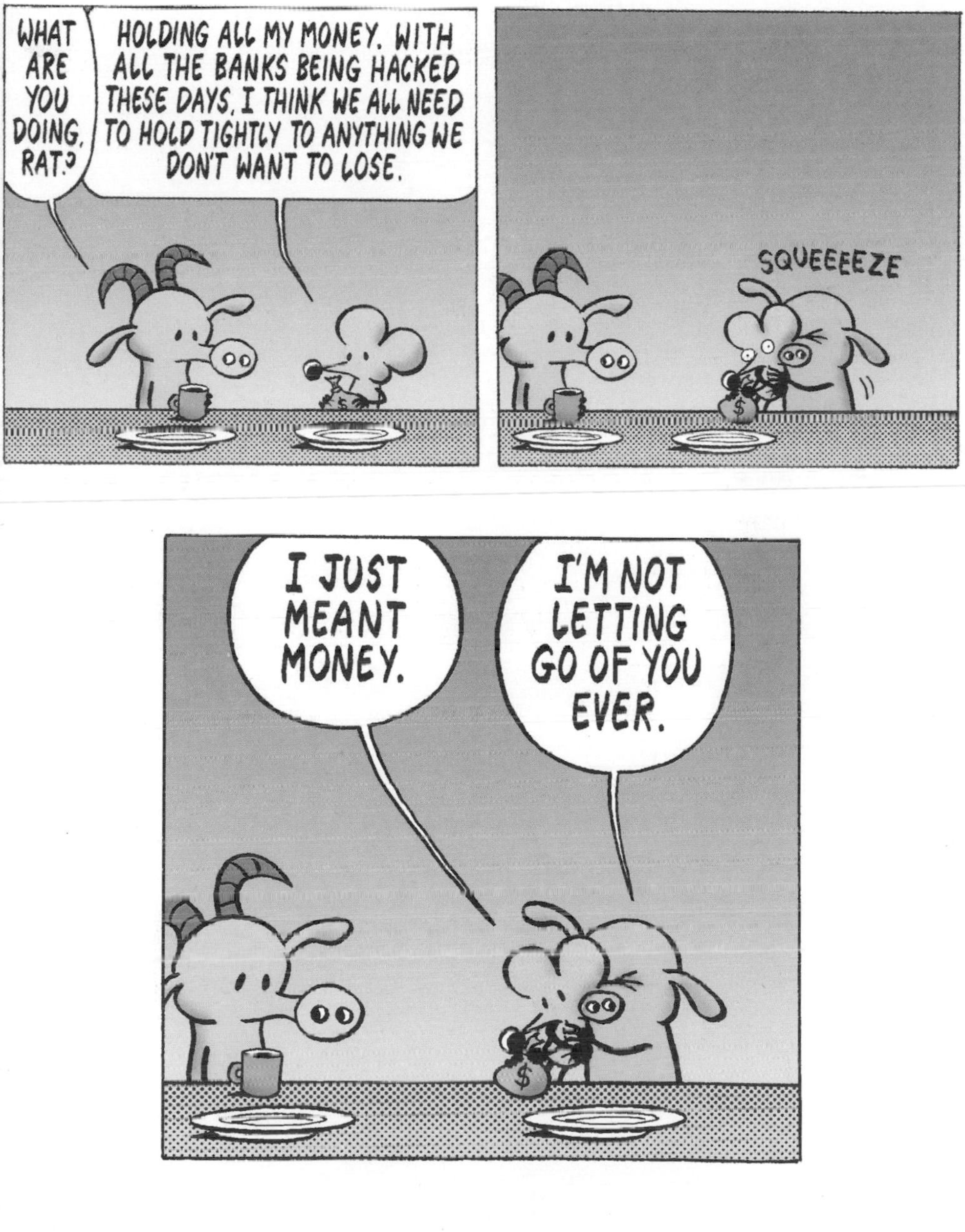
WHAT ARE YOU DOING, RAT?
HOLDING ALL MY MONEY. WITH ALL THE BANKS BEING HACKED THESE DAYS, I THINK WE ALL NEED TO HOLD TIGHTLY TO ANYTHING WE DON'T WANT TO LOSE.
SQUEEEEEZE
I JUST MEANT MONEY.
I'M NOT LETTING GO OF YOU EVER.

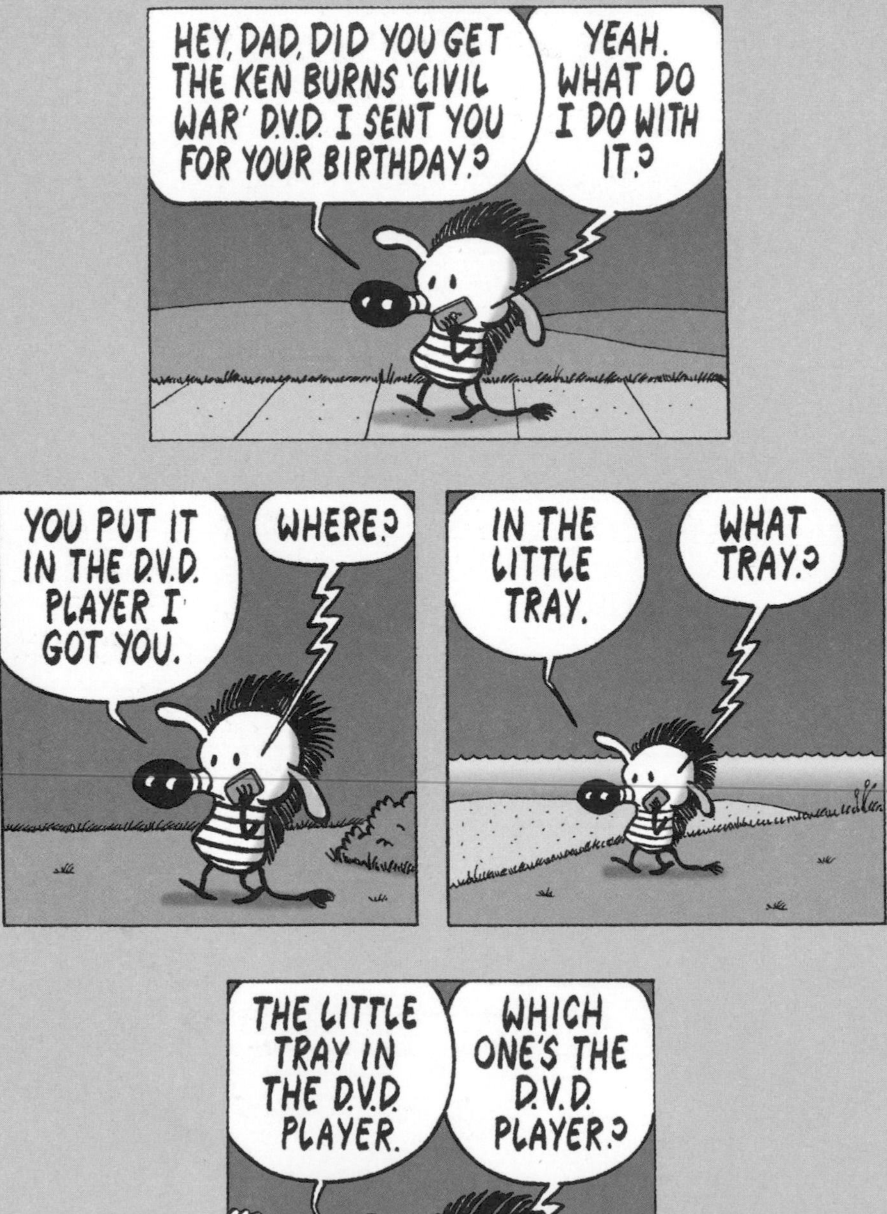
HEY, DAD, DID YOU GET THE KEN BURNS 'CIVIL WAR' D.V.D. I SENT YOU FOR YOUR BIRTHDAY?
YEAH. WHAT DO I DO WITH IT?
YOU PUT IT IN THE D.V.D. PLAYER I GOT YOU.
WHERE?
IN THE LITTLE TRAY.
WHAT TRAY?
THE LITTLE TRAY IN THE D.V.D. PLAYER.
WHICH ONE'S THE D.V.D. PLAYER?

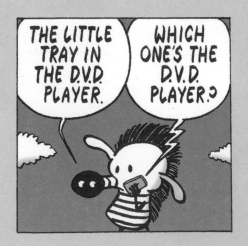

ON TOP OF THE T.V. SET.
OKAY...OKAY... GIMME A MINUTE, WILL YA.?..
...THERE..OKAY...GOT IT IN. AND NOW I'M WATCHING SOME EXPLOSION.
GOOD. YOU'RE WATCHING 'THE CIVIL WAR'?
NO, NO. THE T.V. EXPLODED.
NEVER BUY YOUR PARENT ANYTHING INVENTED IN THE LAST 30 YEARS.

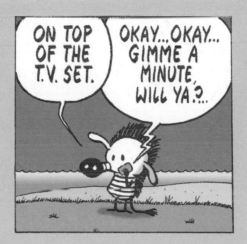

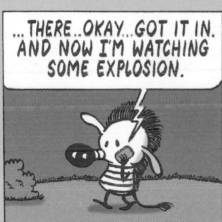

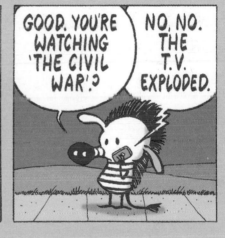

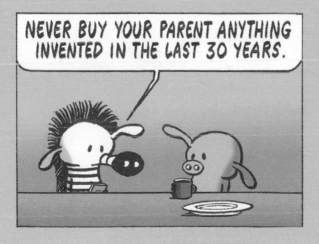

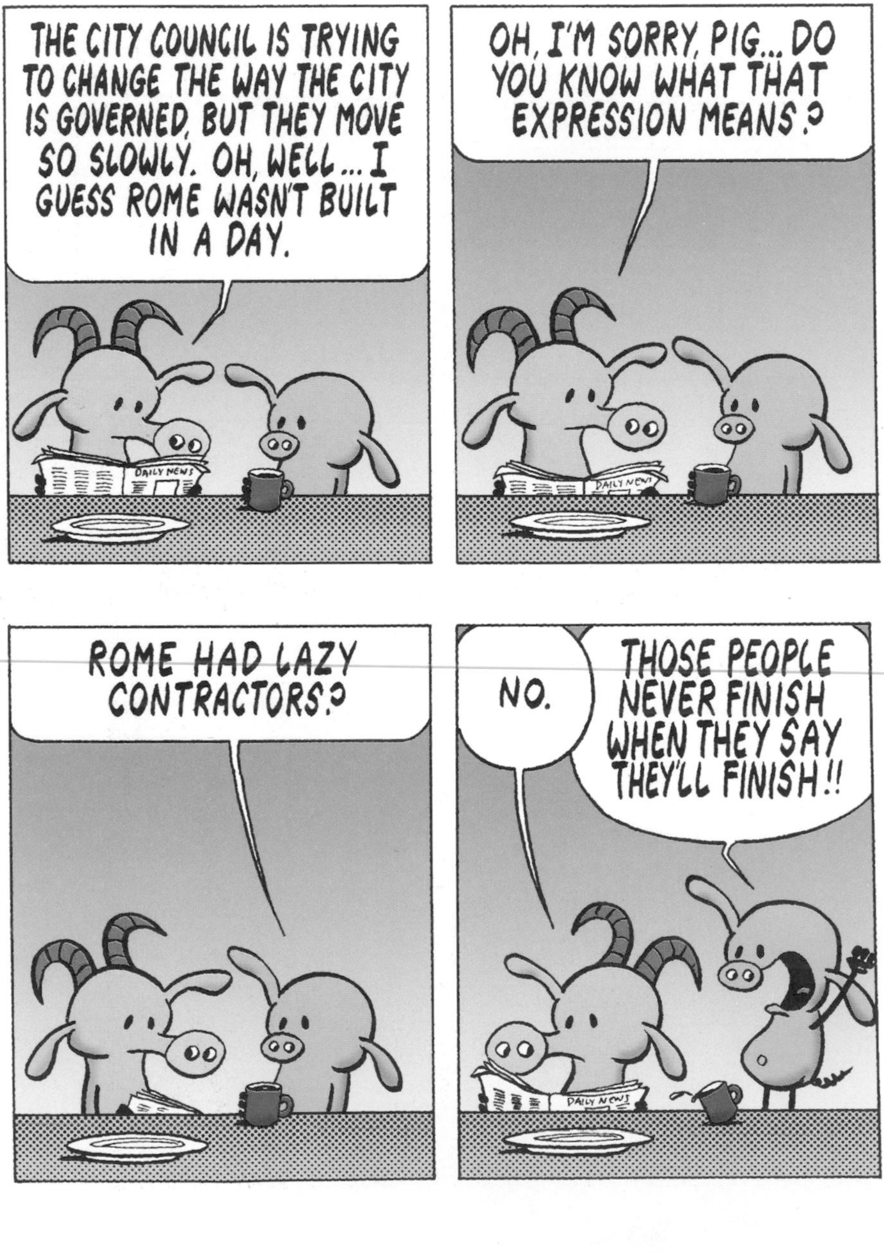
THE CITY COUNCIL IS TRYING TO CHANGE THE WAY THE CITY IS GOVERNED, BUT THEY MOVE SO SLOWLY. OH, WELL... I GUESS ROME WASN'T BUILT IN A DAY.
DAILY NEWS
OH, I'M SORRY, PIG... DO YOU KNOW WHAT THAT EXPRESSION MEANS?
ROME HAD LAZY CONTRACTORS?
NO.
THOSE PEOPLE NEVER FINISH WHEN THEY SAY THEY'LL FINISH!!

WHERE'S PIG TODAY?
HE'S WORKING. HE GOT A JOB AS AN UNMOTIVATIONAL SPEAKER.
YOU MEAN 'MOTIVATIONAL' SPEAKER.
NO, I DON'T.

SO GO OUT AND NAP, NAP, NAP!

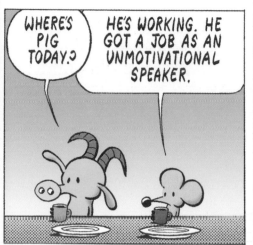

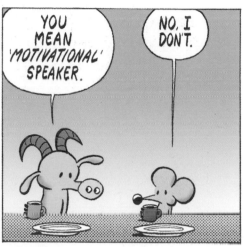

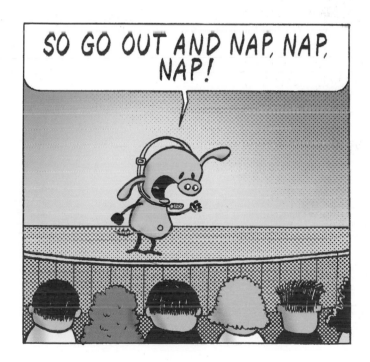

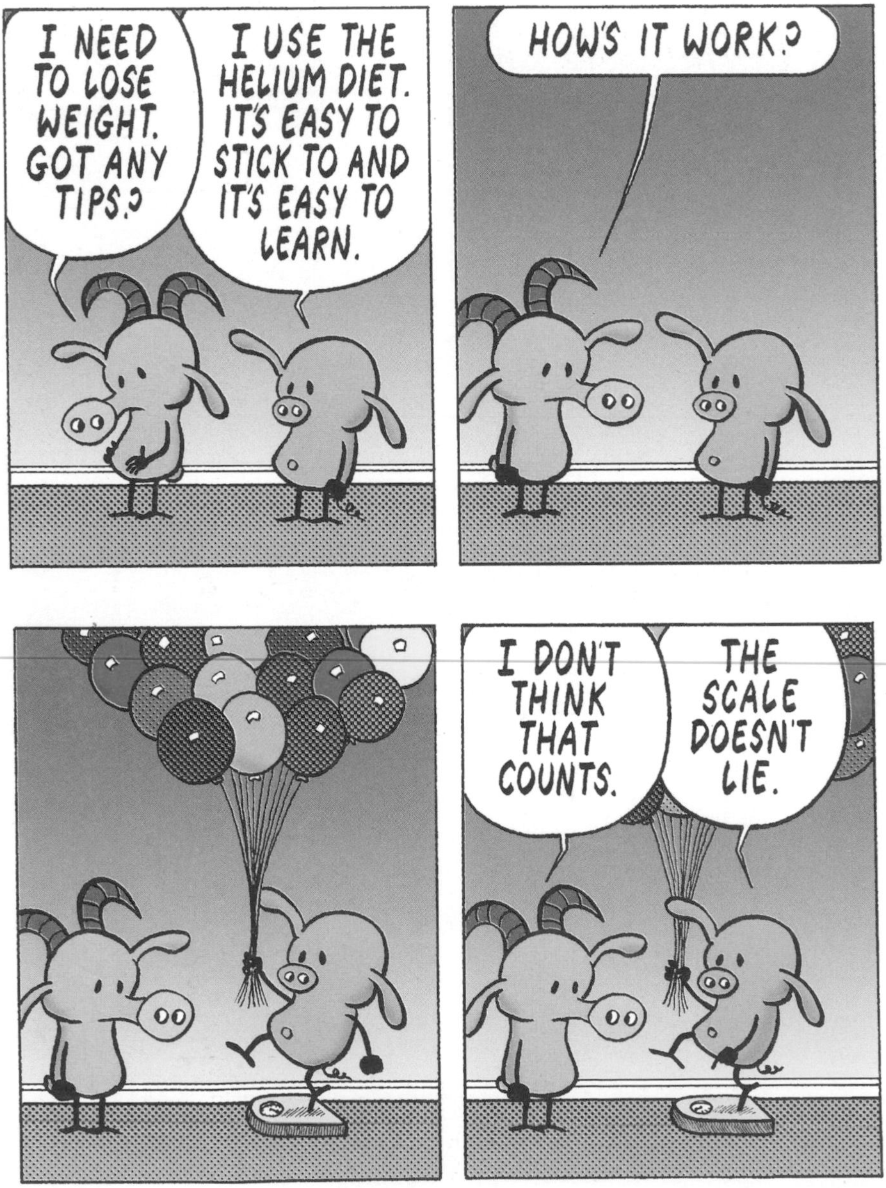
I NEED TO LOSE WEIGHT. GOT ANY TIPS?
I USE THE HELIUM DIET. IT'S EASY TO STICK TO AND IT'S EASY TO LEARN.
HOW'S IT WORK?
I DON'T THINK THAT COUNTS.
THE SCALE DOESN'T LIE.

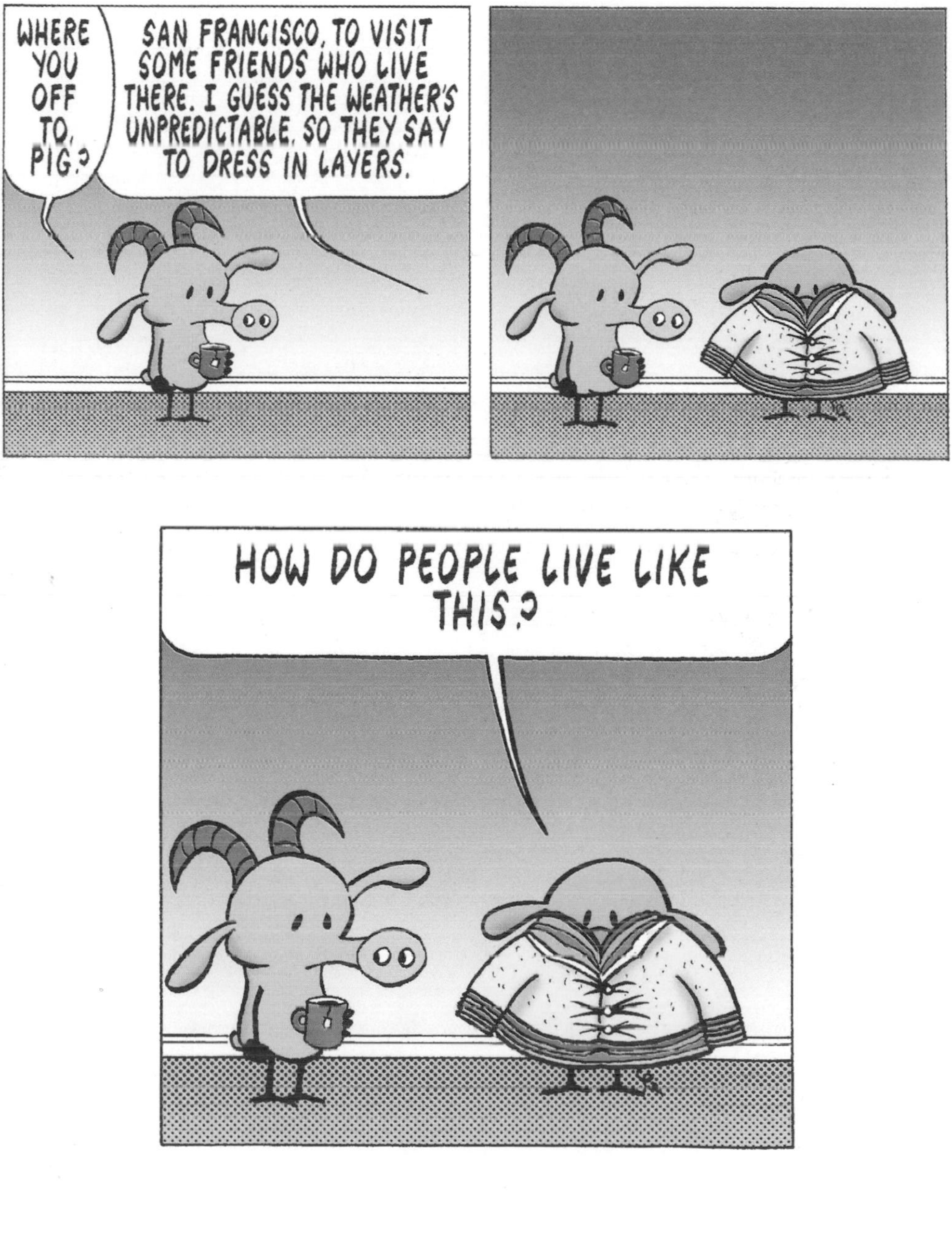
WHERE YOU OFF TO, PIG?
SAN FRANCISCO, TO VISIT SOME FRIENDS WHO LIVE THERE. I GUESS THE WEATHER'S UNPREDICTABLE, SO THEY SAY TO DRESS IN LAYERS.
HOW DO PEOPLE LIVE LIKE THIS?

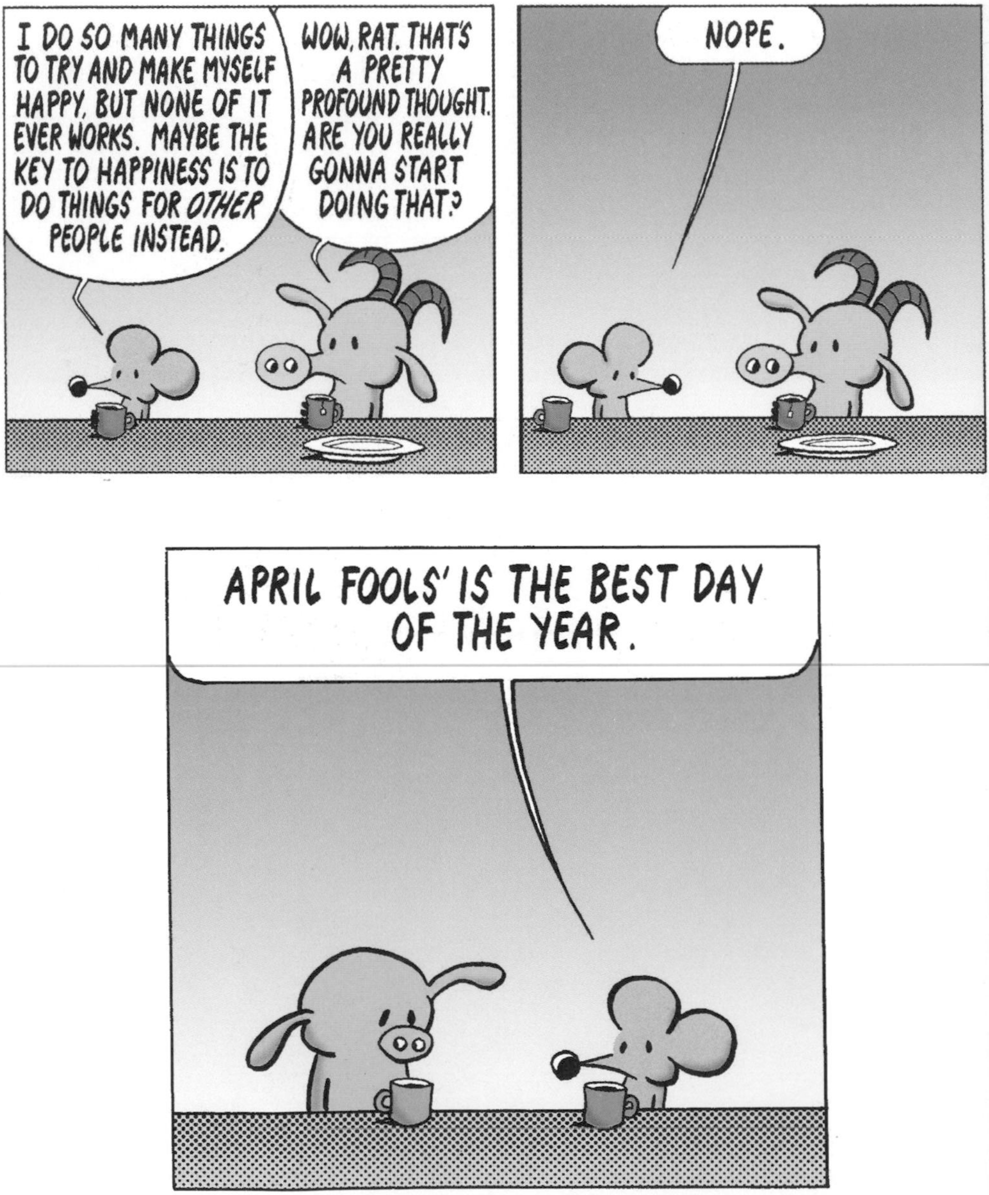
I DO SO MANY THINGS TO TRY AND MAKE MYSELF HAPPY, BUT NONE OF IT EVER WORKS. MAYBE THE KEY TO HAPPINESS IS TO DO THINGS FOR *OTHER* PEOPLE INSTEAD.
WOW, RAT. THAT'S A PRETTY PROFOUND THOUGHT. ARE YOU REALLY GONNA START DOING THAT?
NOPE.
APRIL FOOLS' IS THE BEST DAY OF THE YEAR.

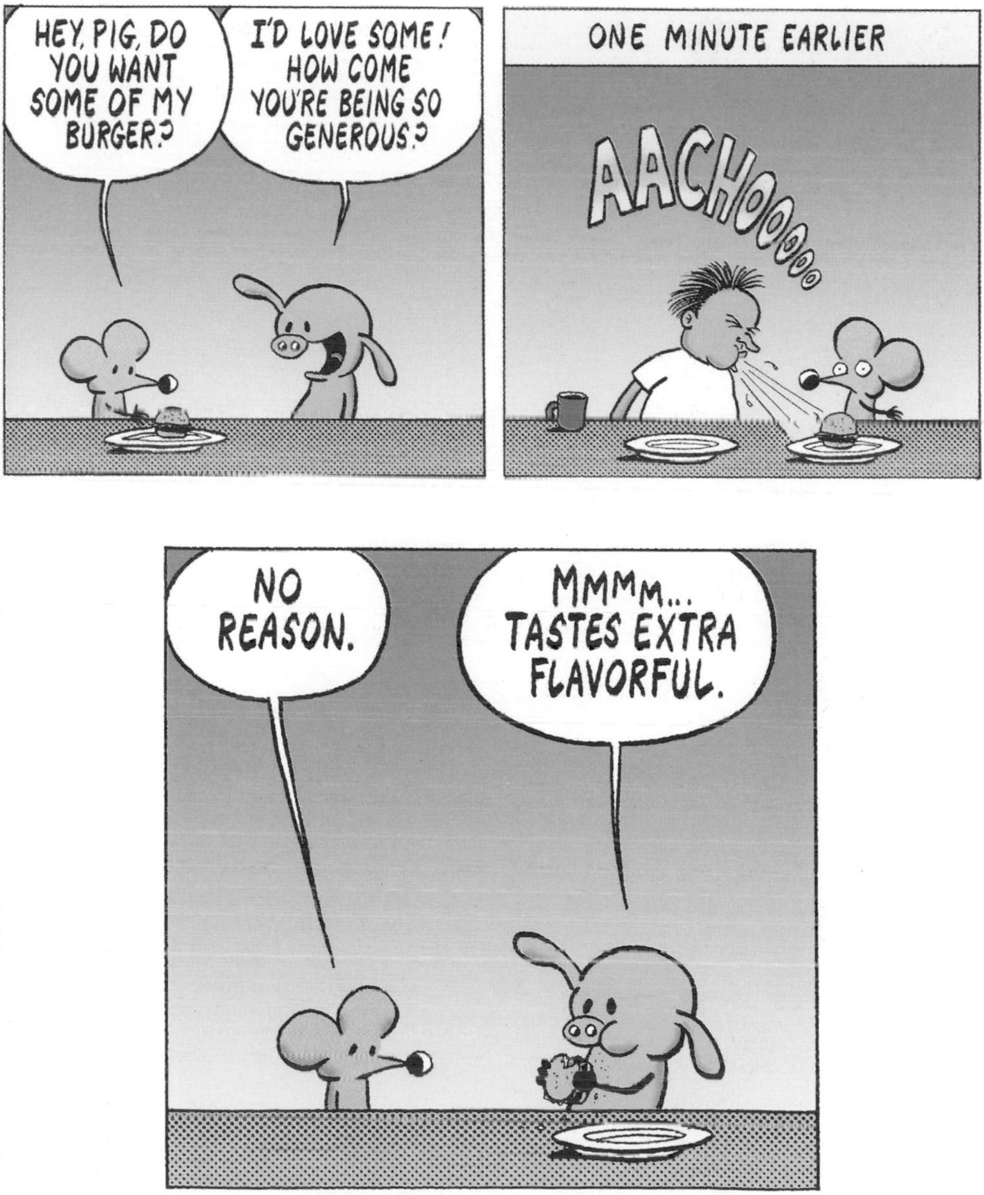

HEY, PIG, DO YOU WANT SOME OF MY BURGER?
I'D LOVE SOME! HOW COME YOU'RE BEING SO GENEROUS?
ONE MINUTE EARLIER
AACHOOOOOO
NO REASON.
MMMM... TASTES EXTRA FLAVORFUL.

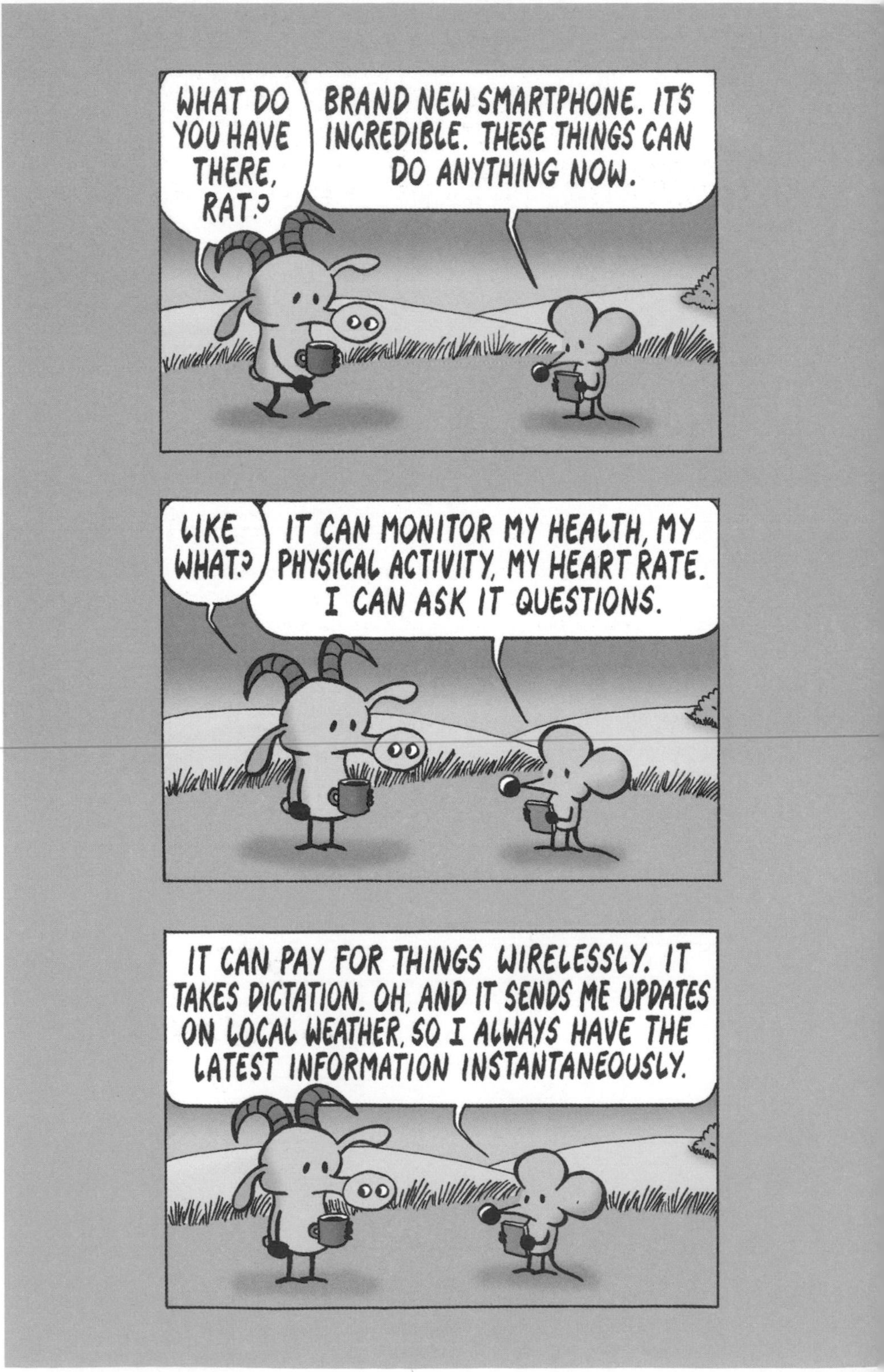
WHAT DO YOU HAVE THERE, RAT?
BRAND NEW SMARTPHONE. IT'S INCREDIBLE. THESE THINGS CAN DO ANYTHING NOW.
LIKE WHAT?
IT CAN MONITOR MY HEALTH, MY PHYSICAL ACTIVITY, MY HEART RATE. I CAN ASK IT QUESTIONS.
IT CAN PAY FOR THINGS WIRELESSLY. IT TAKES DICTATION. OH, AND IT SENDS ME UPDATES ON LOCAL WEATHER, SO I ALWAYS HAVE THE LATEST INFORMATION INSTANTANEOUSLY.

COOL. WELL, SHOW ME SOME-THING.
OKAY, HERE. WATCH IT DOWNLOAD THE LATEST WEATHER INFO.
IT'S GONNA RAIN.
HANG ON. STILL DOWNLOADING.

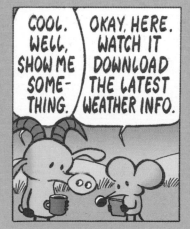

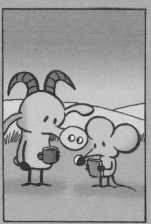

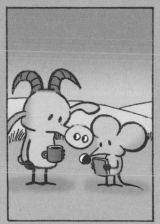

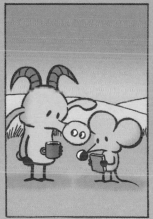

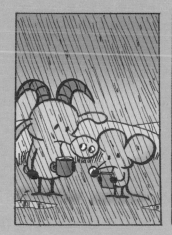

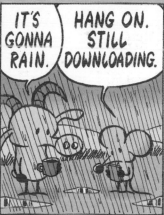

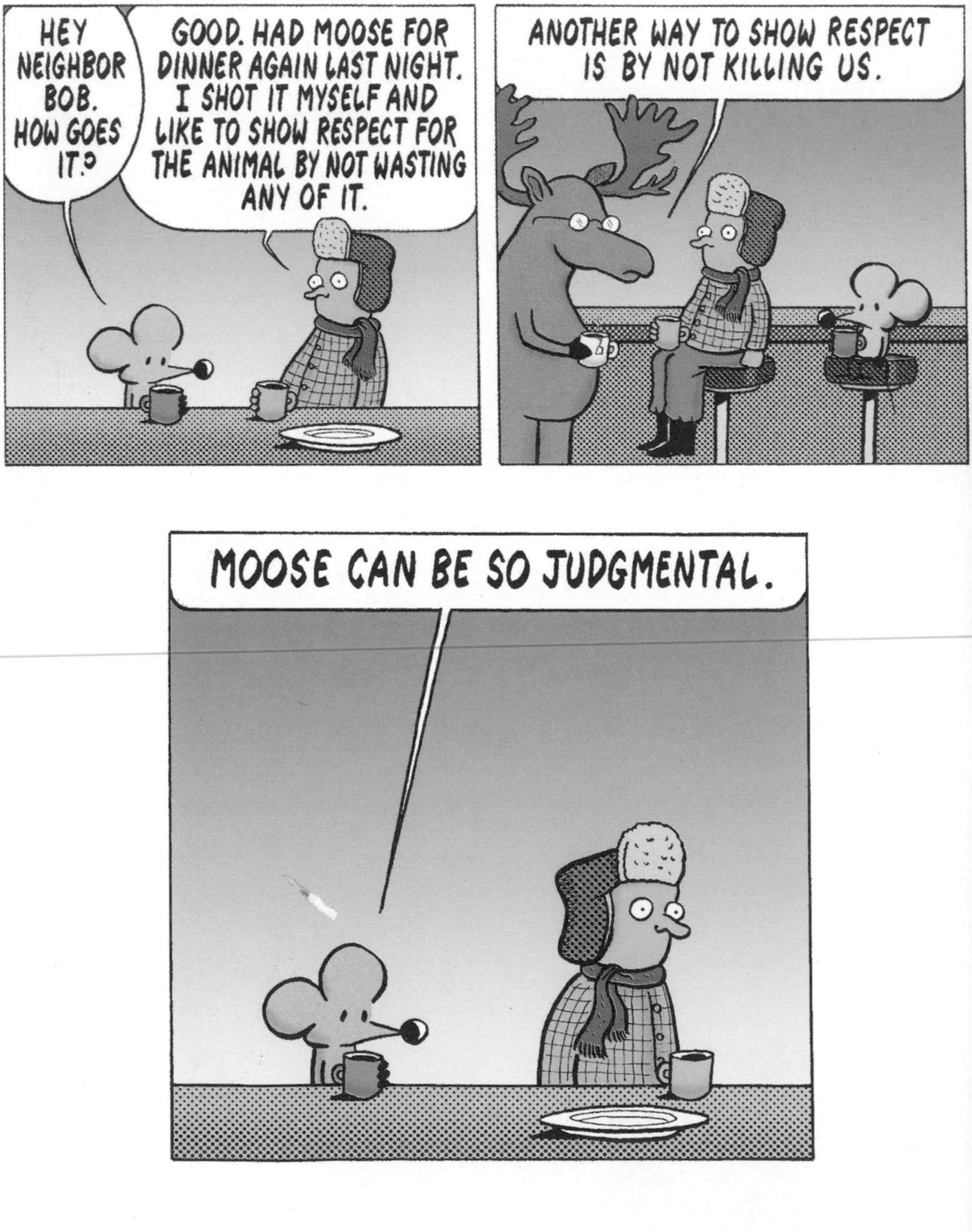
HEY NEIGHBOR BOB. HOW GOES IT?
GOOD. HAD MOOSE FOR DINNER AGAIN LAST NIGHT. I SHOT IT MYSELF AND LIKE TO SHOW RESPECT FOR THE ANIMAL BY NOT WASTING ANY OF IT.
ANOTHER WAY TO SHOW RESPECT IS BY NOT KILLING US.
MOOSE CAN BE SO JUDGMENTAL.

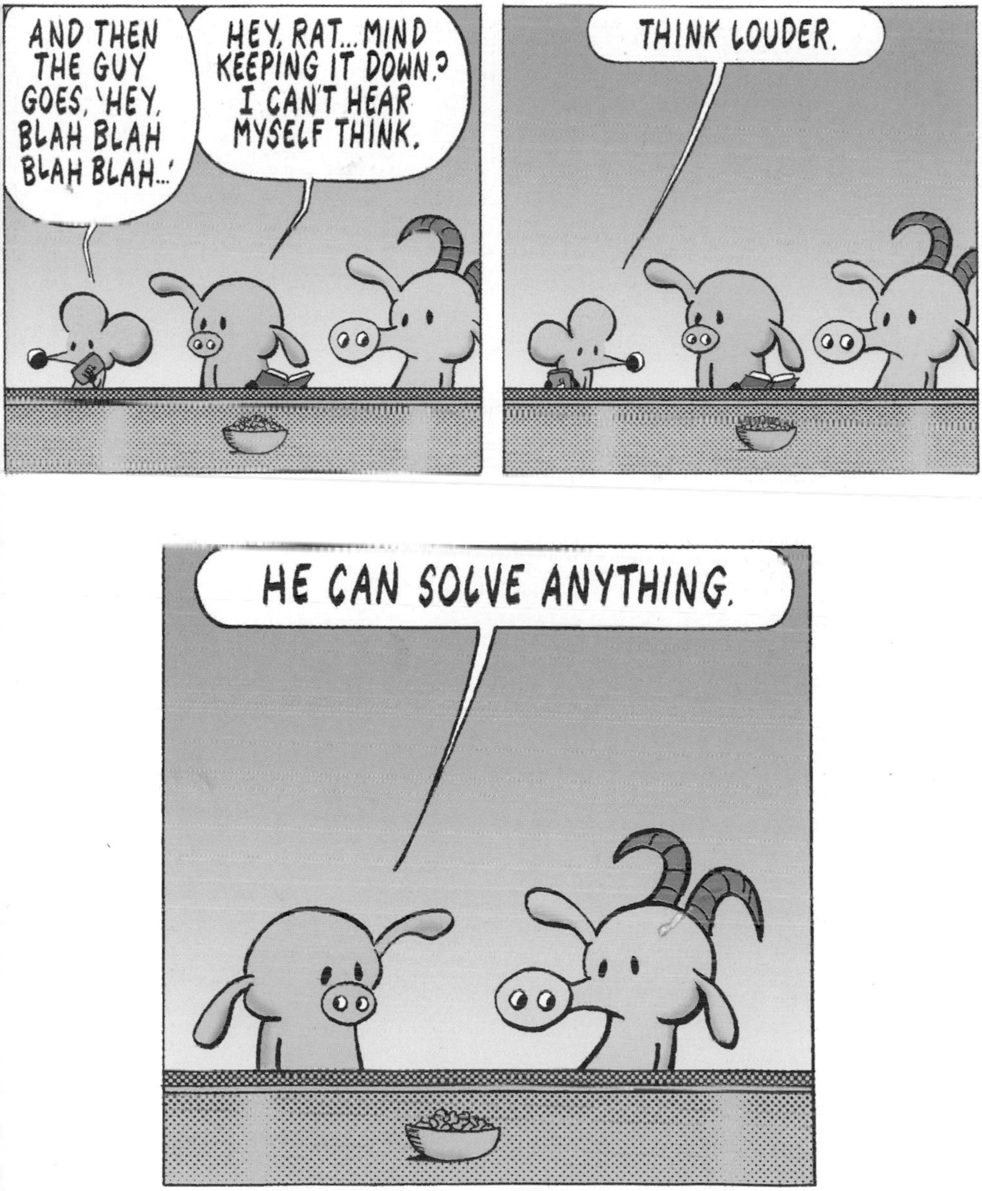
AND THEN THE GUY GOES, 'HEY, BLAH BLAH BLAH BLAH...'
HEY, RAT... MIND KEEPING IT DOWN? I CAN'T HEAR MYSELF THINK.
THINK LOUDER.
HE CAN SOLVE ANYTHING.

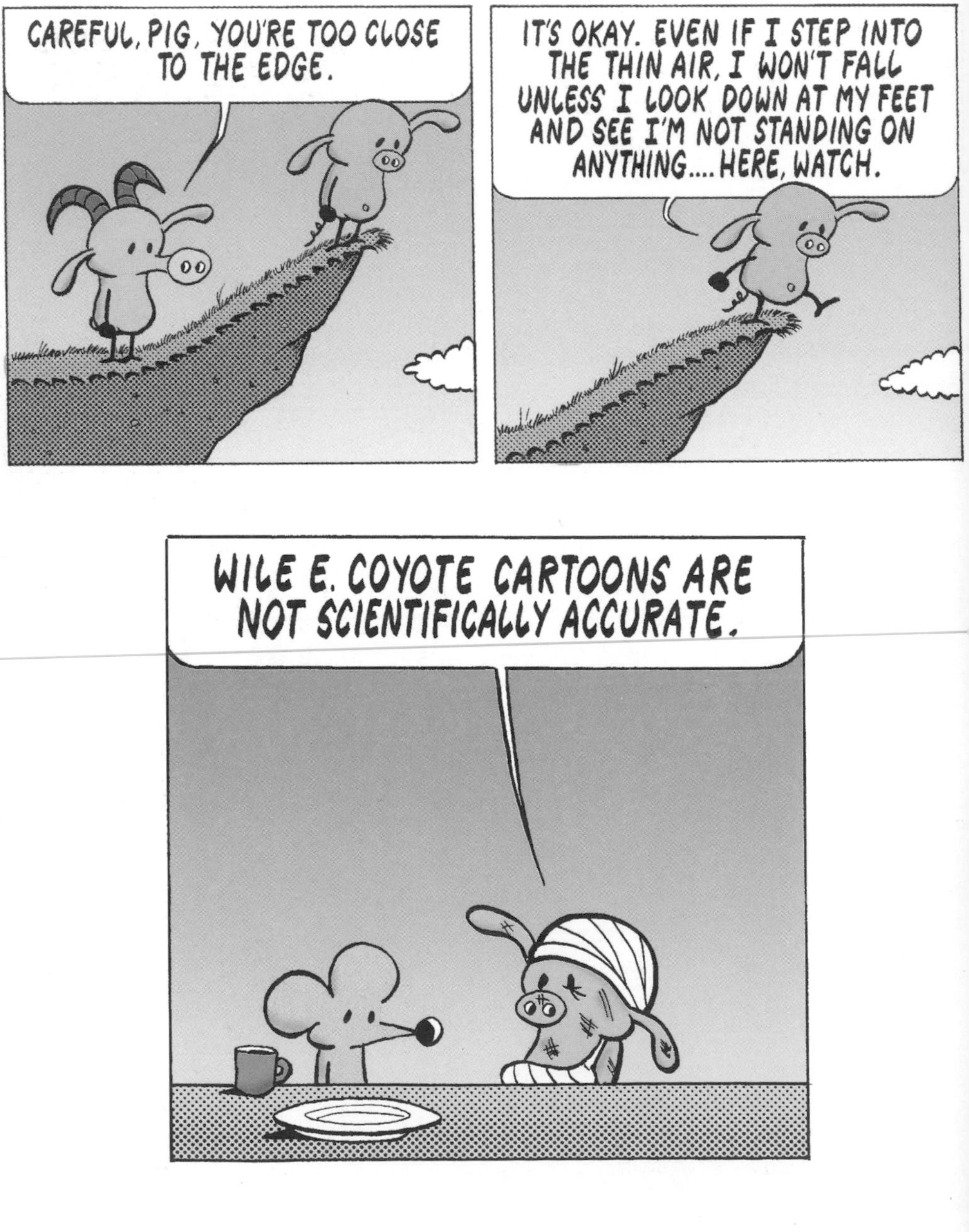
CAREFUL, PIG, YOU'RE TOO CLOSE TO THE EDGE.
IT'S OKAY. EVEN IF I STEP INTO THE THIN AIR, I WON'T FALL UNLESS I LOOK DOWN AT MY FEET AND SEE I'M NOT STANDING ON ANYTHING.... HERE, WATCH.
WILE E. COYOTE CARTOONS ARE NOT SCIENTIFICALLY ACCURATE.

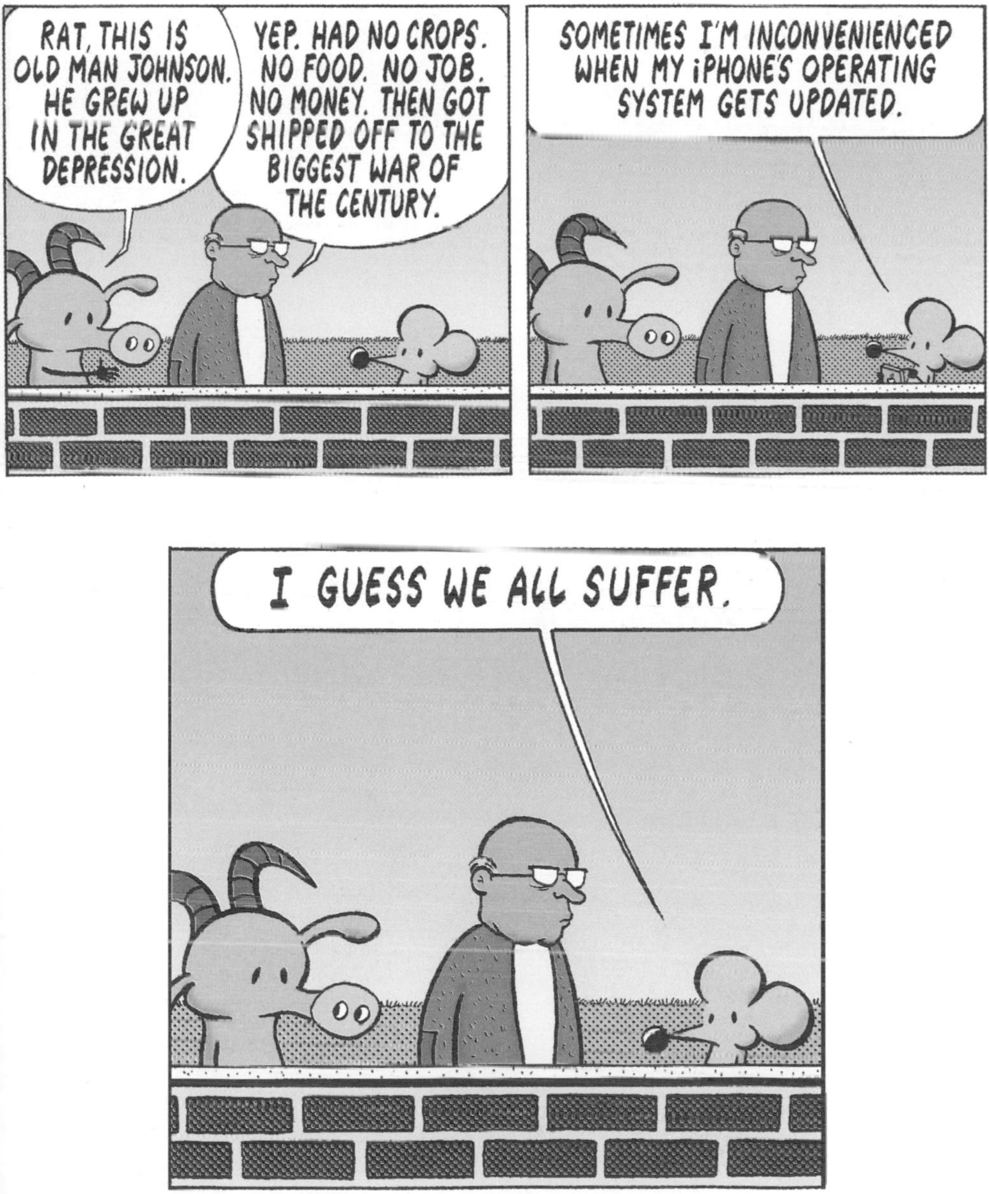
RAT, THIS IS OLD MAN JOHNSON. HE GREW UP IN THE GREAT DEPRESSION.
YEP. HAD NO CROPS. NO FOOD. NO JOB. NO MONEY. THEN GOT SHIPPED OFF TO THE BIGGEST WAR OF THE CENTURY.
SOMETIMES I'M INCONVENIENCED WHEN MY iPHONE'S OPERATING SYSTEM GETS UPDATED.
I GUESS WE ALL SUFFER.

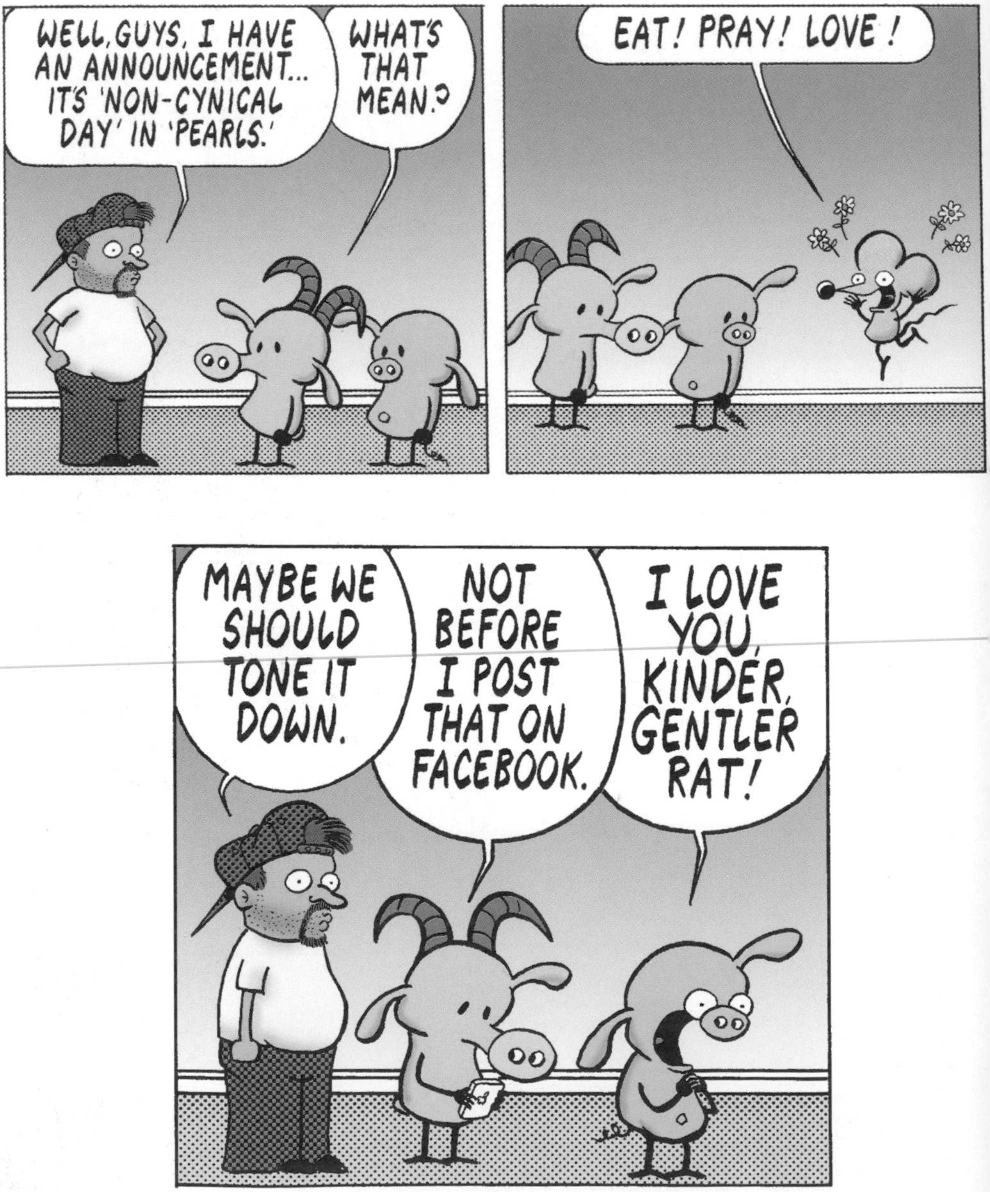
WELL, GUYS, I HAVE AN ANNOUNCEMENT... IT'S 'NON-CYNICAL DAY' IN 'PEARLS.'
WHAT'S THAT MEAN?
EAT! PRAY! LOVE!
MAYBE WE SHOULD TONE IT DOWN.
NOT BEFORE I POST THAT ON FACEBOOK.
I LOVE YOU, KINDER, GENTLER RAT!

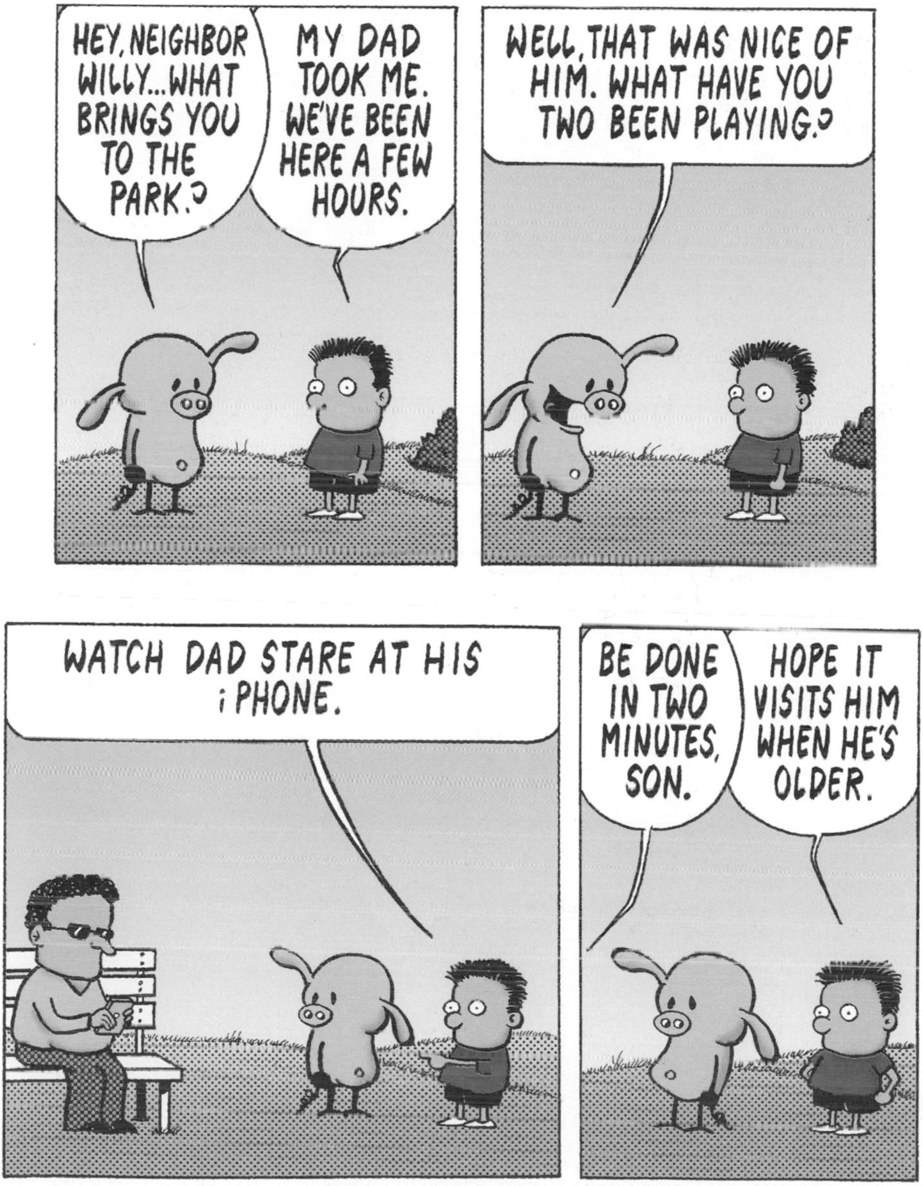
HEY, NEIGHBOR WILLY...WHAT BRINGS YOU TO THE PARK?
MY DAD TOOK ME. WE'VE BEEN HERE A FEW HOURS.
WELL, THAT WAS NICE OF HIM. WHAT HAVE YOU TWO BEEN PLAYING?
WATCH DAD STARE AT HIS iPHONE.
BE DONE IN TWO MINUTES, SON.
HOPE IT VISITS HIM WHEN HE'S OLDER.

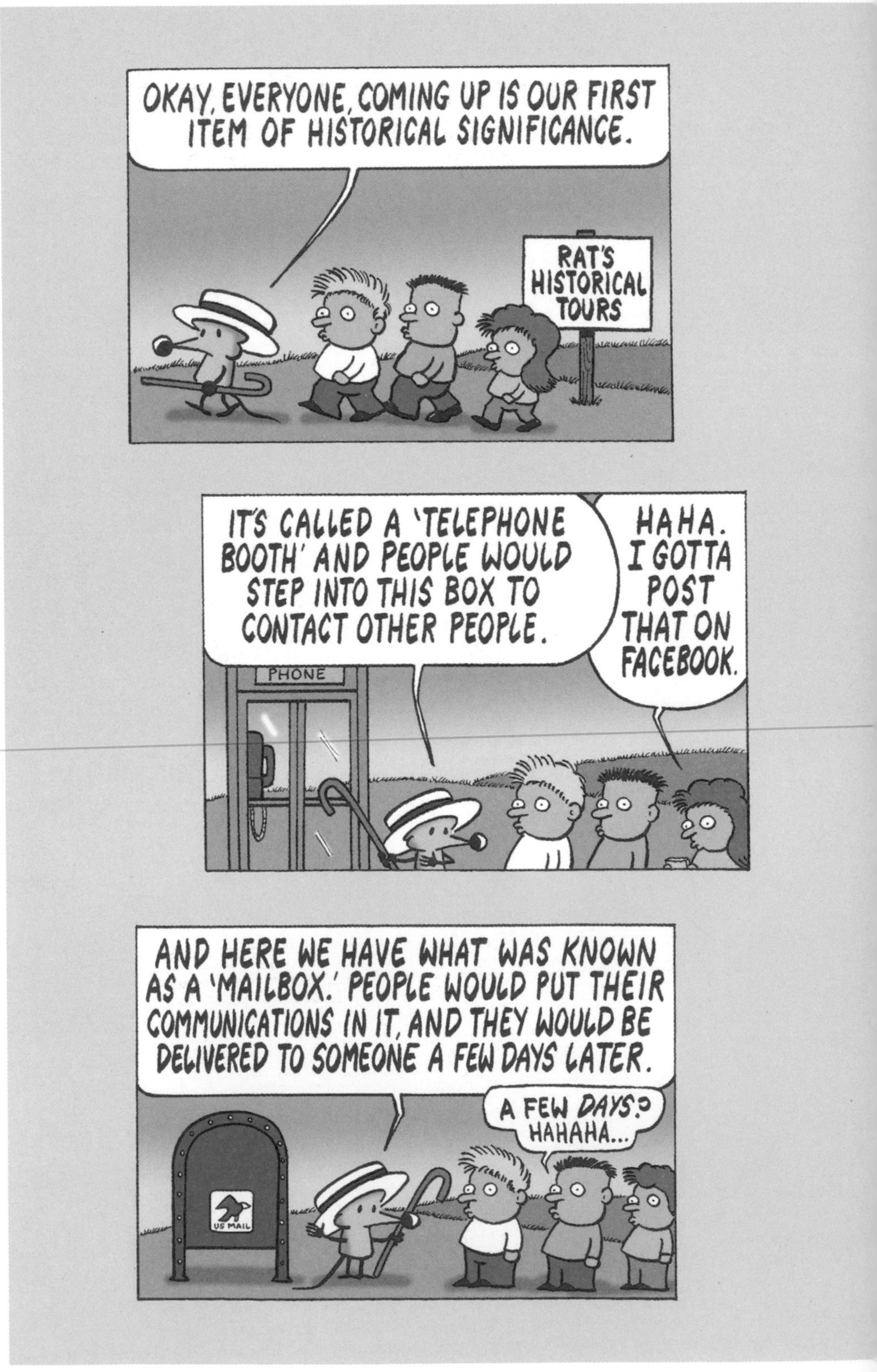
OKAY, EVERYONE, COMING UP IS OUR FIRST ITEM OF HISTORICAL SIGNIFICANCE.
RAT'S HISTORICAL TOURS
IT'S CALLED A 'TELEPHONE BOOTH' AND PEOPLE WOULD STEP INTO THIS BOX TO CONTACT OTHER PEOPLE.
HAHA. I GOTTA POST THAT ON FACEBOOK.
PHONE
AND HERE WE HAVE WHAT WAS KNOWN AS A 'MAILBOX.' PEOPLE WOULD PUT THEIR COMMUNICATIONS IN IT, AND THEY WOULD BE DELIVERED TO SOMEONE A FEW DAYS LATER.
A FEW DAYS?
HAHAHA...
US MAIL

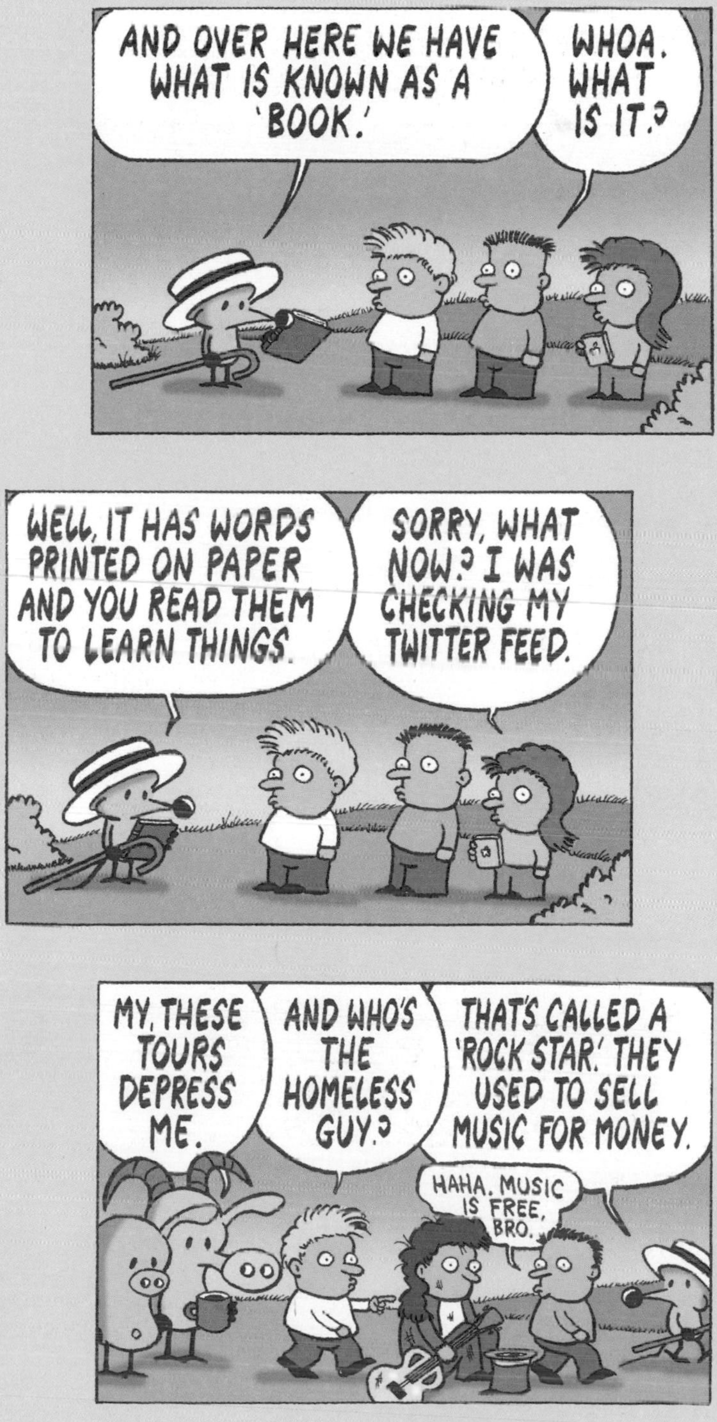
AND OVER HERE WE HAVE WHAT IS KNOWN AS A 'BOOK.'
WHOA. WHAT IS IT?
WELL, IT HAS WORDS PRINTED ON PAPER AND YOU READ THEM TO LEARN THINGS.
SORRY, WHAT NOW? I WAS CHECKING MY TWITTER FEED.
MY, THESE TOURS DEPRESS ME.
AND WHO'S THE HOMELESS GUY?
THAT'S CALLED A 'ROCK STAR.' THEY USED TO SELL MUSIC FOR MONEY.
HAHA. MUSIC IS FREE, BRO.

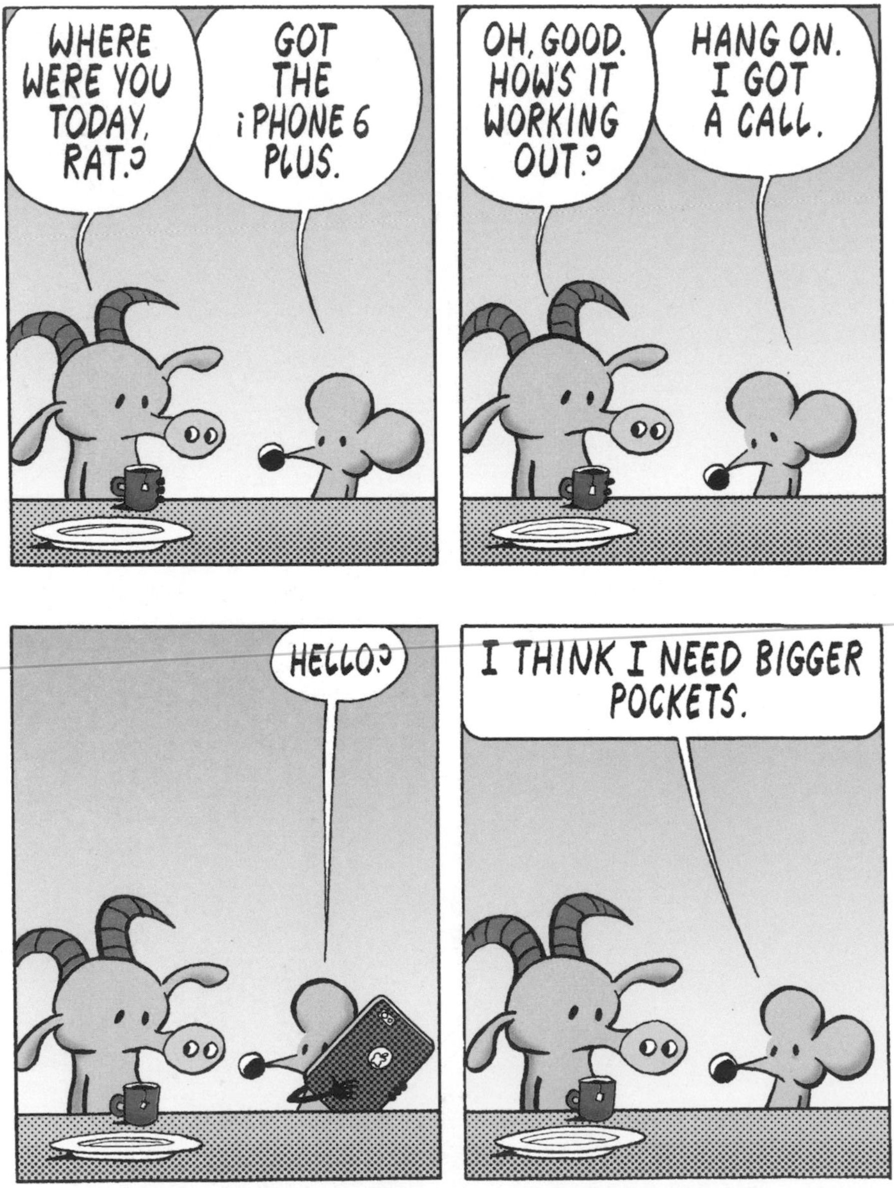
WHERE WERE YOU TODAY, RAT?
GOT THE iPHONE 6 PLUS.
OH, GOOD. HOW'S IT WORKING OUT?
HANG ON. I GOT A CALL.
HELLO?
I THINK I NEED BIGGER POCKETS.

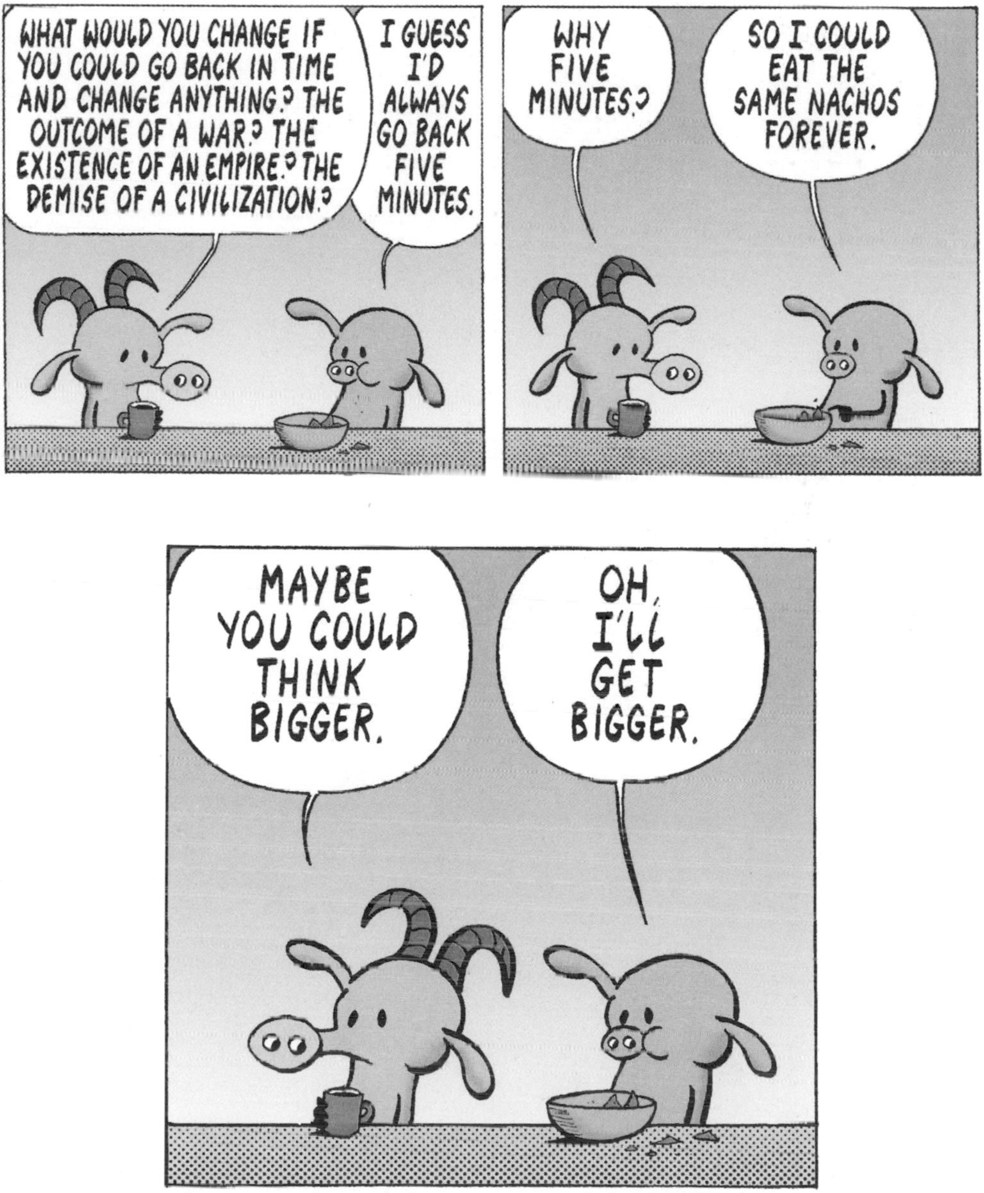
WHAT WOULD YOU CHANGE IF YOU COULD GO BACK IN TIME AND CHANGE ANYTHING? THE OUTCOME OF A WAR? THE EXISTENCE OF AN EMPIRE? THE DEMISE OF A CIVILIZATION?
I GUESS I'D ALWAYS GO BACK FIVE MINUTES.
WHY FIVE MINUTES?
SO I COULD EAT THE SAME NACHOS FOREVER.
MAYBE YOU COULD THINK BIGGER.
OH, I'LL GET BIGGER.

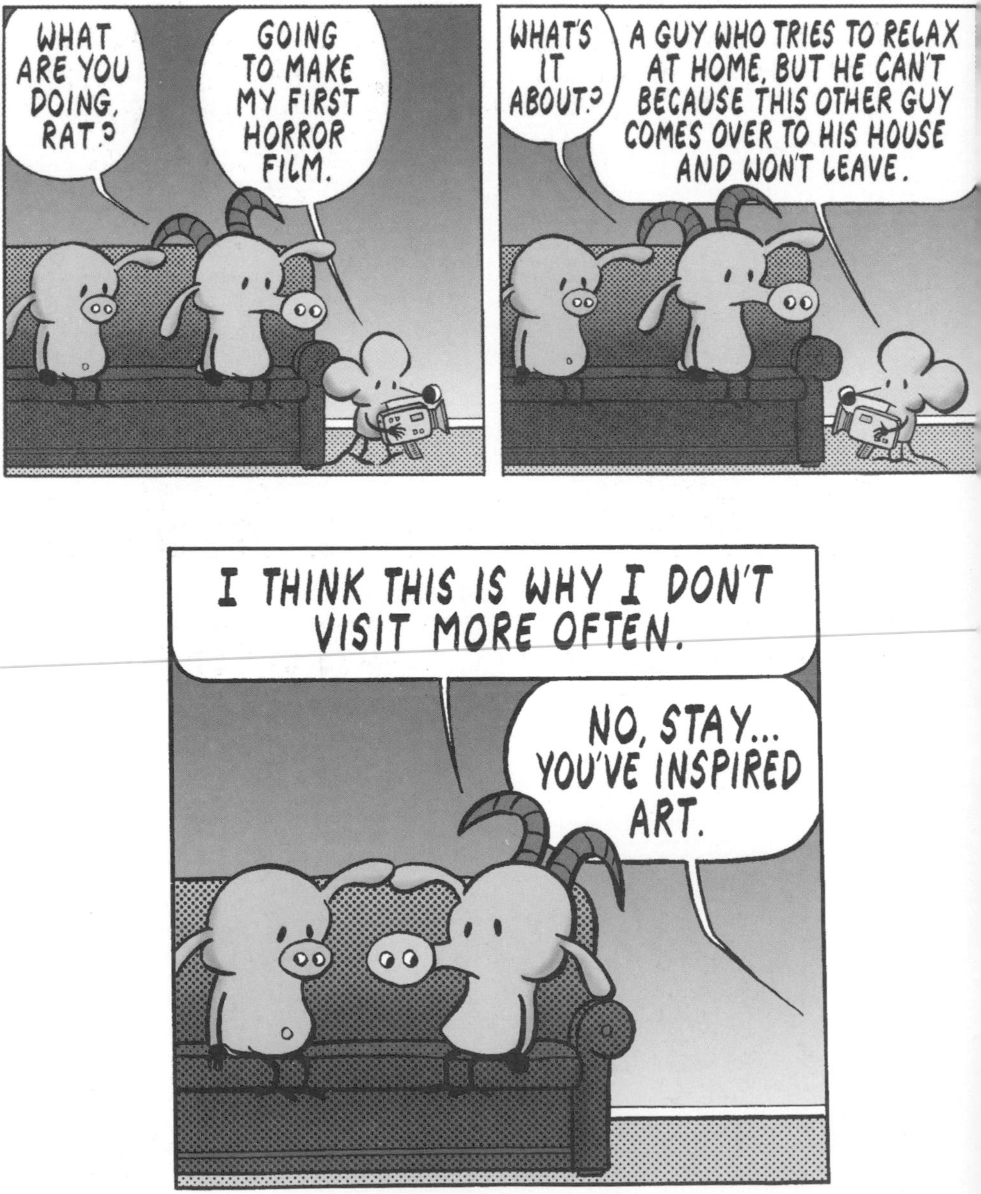
WHAT ARE YOU DOING, RAT?
GOING TO MAKE MY FIRST HORROR FILM.
WHAT'S IT ABOUT?
A GUY WHO TRIES TO RELAX AT HOME, BUT HE CAN'T BECAUSE THIS OTHER GUY COMES OVER TO HIS HOUSE AND WON'T LEAVE.
I THINK THIS IS WHY I DON'T VISIT MORE OFTEN.
NO, STAY... YOU'VE INSPIRED ART.

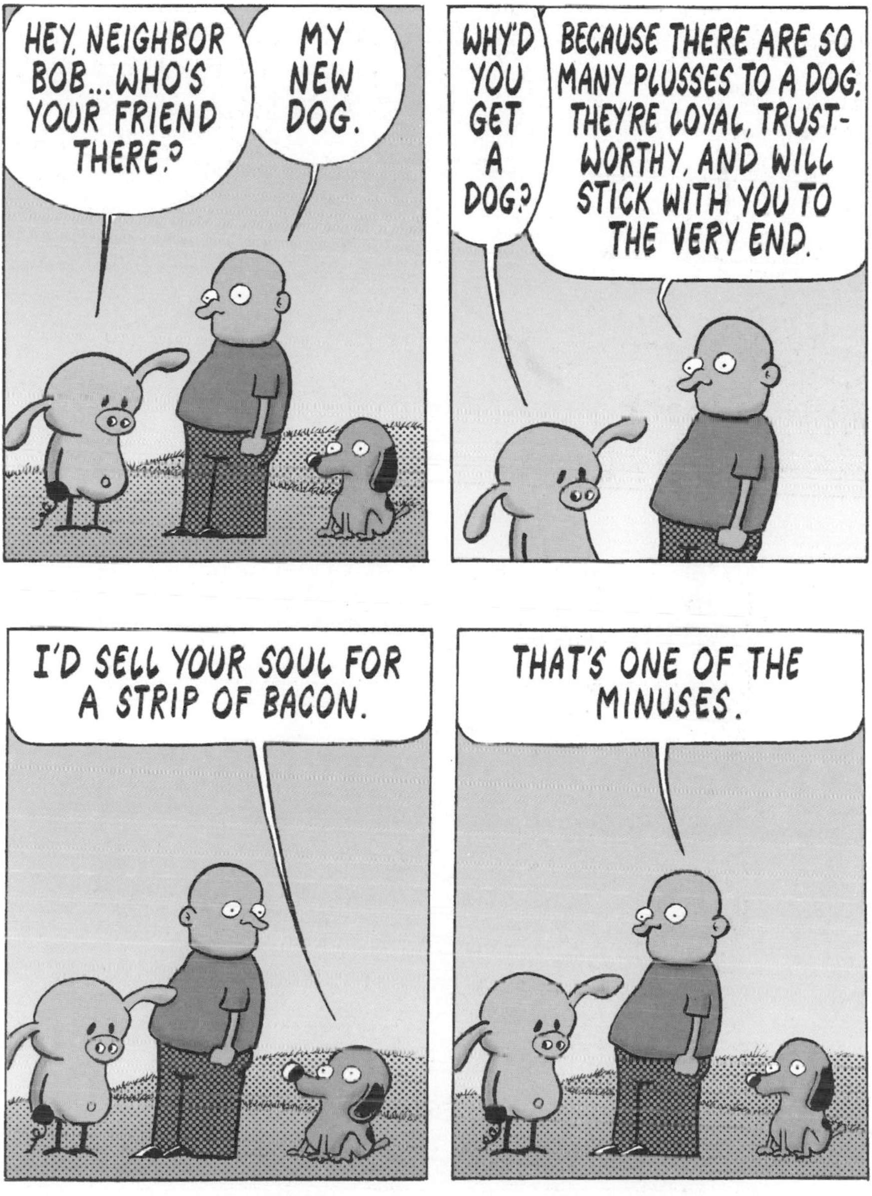
HEY, NEIGHBOR BOB...WHO'S YOUR FRIEND THERE?
MY NEW DOG.
WHY'D YOU GET A DOG?
BECAUSE THERE ARE SO MANY PLUSSES TO A DOG. THEY'RE LOYAL, TRUST-WORTHY, AND WILL STICK WITH YOU TO THE VERY END.
I'D SELL YOUR SOUL FOR A STRIP OF BACON.
THAT'S ONE OF THE MINUSES.

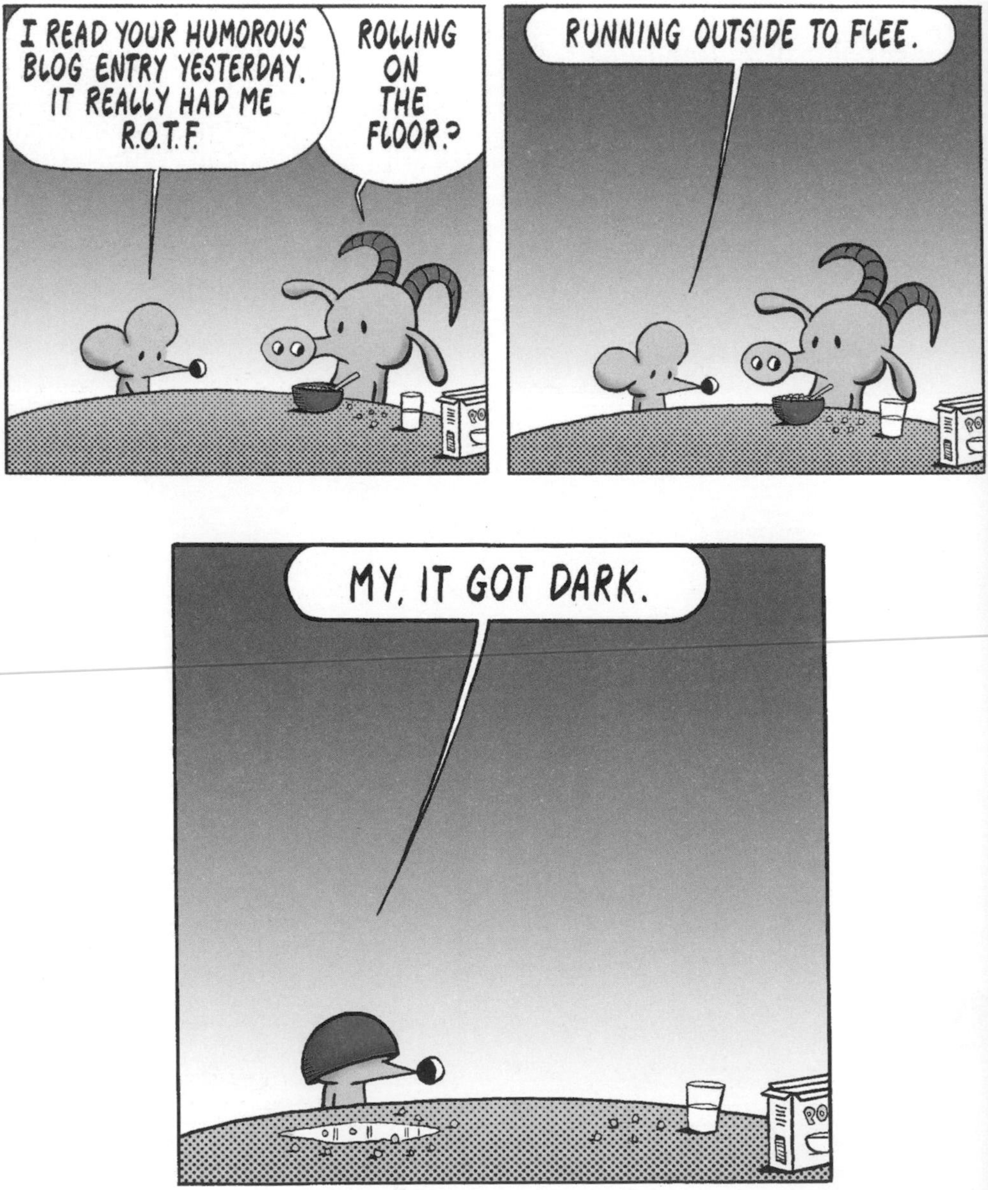
I READ YOUR HUMOROUS BLOG ENTRY YESTERDAY. IT REALLY HAD ME R.O.T.F.
ROLLING ON THE FLOOR?
RUNNING OUTSIDE TO FLEE.
MY, IT GOT DARK.

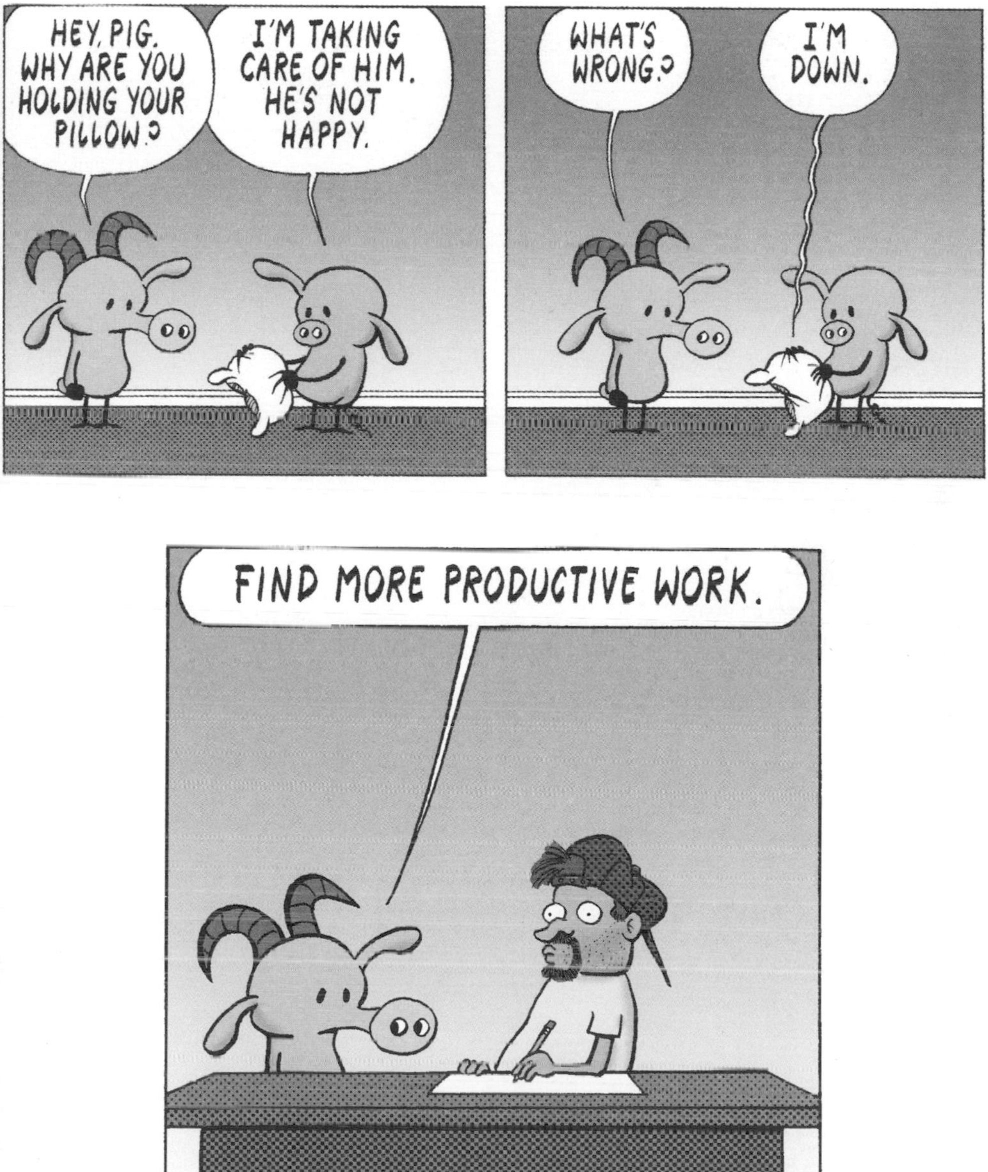
HEY, PIG. WHY ARE YOU HOLDING YOUR PILLOW?
I'M TAKING CARE OF HIM. HE'S NOT HAPPY.
WHAT'S WRONG?
I'M DOWN.
FIND MORE PRODUCTIVE WORK.

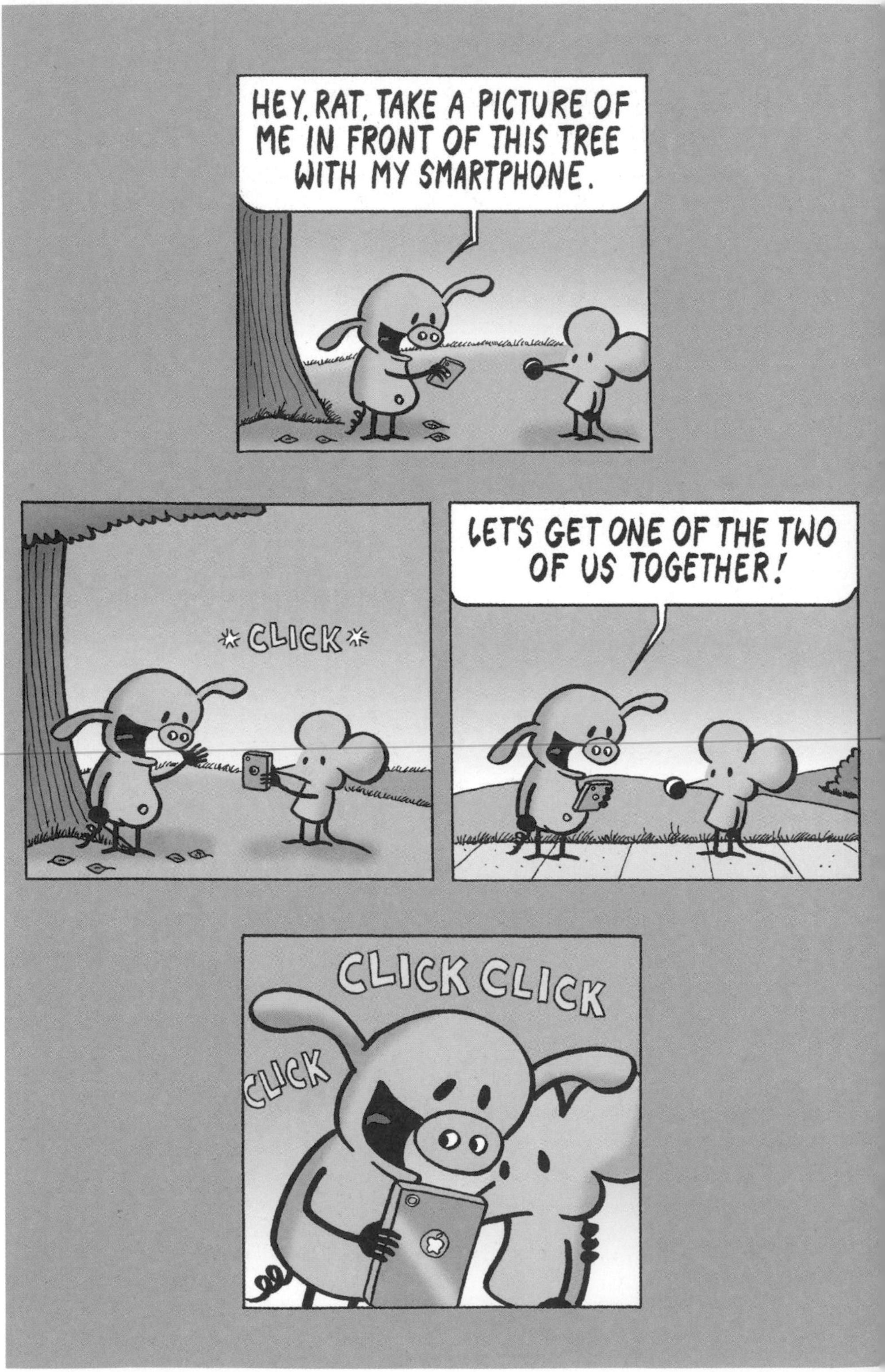
HEY, RAT, TAKE A PICTURE OF ME IN FRONT OF THIS TREE WITH MY SMARTPHONE.
*CLICK*
LET'S GET ONE OF THE TWO OF US TOGETHER!
CLICK CLICK
CLICK

HERE. GET SOME WITH MINE ALSO!
CLICK CLICK
CLICK CLICK
CAMERAS
WHAT THE HECK IS THAT GUY SELLING?
I DUNNO. LET'S TAKE HIS PICTURE.

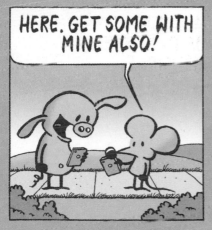

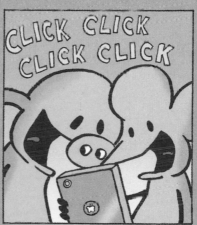

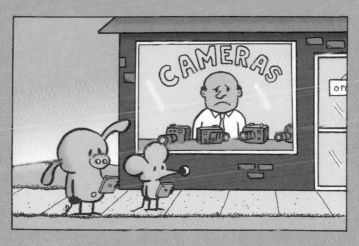

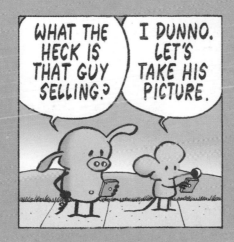

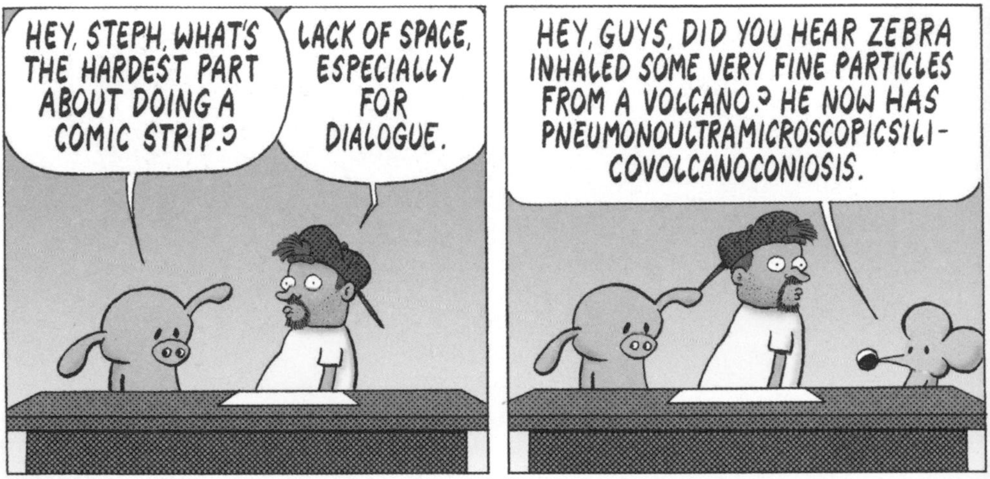
HEY, STEPH, WHAT'S THE HARDEST PART ABOUT DOING A COMIC STRIP?
LACK OF SPACE, ESPECIALLY FOR DIALOGUE.
HEY, GUYS, DID YOU HEAR ZEBRA INHALED SOME VERY FINE PARTICLES FROM A VOLCANO? HE NOW HAS PNEUMONOULTRAMICROSCOPICSILI-COVOLCANOCONIOSIS.

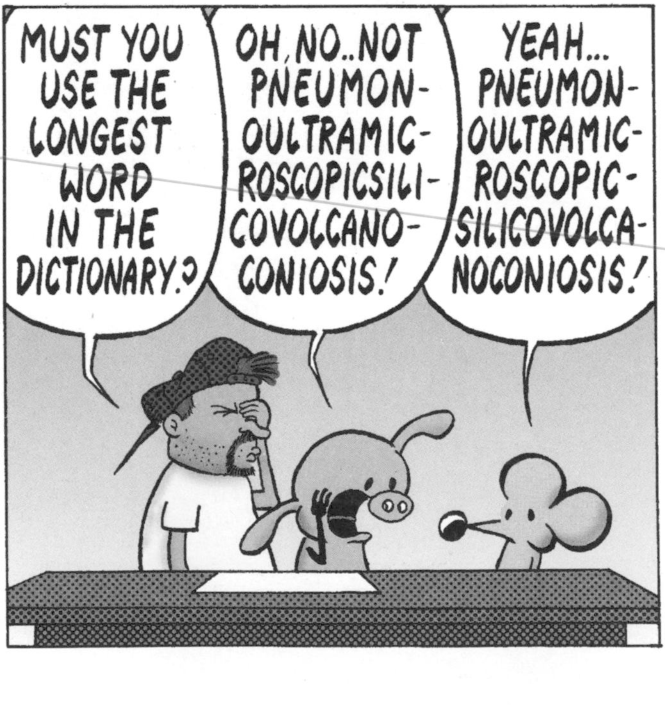
MUST YOU USE THE LONGEST WORD IN THE DICTIONARY?
OH, NO..NOT PNEUMON-OULTRAMIC-ROSCOPICSILI-COVOLCANO-CONIOSIS!
YEAH... PNEUMON-OULTRAMIC-ROSCOPIC-SILICOVOLCA-NOCONIOSIS!

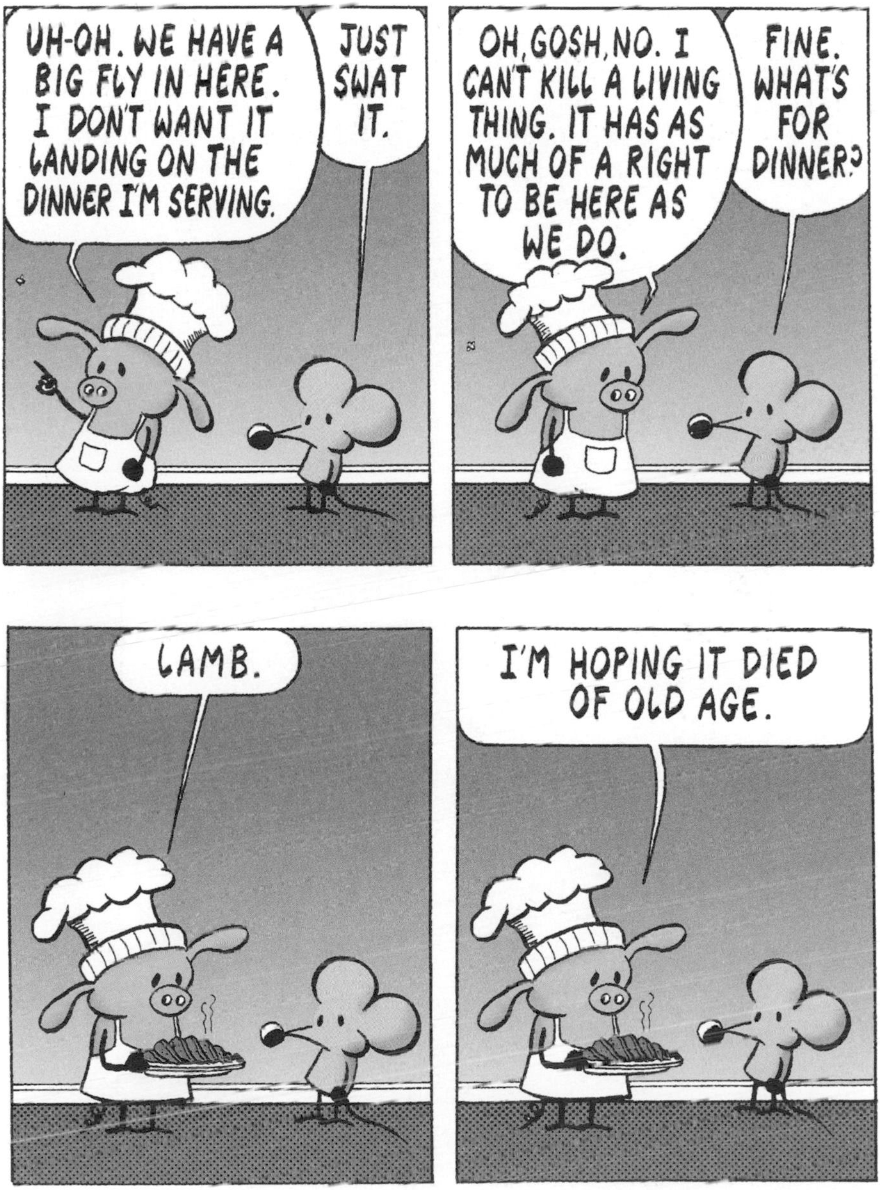
UH-OH. WE HAVE A BIG FLY IN HERE. I DON'T WANT IT LANDING ON THE DINNER I'M SERVING.
JUST SWAT IT.
OH, GOSH, NO. I CAN'T KILL A LIVING THING. IT HAS AS MUCH OF A RIGHT TO BE HERE AS WE DO.
FINE. WHAT'S FOR DINNER?
LAMB.
I'M HOPING IT DIED OF OLD AGE.

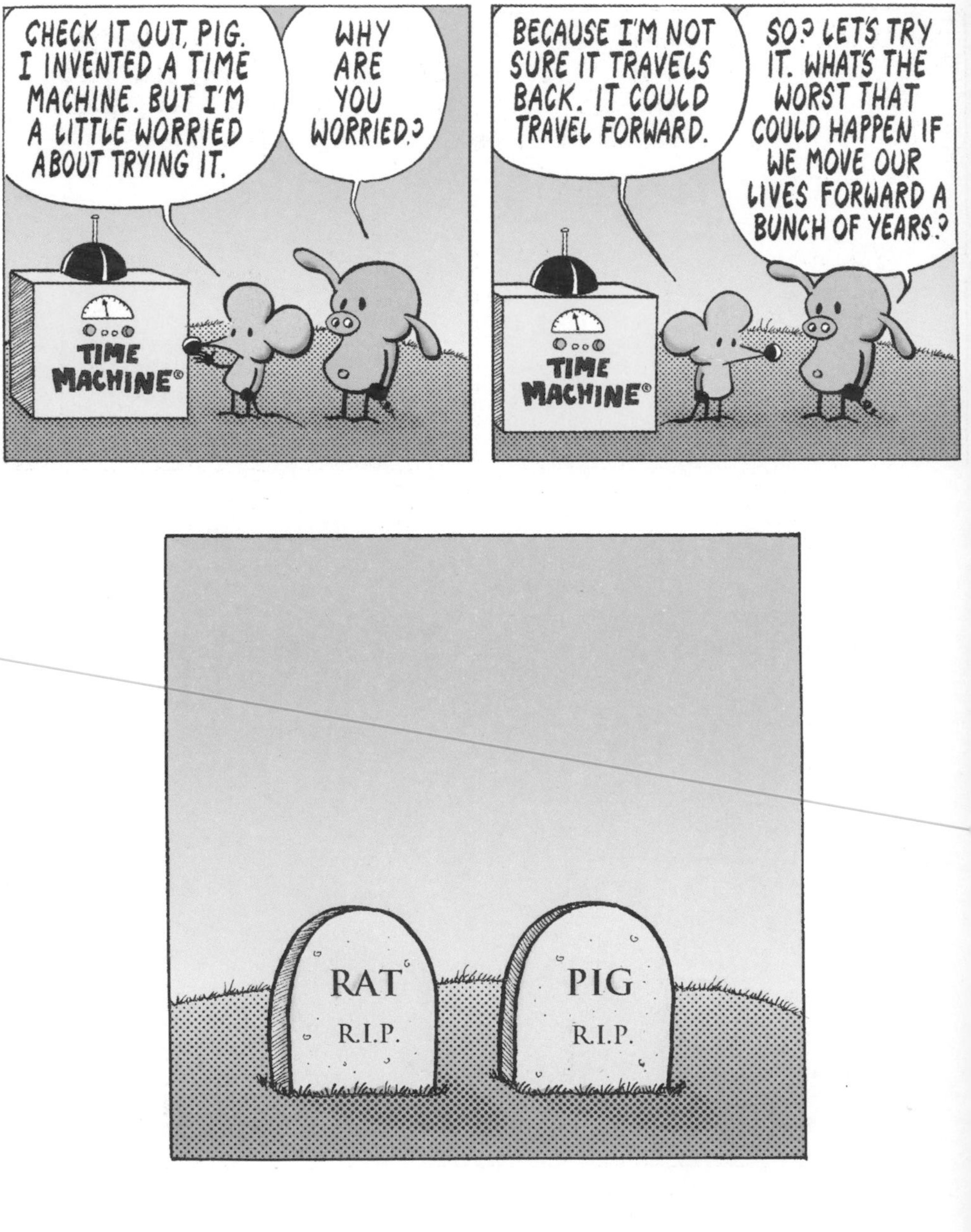
CHECK IT OUT, PIG. I INVENTED A TIME MACHINE. BUT I'M A LITTLE WORRIED ABOUT TRYING IT.
WHY ARE YOU WORRIED?
TIME MACHINE®
BECAUSE I'M NOT SURE IT TRAVELS BACK. IT COULD TRAVEL FORWARD.
SO? LET'S TRY IT. WHAT'S THE WORST THAT COULD HAPPEN IF WE MOVE OUR LIVES FORWARD A BUNCH OF YEARS?
TIME MACHINE®
RAT
R.I.P.
PIG
R.I.P.

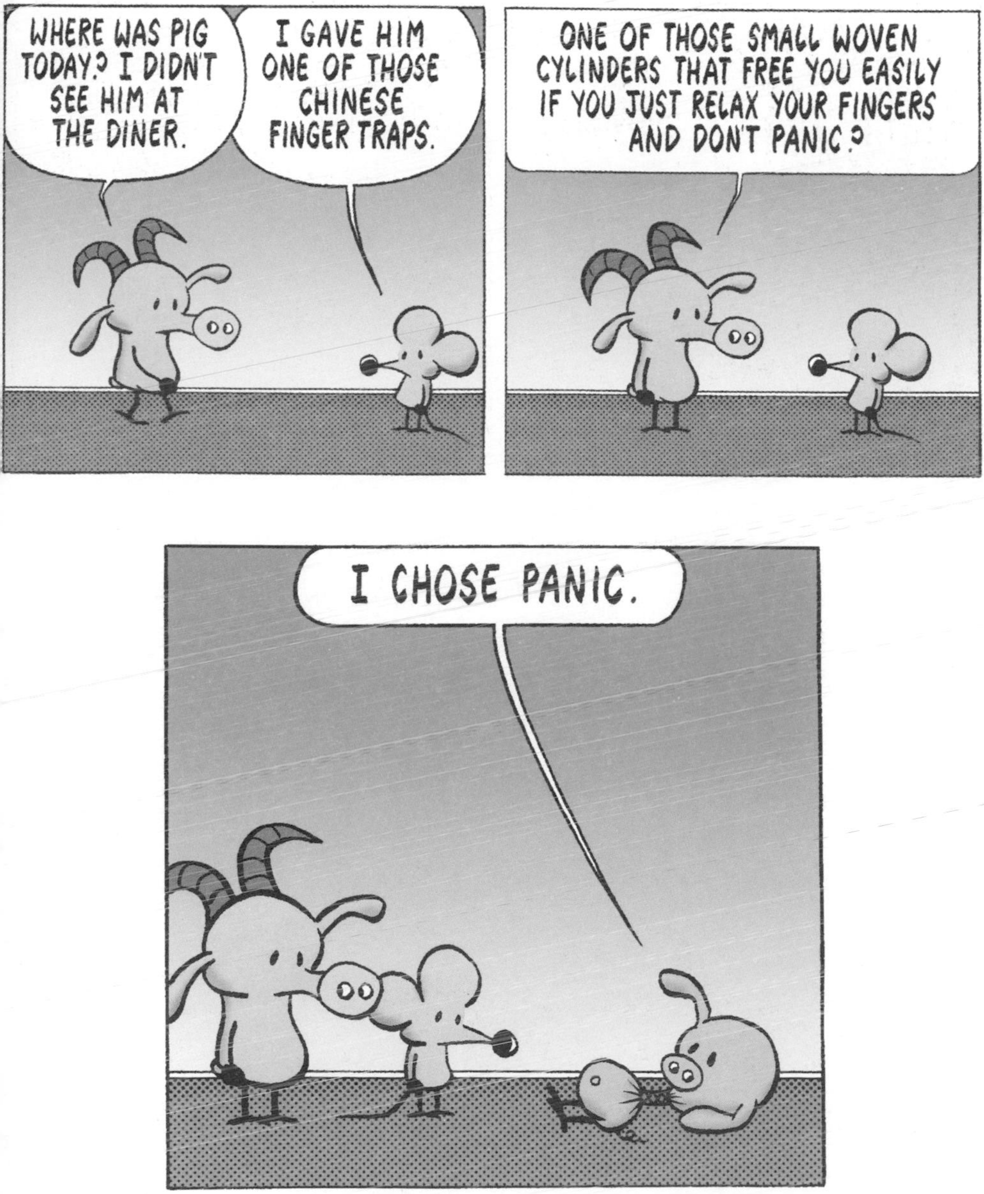
WHERE WAS PIG TODAY? I DIDN'T SEE HIM AT THE DINER.
I GAVE HIM ONE OF THOSE CHINESE FINGER TRAPS.
ONE OF THOSE SMALL WOVEN CYLINDERS THAT FREE YOU EASILY IF YOU JUST RELAX YOUR FINGERS AND DON'T PANIC?
I CHOSE PANIC.

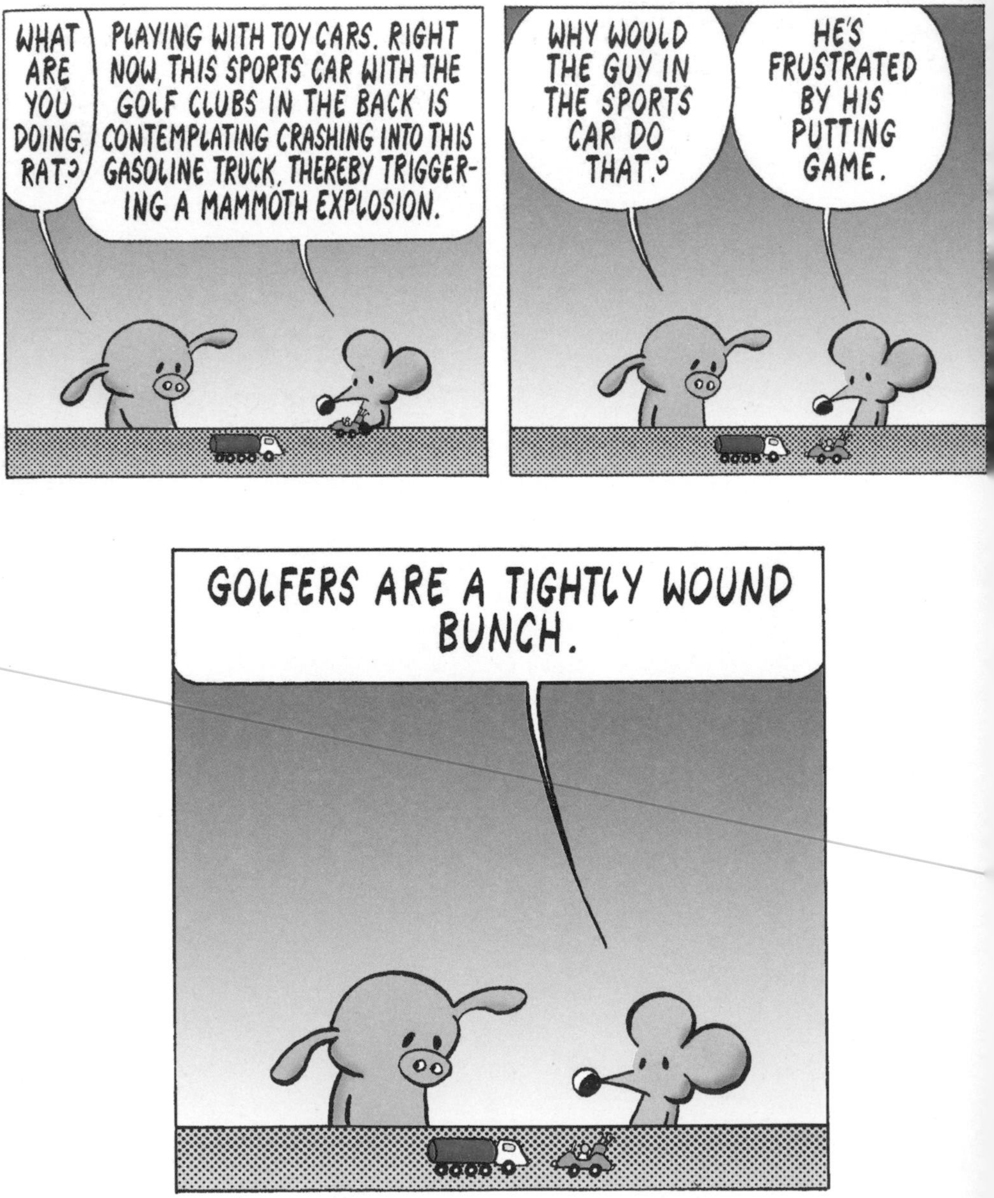
WHAT ARE YOU DOING, RAT?
PLAYING WITH TOY CARS. RIGHT NOW, THIS SPORTS CAR WITH THE GOLF CLUBS IN THE BACK IS CONTEMPLATING CRASHING INTO THIS GASOLINE TRUCK, THEREBY TRIGGERING A MAMMOTH EXPLOSION.
WHY WOULD THE GUY IN THE SPORTS CAR DO THAT?
HE'S FRUSTRATED BY HIS PUTTING GAME.
GOLFERS ARE A TIGHTLY WOUND BUNCH.

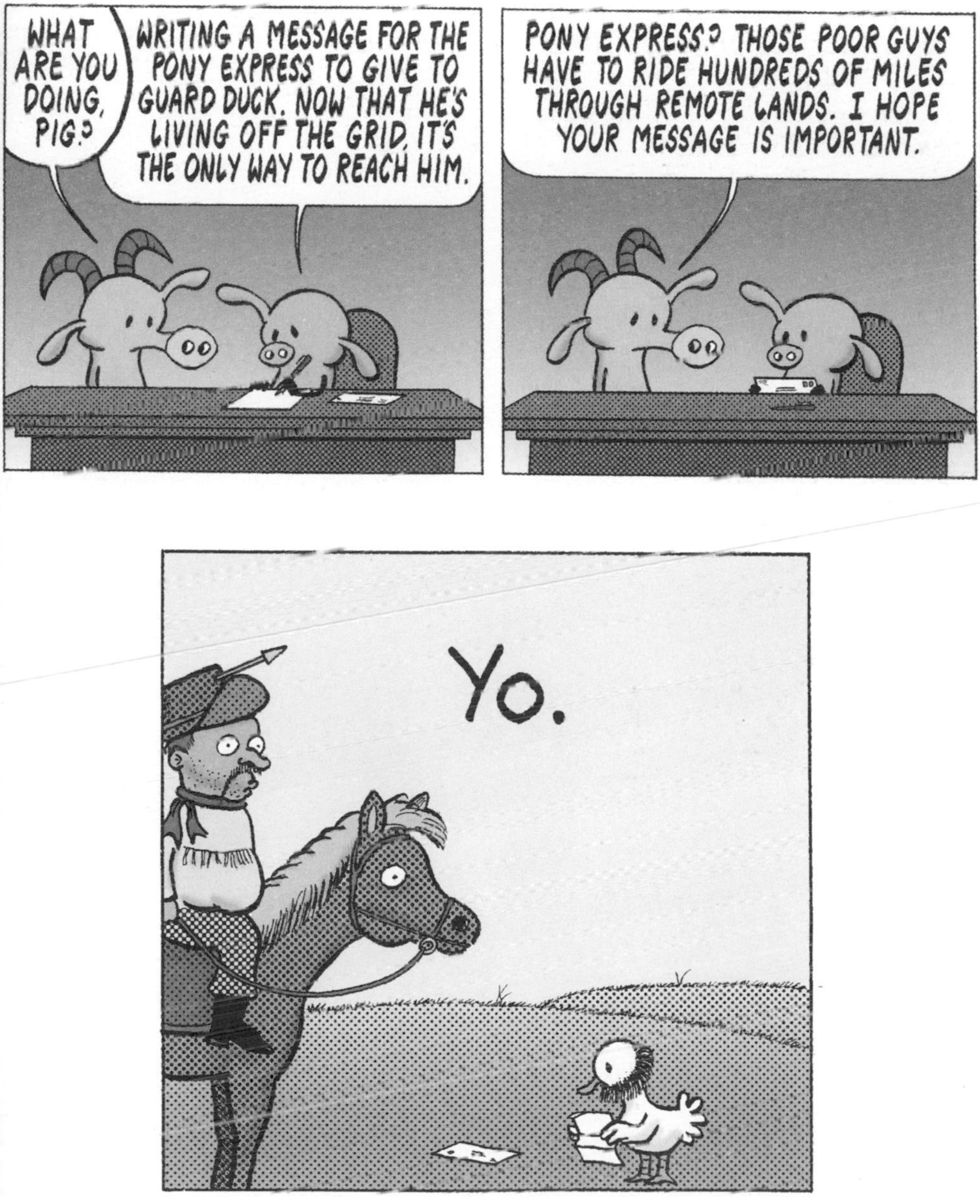
WHAT ARE YOU DOING, PIG?
WRITING A MESSAGE FOR THE PONY EXPRESS TO GIVE TO GUARD DUCK. NOW THAT HE'S LIVING OFF THE GRID, IT'S THE ONLY WAY TO REACH HIM.
PONY EXPRESS? THOSE POOR GUYS HAVE TO RIDE HUNDREDS OF MILES THROUGH REMOTE LANDS. I HOPE YOUR MESSAGE IS IMPORTANT.
Yo.

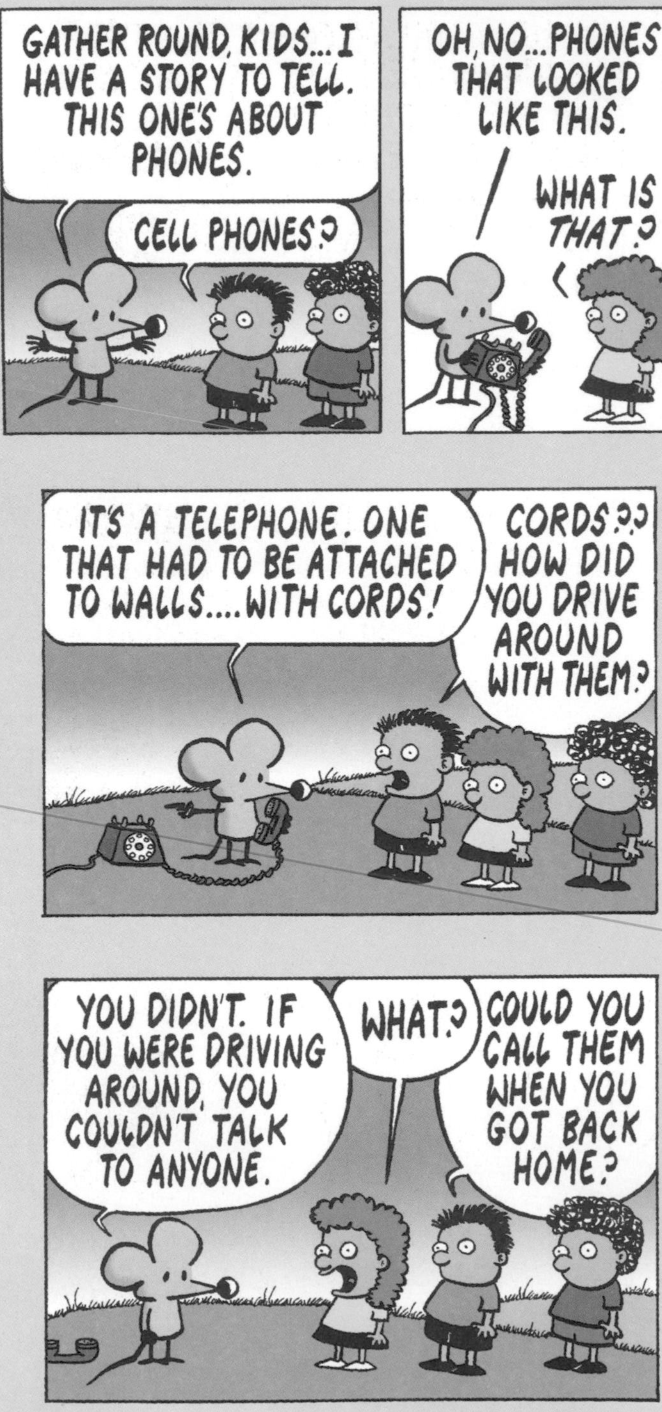
GATHER ROUND, KIDS... I HAVE A STORY TO TELL. THIS ONE'S ABOUT PHONES.
CELL PHONES?
OH, NO... PHONES THAT LOOKED LIKE THIS.
WHAT IS THAT?
IT'S A TELEPHONE. ONE THAT HAD TO BE ATTACHED TO WALLS.... WITH CORDS!
CORDS?? HOW DID YOU DRIVE AROUND WITH THEM?
YOU DIDN'T. IF YOU WERE DRIVING AROUND, YOU COULDN'T TALK TO ANYONE.
WHAT?
COULD YOU CALL THEM WHEN YOU GOT BACK HOME?

YES, BUT IF YOU CALLED WHEN THEY WERE ON THE PHONE, YOU GOT SOMETHING CALLED A 'BUSY SIGNAL.'
WHY DIDN'T YOU JUST LEAVE A VOICEMAIL?
BECAUSE THERE WASN'T ANY. SOMEONE HAD TO WRITE DOWN YOUR MESSAGE WITH PEN AND PAPER.
PAPER?? AAHAHAH HAHAHA HAHAHA
NEVER HAVE I FELT SO OLD.
NOW LET ME TELL YOU ABOUT.... THE TIME LADY!
THE WHO?!

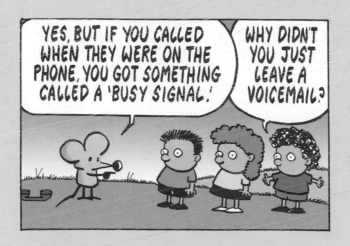

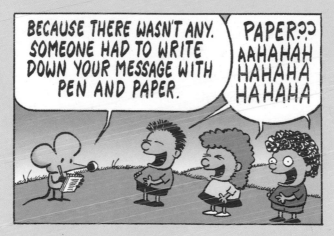

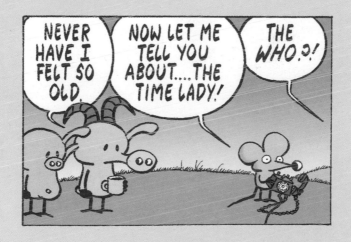

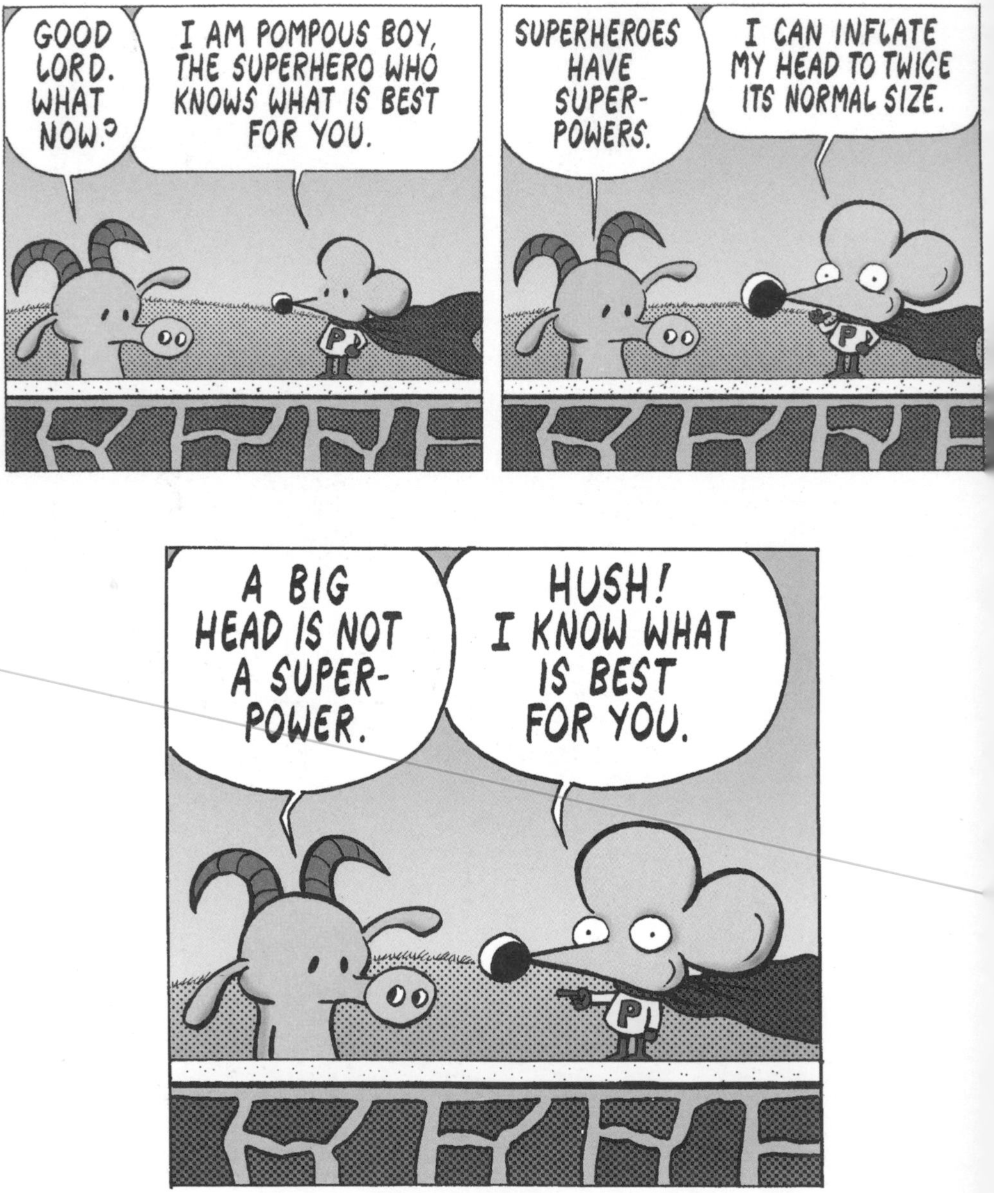
GOOD LORD. WHAT NOW?
I AM POMPOUS BOY, THE SUPERHERO WHO KNOWS WHAT IS BEST FOR YOU.
SUPERHEROES HAVE SUPER-POWERS.
I CAN INFLATE MY HEAD TO TWICE ITS NORMAL SIZE.
A BIG HEAD IS NOT A SUPER-POWER.
HUSH! I KNOW WHAT IS BEST FOR YOU.

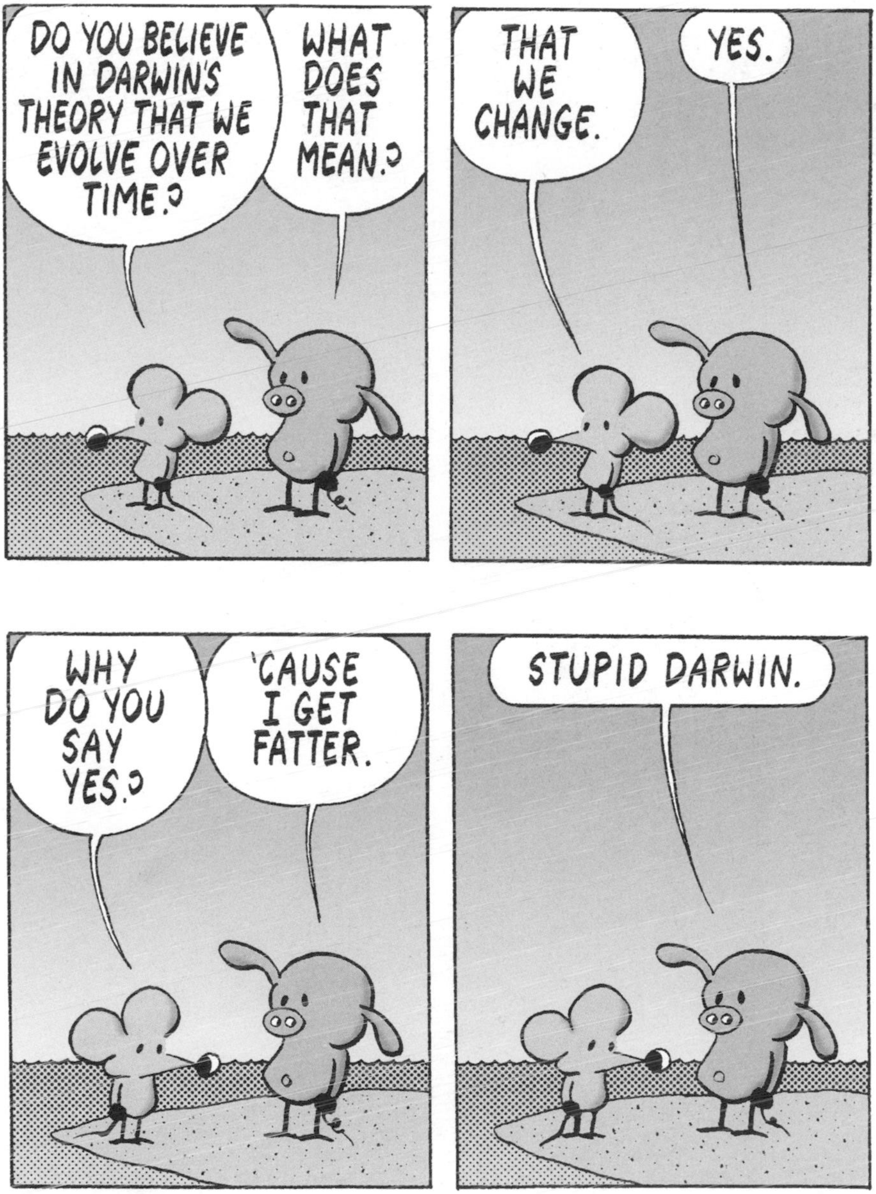
DO YOU BELIEVE IN DARWIN'S THEORY THAT WE EVOLVE OVER TIME?
WHAT DOES THAT MEAN?
THAT WE CHANGE.
YES.
WHY DO YOU SAY YES?
'CAUSE I GET FATTER.
STUPID DARWIN.

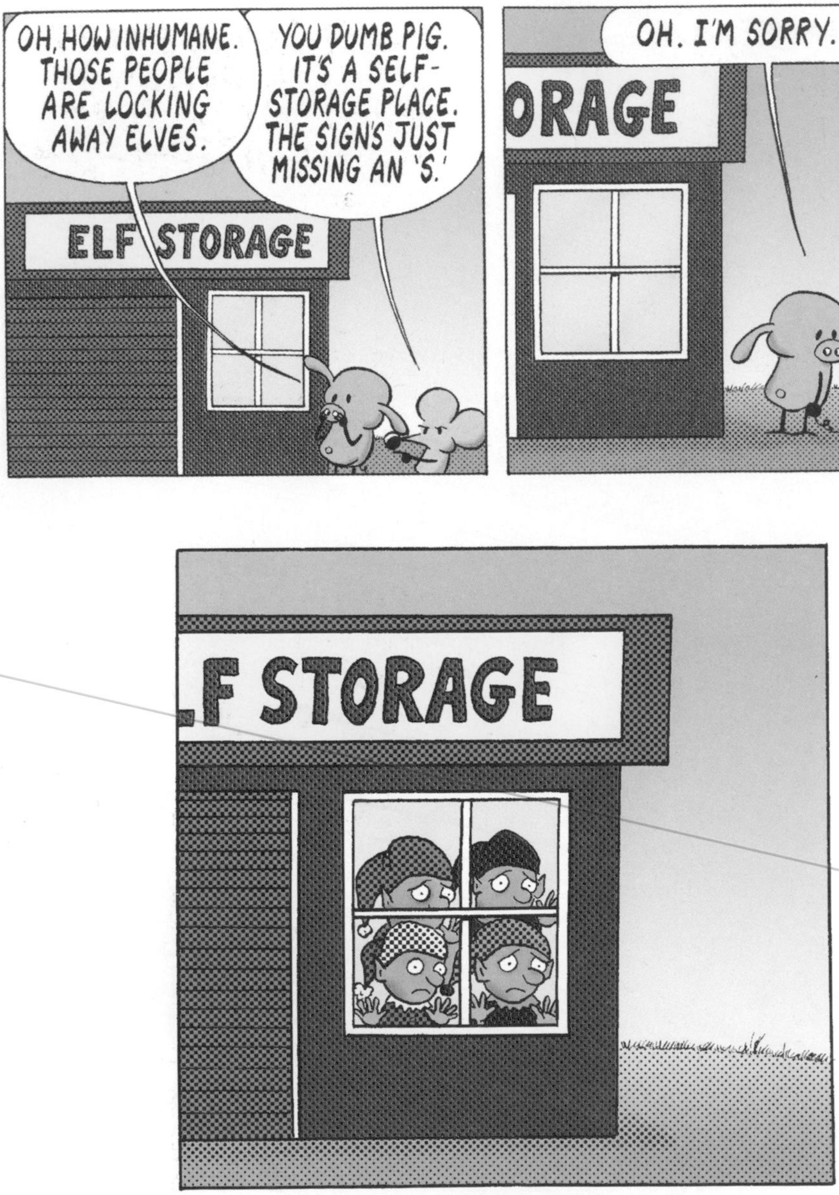
OH, HOW INHUMANE. THOSE PEOPLE ARE LOCKING AWAY ELVES.
YOU DUMB PIG. IT'S A SELF-STORAGE PLACE. THE SIGN'S JUST MISSING AN 'S.'
ELF STORAGE
OH. I'M SORRY.
ORAGE
LF STORAGE

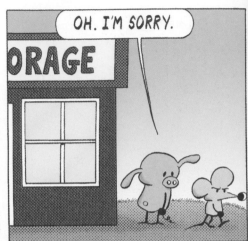

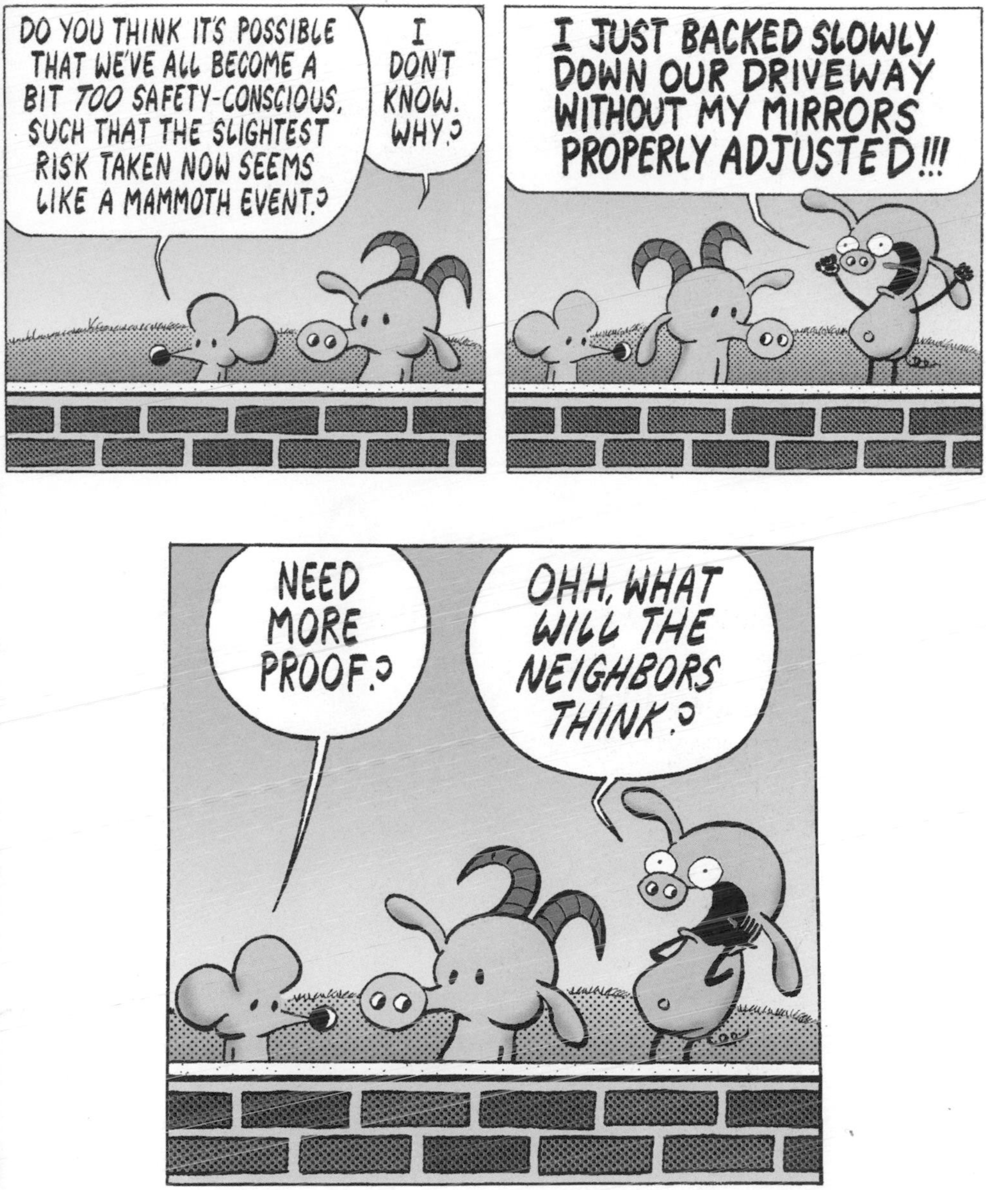
DO YOU THINK IT'S POSSIBLE THAT WE'VE ALL BECOME A BIT *TOO* SAFETY-CONSCIOUS, SUCH THAT THE SLIGHTEST RISK TAKEN NOW SEEMS LIKE A MAMMOTH EVENT?
I DON'T KNOW. WHY?
I JUST BACKED SLOWLY DOWN OUR DRIVEWAY WITHOUT MY MIRRORS PROPERLY ADJUSTED!!!
NEED MORE PROOF?
OHH, WHAT WILL THE NEIGHBORS THINK?

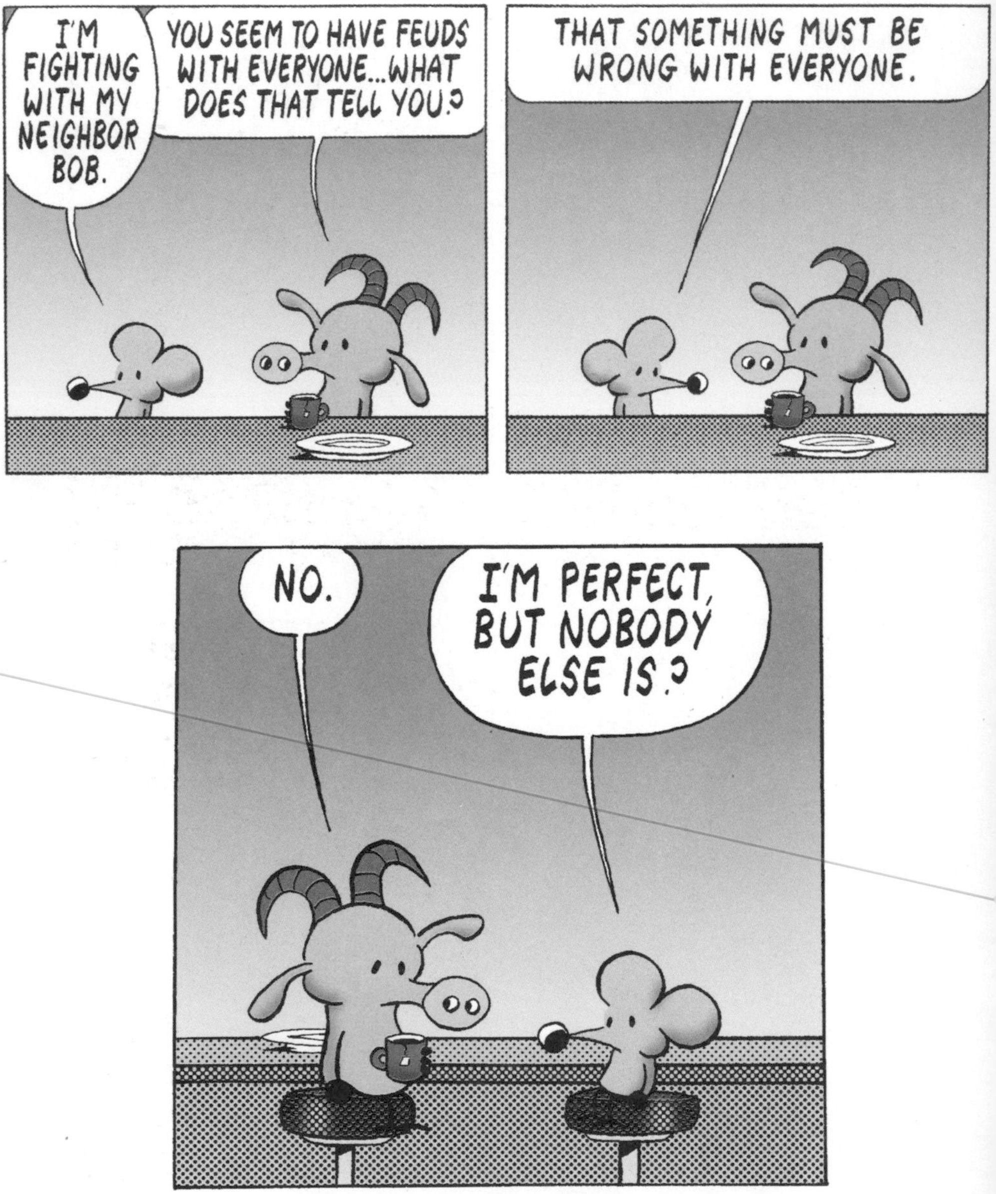
I'M FIGHTING WITH MY NEIGHBOR BOB.
YOU SEEM TO HAVE FEUDS WITH EVERYONE...WHAT DOES THAT TELL YOU?
THAT SOMETHING MUST BE WRONG WITH EVERYONE.
NO.
I'M PERFECT, BUT NOBODY ELSE IS?

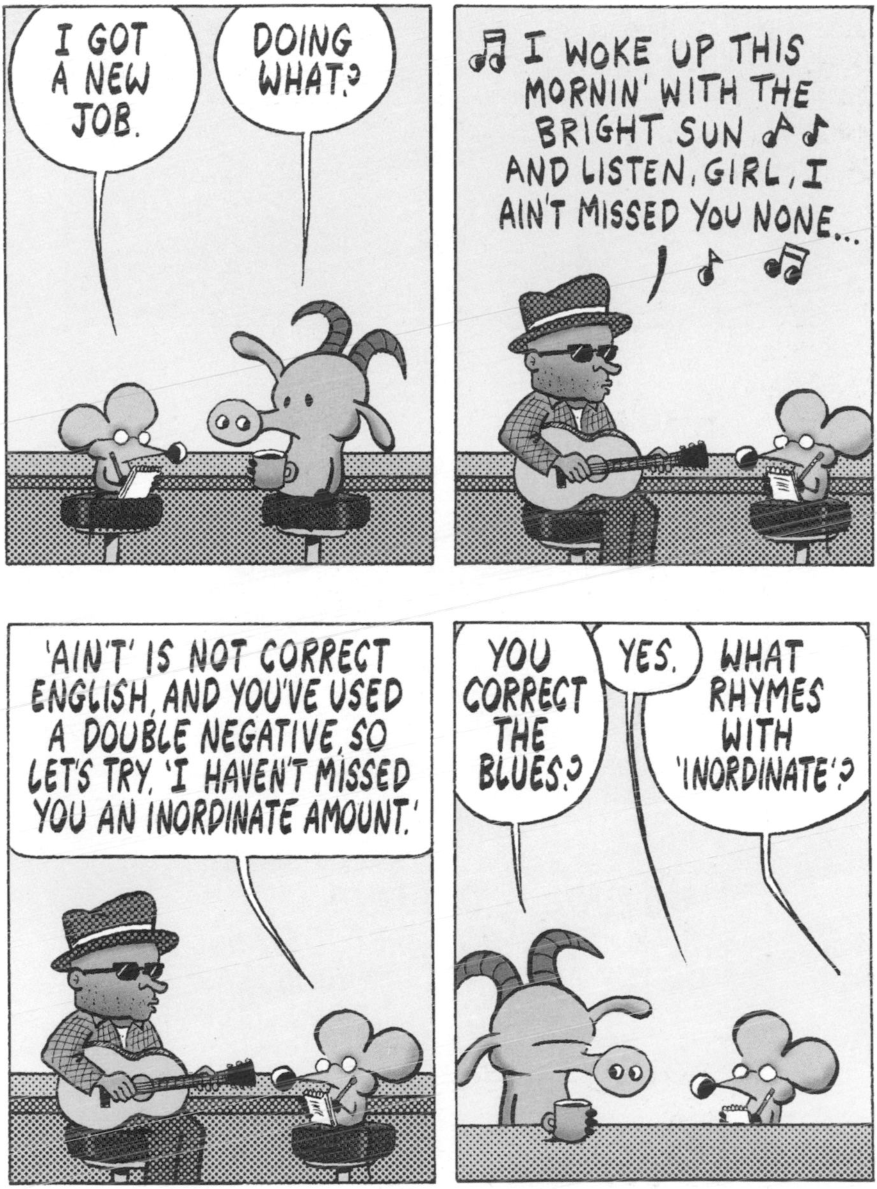
I GOT A NEW JOB.
DOING WHAT?
I WOKE UP THIS MORNIN' WITH THE BRIGHT SUN AND LISTEN, GIRL, I AIN'T MISSED YOU NONE...
'AIN'T' IS NOT CORRECT ENGLISH, AND YOU'VE USED A DOUBLE NEGATIVE, SO LET'S TRY, 'I HAVEN'T MISSED YOU AN INORDINATE AMOUNT.'
YOU CORRECT THE BLUES?
YES.
WHAT RHYMES WITH 'INORDINATE'?

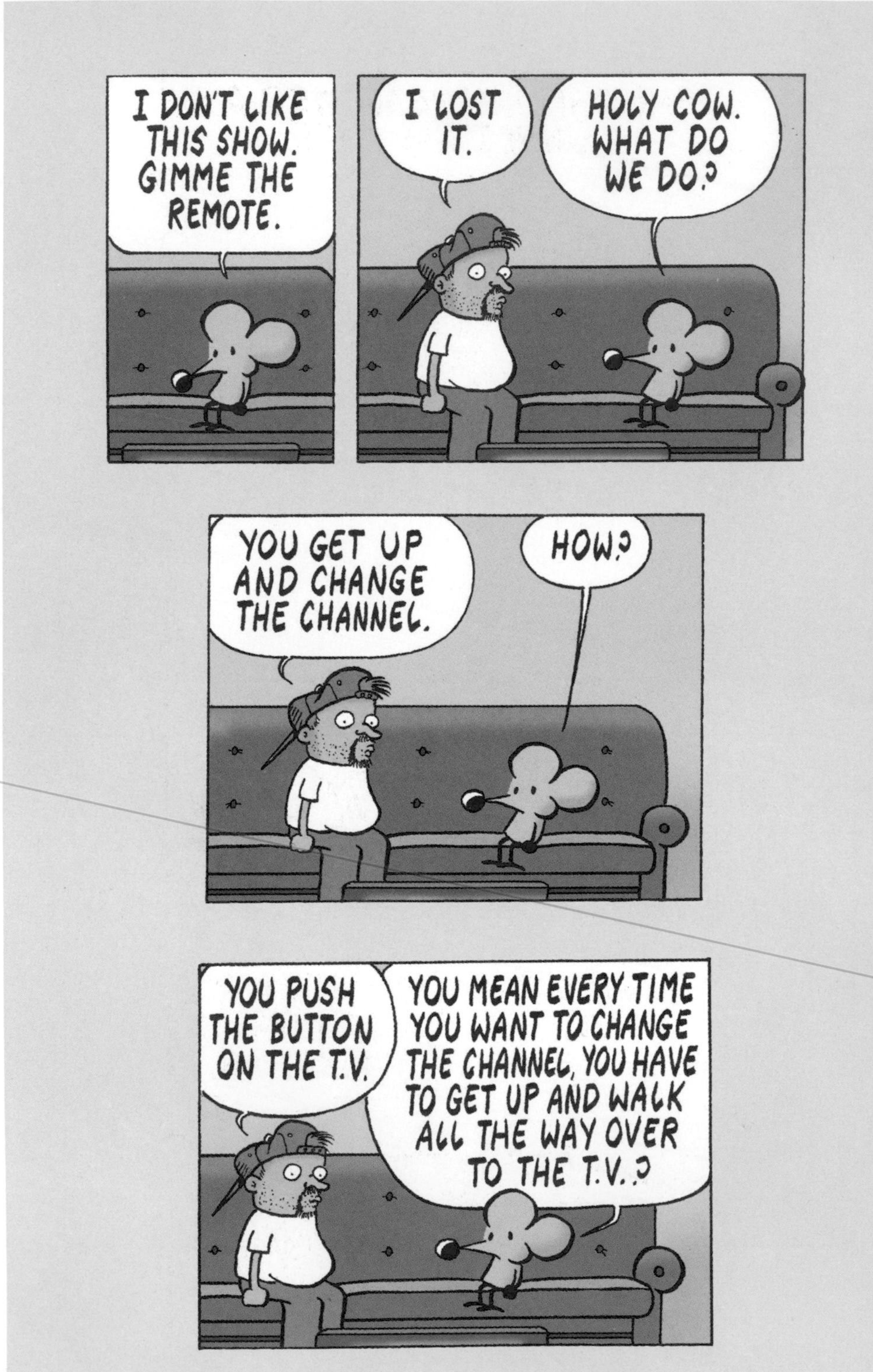
I DON'T LIKE THIS SHOW. GIMME THE REMOTE.
I LOST IT.
HOLY COW. WHAT DO WE DO?
YOU GET UP AND CHANGE THE CHANNEL.
HOW?
YOU PUSH THE BUTTON ON THE T.V.
YOU MEAN EVERY TIME YOU WANT TO CHANGE THE CHANNEL, YOU HAVE TO GET UP AND WALK ALL THE WAY OVER TO THE T.V.?

YEAH. THAT'S HOW WE ALWAYS DID IT WHEN I WAS A KID.
AND YET SOMEHOW I SURVIVED.
LORD HAVE MERCY. WHAT A TRAGIC UPBRINGING.

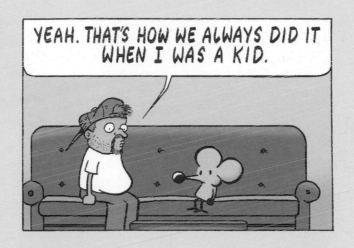

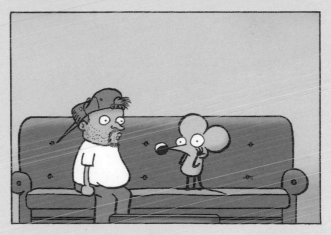

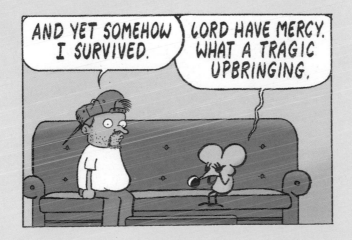

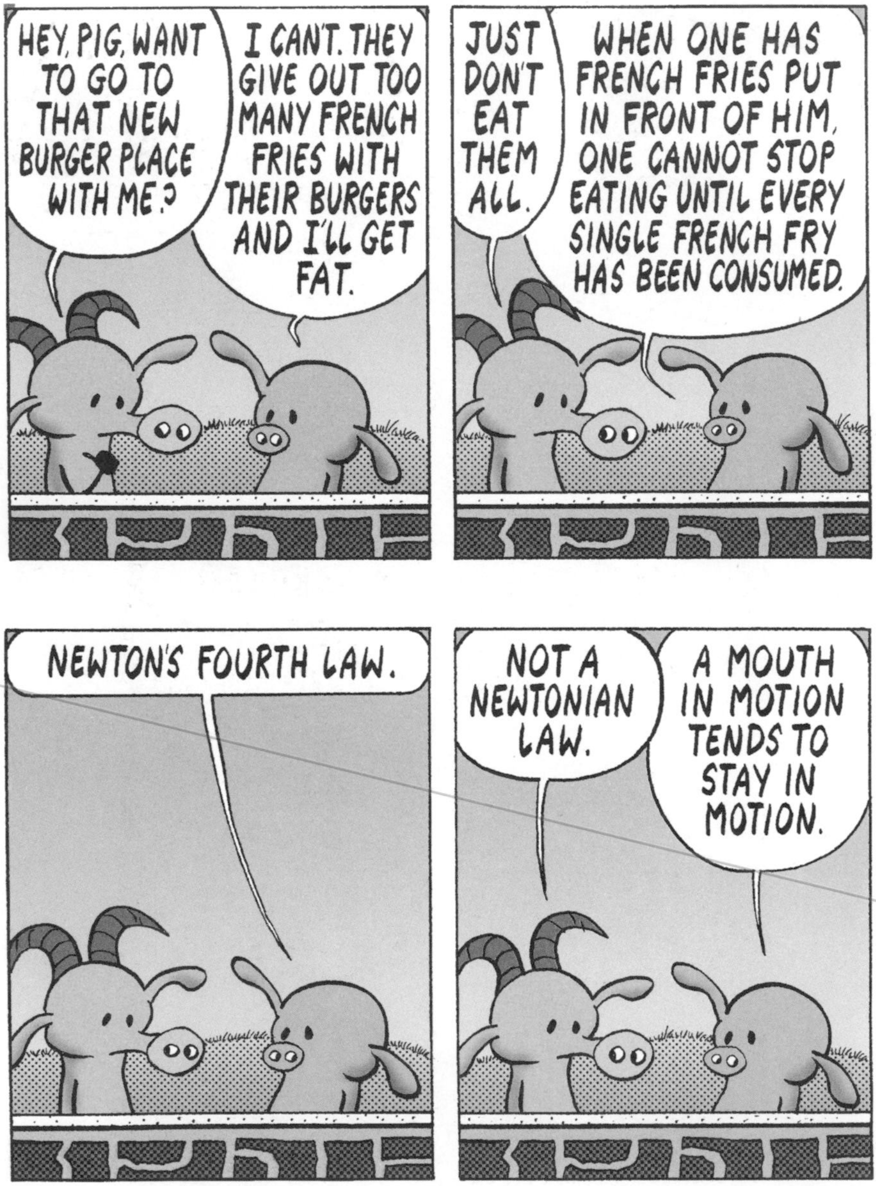
HEY, PIG, WANT TO GO TO THAT NEW BURGER PLACE WITH ME?
I CAN'T. THEY GIVE OUT TOO MANY FRENCH FRIES WITH THEIR BURGERS AND I'LL GET FAT.
JUST DON'T EAT THEM ALL.
WHEN ONE HAS FRENCH FRIES PUT IN FRONT OF HIM, ONE CANNOT STOP EATING UNTIL EVERY SINGLE FRENCH FRY HAS BEEN CONSUMED.
NEWTON'S FOURTH LAW.
NOT A NEWTONIAN LAW.
A MOUTH IN MOTION TENDS TO STAY IN MOTION.

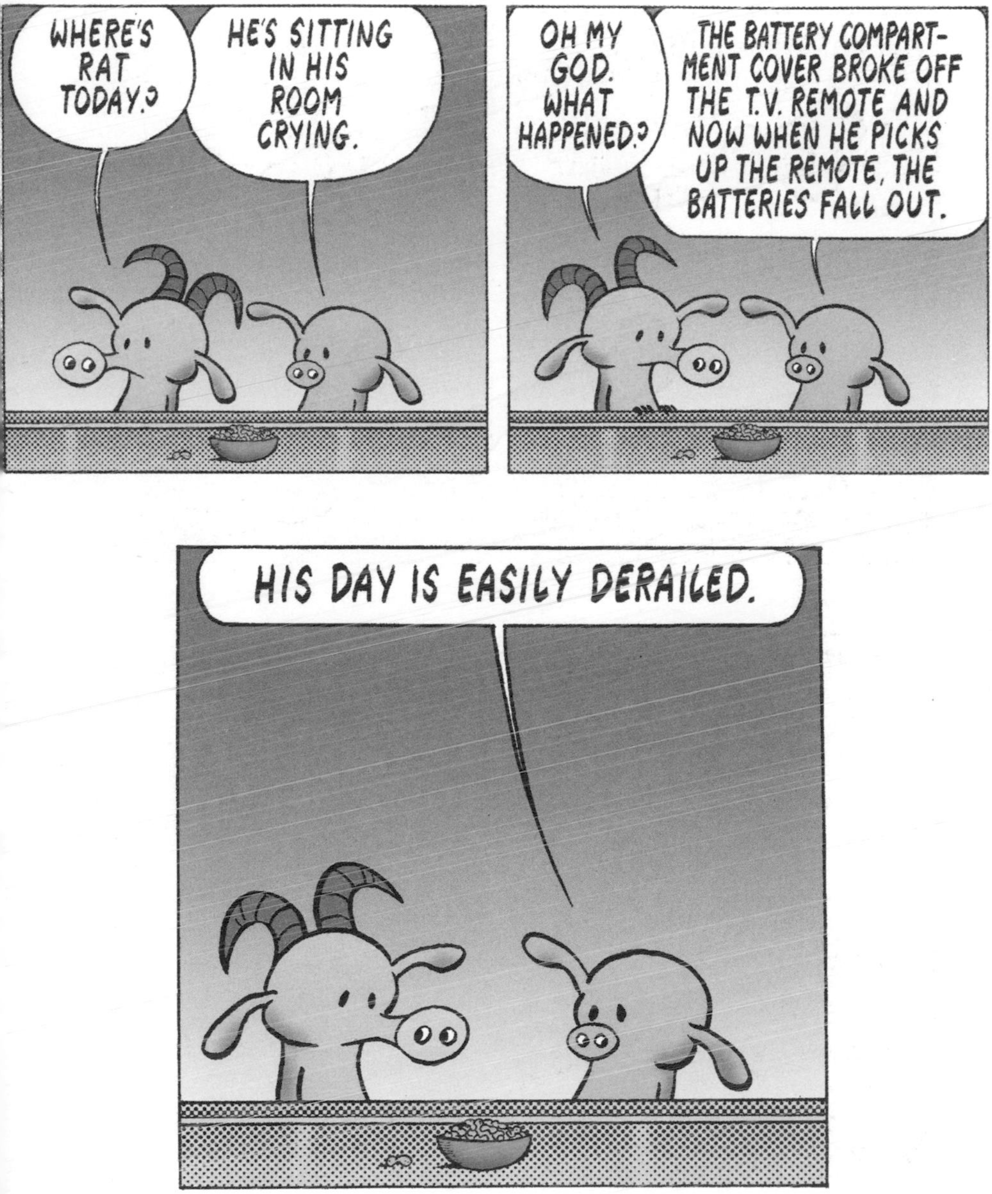
WHERE'S RAT TODAY?
HE'S SITTING IN HIS ROOM CRYING.
OH MY GOD. WHAT HAPPENED?
THE BATTERY COMPART-MENT COVER BROKE OFF THE T.V. REMOTE AND NOW WHEN HE PICKS UP THE REMOTE, THE BATTERIES FALL OUT.
HIS DAY IS EASILY DERAILED.

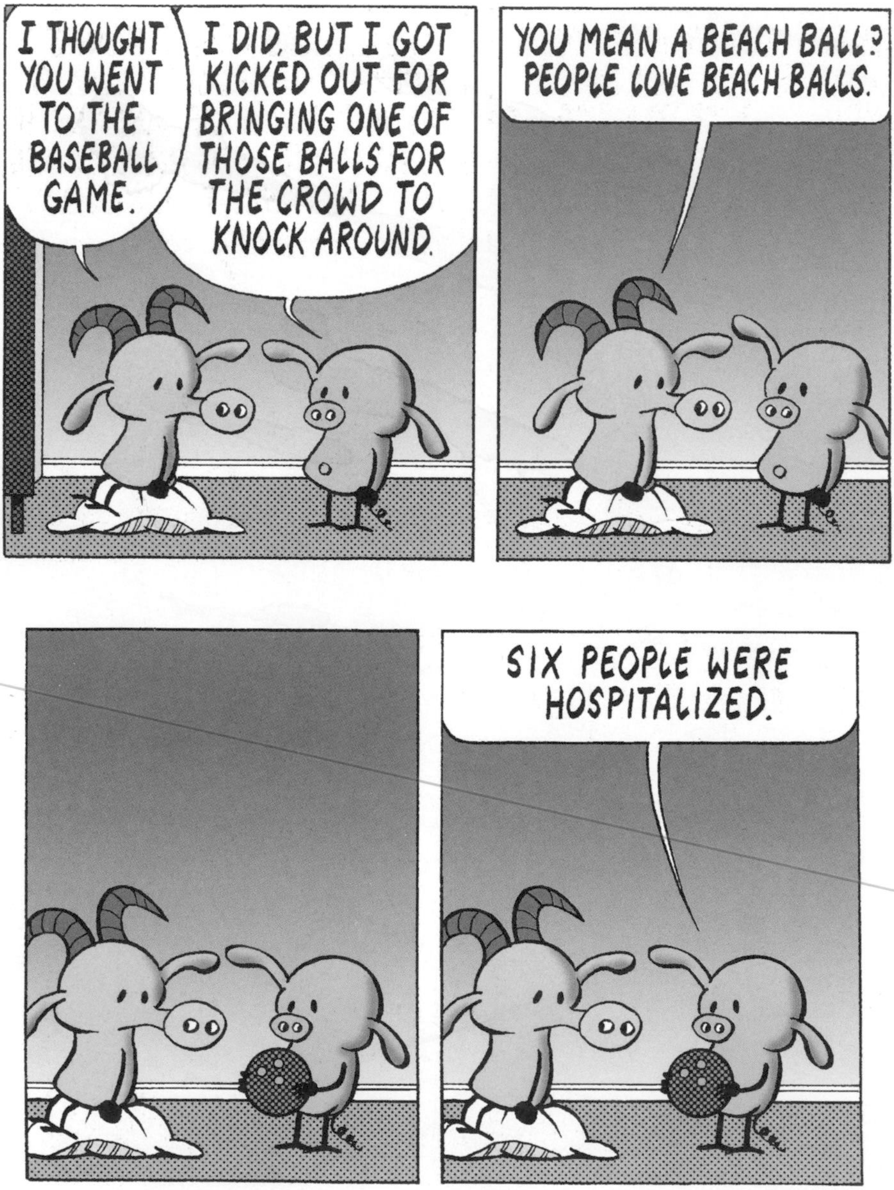
I THOUGHT YOU WENT TO THE BASEBALL GAME.
I DID, BUT I GOT KICKED OUT FOR BRINGING ONE OF THOSE BALLS FOR THE CROWD TO KNOCK AROUND.
YOU MEAN A BEACH BALL? PEOPLE LOVE BEACH BALLS.
SIX PEOPLE WERE HOSPITALIZED.

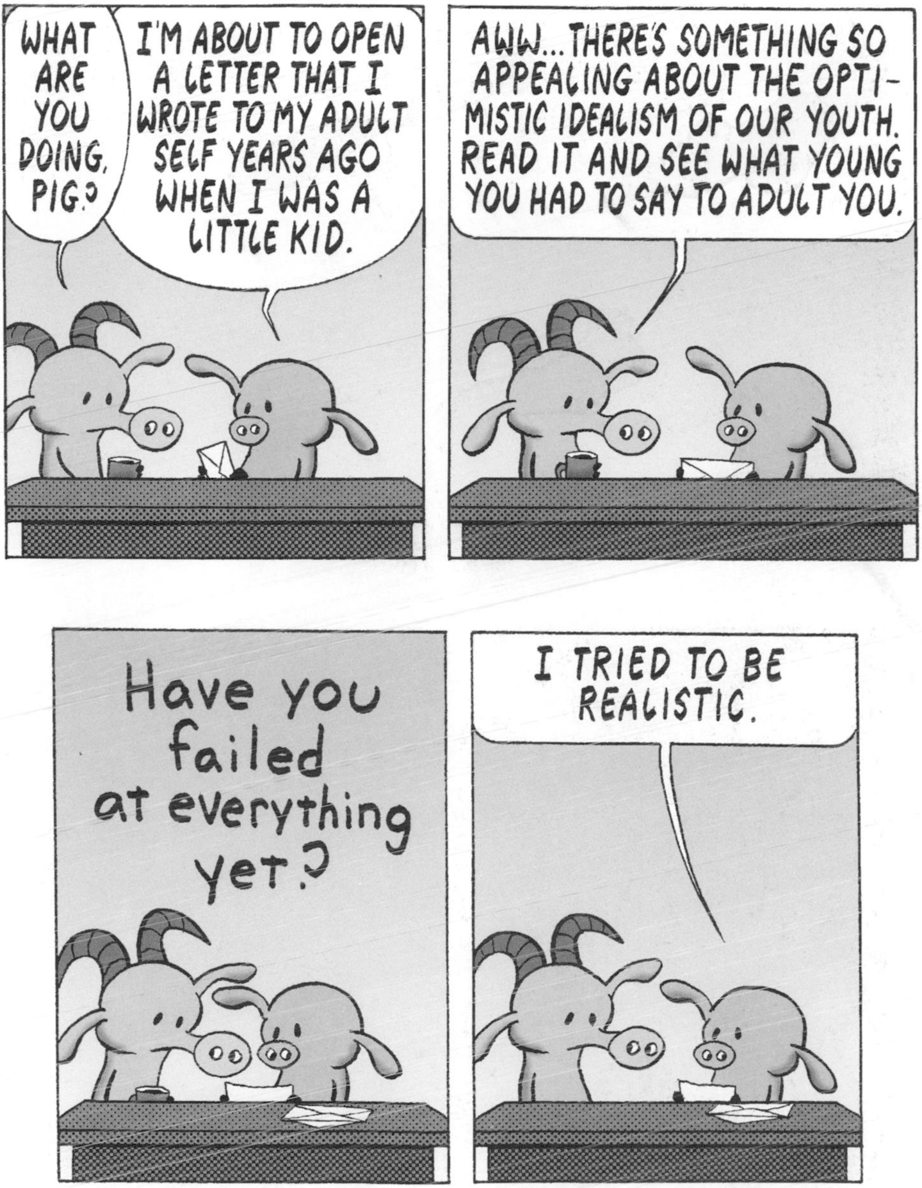
WHAT ARE YOU DOING, PIG?
I'M ABOUT TO OPEN A LETTER THAT I WROTE TO MY ADULT SELF YEARS AGO WHEN I WAS A LITTLE KID.
AWW... THERE'S SOMETHING SO APPEALING ABOUT THE OPTIMISTIC IDEALISM OF OUR YOUTH. READ IT AND SEE WHAT YOUNG YOU HAD TO SAY TO ADULT YOU.
Have you failed at everything yet?
I TRIED TO BE REALISTIC.

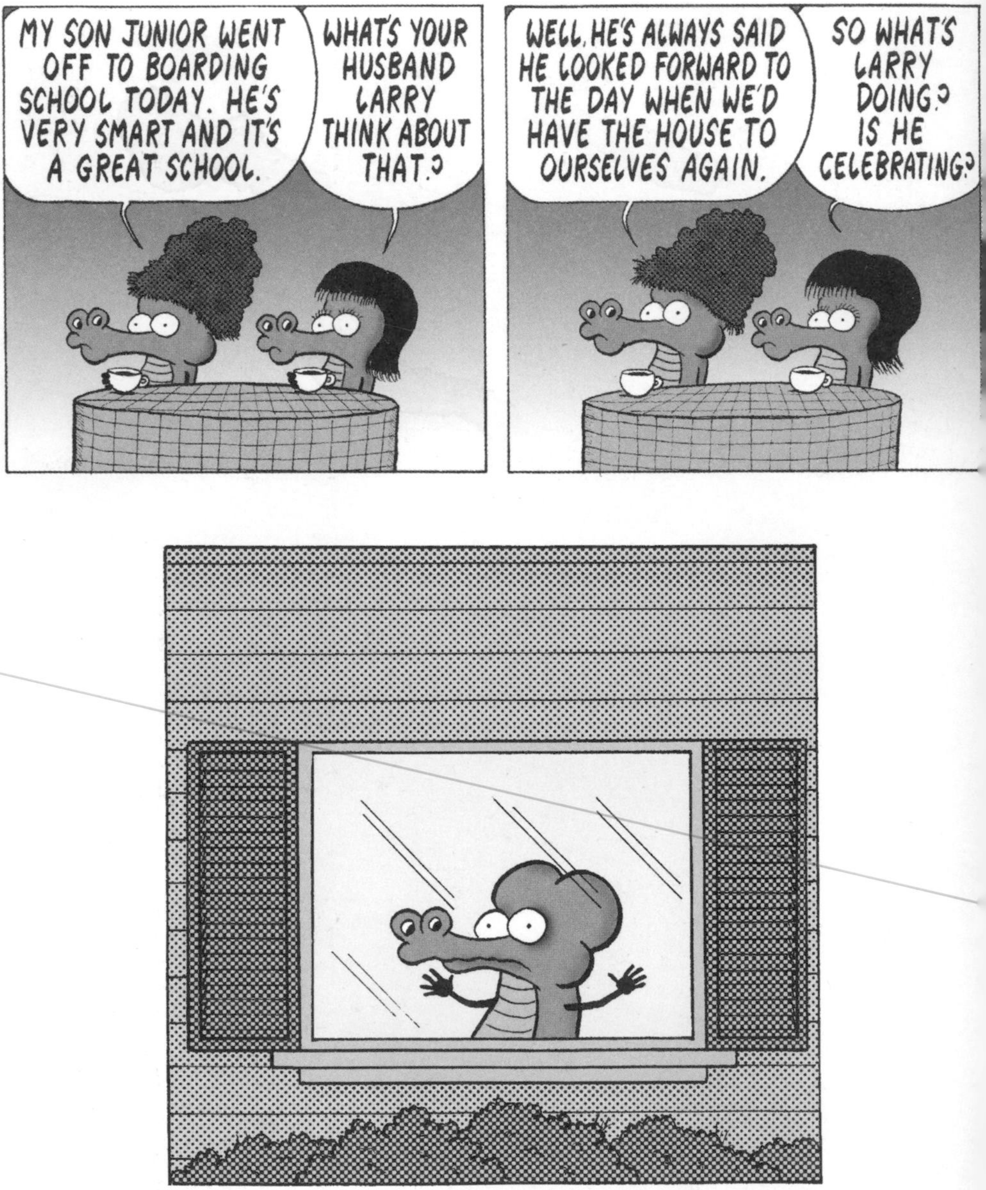
MY SON JUNIOR WENT OFF TO BOARDING SCHOOL TODAY. HE'S VERY SMART AND IT'S A GREAT SCHOOL.
WHAT'S YOUR HUSBAND LARRY THINK ABOUT THAT?
WELL, HE'S ALWAYS SAID HE LOOKED FORWARD TO THE DAY WHEN WE'D HAVE THE HOUSE TO OURSELVES AGAIN.
SO WHAT'S LARRY DOING? IS HE CELEBRATING?

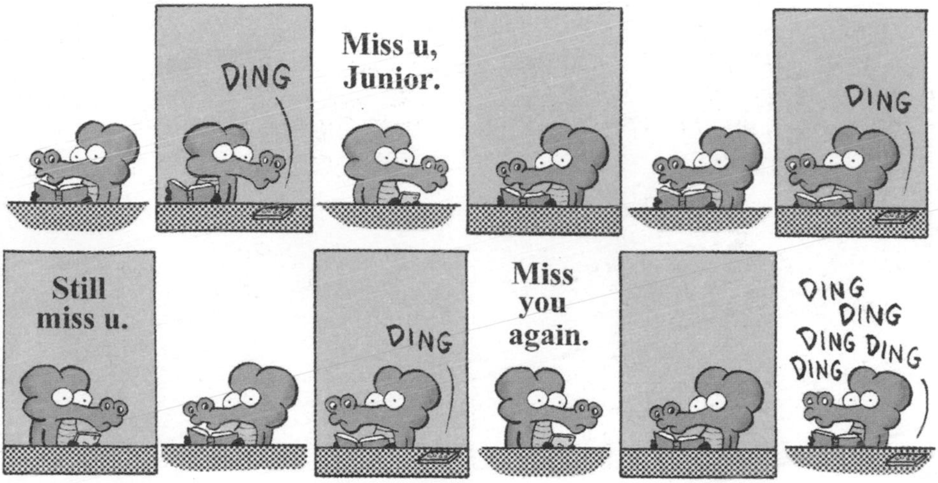
DING
Miss u, Junior.
DING
Still miss u.
DING
Miss you again.
DING DING DING DING DING

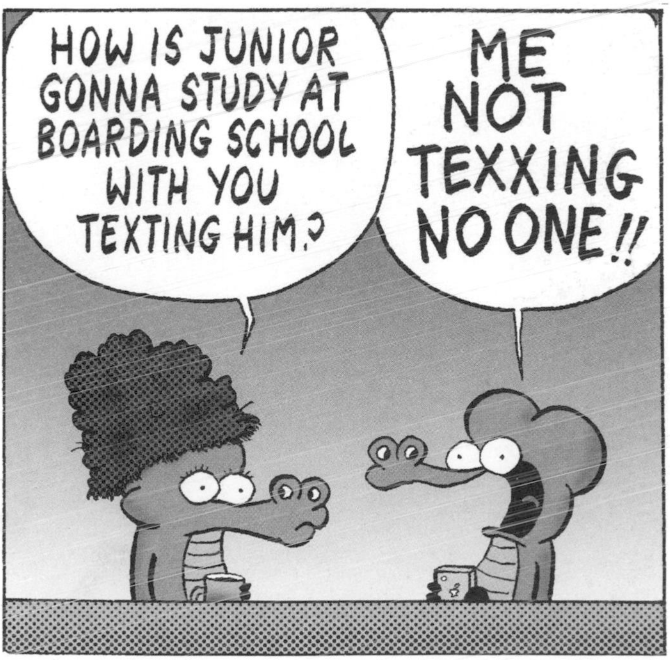
HOW IS JUNIOR GONNA STUDY AT BOARDING SCHOOL WITH YOU TEXTING HIM?
ME NOT TEXXING NO ONE!!

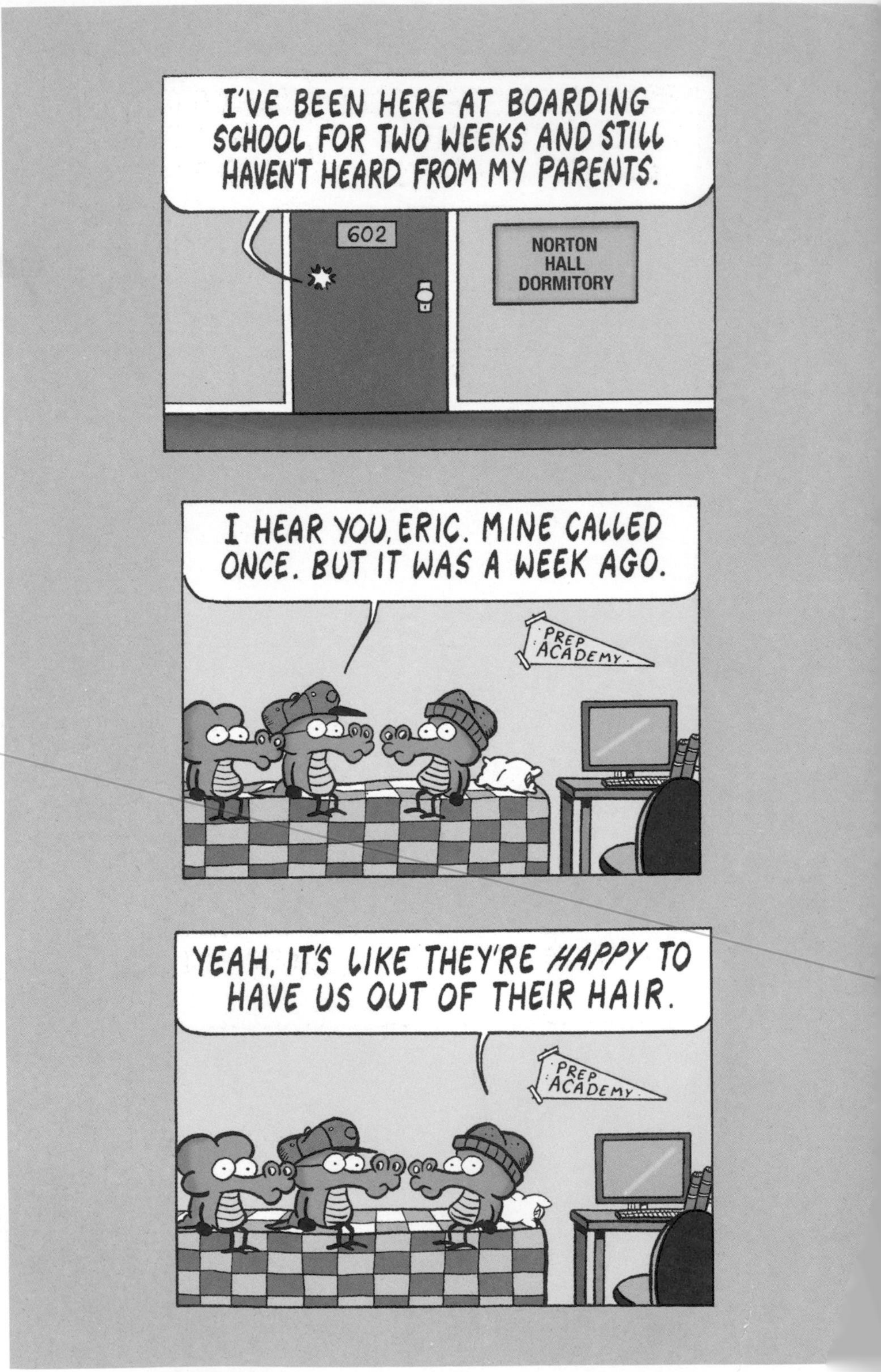
I'VE BEEN HERE AT BOARDING SCHOOL FOR TWO WEEKS AND STILL HAVEN'T HEARD FROM MY PARENTS.
602
NORTON HALL DORMITORY
I HEAR YOU, ERIC. MINE CALLED ONCE. BUT IT WAS A WEEK AGO.
PREP ACADEMY
YEAH, IT'S LIKE THEY'RE *HAPPY* TO HAVE US OUT OF THEIR HAIR.
PREP ACADEMY

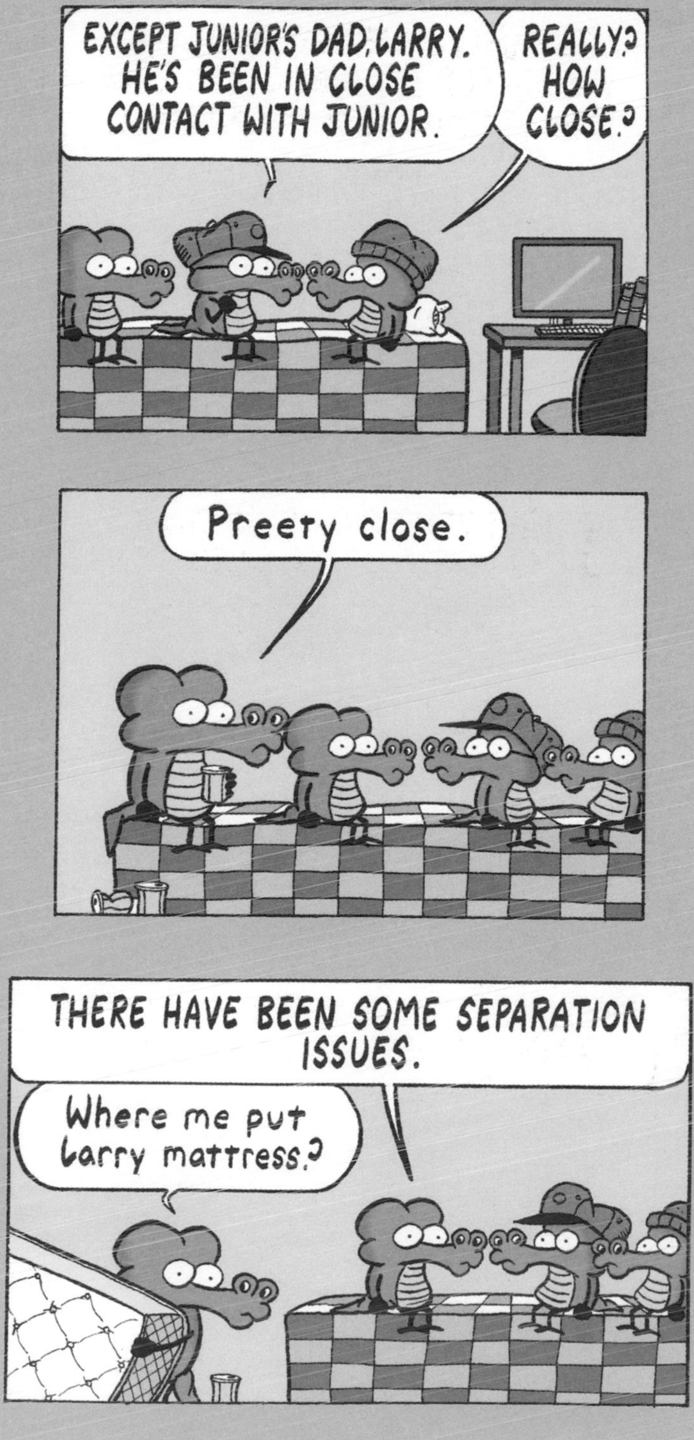
EXCEPT JUNIOR'S DAD, LARRY. HE'S BEEN IN CLOSE CONTACT WITH JUNIOR.
REALLY? HOW CLOSE?
Preety close.
THERE HAVE BEEN SOME SEPARATION ISSUES.
Where me put Larry mattress?

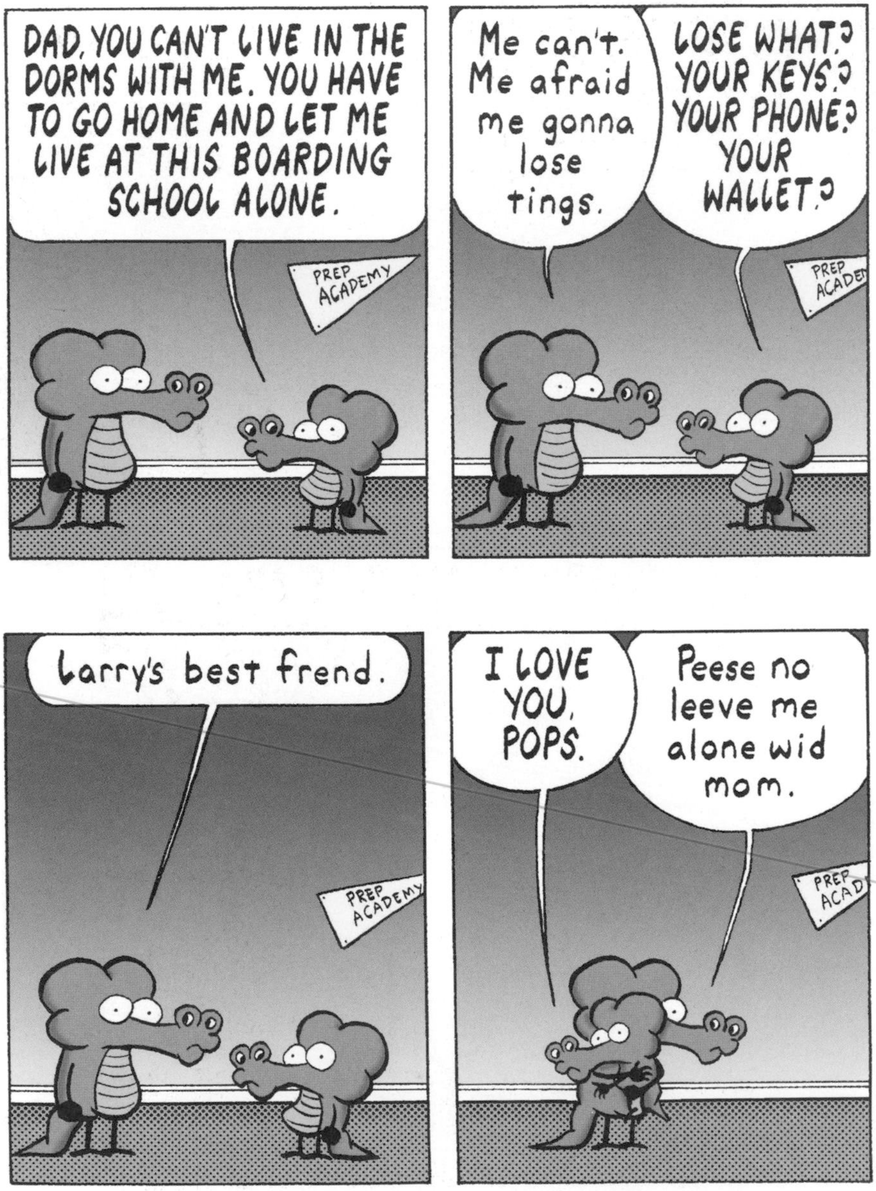
DAD, YOU CAN'T LIVE IN THE DORMS WITH ME. YOU HAVE TO GO HOME AND LET ME LIVE AT THIS BOARDING SCHOOL ALONE.
PREP ACADEMY
Me can't. Me afraid me gonna lose tings.
LOSE WHAT? YOUR KEYS? YOUR PHONE? YOUR WALLET?
Larry's best frend.
PREP ACADEMY
I LOVE YOU, POPS.
Peese no leeve me alone wid mom.

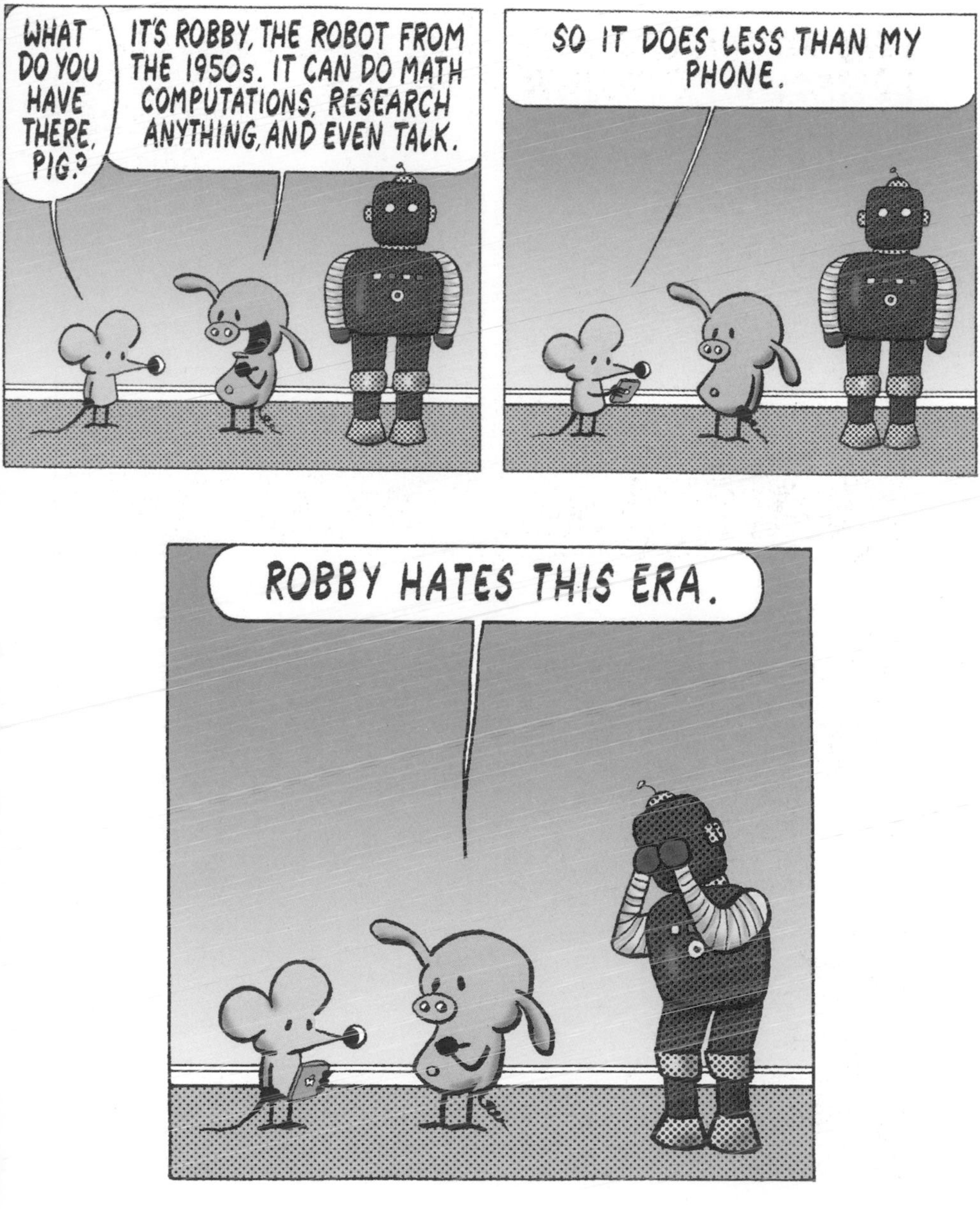
WHAT DO YOU HAVE THERE, PIG?
IT'S ROBBY, THE ROBOT FROM THE 1950s. IT CAN DO MATH COMPUTATIONS, RESEARCH ANYTHING, AND EVEN TALK.
SO IT DOES LESS THAN MY PHONE.
ROBBY HATES THIS ERA.

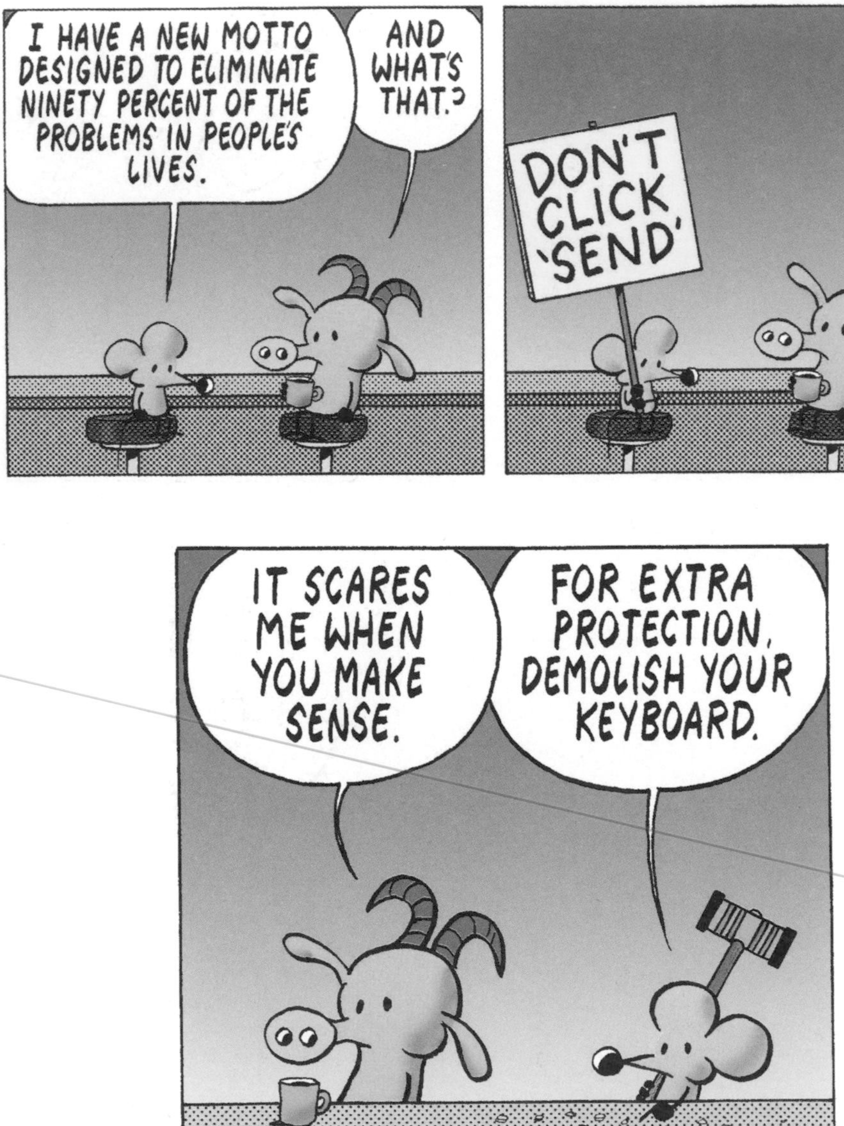
I HAVE A NEW MOTTO DESIGNED TO ELIMINATE NINETY PERCENT OF THE PROBLEMS IN PEOPLE'S LIVES.
AND WHAT'S THAT?
DON'T CLICK 'SEND'
IT SCARES ME WHEN YOU MAKE SENSE.
FOR EXTRA PROTECTION, DEMOLISH YOUR KEYBOARD.

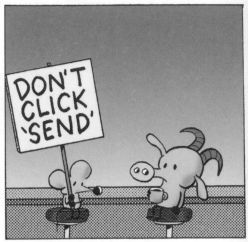

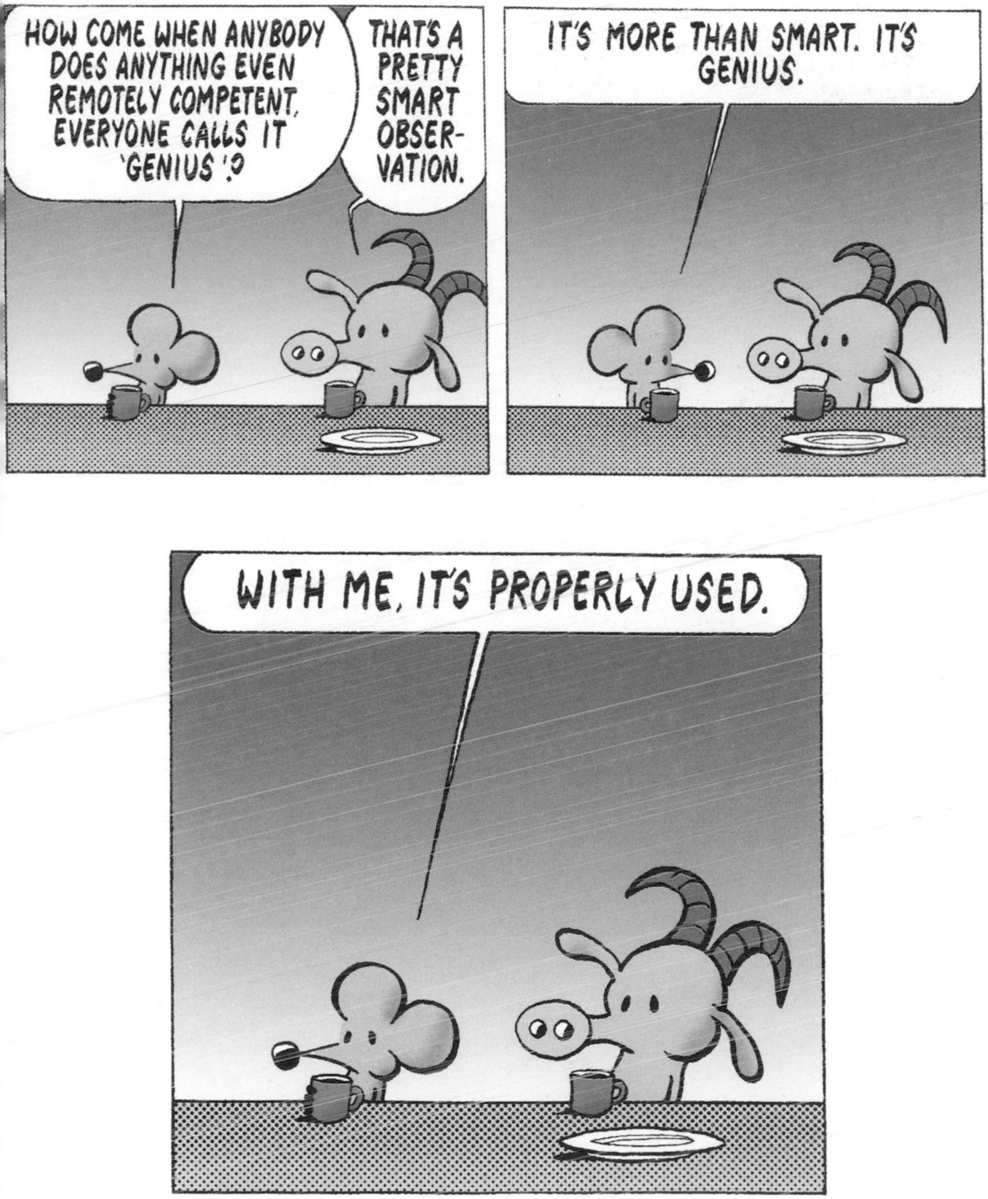
HOW COME WHEN ANYBODY DOES ANYTHING EVEN REMOTELY COMPETENT, EVERYONE CALLS IT 'GENIUS'?
THAT'S A PRETTY SMART OBSER-VATION.
IT'S MORE THAN SMART. IT'S GENIUS.
WITH ME, IT'S PROPERLY USED.

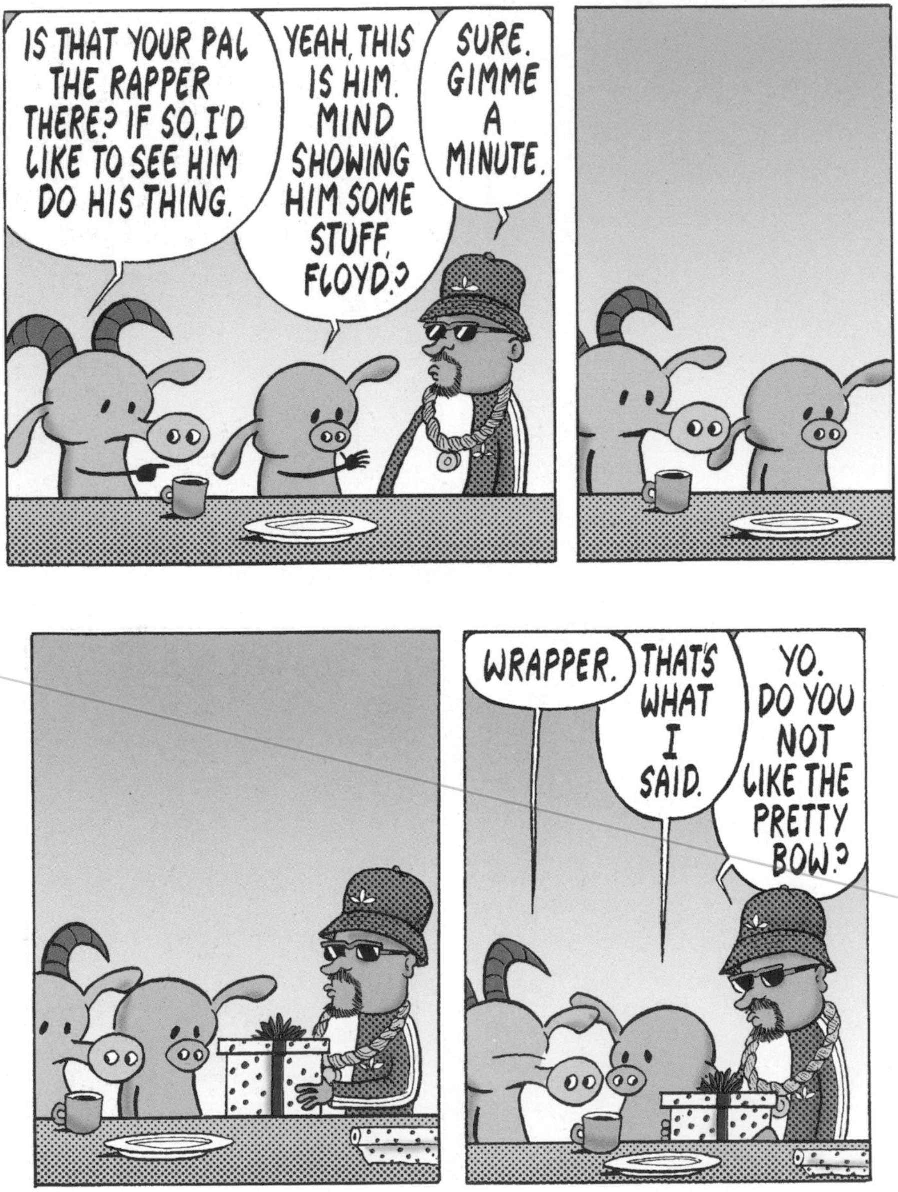
IS THAT YOUR PAL THE RAPPER THERE? IF SO, I'D LIKE TO SEE HIM DO HIS THING.
YEAH, THIS IS HIM. MIND SHOWING HIM SOME STUFF, FLOYD?
SURE. GIMME A MINUTE.
WRAPPER.
THAT'S WHAT I SAID.
YO. DO YOU NOT LIKE THE PRETTY BOW?

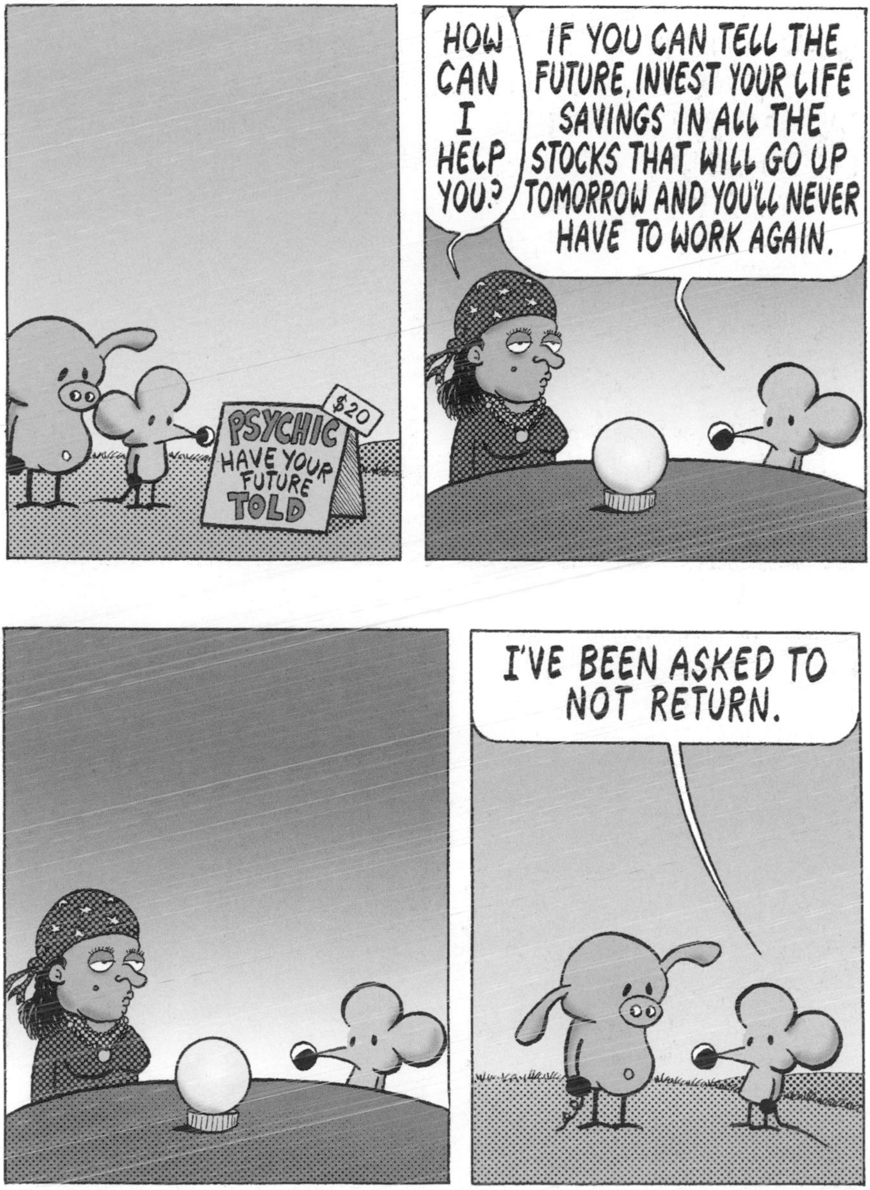
PSYCHIC
HAVE YOUR FUTURE TOLD
$20
HOW CAN I HELP YOU?
IF YOU CAN TELL THE FUTURE, INVEST YOUR LIFE SAVINGS IN ALL THE STOCKS THAT WILL GO UP TOMORROW AND YOU'LL NEVER HAVE TO WORK AGAIN.
I'VE BEEN ASKED TO NOT RETURN.

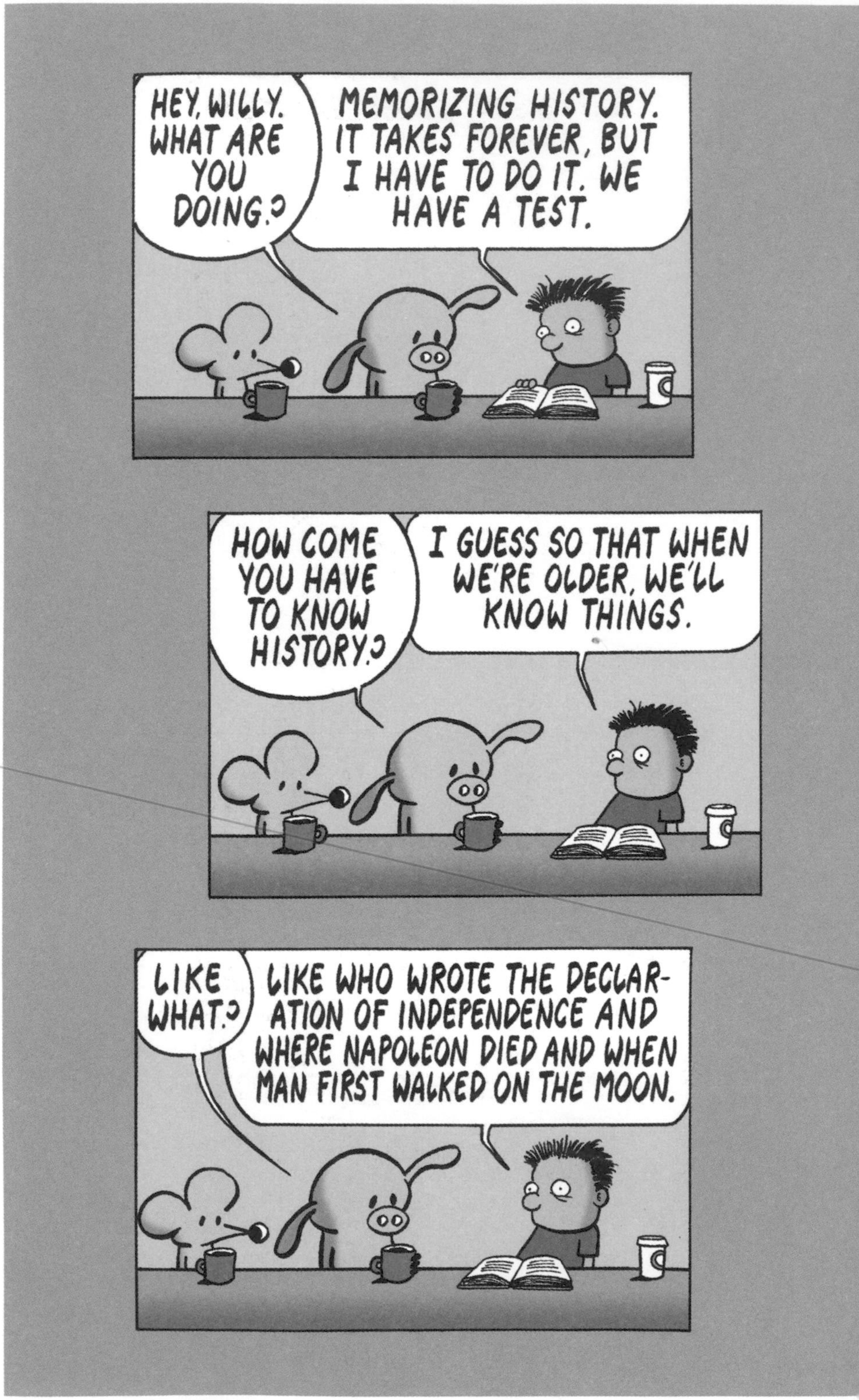
HEY, WILLY. WHAT ARE YOU DOING?
MEMORIZING HISTORY. IT TAKES FOREVER, BUT I HAVE TO DO IT. WE HAVE A TEST.
HOW COME YOU HAVE TO KNOW HISTORY?
I GUESS SO THAT WHEN WE'RE OLDER, WE'LL KNOW THINGS.
LIKE WHAT?
LIKE WHO WROTE THE DECLARATION OF INDEPENDENCE AND WHERE NAPOLEON DIED AND WHEN MAN FIRST WALKED ON THE MOON.

JEFFERSON. ST. HELENA. 1969.
IT'S CALLED 'GOOGLE.'
IS SCHOOL JUST TORTURE?
YES, BUT TORTURE BUILDS CHARACTER.
I GUESS TECHNICALLY, I KNOW EVERYTHING.

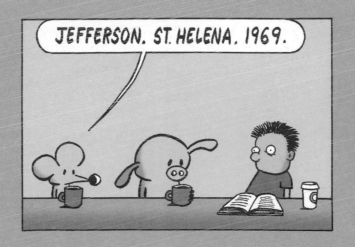

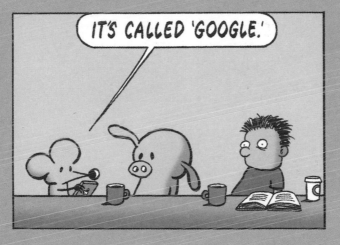

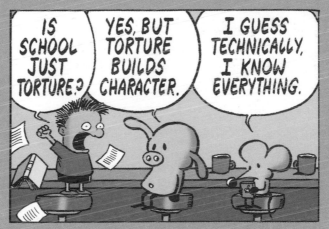

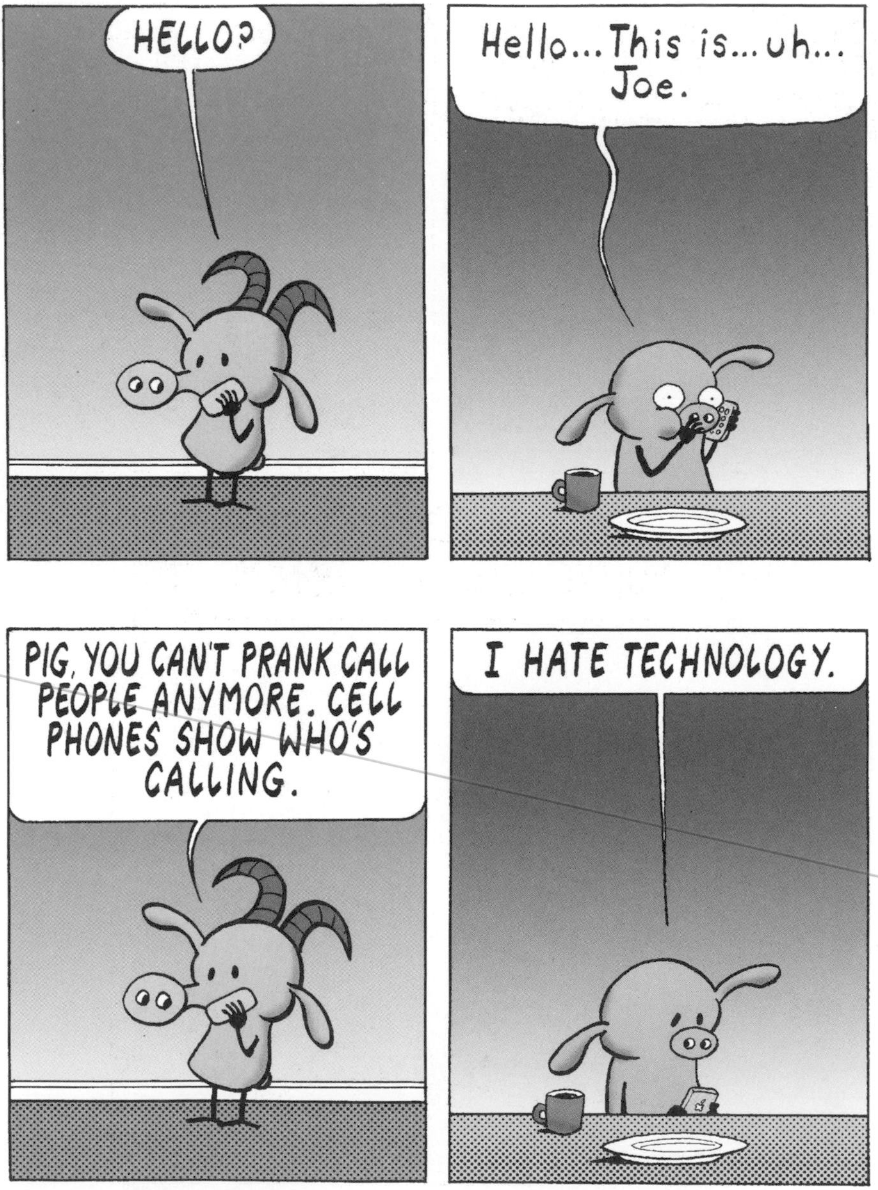
HELLO?
Hello... This is... uh... Joe.
PIG, YOU CAN'T PRANK CALL PEOPLE ANYMORE. CELL PHONES SHOW WHO'S CALLING.
I HATE TECHNOLOGY.

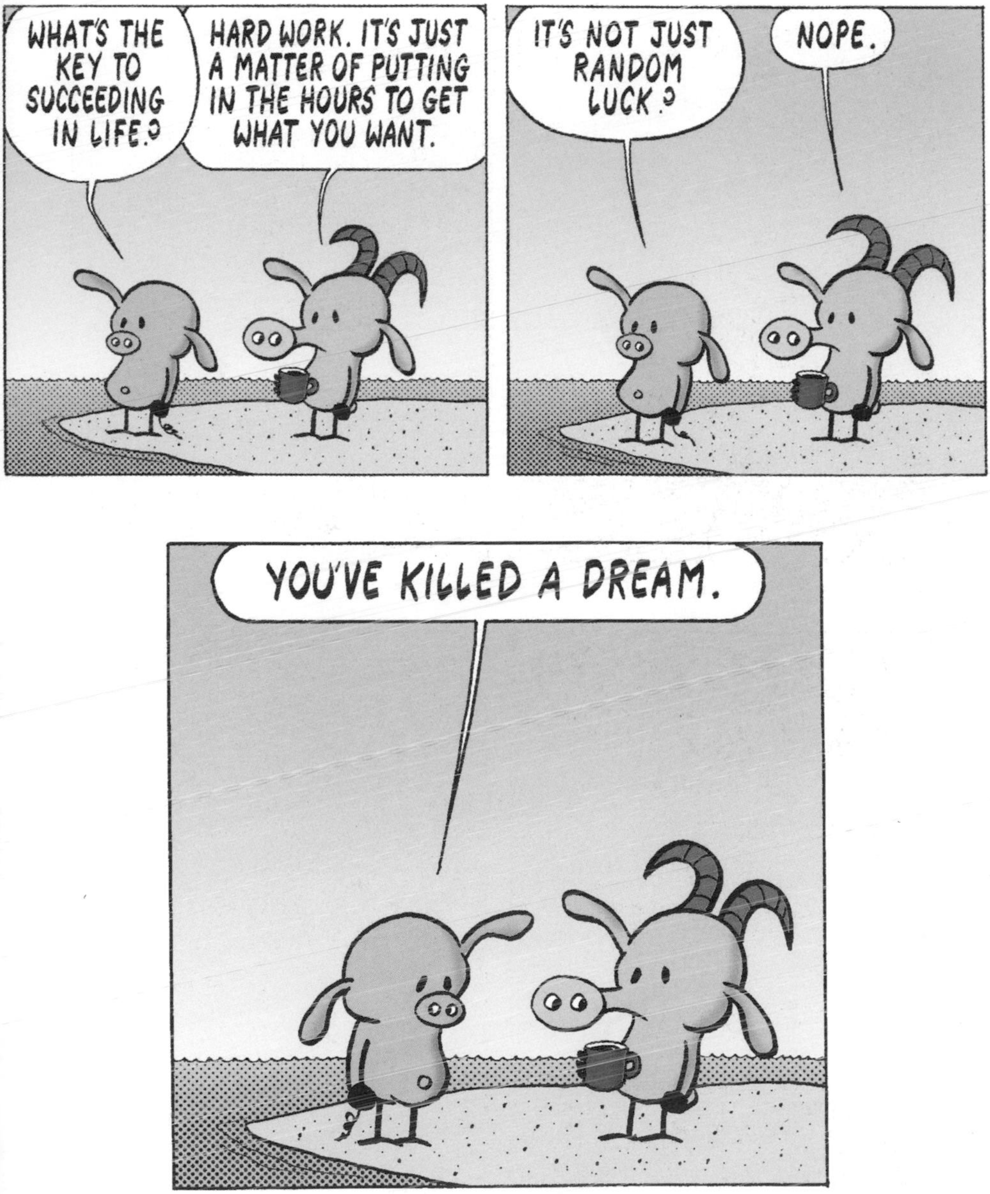
WHAT'S THE KEY TO SUCCEEDING IN LIFE?
HARD WORK. IT'S JUST A MATTER OF PUTTING IN THE HOURS TO GET WHAT YOU WANT.
IT'S NOT JUST RANDOM LUCK?
NOPE.
YOU'VE KILLED A DREAM.

Okay, zeeba...Now you had it... Crocs buy DOOMSDAY device.. If me press button, you house ESSPLODE. So geev up now or face conseekence.
Doomsd device
THAT'S RIDICULOUS. LEAVE ME ALONE.
Ohhhkay, tough guy.. Dat what you tink?... Me will press, you know... You want me press?
Doomsd device
SURE. PRESS IT.
No you tempt me, zeeba neighba... No you *tempt* me.

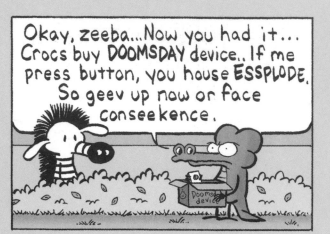

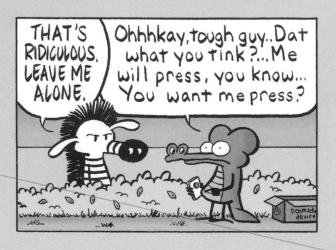

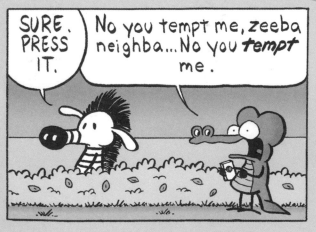

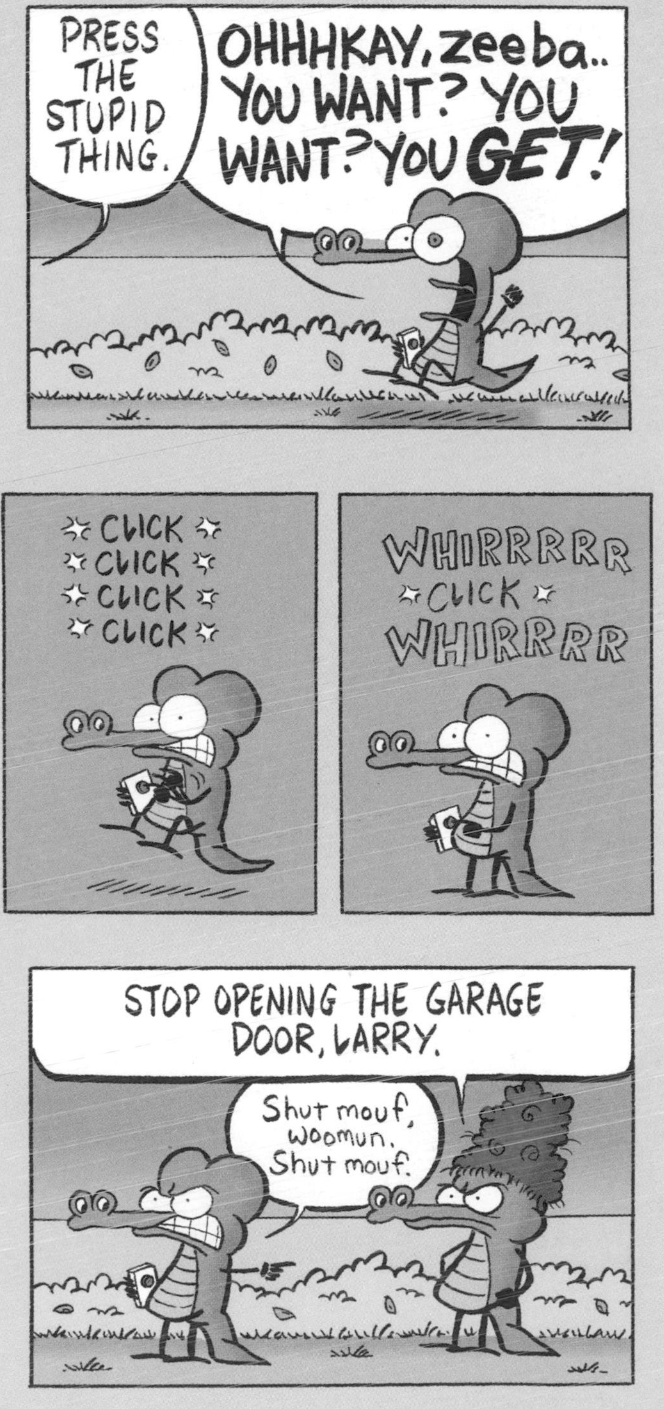
PRESS THE STUPID THING.
OHHHKAY, zeeba.. YOU WANT? YOU WANT? YOU GET!
CLICK CLICK CLICK CLICK
WHIRRRRRR CLICK WHIRRRRR
STOP OPENING THE GARAGE DOOR, LARRY.
Shut mouf, woomun. Shut mouf.

*Pearls Before Swine* is distributed internationally by Andrews McMeel Syndication.

Andrews McMeel Publishing
a division of Andrews McMeel Universal
1130 Walnut Street, Kansas City, Missouri 64106

www.andrewsmcmeel.com

17 18 19 20 21 SDB 10 9 8 7 6 5 4 3 2 1

ISBN: 978-1-4494-8375-3

Library of Congress Control Number: 2016951731

*Pearls Before Swine* can be viewed on the Internet at www.pearlscomic.com.

Made by:
Shenzhen Donnelley Printing Company Ltd.
Address and location of manufacturer:
No. 47, Wuhe Nan Road, Bantian Ind. Zone,
Shenzhen China, 518129
1st Printing – 4/24/17

---

## ATTENTION: SCHOOLS AND BUSINESSES

Andrews McMeel books are available at quantity discounts with bulk purchase for educational, business, or sales promotional use. For information, please e-mail the Andrews McMeel Publishing Special Sales Department:
specialsales@amuniversal.com.

**Be sure to check out other *Pearls Before Swine* AMP! Comics for Kids books and others at ampkids.com.**

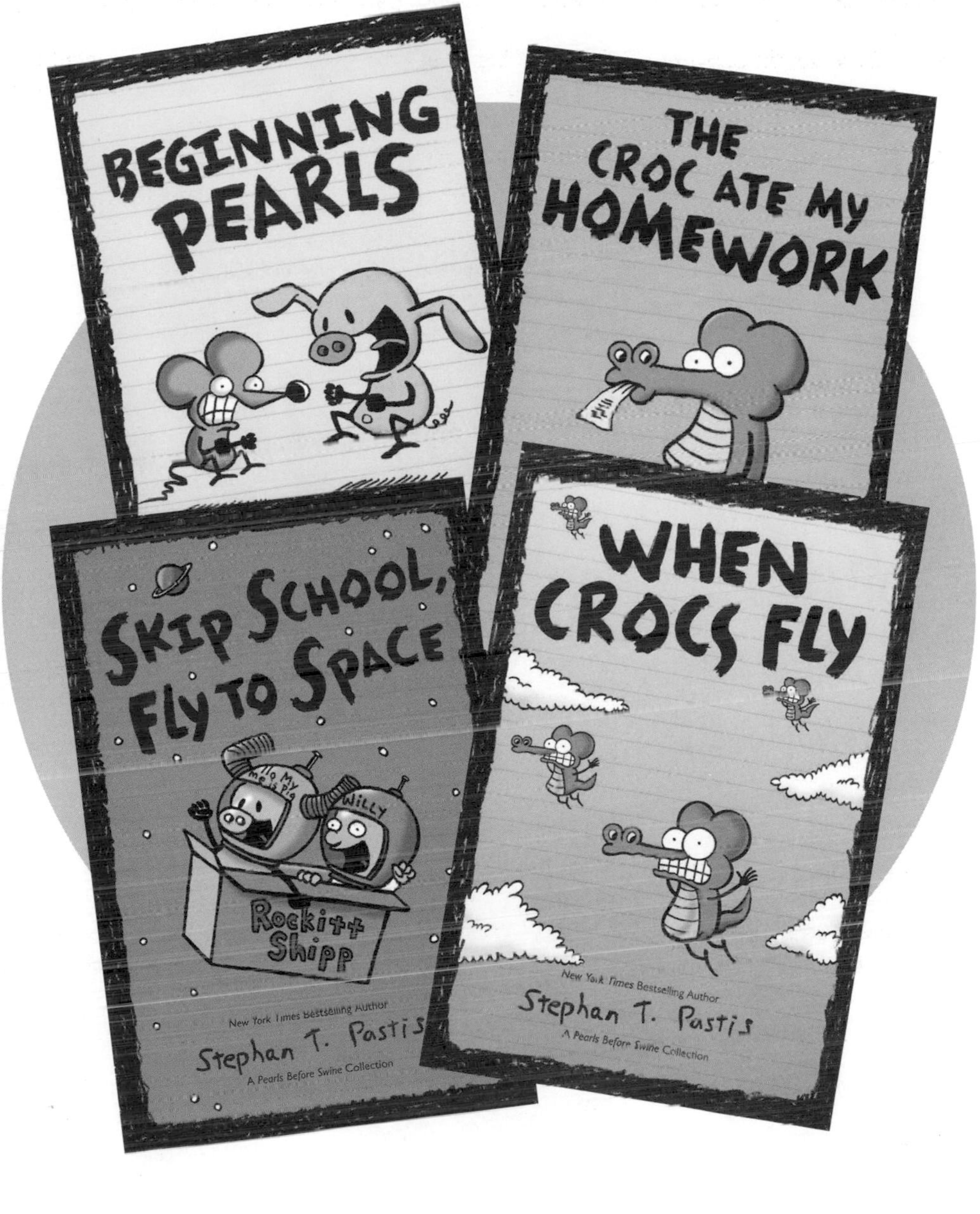
BEGINNING PEARLS
THE CROC ATE MY HOMEWORK
SKIP SCHOOL, FLY TO SPACE
WILLY
Rockitt Shipp
New York Times Bestselling Author
Stephan T. Pastis
A Pearls Before Swine Collection
WHEN CROCS FLY
New York Times Bestselling Author
Stephan T. Pastis
A Pearls Before Swine Collection

# Check out these and other books at ampkids.com

the MUTTS Autumn diaries

· PATRICK McDONNELL ·

SNOOPY TO THE RESCUE

PULL-OUT POSTER INSIDE

A PEANUTS Collection

Tucker Grizzwell's Worst Week Ever

Bill Schorr and Ralph Smith

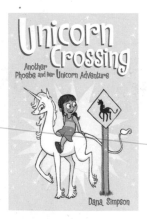

Unicorn Crossing

Another Phoebe and Her Unicorn Adventure

Dana Simpson

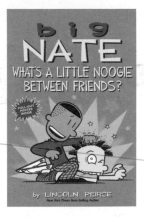

big NATE WHAT'S A LITTLE NOOGIE BETWEEN FRIENDS?

PULL-OUT POSTER INSIDE

by LINCOLN PEIRCE
New York Times Best-Selling Author

THE SCRIBBLE SQUAD in the WEIRD WILD WEST

STINKY CECIL in TERRARIUM TERROR!
BY PAIGE BRADDOCK

LASER MOOSE AND RABBIT BOY

DOUG SAVAGE

SHERLOCK SAM and the SINISTER LETTERS in BRAS BASAH

By A.J. LOW

### Also available:
Teaching and activity guides for each title.
AMP! Comics for Kids books make reading FUN!

www.gocomics.com

HEY, RICKY RAISIN. HOW GOES IT?
GOOD. I WON THE LOTTERY. GOT A NEW CAR. GOT A NEW BEACH HOUSE. GOT A NEW GIRLFRIEND.... OH, WELL. GOTTA GO.
EVERYTHING HAPPENS FOR A RAISIN.

# GATHER 'ROUND THE SMARTPHONE, KIDS!

Even Rat cracks a smile in this fifth *Pearls Before Swine* collection tailored for middle-grade readers. Witty, wacky, and occasionally wise, Stephan and the *Pearls* gang deliver a whole album's-worth of jokes, jabs, and cringe-worthy puns. Say CHEESE!

amp! COMICS for kids
www.ampkids.com
From Andrews McMeel Publishing


**$9.99 U.S.A.** *($11.99 Canada)*
ISBN: 978-1-4494-8375-3
50999
9 781449 483753